M000077175

IT'S ALL
IN THE TITLE

ANN PORT

Ann Port
6/24/11

Copyright © 2011 Ann Port

All rights reserved.

ISBN: 1460973372

ISBN-13: 9781460973370

Library of Congress Control Number: 2011903770

CHAPTER ONE

Caroline Charlotte Cleveland hated her name. She had hated it for as long as she could remember. Actually it had been years since anyone had called her Caroline. She was CC, a nickname her charismatic stepfather, Miles "Flash" MacTandy, had given her when she was only two. CC still recalled, or perhaps Flash had reminded her enough so she thought she could actually remember, his emphatic declaration that she was "far too small to be carrying around a twenty-five letter name." Neither CC nor Flash ever decided if the initials stood for Caroline Cleveland or Caroline Charlotte, but it really didn't matter. CC was how she was to be addressed; she would respond to nothing else.

For months, Mary MacTandy refused to use her daughter's nickname, but Caroline, with childish stubbornness, adamantly stomped her foot, as if forbidding her mother from speaking to her or introducing her to others as anything but CC. The name Caroline never seemed to fit the image that the child, and later the woman, wanted to present to the world; CC always seemed appropriate.

In elementary school, CC was a fitting name for the lively, intelligent tomboy who had absolutely no desire to have a girl's name and who could "fight with the best of them," as Flash often proudly declared. Years later, though being a girl wasn't quite as repugnant to her, the initials suited the athletic teenager, still a tomboy at heart, who was utterly unaware of the hordes of boys who dreamed of dating the sexy girl with the sparkling blue eyes, strawberry blonde hair, fair complexion, and high cheekbones.

When she graduated from high school, CC was an apropos appellation for the undergraduate student at Northwestern University, who flourished in the school's intensely competitive atmosphere. And then for the star of the graduate program at the University of Arizona, who earned her MBA in one year of intense application and study, and as Flash often teased with his bright blue eyes smiling and crinkling up into a squint, an appropriate "handle for a woman with the most mind-boggling tunnel vision" he'd ever seen.

Lately, the short, no-nonsense name was just right for an almost thirty-two year-old woman who was thriving in a world that only a year before had not admitted women: Major League Baseball. Recently named CEO of the Indianapolis Knights, she was the first female in a top-level management position in the sport and the youngest, male or female, ever to be named club president.

It had taken a tremendous amount of hard work and intense effort for CC to gain and maintain respect in the "good-old-boy" world of professional sports, where recycling of presidents, general managers, and field managers was standard practice. However, during the past few months, as everyone in the organization planned and prepared for a new season that was just about to open; her first complete season in the club's top spot, she felt she was finally an integral part of the team. She had reached her goal.

Now, on a late March afternoon, instead of being in the ballpark in Indianapolis watching the ground crew working to prepare the field for the season ahead, CC stood looking out the tall windows in the library of Litchfield Manor, four miles from Oxford, England. At that moment, contract negotiations, arbitration hearings, free agents, and preparations for opening day seemed far away. For the first time since Flash had begun calling her CC, she wasn't sure if that name was appropriate. Certainly no one at Litchfield was calling her Caroline, but they weren't calling her CC either. In this extraordinary place so far from home, she had an entirely new identity. To the numerous servants who waited to do her bidding, she was the Countess of Litchfield, and to her, the new title was both strange and unsettling.

A deer scurried across the open space and darted into the wooded area at the end of the vast lawn in front of the house. *Three days ago who would have imagined that I'd be watching a deer instead of clocking a player running from home plate to first base in a pre-season game?* CC mused as she turned away from the window, crossed the room, and sat down at an antique writing desk.

There was a six-hour time difference between Litchfield and Indianapolis, so it would be eleven in the morning at home, a good time to call the office to talk with Jim Oats, her vice president of marketing and her only perpetual problem since assuming the presidency. The man had bizarre ideas and failed to follow through on projects he began. Because she hadn't wanted to "clean house" immediately after assuming her new position, she was working to bring him in line, but lately she'd begun to wonder if he would be the first casualty of her tenure as CEO. She was sure of one thing, however: there would be no Oats's flashlight fiasco this year. She shook her head remembering that last year his "best ever giveaway" had to be changed at the last minute. It took the stadium staff hours to remove the batteries and hold them to be given out at the end of the game rather than the beginning. Jim never considered that, should the Knights start losing or if an error were committed in the outfield, irate fans might throw the rock-hard cylinders at the players or the umpires. What a mess that had been. Yes, she would conduct a thorough review of Oats's planned promotions.

CC also wanted to talk with Bob Westman, the Knights' general manager. Just before her departure for England, she had received a memo that the members of the U.S. Air Force squadron who were scheduled to do a fly-over before the home opener could not obtain clearance for seven twenty-five, but would be able to perform ten minutes later. The league had to approve a change of start time, but before she could submit the request, she wanted to be certain that Bob and the field manager, Spike Edmonds, had no objections. Her theory was better a happy GM and a contented manager than an unnecessary fly-over. If they didn't want to postpone the starting time, she would scrub the jets.

Next on her list was a call to Bud Sandlin, the chief attorney for the commissioner's office, whom she had met during the 2004 World Series, when she was an assistant GM for the Knights. They'd been dating seriously ever since, though the timing for a wedding never seemed to be right for them.

CC thought about the first time she had seen the handsome man, who at six feet four inches literally stood out above the crowd. They were in Boston and he was a member of the commissioner's entourage. Throughout the evening she tried to concentrate on the game, but for the first time in her life, watching a man was more interesting than paying attention to the player who was stealing second or trying to guess what pitch the left-hander would throw next.

At the post-game cocktail party, Bud approached her and introduced himself. During their brief conversation, CC was impressed by his quick wit and easy charm. She could have stood there talking for hours, but unfortunately, Tim McKinney, the Knights' PR director, had other ideas. "Your presence is requested in the pressroom," he said, a knowing grin on his face. "Apparently our writers have picked up on rumors about a possible trade with Cleveland." As she reluctantly trudged off with Tim, CC was sure that her once-in-a-lifetime chance to get to know Bud was gone forever.

Early the next morning, she caught the American League shuttle. Determined to concentrate on information she needed to absorb before arriving in Atlanta where, as the writers had discovered, she would be watching the series as well as beginning preliminary talks about trading several of the Knights' minor league players to Cleveland for a star pitcher, she opened her briefcase before all the passengers were even on board the plane. However, her resolve to work was short-lived, because when she looked up to greet her seat partner, there was Bud.

The flight passed in a blur. When they reached St. Louis, CC had done no work and was in love for the first time in her life. Before Bud, she had dated casually, but had decided she really wasn't the marrying sort. Her career was her life, her hobby, her avocation, her obsession, and her love. Now she had another love, one that was equally as important as her career.

As they walked toward the bus after the final game of the series, the autumn mist drifted over the ballpark. Uppermost in CC's mind was a quote by A. Bartlett Giamatti, the admired Yale professor and commissioner of baseball who had died much too young. CC recalled his words. *It breaks your heart. It is designed to break your heart. The game begins in the spring, when everything else begins again, and it blossoms in the summer, filling the afternoons and evenings, and then as soon as the chill rains come, it stops and leaves you to face the fall alone...*

For CC, Giamatti's quote epitomized the thoughts of all baseball lovers who faced the end of the season and a long winter without the game they loved. She wondered if autumn would also bring an end to her blossoming relationship with Bud.

Happily, that was not to be the case. Bud and CC began a long-distance romance. They met at all-star games, winter meetings, and owners' meetings and got together for long weekends whenever their schedules would permit. People in the baseball world recognized the striking couple as a two-some, and they did look great together. Bud, with his dark good looks, was a striking contrast to the stunning strawberry blonde. In private they became perfectly attuned to one another, and they delighted in the joy each provided the other.

After Bud was appointed to head the commissioner's law team, CC thought long and hard about giving up her job and moving to New York to be with him. She decided that when he proposed, she would seriously consider marriage, but he didn't ask. He seemed content with their long-distance romance.

When CC's career took off two years later, Bud was comfortably settled in his job and ready to make a commitment. One weekend he surprised her by coming to Indianapolis, bringing with him a huge sapphire ring surrounded by diamonds, but CC refused his proposal that only a year before she would have accepted immediately. It was her turn now, and marriage would have to wait.

After that weekend, their relationship cooled. Bud flew into town whenever he had an opportunity, but the chances for CC to see him in New York grew more infrequent, and as club CEO, when she attended baseball functions, she spent most of her time with other club executives or on the phone. They loved each other, but they had their careers, and as CC joked, she couldn't imagine giving up her life as chief of the Knights for getting up nights with a baby.

CC had called Bud several times before leaving for England, but they hadn't connected. She left messages, but when he returned her calls she was, as her secretary told him, "in conference with the door closed," which meant that unless it was a matter of life or death, she couldn't be disturbed, even for him. When she found time to call him back, he was unavailable for one reason or another. She had made one last effort to reach him just before boarding the plane, but still to no avail. The two of them just couldn't connect. *That appears to be our destiny*, she mused as she sat an ocean away making her "to do" list. Bud was a priority, but he wasn't at the top of her list. Work always came first.

Putting her thoughts of Bud aside to contemplate other calls she needed to make, CC's eyes focused on the beautiful pen she had picked up from the desk to make her list. Entwined in the delicately engraved enamel design were the initials of the pen's owner, WC. How strange. She was actually sitting in her father's house and using his pen to plan her calls to people a world away—and not just in terms of distance.

Aware that her calls needed to be placed in a timely manner or many of her staff would be out for lunch and unavailable, CC picked up the phone. However, without dialing, she quickly returned the handset to the charger. She couldn't help herself. Oddly enough, Indianapolis and baseball weren't on her mind. *What was my father like?* She thought as she leaned back in her chair.

CC had never met William Cleveland, the sixth Earl of Litchfield. He and her mother had met and fallen in love in Paris in 1978. Mary was an army nurse assigned to the military hospital in Wiesbaden, Germany. After working almost nonstop for six months, she had been given two weeks off, so she made train reservations and traveled to fulfill one of her dreams: to see Paris.

Though she had spent an exhausting, though absolutely delightful, afternoon exploring the Right Bank, Mary decided not to waste a minute of her time in the City of Lights. After returning to her hotel near the opera on the Right Bank to freshen up and change clothes, she set off to Le Deux Magot. Being an enthusiastic Hemingway fan for as long as she could remember, near the top of her "to do list" was tasting the Welsh rarebit and sipping a glass of wine at one of the famous author's Left Bank haunts.

Since it was still light outside and despite her sore feet from the long day of sightseeing, Mary decided to forgo a cab ride and walk. She crossed the Seine and strolled to Boulevard St. Germain des Pres, eager to see Le Deux Magot, the famous statues of Chinese monks that had been left when the hosiery store that once stood in the café's locale was closed and from which the café took its name.

Like Mary, William was also taking a much-needed rest from his duties as a pilot in the Royal Air Force. As he often did when in the city, he went to Le Deux Magot to relax and people watch before meeting friends at the Brasserie Lipp for a late dinner. When he arrived at the café, there were no empty tables outside. As he looked around, hoping to find a place to sit, he spotted a lovely blonde woman in an American army uniform sitting alone at a table across from the church of St. Germain des Pres. He made his way through the closely positioned tables and politely asked if he could join her. She smiled, nodded her consent, and pointed to the empty chair beside her.

By the time they finished their second glass of wine, Mary and William realized they both shared a passion for the expatriate author. Minutes turned into hours, and William never made it to Brasserie Lipp. He walked Mary back to her hotel and they made plans to resume their exploration of Hemingway's stomping grounds the following day. Neither William nor Mary had any idea that their encounter at Le Deux Magot or the day ahead would change their lives forever.

After a good night's sleep, Mary met William in the lobby of the hotel at eleven. Hand and hand they walked back to the Left Bank. After lunch at a sidewalk table at Café de Flore, they had a glass of wine at the Dingo Bar where Hemingway first met F. Scott Fitzgerald and another at Café du Dome, the well-known expatriate hangout.

At L'Escargot they, as Hemingway had before them, ate oysters and sipped white wine. Though she was full of food and drink and doubted she could eat another bite, Mary agreed with William: They couldn't forego dinner at the Brasserie Lipp. Since they were not part of the regular crowd, they were seated upstairs, unlike Hemingway who always sat at a preferred table on the ground floor. Despite that, they enjoyed a leisurely repast.

Mary later said that it was Hemingway who brought them together. After that time in Paris, she never read his novels or short stories again.

Mary checked out of her hotel and moved into William's room in the Studio-Apartments Hotel on Rue Delambre across from the Dingo Bar. There they spent hours making love, with only the sounds and smells of Paris intruding on their space. They feasted on cheap wine and crusty bread they bought at the outside market near the Seine and took long walks along the river, stopping to go into Napoleon's tomb and to explore

Notre Dame. Though William had been to these French shrines many times before, they seemed fresh and new to him as he shared them with Mary.

Near the end of the wonderful week, with the threat of parting so near and despite the fact that the young nobleman was formally engaged, they threw all caution aside and, on an impulse, got married. Nothing mattered to them but the moment. They had less than a week left, but they spent a glorious few days as man and wife exploring each other and Paris.

As Mary's leave neared its end, William made the dreaded call to his father to announce his marriage. The old earl's response shattered the hopes and dreams of the young people, who all too quickly realized that any attempt to remain together would be futile.

Despite William's protests, the earl insisted that if the marriage continued, he would no longer have a son. He pulled strings to obtain an annulment on the grounds of William's violation of a binding contract of marriage to Lady Anne Hilliard. Mary was never sure if there actually were legal grounds for an annulment. All she knew was that William would not fight and the earl refused to budge. The lovers had shared two weeks of passion and joy in a place far from England and William's duties. This distance had given him the courage to defy his father and ignore his prearranged marriage—a union he tried solemnly to explain to Mary was "his duty." But when reality set in and family responsibilities came into play, he couldn't oppose the imperious earl or deny his contractual obligation, his upbringing, or his heritage.

William returned home to Litchfield Manor and Mary went back to Germany, where four weeks later, she discovered she was pregnant and asked for a discharge from the army. The news of a grandchild did nothing to move the earl to halt the annulment proceedings. Even the baby's arrival could not induce William to defy his father's wishes. Mary moved to a small flat in London where she awaited the inevitable: her final legal separation from the man she loved so deeply.

The entire legal process took almost a year; a year that Mary would later speak of as the most agonizing, lonely, and painful of her life. Caroline Charlotte was born in London with only her rejected mother to know the joy of having a child. William was nowhere to be seen, though a kindly nurse told the paradoxically happy and sad mother that a man who refused to identify himself called several times to check on her and the baby's condition. She also discovered that a man fitting William's description had come to the hospital and held the child. To the best of Mary's knowledge, William never saw Caroline Charlotte after that day.

Two months later, the day Mary was scheduled to fly home, an envelope containing a great deal of cash arrived from the earl. She had never asked for anything as a condition of the annulment. She stared at the money, realizing she was being paid off because she had not tried to keep the old man from having his way or caused embarrassment to the family. Her first impulse was to return the money with a nasty note saying her feelings couldn't be bought, but she thought of her daughter, the earl's grandchild, and the need to provide her with a secure life. The money would provide that. She considered the cash a gift to her daughter, took the envelope, and, heartsick and shattered, boarded the plane.

The young woman who dreamed of a life with the man she loved had only a daughter to show there ever was a love. With the final annulment papers, she also signed documents promising that she would never try to see William again, that their child would have no claim to the family title, and that she would never cause trouble for the Cleveland family. In return, she was allowed to keep her husband's surname for the sake of the child. Mary never violated the agreement.

Since her own parents had died several years before, Mary had no place to go. Her home had been wherever the army had sent her. So mother and daughter settled in Phoenix to begin a new life. Mary found a job as a surgical nurse at Saint Joseph's Hospital. She bought a three-bedroom house with a maid's quarters in a quiet neighborhood called Palmcroft. The property was expensive, but thanks to the earl's generosity, she could afford it and Ethel Gazuba, the Pima Maricopa Native American housekeeper she hired to live with them and watch Caroline while she was at work.

When Caroline was two, her mother married Miles MacTandy, an ex-Major League ball player who had been with the Los Angeles Dodgers since right after their move from Brooklyn in 1962. After retiring because of bad knees, Flash, as his teammates called him—not because of his speed, but because of his antics—left the team, ignored everyone's advice, and used all of his savings to invest in some "worthless" oil wells. He made a fortune when the wells turned out to be gushers.

Never able to get baseball out of his blood, Flash took his vast earnings, and since no major league team was available for purchase, bought a Triple A Minor League team and moved it to Phoenix. He met Mary when she nursed him after surgery on one of his bad knees.

Flash was a distinguished-looking man with a whimsical smile and a sometimes fiery temper. He was also generous and passionate, and Mary fell in love. With Flash she never knew the kind of passion she had felt with William, but in a way, she was thankful. That all-consuming love came only once, and for her it had meant disaster. Flash made her feel comfortable, secure, and happy. In addition, he willingly accepted her daughter. That alone was enough.

Throughout her childhood, CC lived in the world of professional sports. During the season Flash let her be the team's batgirl, an unprecedented privilege that made every boy she knew green with envy. When she was too old for that job and not too busy with cheerleading and her own sports activities, she worked as a media intern and later as a promotional assistant for the club.

As CC grew older, her love of the game intensified. When she graduated from high school, she begged Flash to let her be his assistant so she could learn the business. He adamantly refused, telling her that a college education was necessary if she wanted to work in the business of baseball. With a degree and her experience in the minor leagues, she might have a chance to break into upper management with a Major League club. Flash finally convinced her the days of the wheeler-dealer, cigar-smoking general managers and their back-room trades were over. The unionization of the players and the umpires along with collective bargaining process had given rise to a myriad of complicated issues. If she wanted to succeed, it was imperative she have a strong business background. CC wasn't sure she agreed, but she listened.

Over the years CC never heard from William. When she was old enough to understand, Mary told her about her father, about the love she and William had shared, and about William's marriage to his heiress, Anne, immediately after the annulment. She explained that with his father's death, William had become the Earl of Litchfield. The title didn't impress CC, but at an age when all children wanted siblings to play with, she asked if she had any half-brothers or sisters living in England.

Her mother's discomfort when CC spoke of her father's wife and the possibility of children from that union was so evident that the intuitive child never asked again. In fact she rarely mentioned William. He hardly ever crossed her mind. Flash MacTandy, the charismatic, fun-loving hulk of a man, was the only father she had ever known or wanted to know. She didn't call him Dad, just Flash, but he was unquestionably her father—and a good and loving one at that. She didn't need anyone else.

Coming back to the moment at hand, CC took her list and the pen to one of the comfortable couches opposite the ornately carved marble fireplace. She still wasn't ready to make her call to the office, so she sat down and pondered the events that had brought her to England.

She had been at her desk in the office when the call came from her mother. Leslie Johnson, CC's friend as well as her private secretary, who had been with her from her early days in the minor leagues, buzzed her. "Your mom's on the phone, CC, and she sounds upset."

"Thanks, Leslie. Please put her through." Mary rarely called her at work, so there was definitely something wrong. Anxiously, CC picked up the phone "Hi, Mom," she said tentatively.

Her mother's voice sounded raspy. "Hello, dear. I hope I haven't interrupted anything important."

"As a matter of fact, right now I'm trying to decide whether to recommend white hats that play 'Take Me Out to the Ballgame' for hat day or go with the traditional blue hats with the silver logo of the knight hitting the baseball with his lance. Now I ask you, does this seem like an earth-shattering decision?"

"I guess." Mary ignored CC's efforts to be amusing.

"What is it, Mother? You sound like you have a cold."

"I feel fine, CC, but I'm afraid I have some bad news."

"Please tell me nothing's wrong with Flash." CC felt her hands and feet grow cold as she thought of something happening to her robust stepfather.

"No, darling, Flash is fine. He's here with me now. About thirty minutes ago I received a call from Harrison Caulfield, your father's attorney."

"Who?"

"Harrison Caulfield, dear, from the firm of Caulfield, Ailesbury and Bedford. They've been solicitors for the earls of Litchfield for many years."

"Litchfield?" CC's mind raced. It had been years since she'd given more than a passing thought to her father.

"I'm sorry, dear. Your father died late yesterday afternoon. I was told he had a heart attack. William's valet found him in his study slumped over his desk when he went to take him his tea."

"I'm so sorry for you, Mom." CC was surprised at her own apathy. This was her father, yet she felt nothing. "I didn't know the man, but I know how much you loved him."

"What your father and I had was a long time ago, CC. I'm sorry you never met him. When I read that Lady Anne died of breast cancer two years ago, I hoped he would come here or send for you, but apparently the embarrassment he felt for letting his father run his life and his guilt for giving you up without a fight was too much. He let time pass until it was too late for the two of you."

CC pondered her mother's words, but she felt no sympathy for William. He had made his choice. "I'm sorry for you, Mom," she said. Is there anything I can do? Would you like for me to come home for a few days?"

There was a pause on the other end of the line. "No dear. You won't need to come home, but you will be traveling, and I'm afraid it won't just be for a few days. Plan to be away for a few weeks or possibly a month."

CC was momentarily at a loss for words as a myriad of thoughts crossed her mind. "CC," Mary said when the silence lasted too long, "did you hear what I said?"

"I did, Mom. I was trying to make sense of all this. You realize there's no way I can leave the club this time of year. In case you've forgotten, spring training is underway. I'm leaving for Florida tomorrow morning. Even coming to see you in Phoenix would be difficult, but if you need me, I'm there."

"I'm afraid you don't have a choice, dear." CC heard that imperious tone of voice her mother only used when she was sure of herself and ready to put her daughter in her daughterly place. "You see, you've inherited all of your father's property and his title. You are now Lady Caroline Charlotte Cleveland, Countess of Litchfield. You have a five thousand-acre estate five miles from Woodstock in Oxfordshire, and you must go and attend to your business."

CC sat quietly, too stunned to respond. How could she be lady anything? She was American, as American as "hot dogs, Chevrolet, apple pie, and, of course, baseball" as Flash used to tell her. She was aware of her dual citizenship, but she never professed to be anything but American, and she was proud of it. "It's impossible for me to go, Mother, and an American can't have a title."

"But you're half-British, darling. Remember? And your father was an earl. Fortunately, or unfortunately for you, he had no children by Anne, and since he was an only child, his title goes to you. Mr. Caulfield said your father's will makes your inheritance clear, though I gather from his tone of voice that your proper British solicitor wasn't too pleased that an American baseball executive was the new Countess of Litchfield."

"Well, I'm not pleased either, and I don't want a title other than the one I already have. I don't see why I have to fly all the way to England to reject my inheritance. Have Caulfield send me the papers, I'll sign, and it's a done deal."

"Let me say again, you have no choice, CC, and it's not as simple as you might think. You have an estate and servants who have been with the family for years. You're going to have to sort this out in person."

"What does Flash have to say about all of this?" CC said, hoping her stepfather would give her a different perspective and secretly wishing he'd tell her to stay home, forget her inheritance, and keep to baseball matters.

"I'll put him on and he can tell you himself."

Flash must have been sitting right by the phone, because only seconds later his booming, deep voice exploded in CC's ear. "Hi, honey. Sorry to have to give you bad news like this."

"It's okay, Flash. I'm fine, but this title I've inherited has left me confused."

"That's no wonder. I suppose you'll have to tie some things up at the ballpark before you leave."

"You mean if I leave."

"As your mother said, you don't have a choice, CC. You have a responsibility to your father, even though it may appear to you that he never showed any concern for you. You need to go to England and attend to the earl's business. Who knows, you might like being one of those English aristocrats. Hey, you could start your own baseball team. Call it the Dukes of Earl."

"Very funny, Flash," CC said sarcastically, "but notice I'm not laughing? Pitchers and catchers reported to camp yesterday, and the rest of the team is trickling in. We're a little over six weeks away from opening day. You of all people should know I can't leave."

"Honey," Flash said sternly, and CC knew that he wasn't going to tell her what she wanted to hear, "you have to go to England. You owe it to your mother, if not to your father. Your people there in Indianapolis can run the organization. You put a good team together, and it's not as if we don't have telephones, fax machines, and e-mail. You'll manage."

"Oh Lord, Flash, I don't see how, but maybe you're right. That said, there's no way I can possibly be gone more than a week, so put Mother on the line and let her give me this Harrison Caulfield's number. Maybe he can have the papers ready for me to sign. As I told Mother, president of the Knights is all the title I need; that is, unless I should decide to be the first woman commissioner of baseball."

"Well, honey, I'm sure if you want to be the commissioner, you'll be the commissioner, but that's in the future. Right now, you go get some advice about managing your inheritance as your father would want you to."

"Now what does that mean?" CC was irritated at her stepfather's evasiveness.

"I don't know what it means. I'm just talking. Anyway, here's your mother. When you get to England, call us and let us know you're okay."

CHAPTER TWO

Two days later CC left Indianapolis for London. It had taken a day and a half to make arrangements for the trip and to deal with matters at the office so she could be away for a week or possibly two. Even though her mother suggested the trip could last up to a month, CC decided she could be away for fourteen days at most.

Despite Jim Oats's arguments in favor of the "Take Me Out to the Ballgame" hat, she chose the traditional cap, and though he protested, Jim ordered fifty thousand. She gave the plans for a salute to the newly retired Willy Snider, the Knights' long-time second baseman, to Wes, and he was going to contact community businesses and organizations to provide gifts in return for the publicity for their companies. Ownership gave final approval for the appointment of Cynthia Arden as vice president of community relations. One of CC's aims was to bring more capable and experienced women into the organization, and Cynthia fit the bill. She had worked for the Padres as assistant PR director for five years, and with the help of the Knights' staff, she would quickly learn the procedures and bring new ideas into a stagnant department in the organization.

She also worked out the final budget projections for the year with Walter Goodman, vice president of finance. She gave Bob ceilings for the two free agents the Knights were actively pursuing. CC wasn't sure she wanted one of the two, the often-difficult shortstop from Atlanta, but baseball was Bob's jurisdiction, and unlike some club presidents, she would not interfere. Only after completing these tasks was CC certain the organization would run well without her physical presence for a week or two.

After a seven-hour flight, she landed at Heathrow and quickly cleared immigration and customs. As she emerged from the restricted area into the terminal, she saw a uniformed man holding a sign saying "Litchfield Manor." All she could think of were the signs tour guides held up to identify themselves to members of their group.

The chauffeur cheerfully introduced himself as Stanley Warham. He took control of her luggage cart and led her to the car that was parked in a waiting zone in front of the terminal. As she settled back in the plush seat of the Jaguar, CC wondered how Stanley had managed to avoid getting a ticket while he waited for her in a no-parking zone.

But for the people driving on the wrong side of the road, CC could have believed she was back home. Factories, businesses, and advertising billboards lined the motorway, and people going toward town to work were caught in gridlock reminiscent of the Indianapolis morning rush hour. But when Stanley turned off the motorway onto the A4, a "dual-carriageway" the sign said, CC knew she was no longer in Indiana. The lush, green, rolling countryside dotted with small picturesque towns, each with its towering church steeple, seemed right out of a picture book. The landscape reminded her of a patchwork quilt with different shades of greens and browns created by the different crops planted in the fields. Those lighter colors contrasted with the deep green hedges, and the lone stands of dark trees scattered throughout the scene acted as the seams dividing the irregular patches. Everywhere sheep grazed alongside black-and-white-spotted cows in the bucolic scene. CC put down her window and took a deep breath of the incredibly fresh air.

During the first part of the trip, Stanley was quiet, allowing his new mistress time to enjoy the scenery. He politely answered the several questions CC asked, but to her, it seemed as if more than a glass barrier separated driver and passenger and she felt extremely uncomfortable. She was aware that class distinction was the British way. She had a title and Stanley was her servant, but this concept was totally foreign to her. There were no artificial titles to divide people in America. CC suddenly felt a rush of pride in her country, but quickly her enthusiasm for her native land gave way to a feeling of uneasiness. To Stanley, she was not an American. England was her country.

Jet lag and lack of sleep during the flight had taken their toll, so she dozed for a while. It seemed as if she had slept for only a few minutes when the different rhythm of the slowing car awakened her. As she looked out the window, she suddenly remembered reading a storybook as a child. She couldn't recall the title, but the tale was about a little English girl who often went to the park with her nanny. From the author's description, CC had decided then and there what an English park would look like in springtime, and her surroundings at that moment fit the picture she had conjured up in her mind. Well-manicured lawns broken up by an occasional well-clipped hedge stretched far into the distance. Giant trees lifted their heavy limbs toward the azure-blue cloud-dotted sky. As she gazed at the landscape around her, CC realized that this beautiful picture was not a scene from her storybook. This was her own English park, her estate.

The narrow, single-lane road slanted upward to the great gray house on the bluff ahead. As the car approached the manor gates, a male peacock that Stanley identified as George spread his feathers and strutted to impress the peahens that strolled nearby. "He's incredibly beautiful," CC said.

"He is, Your Ladyship, but you must remember to be careful of George when you approach him. He can be quite a testy fellow and he doesn't react too well to strangers who come around."

"I appreciate the advice, and if it's all the same, Stanley, I wish you would call me CC instead of Your Ladyship. Somehow, I think the name fits me better."

Stanley's cool response told CC that this would be her first and last attempt to get the staff to address her less formally. "I'm afraid that wouldn't be proper, Your Ladyship. However, I'm certain that you'll soon become used to and even like your new title."

Fat chance of that happening, CC mused. She knew that Stanley had reprimanded her as gently as possible.

As they approached the broad sweep of gravel in front of the main entrance, CC peered out at her father's home. From what she could tell, there were three linked parts, a massive center joined by curving colonnades to a substantial wing on each side.

"Would you like to know something about the house?" Stanley asked.

"I certainly would."

Stanley stopped the car before entering the driveway. "I'll describe the layout as you look at the façade. The house was built in the 1720s. It remained much as it was until your grandfather began a major restoration project about five years before his death. Your father took over where his father left off and the project was completed about a year ago. Every room was beautifully refurbished, that is, except for a chapel that had long since fallen into disuse. None of us knows why the earl skipped that particular room, but I'm sure he had his reasons."

"Did you ask him?"

"No, my lady," Stanley said in disbelief. "It wasn't my place."

Of course not, CC mused. *How could I ask such a stupid question?* She dropped the subject—for now. "

The west wing contains a music room, your father's favorite area on that side of the house; several smaller parlors; a formal dining room; a morning or breakfast room, the last addition to the house, and a state-of the art kitchen which includes a china closet, butler's pantry, and laundry facilities."

"And the chapel you just mentioned," she added, looking for a response from Stanley. For some inexplicable reason, she was drawn in by what Stanley said about a room that was left untouched while the rest of the house was being carefully restored.

"Yes, the chapel is also there," Stanley said curtly, and CC wondered if her chauffeur truly didn't know why the room had been left in its original state, or if he knew and wasn't sharing the reason with her. *Now why would that be?* she asked herself; immediately realizing her contemplations were ludicrous. *What the hell am I doing?* She answered her own question. *I'm making a mystery out of something that's not mysterious. Stanley said my father hadn't restored his chapel. Why would that merit analysis? And yet it's so strange.*

"...Contains only two rooms" was what CC heard. She had no idea what Stanley had said while she was thinking about the chapel, "the long portrait gallery where dinner is served to guests after a ball, and the ballroom at the far end of the gallery."

"Only two rooms on the second level of the west wing?" CC asked, hoping Stanley wouldn't know she wasn't paying attention. "They must be very large."

"They are, my lady, and they're quite beautiful. There's a hidden staircase from the kitchen so servants can deliver food upstairs without entering from the grand staircase."

"I look forward to seeing the rooms and the hidden entry," CC responded, glad she'd figured out what Stanley was talking about without asking him to repeat himself.

"The servant's hall and sleeping quarters are on the lower level of this wing. They are accessible from the kitchen as well as from the delivery entrance at the rear of the kitchen. The third floor has additional rooms for servants of your father's guests as well as storage space."

"And the east wing?" CC asked.

"The east wing has several formal rooms. We will pass through two drawing rooms which your father used when he entertained. There is also writing room where Lady Anne wrote her letters every morning. Several years ago your father had a wireless network installed throughout the house, but Lady Anne never felt email was appropriate for social correspondence."

"Then out of respect for her, I'll set up my computer elsewhere."

Stanley nodded. "You could use your father's private library, if you'd like. It's the last room on the main floor of the east wing. It was your grandfather's office before your father converted it to a reading room and the place where he conducted formal business."

"That would be wonderful," CC smiled warmly. "I will have a great deal of work to do while I'm here and will need a space to spread out."

"Very good, my lady."

"And what about the rest of the east wing?"

"There are two more what I would call important rooms. Your father and Lady Anne spent their private evenings after dinner in the Blue Parlor. It has a large built-in telly with a DVD player and an excellent sound system that your father actually had piped into all the first-floor rooms throughout the house. And when the earl or Lady Anne entertained close friends, they used the White Drawing Room, your father's favorite room."

CC laughed. "It sounds like my father had a lot of favorite rooms."

"I guess I have used the word 'favorite' more than once, my lady, but when you actually see the rooms I'm talking about, you'll understand. Each of the earl's favorite rooms was special for a different reason." Stanley chuckled at his attempt to explain. "I know what I said sounds ridiculous," he said, "but it's true."

"I'm sure it is, and please don't think I'm laughing at you. I'm eager to see all of my father's favorite rooms. However, I do have a question, and perhaps it's because life at my home in Indianapolis is obviously so much more casual than life at Litchfield."

"I'll try to answer all of your questions, Your Ladyship."

He's certainly eager to please, CC thought as she continued. "Thank you, Stanley. If the Blue Parlor has a TV and fantastic stereo system, why wouldn't my father and Lady Anne entertain close friends there?"

Stanley seemed surprised. "Friends who came to dine were never asked to watch television, my lady."

"Of course not." CC smiled, thinking of all the times she had people over to watch the games and how gauche Stanley, and even her father, would find this sort of entertaining.

"The second floor contains several guest suites and your father's and Lady Anne's personal rooms. On the third floor are additional guest rooms, though they're not as elegant as the ones on the second floor."

"What a wonderful place, and the setting is magnificent, Stanley. I look forward to exploring the house." *Including that mysterious chapel,* CC mused. "Would you tell me something about my family's history?" she asked as Stanley turned into the driveway. "I'm sorry to say I don't know much about my family tree."

"Certainly, my lady. Your great-great-grandfather was the illegitimate son of the second Earl of Litchfield, George Henry Lee. Lee was the grandson of Charles II and his mistress Barbara Villiers, Duchess of Cleveland."

"Charles II. Let's see, if I remember my English history, he was restored to the throne after the Commonwealth Interregnum."

"That's correct." Stanley seemed both surprised and pleased that an American would know anything about English history. "The second earl had no legitimate heirs, so their child, Charles Cleveland, was given his great-grandmother's title and surname and, much to the family's disappointment, became the third earl. At his death, the title passed to his son, your great-grandfather, the fourth earl. His son left the title to his son, your grandfather, the fifth earl, and then the title passed to your father, the sixth earl. Now, with his death and no male heirs, the title is yours." *Even if I don't want it at all,* CC reflected. *Wouldn't Stanley be shocked if he knew that?* "You'll hear much more about house once you're inside, my lady. Shall we go?"

"Of course, Stanley, drive on." As soon as she said the words, CC giggled. "Drive on" sounded so aristocratic and so British.

She was certain Dame Judith Evans said the same thing to her chauffeur in some British movie. As they neared the steps, CC noticed a group of people lining the front walkway. Stanley explained that while she was sleeping he had called ahead and these were members of the staff who were eager to see she was properly welcomed to her new home.

About twenty uniformed individuals stood waiting as the car pulled up to the front door. The dignified man at the head of the line, resplendent in his tails and obviously in charge, opened CC's door and introduced himself. "Welcome, Your Ladyship. I am Hastings, the butler."

"Good morning." Without thinking, CC extended her hand. Hastings ignored the gesture and bowed politely.

"Please let me introduce you to some of your staff." He moved beside but slightly behind CC and, without actually making contact, ushered her down the line. "This is Austen, the housekeeper, Your Ladyship. She sees that the activities in the house run smoothly, and besides myself, is the person you should seek out if you have problems or specific needs." The older woman nodded, curtsied, and smiled.

"And this is Richard, my lady. He was your father's valet."

"The earl was an exceptional man," Richard said. "I wish I had known him better."

CC looked puzzled so Hastings explained. "Richard became part of the staff six months before your father's death, my lady. He replaced Hargrave, who retired after faithfully serving your grandfather and then your father. After the earl's death Richard stayed on to help out where he's needed. Now that you've taken up residence, he will once again become a permanent member of the staff."

"If there's anything you need and Hastings is unavailable, I'll be glad to assist you, Your Ladyship."

CC smiled. "Thank you, Richard. I will."

Hastings presented John Claude and Charles, the chefs. "Please let us know what kinds of meals you prefer and we will see that you are well served," John Claude said, and both men bowed.

"Thank you," CC replied.

"Jean and Millie are the upstairs maids who will serve you until you choose your own personal maid," Hastings continued. "And these are our head gardeners, Collins and Conrad." Both men tipped their caps. "And this is Crooks, who is in charge of the stables. He and his grooms will have horses ready for you to ride anytime you like."

The old man grinned and took off his hat. "Morning, Your Ladyship, and welcome."

"Good morning, Crooks." CC smiled.

Hastings quickly introduced the rest of the group. From his tone, CC guessed they were less important maids and kitchen personnel who had come out to greet her. "Of course there are additional servants, Your Ladyship, but since we were unsure when you'd arrive, we allowed those who were scheduled to have the day off to take their time away. You will meet the remainder of your staff tomorrow."

"Thank you, Mr. Hastings."

"Just Hastings, Your Ladyship."

"Of course." CC realized she'd have to brush up on proper British etiquette. With Hastings beside her, she climbed the broad, worn steps into the house and entered an enormous foyer. From the center of the room, a circular staircase split off from a wide set of stairs. One apparently led to the east wing and the other to the west wing of the house.

Jean took her coat and briefcase and CC followed Hastings straight ahead into the hall. She paused to marvel at the remarkable chamber with its central tower that rose through the second story. Hastings remained quiet while CC studied the room and then asked, "While Stanley puts your luggage in your rooms and Jean and Millie unpack for you, would you like to see the house?"

"I would if you'll tell me about each room as we pass through."

"My pleasure, Your Ladyship. We'll begin here in the Great Hall, which was most recently used as the main drawing room. It was originally intended to be a place for the earls to greet their guests, so it was designed to set a tone of scholarship and refinement so important in the eighteenth century when the house was constructed. The sculptured figures above us represent the arts and sciences, and the busts reclining in pairs above the fireplaces and on brackets high above the doors to each of the wings are of well-known eighteenth-century writers and philosophers."

"The hall's magnificent," CC said, suddenly glad she'd been forced to study art and architecture during her freshman and sophomore years at NU when she had to get "those silly requirements" out of the way. At least she could seem semi-knowledgeable. "It's a wonderful example of eighteenth century ostentation." She smiled when she saw Hastings's surprised expression.

Smiling, Hastings ushered her into the first drawing room in the east wing. She admired the walls, which he explained, were covered in early nineteenth-century Lyon silks. On either side of the fireplace, splendid portraits of the first Earl of Litchfield and his countess, painted by Reynolds, stared down from the wall.

They passed through another small parlor into the Blue Parlor Stanley had mentioned. Like a museum docent, Hastings point out the portrait of Barbara Villiers painted by Sir Peter Lely, the seventeenth-century artist and most baroque of English portrait painters. He called CC's attention to the companion painting of Villiers's royal lover at the other end of the room. "It's as if they're staring at each other for all eternity," she said smiling.

"I hadn't thought of it that way," said Hastings, "but I suppose you're right."

Despite the formal wall hangings, the obviously comfortable furniture gave the room a more casual feel than the formal rooms she'd just viewed. *I'll definitely use the Blue Parlor for entertaining,* she reflected as Hastings led her from the room. She frowned when she realized what she'd said, *but who would I entertain in the short two weeks I'll be at Litchfield?* Hastings didn't mention the television or sound system Stanley told her about. She didn't ask, but she guessed they were hidden in a large cabinet opposite the couches and were obviously not important enough to mention.

On the other side of the Blue Parlor was a stunning rectangular room containing a fabulous mixture of priceless antiques; comfortable brocade-covered easy chairs and sofas; an elegantly carved fireplace; marble statuary, and large oil paintings. "This is the White Drawing Room," Hastings said. CC immediately agreed with her father. Besides the Blue Parlor, this was the most comfortable and livable room she had seen thus far.

As they walked back through the east wing, Hastings pointed out the subtly hidden doors at the back of each room. "Those lead to a long hall, my lady. Servants use the corridor to travel from room to room without disturbing our guests."

"Stanley told me my grandfather modernized the house in the 1930s," CC said.

"He did." When he inherited the house from his father, the fourth earl, it had no central heating, no electricity, and only two baths. It was quite unpleasant, or so my father told me. He spent his entire life in the service of the family as did his father. By the by, your grandfather also restored the park and garden to the condition that Capability Brown intended when he created the design in 1770. Have you heard of Capability Brown, my lady?"

"I have." CC said, again thankful for the general courses she was required to take.

"I know you'll enjoy the gardens," Hastings was saying. The spring weather has been delightful. The roses are already beginning to bud. If you'd like, I'll take you on a tour of the gardens later this afternoon, but first, would you like to see the west wing?"

"Please," CC answered, fascinated by her father's house and wanting to see more.

Hastings ushered her through a small parlor off of the Great Hall into the Music Room. The room's main attraction was a magnificent mahogany and satinwood harpsichord. CC walked over to corner. "How old is the piece," she asked.

"It dates from the late eighteenth century, my lady. "This room was used extensively during the Victorian and Edwardian periods. At the time, all proper young ladies prided themselves on their ability to play and sing. Since we now have the telly in the Blue Parlor and a sound system throughout the house, this room isn't used for entertaining, except for concerts the earl sometimes had for his guests. Lady Anne loved music, so your father purchased the grand piano in the other corner of the room. Until just before she died, Lady Anne preferred the harpsichord and played every day."

He gestured toward a French door, and CC entered a splendid formal dining room with tall windows offering incredible views of the gardens; a large crystal chandelier suspended over an exquisite mahogany table that extended almost the entire length of the room, and a highly polished woodblock floor. Two enormous matching sideboards laden with sterling silver serving pieces were on opposite sides of the walls. Beside each side of the French doors that led from the music room were built-in glass-fronted cabinets, which contained an impressive collection of fine English bone china. "If you appreciate fine china, my lady, I'd be happy to explain the dining collection and show you what we store in the china room."

"I'd like that, thank you."

"If you'll follow me." Hastings pushed open the second of three French door. "This is the Yellow Morning Room." CC immediately loved the light, airy atmosphere of the octagonal breakfast room brightened by light flooding in through floor-to-ceiling windows, though she could hardly call a room of this size a breakfast room by definition.

"Lady Anne had the walls covered with this light yellow silk damask, because, as I told you, your father wanted a comfortable and bright place to relax for a light luncheon alone or with her or several friends."

"If you will follow me, my lady, I will show you the last of the main-floor public rooms your father made use of. There is a chapel at this end of this wing, but I'm afraid it has fallen into disrepair and has not been used in years. For some unknown reason, the earl showed little interest in having it restored."

"That's what Stanley said," CC responded, again wondering why her father had redone all the rooms in the house except the chapel.

They passed several closed doors that Hasting didn't offer to open, and CC presumed that what lay behind them wasn't anything she should see. When he finished the tour, he led her back to the Great Hall and up the staircase into the west-wing gallery Stanley had mentioned.

Once again, CC was astonished. The rectangular space, which she estimated was at least one hundred-forty feet long, was magnificent. Portraits of what she assumed were her ancestors lined the walls above pagoda-topped Chinese Chippendale chairs. "Oh my," was all she could say.

"I take it you approve?" Hastings said.

"How could I possibly not?"

"I thought you might, my lady. Though the room was originally constructed only to display family portraits, your father turned it into a functional room, utilizing it for sizeable parties. It and the ballroom through those closed doors at the other end of the gallery could accommodate numerous guests. When we needed to serve more company than we are able to seat in the dining room, we would set up one long table or numerous round tables for more intimate groupings in here."

"How wonderful," CC said, imagining what the room would look like when it was filled with ladies and gentlemen resplendent in their finery.

"As we pass through, you'll note that your family portraits have been hung in chronological order. Your father's likeness is at the end of the hall before the entrance to the ballroom."

Hastings led the way, walking slowly so CC could admire the paintings of her ancestors as she approached the far end of the gallery. When she reached the painting of her father, he stepped aside, leaving her alone in front of the man who had played no part in her life, but who, with his death, had changed it tremendously.

CC studied her father's face. Everyone said she was the spitting image of her mother, but when she stared up at William's portrait, her own eyes looked back at her. William's eyes weren't as blue but they drooped at the corners like hers. *I wonder how many other traits we share,* CC though as she turned wordlessly away from the painting.

After a quick glance at the ballroom, Hastings took her back to the Great Hall where Austen waited to show her to her rooms on the second floor. CC thanked Hastings for the tour and followed the housekeeper up the stairs and into the east wing. They passed several guestrooms, and when they reached her suite, Millie and Jean were waiting.

"I hope this will be satisfactory, my lady." Austen bobbed a curtsey. "If not, there are several other guestrooms you may consider."

"These are lovely, Austen," and CC wasn't exaggerating. The room was furnished in the Victorian style and exuded a sense of family living that had gone back generations. It was comfortable, so everything-that-it-ought-to-be, that even though different in décor, she immediately felt as much at home here as she did in her own room in Indianapolis. She examined the huge walk-in closet; the sitting room; the large, airy dressing room, and the extremely modern bath, complete with tub and shower, something Austen said was highly unusual in English manor houses, where most showers were hand-held fixtures attached to the bathtub.

"These were Lady Anne's rooms," the housekeeper explained as they walked back into the bedroom. "Hastings and

I felt that your father's suite was too masculine for a lady's tastes. However, if you would prefer to be situated there—"

CC smiled. "These rooms will do beautifully, Austen. She wondered if Hastings put her in Anne's suite because her father's rooms weren't appropriate for a lady, or because he felt she'd be uncomfortable in his suite so soon after his death. She would be, but not for the reasons Hastings imagined. She could hardly feel the loss of her father in this house. Her father lived in Arizona. The man who slept down the hall, though she resembled him in some ways, was a stranger who meant nothing to her and who had never cared enough to see her.

Millie and Jean had unpacked and put her clothes away. Instead of exploring Ann's rooms, she lay on the bed to rest for a few minutes.

CC ended up sleeping all afternoon. At four, she dragged herself out of bed, showered, dressed, and went down to the library, where she now sat. She had been at Litchfield Manor for less than a day and already she was able to understand her father's devotion to his home and his heritage. Suddenly her life seemed exceedingly complicated. She realized the decisions she'd be making in the weeks ahead would be difficult. It was no longer as simple as saying her ties and loyalties were only to the Indianapolis Knights and to Major League Baseball. It was no longer as simple as signing some papers and returning home in Indianapolis. She was in England, sitting in her father's office, and suddenly everything was different.

CHAPTER THREE

The telephone interrupted CC's thoughts. Instinctively she jumped up from the couch, but by the time she reached the table, the ringing had stopped. "Of course," she said aloud. "No one would dare let Lady Litchfield answer her own phone."

Moments later Hastings appeared at the door. "There's a call from your office, my lady. Your secretary said she was unable to reach you on your cell phone."

"It must have lost the charge," CC said.

"Would you like to take the call in here?"

"Of course, Hastings." CC realized that her response was too abrupt and added, "Thank you."

Leslie's voice was so clear she sounded as if she were in her own adjoining office rather than thousands of miles away. "Morning, CC. How was the flight?"

"Long, and it's not morning here. How are things there?"

"Pretty routine. Except for another of Jim's wild ideas, everything is on track. Cynthia left for Florida this morning. She actually seemed excited about all of those dinners."

"She'll learn. What's our favorite marketing director doing this time? I thought I left him squared away."

"Apparently not, and Wes is fuming. He just tossed a newspaper ad for opening day on my desk and asked me to call you. It seems that Jim forgot to include the date and the time of the game in the copy."

"Oh God! Get Wes on the line for me. I'll come back to you before I hang up." While Leslie transferred the call, CC seethed. "What am I going to do with this guy?"

"What guy?" Wes heard only the last part of the sentence. "I was talking about Jim. Hi, Wes. Leslie tells me we have a little problem."

"Actually we have two problems, CC. One's solved. I called WBJQ. They're broadcasting the date and time of the game on their sportscasts throughout the day. The paper will reprint the corrected ad tomorrow."

"At their expense, I hope."

"'Fraid not. The paper's not at fault. They didn't design the ad."

"What?"

"You heard me. Jim's hired an independent artist to draw our ads for the paper."

"But the paper provides a free layout designer with the package we purchased. How much is Jim paying this artist?"

"I figured you'd ask that question, so I called Walt. The first bill just arrived."

"The one for the botched ad?"

"Right. The design for the ad cost ten thousand dollars."

"You've got to be kidding? Ten thousand dollars for something we could get for free? Transfer me to Jim, will you Wes?"

"I would love to, CC, but he's out to lunch with clients. I just tried to see him myself."

CC looked at her watch. "It's a little early for lunch isn't it? Did he let anyone know when he might be back?"

"I don't know, but I can transfer you to Susan."

"In a minute. Anything else new?"

"No. Everything's on track."

"Then give me Susan and I'll see if I can find out when her boss will be back in the office. And Wes, don't hesitate to call here at any time. I'm always available. I haven't been here long enough to find out if we have a fax, but I have my laptop and cell, though I have to buy a converter for the chargers. I'll let you know when I'm up and running."

"I will, and CC, are you doing okay?"

"I am. Thanks for asking. I'll be home before you know it."

"Good. We need you. Here's Susan."

Susan sounded slightly flustered when she answered the phone and told CC that her boss would be in by two. "You have got to be kidding," CC barked. "A three-hour lunch?" Quickly realizing that the secretary wasn't the one she needed to reprimand, she regained her composure and asked Susan to have Jim call her when he returned, "no matter the hour."

CC hung up, and as she sat wondering if Jim was going to use her time away from the office to cause trouble or to push through his own agenda, Hastings came in followed by a freshly scrubbed young man carrying a huge silver tray. "Would you prefer tea here or in the White Drawing Room, my lady?"

"Here please, Hastings." The aroma of freshly baked pastries made CC realize she was hungry. Her last meal had been on the plane early that morning.

"This is James, my lady. He works for the kitchen staff in the afternoons after school."

"It's nice to meet you, James. You can put the tray over by the couch." CC smiled, thinking again that England was not much different from the United States. Kids got after school jobs here too; they just didn't work at Burger King. They worked as servants in manor houses.

James poured the tea as CC eyed the freshly baked scones and the strawberry jam. "Would you care for some clotted cream, Your Ladyship?"

"Clotted cream?"

"Clotted cream is cream that forms naturally when fresh milk is warmed. I believe you'll find it to your liking," Hastings said.

"Then by all means I'll try it." Hastings poured the cream, which seemed to remain on the top of the tea. CC stirred the hot liquid that turned a milky brown and sipped. "This is wonderful, and those scones look delicious."

"Then we'll leave you to enjoy them. Will there be anything else?"

"Not at the moment, Hastings, but I do want to alert you that until my cell is charged I'll be receiving quite a few telephone calls. Does the phone ring throughout the house?"

"It does, my lady. All calls coming into the main house will be for you. Calls for the kitchen and staff quarters come in on several other lines that do not ring in the main house."

"In that case, Hastings, if it wouldn't be too inappropriate, I would like to answer the phone personally if I'm at home or unless I tell you otherwise. This way no one will be inconvenienced."

"Of course. I'll instruct the staff, and if any calls come when you're out, we will certainly take messages for you."

"Thank you." CC took another sip of tea and reached for a printed card that lay on the tray.

"Oh, I almost forgot, my lady. You were resting when John Claude planned dinner. He's quite anxious to prepare a meal that will please you on your first night here. Ordinarily he would consult with you, but we decided not to awaken you after your long journey. You're holding tonight's menu. We hope it meets with your approval."

"I'm certain it will, Hastings. What time is dinner usually served?"

"Your father dined at precisely eight every evening. Will that be convenient for you or would you like to make other arrangements?"

"Eight will be fine. Thank you." CC looked at the beautifully printed menu.

Appetizer
Steamed Courgette a Fleur filled with
Salmon and Crab Mousse on White Butter Sauce
Entree
Medallions of Veal Fillet with a Tagliaelli of Vegetables
on a Sweet Meaux Mustard Sauce
Dessert
Rich Chocolate Paved with Cream
Wine
Domaine du Petit Chateau, Muscadet de Serve et Maine
sur Lie
1985
Coffee and Sweets in the Salon

Good Lord! If I eat like this every night, I'll have to pay for two seats just for me when I fly home, she thought as she put the card and the half-eaten scone on the tray. She would wait for dinner.

As she sipped her second cup of tea with clotted cream, a fattening treat she decided she'd have to forego most of the time, Hastings came to the door. "You have guests, my lady. Sir Anthony and Lady Alexandra Chadlington have come to pay their respects. Will you receive them?"

Do I have a choice? was CC's first thought, but she didn't verbalize her irritation at the arrival of uninvited guests.

"Who are Sir Anthony and Lady Alexandra Chadlington?" CC repeated the names so that they would stick with her, a technique she had learned when trying to keep all those baseball people straight in her mind.

"They are your neighbors, my lady. That is, they live twenty miles away at Chadlington Manor. Lady Alexandra is about your age. She rang us yesterday to ask when you would be arriving. I believe they've stopped in to welcome you."

"In that case, of course I'll see them. Please show them in." CC giggled again as she had when she first told Stanley to drive on. How could she sound so British and so proper in just hours? At the office if she said "show them in," Leslie would double over with laughter.

Moments later Hastings's voice boomed from the door. "May I present Sir Anthony and Lady Alexandra Chadlington, Your Ladyship?"

Alexandra Chadlington breezed by the butler and extended her hand to CC. For some unknown reason CC, who was usually quite slow to make a judgment about whether or not she liked a person, warmed immediately. "How do you do, Lady Alexandra." CC took the woman's hand.

"Quite well, and please call me Alex. What should I call you?"

CC appreciated the woman's firm handshake. "I would love it if you'd call me CC. Somehow I can't get used to being called 'your ladyship' or 'my lady.'"

"Then CC it is, and this is my husband, Tony." Tony extended his hand and grasped CC's firmly.

Alexandra Chadlington was a darling woman. Standing about five-feet-one, she was petite and exuded endless energy. Her brown curly hair was streaked with premature gray that only added to her stylish look. Bright blue eyes sparkled above her slightly turned-up pug nose. Her grin was contagious, and CC couldn't help but smile in return. Tony, an attractive man with salt and pepper hair, appeared to be a few years older than his wife and slightly more subdued, but CC immediately knew she would like him too. In fact, his charming face and sympathetic blue eyes reminded her of the GM at Philadelphia, a man she really enjoyed being around.

Tony greeted her warmly. "I'm so pleased to meet you, CC. We know you're tired from your trip over the pond, but we were returning from business in Oxford and couldn't resist stopping in to say hello."

"I'm glad you did. Please sit down and have tea with me. I was beginning to feel rather lonely in this huge old house."

"We would absolutely love to," Alex said enthusiastically. At that moment, as if anticipating Sir Anthony and Lady Alexandra would stay, Hastings arrived with a fresh pot of the steaming brew, a container of fresh clotted cream, and some finger sandwiches.

While they sipped their tea, the three talked nonstop. CC told them about herself, her job, and the reason for her trip. Usually cautious until she got to know an individual, she surprised herself at how open she was with these new acquaintances.

In turn, Alex told her about Chadlington and invited her to come for tea and a tour of the manor the following day. CC accepted and promised to call and confirm after she found out what her schedule would entail. Her first priority was to see her father's attorneys in London, and she could not plan a definite time to visit until she knew when the meeting would take place.

It was six-thirty when Alex and Tony got up to leave. CC wondered if she should have invited them to dinner, but she didn't know the procedures at Litchfield or if there was enough food being prepared to serve guests. She would have to find out from Hastings for future reference. She walked her new friends to the front door, where the two women embraced warmly. CC hoped that her schedule the next day could be arranged to include tea with her neighbors.

No one had told CC what to wear for dinner, but she imagined from the looks of the menu, elegant casual would be apropos. She went upstairs to her room. As she was freshening up her makeup, the phone by her bed rang. CC glanced at her watch. It was too early for Jim to be back from lunch. Pleased that Hastings had told the staff she'd be taking her own calls, she answered and breathed a sigh of relief. It wasn't Jim; it was Bud calling from New York. "Hi, sweetheart, I can't believe we're actually talking," he said cheerfully. It seems we've been playing phone tag these last few days."

"We have. How are you?"

"I'm fine. How are you doing? I was sorry to hear about your father, CC."

"Thanks, Bud, I'm fine. I never laid eyes on the man you're calling my father. It's not like something happened to Flash. Litchfield Manor is quite a place. I'll tell you all about it when I get home, hopefully next week. If it fits into your schedule, I'll have Leslie book a flight so I can clear customs in New York rather than Chicago. Maybe we can have dinner together."

"I hope we can do more than that. I miss you."

"I miss you too, but I'm not sure how much time I'll have. I have to be back in the office as soon as possible."

"Of course you do, CC." CC noted the quick change from warmth to exasperation in Bud's voice. She frowned and made an effort to make things right.

"I'll really try, Bud. Let me deal with the issues here. Then we'll make plans. I don't like being apart any more than you do, but this is my first season—"

Bud cut her off before she could give him the excuse he'd heard so often in recent months. He wouldn't argue across an ocean. "I know it," he said glumly and CC could hear the irritation and frustration he was feeling. He quickly changed the subject. "Is there anything I can do for you?"

"Actually, there is. Everything's under control at the office, but there may be one problem."

"Don't tell me, Jim Oats? What's he doing this time?"

"Nothing I haven't been able to handle, but would you keep your ears open while I'm away? If you get wind of anything out of the ordinary, let me know so I can deal with the problem before it gets out of hand. I mean if Jim applies to have the logo changed, I'd like to know."

Bud laughed. "I doubt he would do anything that brazen, but I'll listen. Anything else I can do?"

"Take care of yourself and know I love you and miss you."

"I love you too, CC. I'll talk with you soon."

CC hung up feeling quite dejected. She loved Bud, but lately, saying I love you had become almost rote. She wondered if she and Bud would ever get it right. Would they ever be at the same place at the same time? She finished dressing and went downstairs for her first meal at Litchfield Manor.

CHAPTER FOUR

Dinner was delicious. CC was particularly impressed with the presentation of each dish. She wondered if she dared ask John Claude to give her the recipes for his sauces and sent her compliments to the chefs after each course. The only downbeat aspect of the meal was the setting. She sat alone at the huge mahogany table that would easily seat eight down each side and two at each end without adding any leaves.

James stood dutifully by like a sentry waiting to obey orders, but he never spoke. CC guessed the French door he guarded led to the kitchen, but she was not sure since her initial tour hadn't included a room that Hastings obviously felt would be of no interest to her.

It was apparent that James was there to clear dishes, to see that CC always had a full glass of wine, and to ring the bell cord to indicate that she was ready for the next course. Hastings stuck his head in from time to time, but always without comment.

The china and silver were elegant, and CC was eager to know their age and history, but there was no one to ask, and James certainly wouldn't know. When she finished the last bite of her rich chocolate dessert, James was behind her to pull her chair out for her. "Coffee and sweets will be served in the Blue Parlor, my lady," he said politely.

"Just coffee, thank you, James. I couldn't eat anything else."

"As you wish. I will inform Hastings."

CC moved through the Great Hall toward the Blue Parlor, marveling again at the beauty of the decor that she planned to study in more depth in the days ahead. Coffee was waiting on a silver tray placed on a small highly-polished table in front of a lovely blue and rose-colored tapestry chair. CC poured the steaming brew into a small demitasse cup. She took a sip and shuddered. This was unquestionably the strongest coffee she had ever had. She added cream to fill the cup to the top, doubting that she would ever get to sleep if she drank very much.

She wanted to call Hastings and ask for a larger cup so that she could dilute the brew with more cream, but she had no idea how to summon the servants. Each time she'd needed him in the hours before, Hastings had appeared as if he'd sensed her needs. Now, when he was leaving her alone to enjoy her coffee, she wanted to talk with him and had no way to let him know.

She got up and roamed back toward the dining room where James and several servants were clearing away the last of the dishes. "Excuse me, James. I'd like to speak with Hastings. Is he anywhere in the vicinity?" James rang the tapestry cord by the dining room door, and minutes later Hastings appeared. "I'm sorry to bother you, Hastings, but I would like a larger cup for my coffee. It's delicious but a little too strong for me."

"Of course. James will see to it right away, my lady. Will there be anything else?"

"As a matter of fact, this may seem like a silly question, but I wonder how to call you if I need to speak with you."

"I apologize, my lady. There is so much I should have gone over with you this afternoon, but I hated to awaken you. In the future, if you need me, just pull a tapestry cord like this one." He pointed to the cord James had just pulled. "You'll find one in each room. They look rather old fashioned, but they are electronically connected to my rooms, Austen's room, the servant's hall, and the kitchen. Someone will see to your needs immediately. Incidentally, my lady, this fax just arrived for you. I didn't want to disturb you during dinner and was going to bring it to you after you finished coffee, but since you're here—"

"Thank you." CC took the fax, pleased to know Litchfield had a modern communications system.

She walked back toward the parlor, sat down and read the message. It was from Harrison Caulfield from the firm of Caulfield, Ailesbury and Bedford requesting that Lady Litchfield come to their offices in the Chesham Executive Suites, 150 Regent Street, London at precisely eleven the following morning. Luncheon at Wilton's on Jermyn Street would follow at twelve-thirty.

CC was amazed there was no number to call if the time of the meeting or luncheon was unsatisfactory. She assumed this was as near a command performance as she would ever have. She rang for Hastings, who appeared promptly. "I need to be in London on Regent Street tomorrow at eleven, Hastings. What time should I plan to leave here?"

"I would recommend that Stanley bring the car up at eight forty-five. With morning traffic heading into London, that should be sufficient time to deliver you to your appointment at the time Mr. Caulfield specified. I'll let Stanley know of your plans before I retire. That will mean breakfast will need to be served at seven. Would you care to come down to the breakfast room or would you prefer to eat in your rooms?"

"After tonight's feast, I hardly think I'll need much to eat in the morning. If I could just have some coffee, fruit, and wheat toast in my room that would be lovely."

"Of course. Would you like to be awakened earlier than seven?"

"No thank you. I have a travel alarm clock with me."

"In that case, unless you need something else..."

"Nothing, Hastings, thank you."

"I'll say good night then, but if you should require anything else or need additional assistance, please ring. I won't retire until I know you're in your rooms and need nothing more."

"I'm sure that will be all." *There's that formal aristocratic response again.* CC frowned, thinking that she didn't even sound like herself anymore. Hastings turned to leave when she interrupted him: "And Hastings, thank you again."

The butler smiled and bowed, but before he could pull the doors closed, CC stopped him once more. "Oh, Hastings. I almost forgot. Sir Anthony and Lady Alexandra have invited me for tea tomorrow afternoon. Would you please ask Stanley to plan our route so that we could stop by Chadlington Manor before returning home?"

"Certainly, and would you like for me to inform Mason, the Chadlington's butler, that you will accept their invitation?"

"I'd appreciate it. I forgot to ask Alex, uh, Lady Alexandra, for her phone number, and I imagine I'll be on my way to London before an appropriate time to call."

"I'll take care of it early tomorrow. Good night, my lady."

"Thank you and good night."

CC returned to the Blue Parlor and sat for a few more minutes, trying to enjoy the diluted but still-too-strong coffee. Tomorrow night she would make it half-and-half, half coffee and half milk. The fire blazing in the fireplace relaxed her and made her feel rather drowsy. She left the coffee cup on the silver tray and went upstairs to make her calls from her bedroom and then get to bed so she would feel rested for her appointment in the morning.

When CC opened her bedroom door, the bed was turned down and Millie was waiting. "Would you like for me to draw a bath, Your Ladyship?"

"That won't be necessary, thank you, Millie. In fact I don't need anything else tonight."

"As you wish." Millie curtsied and left the room. *Such formality*, CC mused. She crossed the room and opened the closet to take out her robe. She hadn't spent much time in her rooms except for sleeping or freshening up for dinner. She undressed, put on her robe, and went into the attractive, airy sitting room.

"This is lovely," she said as she admired the autumnal color scheme of green, gold, russet, and deep peach-pink room. A fire blazed in the carved wooden fireplace, further adding to the warm, cozy atmosphere. The room was furnished with two comfortable settees, one on each side of a table upon which rested a stack of current magazines and newspapers. A myriad of antique figurines, cups and saucers, plates and teapots attested to the fact that this was a lady's room.

Numerous books, some which looked like leather-bound first editions and other more recent bestsellers, filled the shelves of a beautiful eighteenth-century secretary. CC pulled out a first addition of *Gulliver's Travels* and carefully turned the pages before putting the book back, fearful she would somehow damage the fragile paper.

An arrangement of fresh flowers adorned the coffee table and another larger arrangement decorated the mantle. Opposite one of the settees was a large console television with a built-in VCR/DVD player. *All the modern conveniences in an ancient house*, she thought. *I wonder if ESPN telecasts baseball games to England.*

On the wall opposite the double door she had come in, CC noticed an identical double door. She went over to investigate. The door opened into another bedroom, this one much more masculine than the one she occupied. *Obviously this was my father's suite,* she mused. With apprehension she entered William's private domain.

The heavy satin draperies, bed curtains, and bedspread of the swaged canopy bed revealed the dominant colors of the room, deep maroon and forest green. Two maroon leather wingback chairs with a mahogany table between them stood near the window, which was almost entirely covered by the draperies, adding to the overall darkness of the room. The dark wood paneling did nothing to add any brightness. CC was glad that she had been put in Anne's rooms. She wondered if her father was as gloomy as the room he occupied.

CC walked to her father's dresser. On it was a cut glass decanter of sherry and two matching glasses on a silver tray. A silver initialed comb and brush rested nearby. CC picked up the brush and turned it over in her hands. Strands of gray hair remained in the bristles. She put the brush back in its place and picked up a photograph of two men carrying hunting rifles. She looked closely at their faces. The man on the right was definitely her father. It was the same face she had seen in the gallery, though in the picture William was at least twenty years older. As she put the photo back by the brush CC realized she didn't know what her father looked like when he died. She made a mental note to ask Hastings if there were family pictures more recent than the one on her father's desk.

She opened a small drawer at the base of the dresser mirror. There before her were perfectly pressed initialed linen handkerchiefs. *My, William was fastidious,* she thought as she opened the large top drawer of the dresser where her father's underwear was neatly folded. The next drawer contained neatly rolled socks, and the last was filled with beautiful silk shirts, ironed and folded neatly. CC wondered if her father really was this orderly or if the servants saw to it that his clothes were flawlessly arranged. How strange it felt to be holding clothing that her father had worn when she knew nothing about the man.

Hoping to get another clue to William's character, she crossed the room to his bed. A table made of the same rich wood stood beside it. CC opened the small table drawer. In it was an address book, several pens similar to the one she had used to make her lists downstairs, and a small photograph album. *Maybe I won't have to ask Hastings*, she reflected as she opened the album. The first picture was of a smiling woman, dark-haired, petite, and very English looking. CC guessed this was her stepmother. She studied the woman's face, wondering what kind of person would marry a man she knew loved someone else. An English woman with a duty, her mother would say.

The second picture was of a beautiful golden retriever. CC guessed the dog belonged to her father. "Well, that's something positive," she said. CC loved animals and had two German shepherds of her own at home. At least she and the earl shared one common interest.

She turned the page again. There, staring out at her, was her silver-haired father. This was the man whose hair was in the brush on the dresser. Despite the fact that he was older, his face remained boyish and handsome. He was grinning but CC detected sadness in her father's eyes that hadn't been there in the picture taken during the hunt. This was not something others would have noticed, but she knew. His eyes looked like hers did when she was unhappy or discontented. The expression was not something she could explain. Maybe the eyes just drooped on the sides a little more than usual. For the first time CC felt a connection: This was her father.

She sat and studied the picture. William was dressed in riding gear, and the same or a similar golden retriever as the one in the previous picture was with him. Tears welled up in CC's eyes. She had not expected to be affected this way, and she had certainly not anticipated feeling any emotions for the man.

She started to put the album back in the drawer when she saw something protruding from the back of her father's picture. She looked more closely and saw that a second photograph seemed to be hidden there. She pulled it out with her fingernail and gasped when she looked into the eyes of her mother, thirty years younger, but her mother nonetheless. "So he did love her! I'll have to tell Mom about finding the picture," she said, but quickly thought better of her idea. She wouldn't open old wounds. The picture would remain a secret between her and her father.

CC put the album back in the table drawer and glanced at the clock on the mantle over the fireplace. It was ten-thirty. She'd have to continue her explorations in the morning. It was three-thirty in Indianapolis, and she needed to reach Jim before he left for the day. She went back into her own sitting room, wondering if her father had often joined Anne there, and sat on the bed to make the call.

"Anything new?" she asked Leslie.

"Nothing important. Let's see. Cynthia called from Florida. She needed information on several players. I put her in touch with Wes. Bob called and left word that he would call you. Still no news regarding the free agents, but he'll keep you in the loop. He did say that the Atlanta shortstop was most likely out of the picture, so they would be concentrating on the catcher from St. Louis. He didn't say if they're close to an agreement. Oakland's bidding for him too."

"That doesn't surprise me. What else?"

"Walter came down. He wants to talk with you. I guess that's all. So how are you?"

"Ten pounds heavier in one night. You wouldn't believe the food here. Actually, I'm fine. I have a meeting with my father's attorney tomorrow morning. After that I'll know more about my plans and when you can make my reservations home. By the way, would you find a flight that will allow me to clear customs in New York rather than Chicago?"

"Will do. I should have thought of that when you left. You could have seen Bud on the way to England."

"There wasn't time to plan or to stop in New York, for that matter. Anyway, if it can be arranged, so be it. If not, that's fine too." CC couldn't believe she'd said that, or much less that she felt so nonchalant about a visit with Bud. "If that's all," she continued, "you can head home early. "Transfer me to Walter and I'll have him put me through to Jim, not that I look forward to that conversation."

"I'll bet you don't. I'll talk with you tomorrow."

"You will, but I don't know when. I'll be in London for meetings throughout most of the morning. After that I'm having lunch with my father's attorney and tea with neighbors about the time you get to work."

"Tea? Now aren't we becoming British?"

"Knock it off and transfer me."

"Okay." CC heard Leslie laugh and then the clicking of the phone as the transfer was completed. A few seconds later the CFO's voice came booming over the line.

"Hi, CC. I've been waiting for your call."

"I just finished dinner, Walter, and you don't have to yell. Modern phone service is wonderful. What's happening?"

"I just wanted to make sure you were clear on the advertising situation."

"Wes filled me in earlier. Anything since then?"

"As a matter of fact, yes. Our marketing director, with no one's knowledge or approval, has signed a contract with the advertising company. He's going to provide the information and they will design the ad to run in each week's paper. The cost will be $10,000 per ad."

"You aren't serious! What can the man be thinking? Is he totally out of it? Is he aware that we function on a budget and that the layout service is provided free of cost by the paper?"

"He thinks we can get better service and better quality by using our own people."

"Quality such as leaving out a date and time for a game? How firm is the contract?"

"I don't really know. I haven't seen it, only a memo from Jim saying I would be receiving bills from Advance Advertising Company."

"I'll see what I can do. Go ahead and pay the bill for the botched ad, but send Jim a memo telling him you will pay no more bills without written authorization from me."

"Will do. I'm sorry to cause problems for you now, CC."

"It's inevitable. I didn't think Jim could get things right, but don't worry, I'll handle him. Anything else?"

"Only good news. I thought I'd end the conversation with something positive. I spoke with Stuart in the ticket office. Our season ticket sales have topped twenty-six thousand, the best number ever."

"Wonderful! And with over six weeks before the home opener. Let's hope for even more. Tell Stuart he's doing a great job."

"I'll do that. Are you ready to deal with Jim?"

"As ready as I'll ever be. I'll talk with you tomorrow."

After several seconds, CC heard a gruff "Jim Oats here."

"Jim," CC decided not to mince words. "We have a problem."

"A problem?" Jim was obviously going to play dumb and let her tell him what she meant.

"That's what I said. What's this about hiring an advertising firm without my approval?"

"CC, you're not here, and I had to make a decision. I felt that an independent firm would provide better service for us, so I signed a contract."

"First, have you heard of telephones or fax machines or even e-mail, Jim? We do have all of these over here. In fact, I'm sitting in my room talking to you from England right now, and had I not been here, I always carry my cell phone. I believe you have that number." She didn't wait for Jim to respond. "Secondly, are you aware that I have instituted a procedure for long-term contracts? If you'll check your memos and notes from past meetings, you'll see that all of these contracts must be approved by me before they're signed."

"But this is different. I had to act right away or—"

"Or the company would have told you to take a hike? I doubt it. Now listen carefully to what I'm telling you. Call them now and tell them that the contract is not valid without my signature."

"But CC—"

"No buts and no arguments, Jim. You've gotten yourself into this mess, and you'll have to get yourself out of it or pay the damn bill out of your own pocket. Let's see, with roughly six months of baseball ahead of us, not counting post-season play, and one ad per week at ten thousand dollars for each, I'd say that's more money than you can afford. Do I make myself clear?"

"Perfectly." CC could hear fury in Jim's voice.

"Good. I'll call tomorrow to find out how you handled the situation, and Jim, remember I can be reached any time. In the future, if I am out of the office even for lunch and you have to make a decision which involves spending this much money, call me."

"Fine!" Again CC heard animosity.

"I'll talk to you tomorrow. Now transfer me to Wes."

Jim didn't respond, but seconds later CC heard Wes's voice. "Hi, CC. Everything go okay?"

"I have no idea, but I laid down the law. Only time will tell what our friend will do next. In the meantime, would you please contact the paper and tell them that in the future we will expect their people to do our layouts."

"Will do. I don't think tomorrow will be too pleasant around here."

"You can count on it."

CC hung up the phone. Jim Oats had to go. It wasn't pleasant firing anyone, but as soon as she got back, she would happily do the deed. She didn't know if the man was stupid or sly, but it didn't matter, she had given him his chance and he'd blown it.

After a hot bath, CC cracked the window to let in some air, set the alarm for six o'clock to jog before breakfast so that her dinner wouldn't translate into several pounds, and turned off the light. Her last thoughts before falling asleep were not of Jim Oats and the office, but rather of her father's face and the hidden picture of her mother.

CHAPTER FIVE

After a wonderful night's sleep and a thirty-minute jog that convinced CC she would have to find time to explore the grounds of Litchfield as well as the inside of the house, she showered and made notes of topics she wanted to discuss with her father's attorney during their meeting.

As Hastings had promised, Jean brought breakfast at seven. The morning coffee was not as strong as the night before, and CC continued to write as she sipped the delicious brew, ate strawberries, and munched on toast with orange marmalade. She was basically a morning person, if one were to believe the theory of morning and night personalities, and she liked to get up early and plan her day when she was rested and thinking clearly. In order to be sure she hadn't forgotten anything, she numbered the questions she planned to ask Harrison Caulfield:

1) What if I refuse the title and the property? To whom does it go?

2) Am I empowered to sell Litchfield Manor?

3) If I choose to keep the title and property…

CC stopped writing. This was the first time she had even considered keeping the land or the title, and she hadn't actually thought about doing so until she wrote the question. Before seeing her father's picture and the concealed photograph of her mother the night before, keeping her inheritance wasn't even a distant possibility. But now? She continued to write.

4) If I were to keep the title, would I have to renounce my American citizenship?

There it was again, that possibility of keeping the title. Wasn't it just yesterday when she said that being president of the Knights was all the title she wanted?

5) What are the terms of my father's will? Is there money to run the estate?

6) What did my father do to remain financially solvent?

All of these questions and probably many more she had not yet imagined had to be answered.

CC showered and dressed in a charcoal gray business suit, dark off-black nylons, and black heels with gold buckles. She accented the off-white blouse with a red and yellow Hermes scarf pinned with a gold brooch that matched her gold earrings. When she finished dressing, she looked in the mirror. "Acceptable," she said. "I don't think Harrison Caulfield will think me a hick from the colonies."

As she was about to leave the room, there was a knock on the door. She opened it to greet Hastings, who was carrying a very large wooden box. "Come in, Hastings," she said cheerfully.

"Good morning, my lady. I trust you slept well."

"Wonderfully, thank you."

"Stanley is waiting with the car, but before you go, I thought you might like these." He placed the box on the bench at the foot of the bed. "They belonged to Lady Anne and to the wives of the past earls. They're yours now. I'll leave them with you and tell Stanley to expect you directly."

When Hastings closed the door, CC opened the box. She gasped when she saw what was inside. The top tier was filled with jewels. There were four diamond rings, several diamond bracelets, two stunning diamond necklaces, and four pairs of diamond earrings. CC picked up the pieces one by one. She knew something about jewelry, and from the fire and color of the stones, she knew these pieces were exceptional. Some cuts appeared to be old, and some of the stones had more modern cuts indicating they were purchased by her father for Anne.

She removed the top tier and gasped again when she saw what lay below. The second tier contained two matching sets of jewels. One contained fiery diamonds intricately interwoven with brilliant sapphires. There were two rings, a bracelet, an incredible necklace, and a pair of drop earrings, each with a large sapphire surrounded by diamonds and a similar stone and design at the end of a rope of diamonds. The other set contained a necklace, ring, bracelet, and earrings made of diamonds and blood-red rubies.

The third tier was filled with pearls of all lengths, ranging from a short three-strand choker to a double opera-length knotted strand. One particularly impressive piece was a gigantic single pearl drop surrounded by large diamonds. The clasps of several of the necklaces were encrusted with diamonds and other valuable stones.

In the fourth tier were gold necklaces and bracelets with earrings to match. One gold V-shaped necklace contained a large pear-shaped diamond suspended at the tip of the V. CC picked up the magnificent piece and examined the extraordinary stone that she judged weighed over ten carats. She replaced it carefully and uncovered the final layer that was quite deep. In it lay a diamond tiara. At first estimate, CC guessed that the total diamonds in the piece exceeded a hundred and ranged in size from one to well over six carats. *My God*, she pondered, *the Earl of Litchfield was certainly not a poor nobleman who worried about how to pay his taxes.*

Feeling that she should wear at least one piece, since Hastings had made the effort to bring them to her before her meeting in London, she chose a large ruby ring surrounded by diamonds because the red matched the color in her scarf.

She replaced each tier carefully. "Now what do I do with these? I can't leave them lying around in the room." She walked over and rang the cord by the door. Hastings knocked a few minutes later. "These jewels are truly magnificent, Hastings. I'll love wearing them, but I'm not sure what I should do with them right now."

"I'll take them for you, my lady. Later this evening I'll show you the safe where they're kept and give you the combination in case I'm unavailable when you're ready to choose a piece to wear. I'm the only one at the house who can open the safe. Of course your solicitors have a copy of the codes should anything happen to me. There are two dials and the safe is bolted securely to the floor and to the walls, so I assure you your jewels are safe. By the way, I almost forgot, it also contains letters and several bundles of papers your father left for you. Perhaps you will have time to begin going through them this evening or tomorrow."

"I'll make time." CC was suddenly quite curious about what her father had left for her to read. "And thank you for bringing the jewelry to me."

"It's yours, my lady. I'm certain your father would approve."

"I consider that a compliment. Please tell Stanley I'll be right down."

Hastings excused himself and CC sat on the bed. Pictures, jewels, papers, letters; her father was truly becoming more of a mystery every minute. At that moment she realized she hadn't thought of the office all morning. She rationalized her lack of attention to the early hour in Indianapolis. "I couldn't reach anyone now if I wanted to," she said. After checking her appearance one final time in the mirror, she decided she was ready to take on Harrison Caulfield.

"Good morning, Your Ladyship," Richard said as he opened the front door. "Have a nice day."

As she walked down the front steps, CC expected to see the same plush Jaguar she had ridden in the day before, but Stanley was holding open the door of a spectacular silver Rolls Royce. Again, CC was amazed. "We have two cars, Stanley?"

"Actually, my lady, there are currently five cars in the garage. If this car isn't satisfactory for the trip—"

"It's wonderful. I was surprised because I expected to see the Jag."

"I alternate. Lady Litchfield liked to be driven in the Jaguar, and your father preferred the Rolls. He was the only one to drive the antique Bentley, and he only did so here in the country. He bought the little Mercedes last year, but he didn't drive it much."

"Well, I'm sure I'll put some miles on it before I leave. And the fifth car? "

"It's a Range Rover, my lady. Your father took it when he went hunting or wanted to drive around and take a look at parts of the estate that are inaccessible by road."

So my father was an outdoorsman, CC mused as Stanley pulled out of the driveway.

As she settled back in the comfortable leather seat, CC tried to figure how her father had so much money. The papers were full of stories about English peers forced to open their manors as small country hotels and dukes who allowed tours of their homes so that they could pay taxes, yet her father had five cars and jewels that looked as if they should belong to the queen. And then there was the estate itself. It was in excellent shape and the art and antiques were priceless. Perhaps Caulfield would shed some light on the mystery.

CC was so deep in thought that she failed to realize they had arrived in the city until the car slowed down to avoid a brazen cabbie who demanded the right of way. Several famous red double-decker buses passed them as they drove by Hyde Park toward Piccadilly. As they drove by St. James and Piccadilly, Stanley, who was now acting as tour guide as well as a chauffeur, informed her that Christopher Wren had designed the little church and the café in the basement served delicious homemade soup. "If there's time before I leave, I'd love to see London. Would you be my guide, Stanley?"

"I would consider it an honor, my lady, but I'm quite certain we'll come to London many times in the weeks and months ahead. In fact, once you're used to our English method of driving, you might wish to motor in by yourself for a day or so. Your father always had a suite available at the Ritz, and I'm sure it will be available for your use."

A suite at the Ritz? That requires big money, CC mused. Her curiosity was again aroused. "That sounds like a good idea," she said, "but with one slight modification. I can't imagine driving in London traffic."

They turned onto Regent's Street. Stanley stopped the car in a waiting zone in front of an impressive office building, jumped out, and dashed around to open CC's door. As she stepped out, he told her that he would be waiting in that same location at two-thirty.

"I'm not certain I'll be ready exactly on time. I hate to make you wait."

"When I drove your father to town, I always dropped him here at ten forty-five and picked him up at precisely two-thirty.

He also joined Mr. Caulfield for lunch, but please don't worry, if you're late, I'll wait for you."

"Did my father come here often?"

"About once a month. He had dealings with others in the building besides Mr. Caulfield."

"Thank you, Stanley. I'll be here as close to two-thirty as possible, and I appreciate your guided tour."

"Very good, my lady. I hope your meeting is successful."

CC nodded to the doorman, who ushered her into the lobby of the building. She looked around for a directory of offices, but none was available, so she approached the concierge and asked for directions to the offices of Caulfield, Ailesbury and Bedford.

"The firm occupies the entire seventh floor, Madam. May I have your name so I can announce you?"

This was certainly different. She had to be announced before going up in an elevator. "CC or Caroline Cleveland," she said.

The concierge scanned his list several times. "I'm afraid, Madam—"

"Try the Countess of Litchfield. I could be listed that way. At any rate, I have an appointment with Mr. Caulfield at eleven."

The man stood. "Your Ladyship, please excuse me. You are certainly on this list. Please take the lift around the corner while I announce you."

CC rode to the seventh floor. The lift opened onto a large foyer where the face of a huge old grandfather clock stared back at her as she stepped into the office. She turned toward a reception desk where a spectacled elderly woman sat. "Good morning, Lady Litchfield, Mr. Caulfield is on his way to greet you.

Would you like to sit while you wait?" She looked down the hall to her right. "Oh, here he is now."

A stern-looking gray-haired man about five feet ten inches tall strolled into the room. He was older, in his mid-sixties, CC guessed, and he exuded power and success. "Cocky" was the first word that came to CC's mind. Cocky, but for good reason. He was not the Perry Mason type. In fact, he didn't fit into any category, but the moment he appeared, CC knew he was in charge. "Good morning, Lady Litchfield." Caulfield extended his hand and CC took it.

"Mr. Caulfield. It's nice to meet you."

With his alert green eyes Caulfield studied his new client. CC felt that she was being appraised and wondered if she was making a positive first impression. She assumed she passed the test because Caulfield smiled approvingly. "Won't you please come to my conference room? Tea will be served, or if you would prefer, I can have coffee sent over."

"Tea will be fine. Thank you."

They walked down a richly paneled corridor that ended at double doors. Caulfield opened one for CC, who led the way into a room richly decorated in dark colors, not unlike the colors of her father's bedroom. Mahogany chairs faced a large, shiny mahogany table. A comfortable couch with two side chairs sat against the wall opposite the window framed in forest green velvet curtains that stretched almost floor to ceiling. A Reynolds and several Gainsboroughs decorated the walls. The office radiated old money and good taste.

"We will have tea over here." Caulfield gestured toward the couches. "We can relax and get to know one another better before beginning our business. The matters we need to discuss today will only take an hour or so. My driver will take us to Wilton's at twelve-fifteen."

He certainly is organized, CC thought and said, "That will be fine, Mr. Caulfield."

As the two sipped their tea, Caulfield asked numerous questions. CC knew he wasn't making small talk. He wanted to learn as much about her as possible. She did most of the talking. She told him about her career, her home in Indianapolis, and her family in Arizona. When she started to explain the relationship between her father and mother and the fact that she had never seen her father, he interrupted. "I am aware of all of the circumstances, Your Ladyship."

"Would it be too improper for you to call me CC?" she asked, remembering the response she had received when she asked Stanley the same question.

"If you prefer, that would be acceptable to me. I always called your father William at his request. CC it is, though I wonder why you choose to use CC. Caroline is such a charming name."

"I've been called CC for as long as I can remember. My stepfather gave me the name when I was very young, and it stuck with me."

"Then CC, if you'll have a seat at the table, there are some matters we need to discuss. Of course, you realize this is a preliminary meeting to familiarize you with your father's will and your responsibilities as his heir. We will meet again in several weeks, after you have read the documents I will give you and after you've had time to adjust to your new situation."

"I'm not certain I have several weeks, Mr. Caulfield. The baseball season will begin soon and I'll have to get back to the office as soon as possible."

"We shall see," Caulfield said nonchalantly. Obviously what she said hadn't fazed him. He pulled the Queen Anne chair out for her to sit.

Caulfield didn't join her at the table, but rather walked to his desk and pushed a button. Several minutes later a man in his late twenties entered the room carrying a wooden file box. He nodded to CC and placed the box on the table. Caulfield sat down, opened the file, took out a letter, and handed it to CC. "If you'll read this letter while I am sorting through these files, CC, perhaps what I intend to tell you will be easier for you to understand."

CC opened the sealed envelope and read:

My Dearest Daughter, Caroline Charlotte,

Though I have never actually met you, I feel that I know you well, and over the years I have come to love you. I have managed to keep track of you through news from individuals who I asked to keep watch over you. I so much appreciate your wonderful stepfather who has taken such good care of my beloved Mary and my cherished daughter. For that I am grateful, and as Caulfield will tell you, I intend to show my appreciation to Mr. Miles "Flash" MacTandy.

There were many times over the years when I especially wanted to contact you, but for reasons you will eventually come to know, for your mother's sake and for yours, I chose, however painful it was for me, to keep my life entirely separate from yours.

It's quite important to me now, when I embark upon a road that might well cause my death, that you understand my motives and me. I loved your mother, Caroline, or as you prefer, CC. Never before and never again will I love anyone as I loved her. I married Anne, but our life together was based on a good friendship and mutual respect. She knew of my love for Mary, but as a true Englishwoman, proud of her family and always willing to do the proper and responsible thing, she married me.

You may have wondered why I never stood up to my father, defied him, and remained married to your mother. Perhaps you think me less than a man for abandoning her and you. This is not so, but nothing I could say to you now would make you understand. You will have to become more English and develop a love of your new country and your heritage. Then you will not need to ask why I did what I did. My motives will be clear.

At this point I'm sure you are denying your English half, quietly thinking that there will be no time for you to discover your birthright and planning your trip back to America to your career in that strange game, baseball. However, I believe when Caulfield is through with you today, and when you have done as I ask, you will not be so quick to leave England or Litchfield Manor. I am counting on this.

Perhaps now you're thinking, what right does this stranger have to expect me to do anything for him? He did nothing for me. This is not entirely true. In a way, all that I have done and all that I will do in the next months is for you. Please know that. Know also that I am in perfect health. Only last week the doctor told me that I could expect to live for years to come. I tell you this in case something happens to me in the near future. And if you are reading this I imagine I am incapacitated or I will have met my maker.

Caulfield will tell you as much as he knows, which is not a great deal. There is certainly not enough space here to write the volumes I would like to write to tell you about me or about how I have always felt about you. Always know that I love you. You will soon learn more about that love.

Now comes the part where I ask you to do something for me, something that may help you to understand me better. Go to the old chapel in the servant's wing of the house. Go alone. Behind the altar, which with a little effort and your athletic ability (you see I do know about you), you will be able to move away from the wall enough to get behind. You will find the back is hollow. What actually looks like solid stone from the front is, in reality, a huge container. On a shelf in the top right corner there will be a diary and a folder. These, along with the papers and letters Hastings will give you, will help you to understand me and why I have lived as I have.

Caulfield will read my formal bequeaths to you after you have read this letter, which by the way, no one has read, not even Caulfield. It is my sincere wish that though you reject your heritage and your inheritance at this moment and though you have no desire to be Lady Litchfield, when you are through examining all of the evidence, you will change your mind and trade your American title for a title that is generations old. When you do that you will be accepting me as a father who loved you always, though by necessity from afar.

Know how proud I am of you, my darling daughter. Never forget that.

I remain your loving and devoted father,
William, Earl of Litchfield

CC was stunned. She had expected a formal reading of her father's will, but she hadn't expected a personal letter, and definitely not one like this. She folded the papers. "I assume this letter is for me to take?"

"It is. I've kept it for years. That is, I have kept a series of letters. The first was written on your first birthday. Your father gave me an updated letter on the same day each year. This particular letter was written last April. When your father updated one, he would take the other with him. Perhaps he destroyed them. Perhaps he kept them. I have no idea. But now, if you're ready, we can proceed with the reading of your father's will. Then if you have any questions I will try to answer them."

CC put the letter in her purse. Caulfield settled back in his chair, her father's will in front of him. Even in a seated position, the man was the epitome of power. It wasn't often that CC let another individual dominate a meeting, but with Harrison Caulfield she had no choice. "We will skip the introductory paragraphs, which I assure you are in order, and go straight to the bequests, if that meets with your approval."

CC nodded and the attorney continued: "Except for bequests to the staff members who have been with him for years and a very generous gift of 250,000 pounds to Mr. Miles MacTandy…"

CC gasped at the mention of Flash's name and Caulfield looked up from his reading for a moment before continuing. "Your father leaves all of his lands and everything on them to you, his daughter by his beloved Mary. Included in these properties is Litchfield Manor, a hunting lodge near Inverness in the Highlands of Scotland, and a penthouse suite which he owned at the Ritz."

"Owned?" CC couldn't help interrupting. "Do people actually own suites at the Ritz?" She remembered Stanley mentioning a suite her father used when he was in London.

"It is rather unusual, but then your father was not a typical man in many ways. He purchased the suite in 1987. The agreement says that the suite remains in the family and goes to you upon his death. In addition to the real property and the title, there is a substantial bank account in the Bank of England. I receive a statement each month, as does your accountant John Norris, who also has an office in this building. I will arrange for you to meet him when you come to town in a few weeks."

There he goes again, CC fumed. *He takes it for granted that I'll stay. It's as if I have no say in the matter.* She was surprised when she answered, "That will be fine," instead of what she was thinking.

"At the end of last month, after subtracting the bequests to your stepfather and the servants at both Litchfield Manor and Knockie Lodge, the account contained approximately 1.5 million pounds."

CC caught her breath. "That much money? What about the newspaper articles I've recently read about the impoverished nobility?"

"As I told you, CC, your father was not a typical English lord. In addition to the account in the Bank of England, there's money in the Bank of Zurich, though I'm not privy to information regarding that account. If you call the bank president, he will ask you a question. Answer it, give him this number, and he'll tell you what you want to know." He handed her a paper with a seven-digit number on it.

"What if I can't answer the question?"

"I have no idea what the actual question will be, but I can assure you it will be something personal that only you will be able to answer."

To say CC was shocked would be an understatement. A Swiss bank account, a penthouse in London, a lodge in Scotland, a manor in England, jewels beyond even a princess's wildest dreams, and a fortune in the Bank of England. Who was her father? Who had been watching her for years and reporting her every move? Why did William leave all that money to Flash? Harrison Caulfield had told her too much for her to absorb yet too little to satisfy her curiosity.

Caulfield stood. "I believe it's time for lunch, CC."

CC looked at her watch. How could time have passed so quickly? She rose, but her knees felt wobbly and she reached for the back of the chair to steady herself. By the time Caulfield had put the files back in the box, given her copies, and buzzed the same young man to come for the originals, she felt better. However she didn't really want to go to lunch. She wanted to go home. *Oh Lord*, she thought. *I can't go home. I have to go to Chadlington. Well, the day's blown anyway, so I'll enjoy the next two hours and see what else I can learn about my mysterious father.*

CHAPTER SIX

Much to CC's surprise lunch with Harrison Caulfield was enjoyable. The attorney's formal office decorum vanished as he talked with pride and enthusiasm about English food, British traditions, and the parts of England he loved. As she listened, CC gained insight into the feelings she knew her father had for his country. She wondered if this was Caulfield's intent or if he were merely making conversation.

Deciding not to allow the entire time to center on small talk, when coffee was served, she turned the conversation back to her father's will. "Mr. Caulfield, what would happen to Litchfield lands and my father's title if I rejected my inheritance?"

As he answered, Caulfield again became all business. No longer the pleasant luncheon companion, he quickly adopted the persona of the aloof attorney CC had first encountered. "Why, CC, I never considered the possibility that you would not accept your heritage and the title your father left you, but should you ultimately decide to give up your legacy, we would begin a search for your nearest relative who would inherit. You can be sure the Litchfield title will not pass into obscurity."

"And if I give up the title and the real property, does the money in the accounts go with what I leave behind?" CC was afraid she was sounding greedy, but felt the question was pertinent.

"It does. Your father's will specifies that you accept your entire inheritance or sign papers rejecting all of it. There can be no in-between. Of course William believed that when you spent some time in England, you would understand your duty and accept all that he left to you."

There was that word "duty" again. CC wondered if it was used synonymously with the word "Englishman." "Would I have to renounce my United States citizenship to accept the title, Mr. Caulfield? I've always considered myself an American, and I can't imagine changing my nationality so I can be Lady Litchfield."

"I'm afraid it would be impossible for you to inherit the lands without the title and the title without being a British citizen."

"Then I would need a green card to work in the United States?"

"I'm not absolutely certain. We will deal with that situation if and when we are faced with it. For now, I suggest that you do as your father asked. Read his letters and papers. Then take some time to see your properties in Scotland and London. Stay at your suite at the Ritz before our next appointment. I'm quite sure you'll find the city to your liking."

"I'm sure I will, but right now I have so many questions. For one, what did my father do to make such an incredible amount of money?"

"He managed his money well and made good investments. Beyond that the information is privileged, but CC, never doubt that your father was a special and courageous man who served his country with great honor. You needn't worry that he was dishonest. He was one of the most ethical individuals I've ever known. To be honest, there's a great deal I didn't know about the earl, and some of what I do know, I'm unable to reveal because of an agreement we made. If you truly wish to know your father, you'll make time to determine who and what he was. If not, then he must forever remain a mystery."

CC was puzzled. Was this what her mother had meant when she said that a week's stay in England wouldn't be long enough; that she should plan on remaining a month? What secrets did her mother know about William? She had always believed Mary's reluctance to talk about her first love was due to the pain she felt at being rejected and abandoned. Now CC wondered if there were other reasons that her father's name was rarely mentioned. She made a mental note to ask her mother more about William Cleveland, Earl of Litchfield.

The appointment ended at precisely two-thirty, and as promised, Stanley was in front of the office building to pick her up. CC shook hands with Caulfield, who said he would call the house to let her know the time of her next appointment.

During the ride back to the Cotswolds, CC tried to shift her thoughts from the events at hand to what she needed to deal with the office. When she was certain Leslie would be in, she closed the partition between her and Stanley and using the car phone, dialed the familiar number. Her secretary's voice brought her back to her own reality and she quickly settled into the comfortable role as the baseball executive, forgetting for the moment how awkward she felt when she assumed the role of Lady Litchfield.

"Hi, Les. What's happening today, or do I want to know?"

"Want the good or the bad news first?"

"What now?"

"I guess that means you want the bad news first. Do you want me to tell you or do you want to hear it from Wes?"

"What's with the twenty questions? Just tell me."

"The T-shirts for the July Fourth promotion came in."

"That's good."

"That's not good. They say Indianapolis Knights across the front in blue and below it is the Knights' logo."

"Good."

"Not good."

"Will you cut it out and get to the point, Leslie?"

"Sorry, CC, I didn't mean to be glib. Our problem is that what should be spelled K-N-I-G-H-T-S is spelled N-I-G-H-T-S."

"You're kidding. Was it our fault?"

"It looks like it. Jim said he can't imagine who wrote the name on the order form so illegibly. He called the T-shirt company to ask why they hadn't checked with him to see if the spelling was intentional and they told him they thought the team was trying to promote 'nights' at the ballpark."

"Oh my God! Does he really expect me to believe that?"

"It seems so. He wants me to ask if you would like for him to reorder."

"What would that cost us?"

"I thought you might want to know that. I called Walter this morning, but he's been in a meeting with the city and won't be in until after lunch. I left word for him to call me when he gets back."

"What did Wes say?"

"He only shook his head, but he did say the calendars, *The Lance*, and the huge posters that hang in the various businesses all have the T-shirt promotion advertised for the Fourth."

"Then I guess we're stuck and have to reorder no matter the cost. Does Wes think we can get fifty thousand more shirts printed and delivered in time? I think these were ordered back in November."

"I didn't ask, but I know he wants to talk with you, so when we're finished I'll connect you. I just saw him pull into the parking lot."

"Would you like to tell me the good news now?"

"With pleasure. Bob signed Paul Singleton." Singleton was a holdout who was trying to get his contract extended another year. He was definitely a favorite with the fans, who were protesting the Knights' treatment of him in letters to editors and comments on sports talk shows.

"What did we have to do to make the deal?"

"He added another year at the club's option, so really nothing."

"After all that rhetoric with his agent, I wonder how Bob managed to get off so easily. I'll call him later. I imagine he's on the field now. What else?"

"Cynthia called. Her speech last night was a rousing success and she's excited about tonight's dinner. Can you believe it?"

"Let's remind her of this next year, okay? Make a note of the call. She'll laugh when she hears what she said after all of the off season speeches she'll have to give. Anything else?"

"That's about it. Shall I tell Walter to expect your call this afternoon?"

"Yes, but I don't know when. I'm on my way to tea with neighbors now, and after that I have some things to do at Litchfield. Now transfer me to Wes. I want to hear more about this T-shirt fiasco."

"I'm transferring now. Have a good day, or what's left of it for you."

CC heard the click on the line and then Wes's greeting. "Just another day at the madhouse, CC. Aren't you glad you're not here? I suppose Leslie filled you in on Jim's latest?"

"She just did, and to answer your question, I'm glad I'm not there. If I were, I would be spending the rest of my life in jail for murder, though a jury might accept justifiable homicide a valid motive."

Wes laughed. "I almost did the job for you thirty minutes ago," he said, "but I managed to think of Carol and the kids."

"Good, I need to have someone sane around there. Can we possibly get fifty thousand T- shirts by July Fourth? I realize it's not in your job description, but I would appreciate it if you would follow through."

"No problem."

CC thanked him and hung up. She opened the partition. "How far are we from Chadlington, Stanley?"

"About thirty-five minutes, my lady."

"Oh, good, then I have time to make one more call." CC closed the partition again and dialed Bud's private number in New York. Much to her surprise, he answered. "Bud?"

"CC, I didn't expect to hear from you this morning."

"Where's Alice? Isn't she answering the phones today?"

"She's down the hall getting me a cup of coffee. Awfully chauvinistic, isn't it? What's up?"

CC told Bud about her father's room and the picture of her mother she had found. She talked about her trip to Caulfield's office, the letter, her father's will, the Swiss bank account, and the papers hidden at the house. As she talked, Bud heard the excitement in her voice. "You sound as if you're actually thinking about staying in England to unravel the mystery."

"All I can tell you right now is that things are far more complicated than I originally expected. I do know there's no way I can be back this week. I expect to see Caulfield again in two weeks and hope to have everything resolved by then."

"Still planning to come home through New York?"

"I told Leslie to see what flights are available, but I really don't know. It depends on how long I have to be here. At this point I just hope to be back in Indianapolis for opening day. No CEO should be out of the country during the first part of the season."

"Is everything going well at work?" CC told Bud about the T-shirt fiasco. "It never stops, does it, sweetheart?"

"I wish it would. And it's always Jim who causes the problem. Remember to keep your ears open for me, will you?"

"I told you I would. And I'll talk with you soon. Take care of yourself. I love you."

"I love you too." CC hung up and gazed out the window. "I can't think of this anymore," she said quietly. She put down the partition. "Are you ready to be my tour guide during the remaining part of the trip, Stanley? I would enjoy hearing about this lovely countryside."

CHAPTER SEVEN

Stanley drove through delightful villages containing picture-squeue houses, all with lovely gardens blooming profusely with combinations of purple and white foxglove, purple bellflowers, pink geraniums, cosmos, cleome, and yellow English daisies. The untamed landscape surrounding each of the villages was a mélange of different shades of green with an occasional bright red field of wild poppies to add a splash of color.

"What does Cotswold mean?" CC asked as they passed through the quaint town of Stow-on-the-Wold and approached the turnoff for Upper and Lower Slaughter.

Stanley proved to be not only a tour guide, but also a bit of an historian as well. "The name is a derivation of the Anglo-Saxon words 'cots,' which meant sheep shelters, and 'wold,' or rolling hills, my lady. Sheep are an important part of England's past history and were once mainstays of the economy. This area has a history that dates back to approximately 6000 BC."

"How do you know so much about the area, Stanley?" CC realized how little she knew about the history of Indianapolis or even Phoenix, where she had lived most of her life.

"I made it a point to learn about my country, my lady, particularly since your father often asked me to serve as a guide for his friends from other countries who would come and stay at the manor."

"Did my father have many visitors from abroad?"

"Quite a few. Business acquaintances for the most part, but even people who came here to work took a little time out for sightseeing. When his schedule permitted, your father would be a tour guide, driving them in the Bentley, but when he was unable to find a spare moment, I would take them and tell them about our part of the world."

"Was my father so busy that he couldn't get out to show his guests around? I would think a country gentleman would have all the time in the world."

"Oh, your father wasn't just a country gentleman, my lady. He was quite an important man." There was obvious pride in Stanley's voice.

"How do you mean?"

"Well, he certainly had many important friends. Did you know that the Iron Lady once visited us at Litchfield?"

"Margaret Thatcher!" CC was surprised that a British prime minister would visit her father's country house.

"She surely did, my lady, and there were others also." Stanley rattled off a few names that CC didn't recognize, but he obviously thought they were important people and she intended to find out who they were when she had a spare moment. She took out her ever-present notepad and wrote down all of the names as best as she could spell them, particularly the foreign ones that Stanley offered as examples of her father's celebrity. She also decided that she needed make a "to do" list so she wouldn't forget her plans to learn more about her father. She wrote:

1. Call Mother and see if I can pry some information from her after all these years of silence.
2. Go into the safe for the papers Hastings spoke about.
3. Go to the chapel and remove the diary and papers from behind the altar.
4. Search the internet to try and identify the people Stanley said came to Litchfield Manor.
5. Pump Hastings about the prime minister's visit.

6.   Make arrangements to see my property near Inverness.

My property? CC was surprised that in her mind her father's property had become her own. As she tried to think of more things she wanted to do, Stanley turned into the gates of Chadlington and drove up the long driveway toward the house. "What can you tell me about Chadlington?" she asked.

"I don't know much about the manor itself, my lady, but I do know something about Anglo-Saxon derivation. 'Ceadda' was a short form of 'Ceadwalla,' a common Saxon name, and 'tun' was the Saxon word for a small cluster of homes or a farm. The village is recorded in *Domesday* as 'Cadilintone.'"

"Domesday?"

"Yes. The *Domesday Book* was a census William the Conqueror conducted right after he invaded England in 1066. He not only counted the people, he took a survey of the animals as well. The people called it 'Domesday' because they feared being taxed even more based on the census. Today the document gives us a wonderful picture of Anglo-Saxon life as it must have existed."

"Interesting," CC said. "I want you to know how much I appreciate all the information you've provided since my arrival, Stanley."

Stanley delighted in the praise. "My pleasure, my lady, but I'm afraid the sightseeing must end for the moment. We've arrived at Chadlington Manor."

When they pulled up to the door, a man in his early fifties immediately came out and opened CC's door. "Welcome to Chadlington, Your Ladyship. Sir Anthony and Lady Alexandra are waiting for you in the library."

"This is Mason, the butler," Stanley said.

Mason bowed. "If you'll follow me, Your Ladyship," he said and stood aside for CC to go into the house.

"Thank you, Mason."

Mason ushered her into a charming entry hall. Though not as resplendent as her own at Litchfield, CC found it remarkably welcoming. They passed through several rather formal sitting rooms before arriving at what was obviously the library. The walls of the room were richly paneled in a light mahogany, and bookcases of matching wood lined the walls on either side of the fireplace. In them were what appeared to be very old leather-bound volumes interspersed with bright pieces of English china and charming knickknacks. Chairs with bright yellow and blue floral print fabrics matching the floor-to-ceiling draperies were grouped for informal conversation.

When CC entered the room, Alex and Anthony were seated on one of two overstuffed light-blue sofas that faced each other on either side of a blue marble fireplace. Alex immediately leaped off the couch and hugged CC warmly. "We're so glad you were able to stop by, aren't we, Tony?"

"That we are, CC." He rose, extended his hand, and then turned toward his butler. "We will have tea now, Mason."

Arm in arm, Alex led CC to one of the couches and Tony sat opposite them. "Now tell us all about your day. Did you enjoy London? Though I can't imagine you had much time to explore."

"No, I didn't see very much," CC answered, "though Stanley provided excellent commentary about every area we passed through. I was able to see enough to know that I want to see more."

"Wonderful. Perhaps we could go to town after Tony and I return from our trip."

"You're leaving Chadlington?" CC was disappointed that she wouldn't have the opportunity to invite these delightful people to dinner over the weekend.

"Just for the weekend. Say, why don't you join us?" Alex turned to Anthony. "She could, you know. There will just be the two of us at Charlie's lodge."

"Charlie? Lodge? You're way ahead of me, Alex. You haven't even told me where you're going."

The arrival of the tea delayed Alex's response. A young man carrying a large silver tray containing a silver teapot, lovely English bone china cups and saucers, and a plate of biscuits and scones followed Mason into the room. "Put them here on the table." Alex waved toward the cocktail table in front of the fireplace.

"Very good, my lady." Mason stood aside while the young man put the tray down. "Would you like for me to pour?"

"That won't be necessary. Thank you." Mason and his assistant left, and Alex poured the steaming tea. "Would you like milk or lemon, CC? We don't serve your clotted cream here. Not good for either of our figures, is it, darling?" She grinned at Tony who nodded in agreement.

"We do eat biscuits, though. I must say, I never could figure out why we eliminated one fattening food and not the other. I suppose this way we'll only be half as heavy." Alex passed a biscuit to CC. "These biscuits are made from the recipe given to me by the Duchess of Marlborough. You may have passed Blenheim Palace on your way through Woodstock. You have been through Woodstock, haven't you?"

"Not yet, I'm afraid, and though I hate to admit it, I'm not familiar with Blenheim or the Duchess of Marlborough."

"Oh, my dear." CC sensed that her hostess felt sorry for her lack of knowledge. "Blenheim is the birthplace of our beloved Winston Churchill. The duchess is one of his relations. Though I would not normally be in the duchess's circle of friends, we met at one of the queen's garden parties several years ago and hit it off splendidly. Since then, I've been a frequent guest for tea. I would love for you to meet her. Perhaps I could persuade her to give you a personal tour of Blenheim. By the way, your father was also a regular guest there. He and the duke seemed to have a great deal in common. At least they had their heads together quite often."

Another piece of a puzzle, CC mused. She clearly understood why the duchess would be so attracted to Alex. The woman was absolutely delightful. But why would her father and the duke be close? Why would her father be a guest at Blenheim? "I would love to meet the duchess and see Blenheim," she said, thinking that she might be able to get some information that would help her learn more about her obviously complicated and enigmatic father.

"Good, we'll plan on it. I believe the duchess is in Edinburgh at the moment, but I imagine she would be able to find a spot for us on her calendar within the next month or so."

"Month? I'm afraid I'll be home running a ball club by then. Perhaps during another trip."

"You mean you still plan to go back to America? You won't be living at Litchfield?" Alex was plainly shocked that CC would even think of leaving. "I imagined you would be our permanent neighbor."

"I don't think that's likely. We're just about to begin a new baseball season, and there's no way I can miss the opener or get away during the next six months to spend time here."

"Then you intend to leave in the near future?"

"Just as soon as I complete my business in London and visit some property I own in Scotland, as Mr. Caulfield, my father's attorney, suggested."

"Scotland. When do you plan to go to Scotland?" Alex asked.

"I have no idea. I planned to ask you and Anthony over for dinner this weekend, but since you'll be away, I may try leave tomorrow; that is, if Hastings can make the necessary arrangements. Come to think of it, I don't even know how I'll get there. Should I take a train or fly or should I ask Stanley to drive me? Do you think I dare drive myself?"

"No need to worry about any of that. Your problem is solved! Tony and I are visiting my older brother in Glencoe. Five years ago Charlie married the daughter of the chief of the MacDonald clan. They moved to the family hunting lodge near Glencoe, though I doubt you would really consider it a hunting lodge, since the house is actually larger than this one. Lord Dougall, who lives at the family home, Dunollie, gave the lodge to Flora and Charlie as a wedding gift. If I remember correctly, your father's lodge is only thirty minutes from there. I believe it's near Whitebridge, which is about twenty-five minutes from Inverness."

"I'm not sure where it is. I only found out about it the morning, but I seem to recall that Mr. Caulfield mentioned Inverness."

"Then that settles it. You'll come with us tomorrow morning. Anthony will drive. It's a push, but even with a stop for lunch, we can make it to Glencoe by nightfall. You can stay the night with us at Charlie's and we'll drive you to Knockie in the morning. I imagine Charlie would like to go with us. I believe he joined your father for hunts at the lodge once or twice."

"It sounds tempting, and I appreciate your offer." CC, said though, she hadn't considered leaving as early as the next morning. Before going anywhere she wanted to retrieve the papers and diary from the chapel, so she tried to make an excuse to remain behind without offending Alex. "I would love to go, but I left home for what I thought would be a short stay, a week at most. I'm afraid I didn't pack for a weekend in the country. All I have with me are jeans and sweats for jogging."

"Jeans will do beautifully for the drive, and believe it or not, the lodge is not in the middle of nowhere. You can get anything you could possibly need in Inverness, Fort William, or Fort Augustus, and you won't believe the woolens."

CC tried again. "But Flora and Charlie—you did call her Flora, I believe—won't be expecting guests. I don't want to intrude."

"Don't be silly. Charlie will love it. He's really quite lonely out there in the Highlands. I guess I forgot to mention it, but Flora died a year and a half ago. With our modern medicine one doesn't worry about a woman dying in childbirth, so my sister-in-law's death was a tremendous shock to all of us. Right after she delivered little Charlie she developed toxemia, lapsed into a coma, and died the following afternoon. No one could believe she was gone, especially after she had such an easy pregnancy and delivery. Charlie was devastated, but he finally seems to be doing better. Time heals. I used to think that was a trite saying, but it seems to be true. Anyway, only he and the baby and a house full of servants live at the lodge, and I know he would enjoy meeting you."

CC gave up trying to think up excuses for remaining behind. "In that case, I would love to go; that is, if I can deal with several business issues tonight. If you'll give me your brother's phone number, I'll leave word with my office. I want them to know how to reach me. To date I haven't found time to buy a converter for my charger."

"You do have servants," Alex said. "Ask one of them to purchase the converter for you. In the meantime I'll give you the number." She went to the writing desk across the room.

Tony leaned over conspiratorially and whispered, "I'm quite glad you'll be joining us, though I believe I must warn you, CC, I really don't think Alex has invited you solely for your charming company, or for that matter to furnish you with transportation to Scotland, though it seems a marvelous coincidence that we are going to the same area and can travel together. I confess that from the moment she saw you yesterday, Alex decided you would be a perfect wife for Charlie."

"You're kidding!"

"Absolutely not, and neither is Alex. I guarantee that she will enthusiastically go about this matchmaking, and once she makes up her mind—"

"Makes up her mind to what, dear?" Alex returned with the phone number on a piece of paper.

"I was just telling CC that once you made up your mind to have her accompany us to Scotland, no argument could have persuaded you differently." He winked at CC.

"That is absolutely right, so if I am going, I'd better go home and pack." CC stood.

"Wonderful." Alex pushed a button on a box that lay on the table by her chair. Almost immediately Mason appeared. "Would you please see that Lady Litchfield's car is brought around?"

"Right away, my lady."

Alex put her arm around CC and led her toward the door. "We will be by the house to pick you up in the morning. As I said, Tony likes to get an early start. Shall we say seven-thirty? Is that all right, darling?"

"Perfect, if that's not too early for you, CC?"

"Not at all. By then I'm usually at the office."

Stanley held the door for CC while she said her good-byes. When she was settled in the back seat of the Rolls, CC sighed.

She was exhausted from listening to Alex chatter. *She is a fireball,* CC mused, *both in actions and in speech.*

During the drive, she tried to put the additional pieces of the puzzle together. With all that she'd learned about her father during her trip to London, she could now add that he was a frequent guest at Blenheim, he knew Alex's brother, and Charlie and often hunted with him. Was that a coincidence or was there a connection? Was she looking to create a mystery that really wasn't there? She was glad to be meeting Charlie, but not for the same purpose that motivated Alex. *Wouldn't Bud just love knowing I'm going to Scotland with my neighbor, whose ulterior motive in taking me is to marry me off to a Scottish lord?* CC reflected. *This is the kind of plot a person reads about in a silly romance novel, and I never liked romance novels.* She had never liked mystery novels either, but now it seemed she was involved in an authentic mystery. Suddenly she looked forward to her trip.

CHAPTER EIGHT

During the drive back to Litchfield, CC formulated a plan so she could be alone in the chapel long enough to move the altar and retrieve the papers. She would ask Hastings to give her a tour of the servant's wing of the house, and when he showed her the chapel, she would tell him she wanted some time alone to sit and think. Certainly he wouldn't find that a strange request.

When CC entered the house, Hastings was coming from the direction of the servant's wing. "Welcome home, my lady. I trust your day was a beneficial and pleasant one."

"It was, and a long one too."

"Would you like to rest before dinner? That is, after you've returned your calls." He handed her three slips of paper. "These are messages we took for you during your absence."

"Thank you, Hastings." One message was from Jim Oats who wanted to talk with her when she returned. "Oh God, what now?" she groaned.

Her mother had also phoned and wanted CC to call her, regardless of the hour. CC sighed. She had forgotten to phone her and Flash when she arrived at Litchfield, but maybe it was just as well. Now she could talk armed with what little knowledge she had obtained from Harrison Caulfield. CC was eager to know if Mary had any information that would help her better understand her mysterious father. The third message was from Bud, who reminded her that he would be leaving New York for Los Angeles and left the number where he could be reached. CC turned to Hastings. "I'll return these calls from my room."

"Very good. Would you like tea or some other refreshment? Millie can bring whatever you like while you dress for dinner."

"A glass of wine would be wonderful. I don't suppose we have a California Chardonnay?"

"We have a Chardonnay from America, though I'm very much afraid it's not from California. If I may say so, your father kept an excellent wine cellar, one of the best in the country. Over the years I've become a bit of an amateur sommelier. Several years ago we purchased a case of Chardonnay from Rose Creek, Idaho. It is a 2008 vintage, which I'm quite certain you will find to your liking."

"I'm sure I will. Would you please have Millie bring me a glass, though I hate to ask you to uncork a full bottle for one or two glasses.

"That won't be a problem. If you like the wine, you can have a more with your dinner."

"Good idea," she said, though she really didn't feel like eating so soon after having tea and biscuits. When she returned from Scotland, she would have to make some other arrangements for the evening meal. She didn't want to offend John Claude and Charles, but a heavy dinner wasn't necessary every evening. And then there was the dining room. It was so large and lonely for just one person. *I've got it*, she thought. *I can eat in front of the TV in the Blue Parlor*. She chuckled to herself, wondering if Hastings had ever considered anything as gauche as a TV tray, or for that matter, if he'd ever heard of eating a meal in front of a television.

"By the way," Hastings continued, "John Claude and Charles send their apologies. Since you were away, they selected the entrees for this evening. Beginning tomorrow, you will be able to plan the menu for a full week, if that meets with your approval, of course."

"It does, but I'm afraid planning the dinner menus will have to wait until I return from Scotland. Sir Anthony and Lady Alexandra have invited me to her brother's home in Glencoe. We'll spend the night there and then they'll drive me to my father's lodge the following morning."

"Excellent! Your father was very proud of Knockie and entertained there quite often. The house overlooks Lan Nann, your father's own private loch."

"You said my father frequently entertained at the lodge."

"He did. I often accompanied him, though he has an excellent staff in attendance there. I'll call ahead in the morning and tell the servants to expect you on Saturday."

"Have the same individuals worked there for a long time?" CC asked, hoped there would be someone to talk with about her father.

"The housekeeper, Mrs. Lauriston, worked for your grandfather and then your father. She's a fine woman, and Henry's been there for at least thirty years. I think you'll find them both amiable and eager to please. "But if you don't need anything else, I'll prepare your tray. Millie will bring it to you."

"Thank you, Hastings."

CC started up the stairs. She'd gone partway when she suddenly remembered her plan for the evening. *Oh my Lord, how could something so important have slipped my mind?* She turned, dashed back down the stairs, and headed toward the kitchen. "Hastings, one more thing," she said breathlessly when she caught up with him in the dining room.

"Of course, my lady," he said reproachfully.

Okay, I should have pulled the cord and not raced after him through the house, CC realized when she saw the disapproval on her butler's face. *Oh well, once again he'll have to put up with a gauche American.* "Hastings, after dinner would you get my father's papers and letters, and show me the safe where my jewelry is kept? I may want to take several pieces to Scotland and I'd like to have the papers so that I can read them in my spare time while I'm there."

"I would happy to do so, my lady."

Hastings turned toward the kitchen, but CC wasn't finished. "Also, when you have a few moments, I would like to speak with you about my father. I'm eager to know more about him, and Mr. Caulfield said that you would know him as well as anyone."

Hastings hesitated and CC sensed apprehension in his voice when he responded, "Of course. I will be glad to tell you what I can."

CC sought to allay the man's obvious discomfort. "I don't want to know any deep, dark family secrets, if there are any. I've heard so many people talk about what a fine man he was, and I want to hear about him. That's all."

Obviously relieved, Hastings smiled. "In that case, I would be proud to tell you about your father whenever you have time, and I'm sure Richard would be glad to expand upon what I tell you. But now, if there is nothing else, I'll go to the wine cellars and have Millie bring you the Chardonnay"

"As a matter of fact, Hastings, there is one more thing."

"Yes, my lady."

Am I pushing it? CC wondered. Though Hastings didn't look pleased, she continued, "When you first took me through the house, I believe you mentioned an old chapel."

"I did, but as I said then, the chapel hasn't been used for years."

"I would like to see it."

Hastings was obviously surprised. "This evening?"

"Yes, please."

Hastings hesitated, and CC wondered if her servant could refuse to do what she asked. "Of course," he finally replied, though not enthusiastically. "Would you like for the maids to tidy it up before you see it?"

"That won't be necessary. I don't want anyone to go to any extra trouble. I'm curious and would like to take a peek."

"Then of course I'll take you there and any other place you wish to go. You haven't had time to see much of Litchfield, and as I said when we toured the house, I'd like to show you the gardens and the stables. Do you ride, my lady?"

"I rode when I lived in Arizona. My stepfather had horses, but I'm afraid I haven't had much experience with an English saddle, and it's been years since I've even been on a horse."

"You were one of those real western cowgirls?"

CC laughed. "You might say so. I rode in junior rodeos, and if I do say so, I was pretty good at barrel and flag races. However, we didn't learn to jump like English riders do."

"Perhaps you would like to ride when you return from Scotland. Your stepmother had a wonderful mare that could use some exercise, and I know Crooks would be pleased to accompany you around the grounds."

"That sounds good, thank you. Now if you'll excuse me, I'll take care of these calls." CC grimaced. "And speaking of calls, I wonder if you'll ask one of the servants pick up a converter for my cell phone charger while I'm away. I'll leave the phone here so you'll know what to buy. Perhaps you could plug it in so it's charged when I return."

"Certainly, my lady." Hastings bowed as CC went up the stairs to her room and the only privacy she had enjoyed since early that morning. The maids had put fresh flowers on the dresser and opened the windows to let in the fresh, cool air.

CC walked to the window and looked out at the grounds. Sheep grazed peacefully in the pasture area beyond the formal gardens. Clouds were moving in rapidly, blown by the wind that moved the tops of the huge trees on the front lawn. A white wrought iron table and four chairs under one of the trees looked like a wonderful place to have after-dinner coffee, and CC decided she would ask James to serve her there, but she wouldn't linger long in the pastoral surroundings, since the chapel and her father's diary and papers waited.

CC turned on the tap to fill the tub, added some bath salts from a silver tray that provided several selections of bubble baths and bath oils. As she undressed, she looked around the ultra-modern bathroom. A separate shower had been installed as well as a French bidet. Electrically heated towel racks held soft, plush towels with the Litchfield crest emblazoned on them. *All the conveniences of home,* she mused.

She finished undressing, wrapped her hair in a towel, and climbed into the warm, scented water to soak. "I could become used to a life like this," she said as she lay back to relax, once again surprised by what she was thinking.

When her body could take the warmth no longer, she got out and took a cool shower to rinse off and to bring her back from the lethargic state the hot bath had produced. The cool water did the trick and she emerged from the shower refreshed and ready to call her mother. She was very much aware that she had to choose her words carefully and not sound threatening or demanding as she sought information about William. She had long since discovered that Mary could be a stubborn and silent adversary when confronted or backed into a corner. CC put on the blue terry robe the maids had laid out for her, stepped into the matching terry slippers, and removed the towel from her hair.

When she went into her bedroom, a glass of wine waited on a tray beside her bed. She smelled the bouquet, sloshed the liquid around in the glass, and took a sip. "This is delicious, and to think it came from Idaho," she said. "I had no idea they made anything but potatoes in Idaho." She laughed as she thought about what she'd said. *Made potatoes? Wow, I'm either very tired or I'm losing it.* She sat on the bed, dialed her mother's number in Phoenix, and listened to the familiar ring.

"MacTandy residence," CC heard the familiar voice of Martha, the housekeeper. Ethel Gazuba had left them right after Mary's marriage to Flash, and in her place, her mother had hired Martha. CC loved the sweet, caring woman and often thought of her as a second mother. So many times in the past she had been left home with Martha in charge when her mother and Flash had traveled on baseball business or private trips.

"Martha, it's CC. How are you?"

"CC, it's wonderful to hear your voice, honey. I was so sorry to hear of your father's death."

"Thank you, Martha. How's everyone? Is Mom okay?"

"She was very quiet when she first received the news. Today she seems much livelier, but then she's always happy when she entertains. Are you back in Indianapolis already?"

"Not yet. To tell you the truth, I have no idea when I'll be home."

"You sound like you're right next door."

"Modern technology. Is Mom around?"

"She's out back by the pool. Let me take the phone to her. As I began to tell you, she and Mr. Flash are having a barbecue tomorrow night for some of the club sponsors. She's telling the gardeners how to set up the patio. I know she wants to speak with you."

"I'll wait then. Talk to you soon, Martha."

"You sure will, honey, and you take care of yourself over in that strange country."

As CC waited for her mother to answer the phone, she pondered Martha's words. *If you only knew how strange*, she thought.

Moments later her mother answered. "CC, darling, I thought you were going to call us when you arrived.

"It's been rather hectic. I know that's not a valid excuse, but it's the truth. I'm fine, though."

"How do you like England?"

"It's beautiful. I love the countryside and Litchfield Manor is fabulous. I also saw a little of London when I went to see Harrison Caulfield today."

"Then you saw Mr. Caulfield. What did he say?"

"Quite a lot actually. For the most part he talked about the choices I'll have to make. They're pretty clear cut. I can give up everything here, the title, the house, the lodge in Scotland, and a suite at the Ritz in London, and return home as Caroline Cleveland, a.k.a. CC, president of the Indianapolis Knights or I can do as my father specified in his will, keep the title and lands, and remain here as Caroline Charlotte Cleveland, Countess of Litchfield."

"Have you decided what you're going to do?"

"I honestly have no idea, and admitting that to you shows a tremendous shift from the mindset I had before I left. Yesterday morning I would have told you in no uncertain terms that I would be home running the Knights within two weeks, but now I'm not a hundred percent certain when I'll be back or what my future plans will entail."

"Then you're considering remaining in England?"

"Not really. Oh, I don't know. I have no idea what I'm thinking, but you'll surely play a part in whatever decision I do make."

"I will? What could I possibly say to persuade you one way or another?"

"I need some information, Mother. We've never talked much about my father because I never wanted to push. I knew that talking about him was painful for you, but since my meeting with Harrison Caulfield this morning there are things I really need to know, and I'm counting on you to help me."

"What can I possibly tell you, CC?"

"I'm not really sure, but I have some questions. What did you know about William Cleveland; that is, beyond the fact that he would inherit a title and that you loved him? What did he do for a living?"

"Why, he was the son of an earl. He was in the Royal Air Force, but he was doing his duty. He had no plans to continue in the service."

"Was the family rich?"

"I think so, though I don't really know. Your father never mentioned the family's financial status, but there didn't seem to be a lack of money. I don't think we ever talked about it, but when I left England for home after the annulment proceedings were over, your grandfather gave me a very large sum of money, approximately a hundred-fifty thousand dollars, which was quite a large sum in those days. I felt it was his way of paying me off for not fighting him and the annulment. I took the money for you, not for me."

"You never told me that, but from what I've seen here, the old earl could afford the payoff. In fact, he probably could have afforded much more."

"I never got the impression that William was extremely rich, but I knew he was comfortable. Are you telling me that your father left you a great deal of money?"

"At this point I have no idea how much. There's a Swiss bank account that I haven't had time to check out. But there's also an English account that contains well over a million and a half pounds."

"That much?"

"There's also Litchfield; a lodge in Scotland, which, by the way, I'll be visiting this weekend, and a suite at the Ritz in London, a suite he owned, not leased."

"CC, I'm astonished. I can't imagine how your father made that kind of money."

"Do you recall anything unusual about the time you spent together in France? Did he meet anyone he didn't introduce you to? Did he go anywhere without you? Anything?"

"It was so long ago and I was so much in love. I really can't remember, but I did keep a very detailed diary of our time together."

"A diary?"

"Yes. Keeping a diary was quite the rage back then. I haven't looked at it since I left England. In fact, the last entry is the day you and I flew to the United States."

"Where's the diary now?"

"In my safety deposit box, the one I've had since before Flash and I were married. I keep personal items in it: pictures of my mother and father; the license when I married your father; the annulment papers; a lock of your baby hair; your first teeth, the ones the tooth fairy took; your elementary and high school report cards, things like that."

"Does Flash know about the box?"

"He does. In fact he's also a signer on it in case something happens to me, but he doesn't go into it. I know that for sure. We both have our secrets. I don't ask him about some of the strange things he does in business and he allows me my privacy. That's one of our strengths and one of the agreements we made when we married. Flash knew everything he needed to know about William and me, but he never intruded into my personal feelings."

CC wondered about her mother's reference to "strange things" Flash did, but decided not to pursue that subject. "Could you possibly read the diary, Mother? I know it won't be easy, but—"

"Of course, darling, if it will help you know your father better. I no longer feel pain when I think of William. I will always have feelings for him, primarily because of you, but I love Flash, and my life with him has been everything I could have wanted."

"When do you think you might get to the bank?"

"If I can get this party situation in hand, I'll drive over this afternoon. If not, I'll go tomorrow morning. The bank's open from nine to noon on Saturday. I should be able to read the diary this weekend. Why don't you call me Monday?"

"Great. I'll do that."

"Now what specifically do you want to know? I'll write it down."

"I want to know if my father left you to go to a meeting or to rendezvous with someone he didn't feel you should meet. Did he introduce you to someone he didn't want to talk about or someone with whom he acted strangely because you were around? I also want to know if he spoke of the family's financial situation or his reason for marrying Anne when he loved you so much. I imagined he married for money. Maybe that's because I'd always heard that two British houses are often united to save one house from financial ruin."

"I think that's probably a motive from some romance novel, CC. Anything else?"

"Not that I can think of specifically. Look for anything that strikes you as being in different or strange. Now that you can objectively look at what you wrote without a romantic interpretation, maybe something will strike you."

"Did you learn anything else from Mr. Caulfield?"

"As a matter of fact, I did. Do you have any idea who might have been watching us all of these years?"

"Watching us? What do you mean?"

"Caulfield gave me a letter. William knew a great deal about what we were doing. In the letter he said that he was rewarding Flash quite generously for taking such good care of us."

"That's impossible. In fact, I'm surprised he knew about Flash. CC, I can assure you, after he left me I never heard from William Cleveland or any of his representatives again. It's as if he never existed for me and I never existed for him. To tell you the truth, I often wondered why he never showed any interest in you. I thought about sending him pictures, especially when I read that his father died, but I never did. I waited for him to contact me about you. I was afraid to make the move."

"I have no idea how he knew about me, but he did. I'll work on finding that out later. Now I want to get that diary. Hastings, the butler, also has some letters and papers for me from William. Maybe they'll provide clues."

"Does it really make that much difference to you what William did or how he made his money, CC? Will this information help you make a decision about your own life?"

"I have no idea. Maybe it's my perpetual curiosity that's been aroused. Remember you once told me that trait could get me into trouble?"

"I don't want to hear that. You're not to do anything dangerous. Do you hear me?"

"Mom, there's no trouble to get into. As I said, I'm curious. From what others have told me about my father and how wonderful and special he was, he doesn't seem like the kind of man who would refuse to stand up to his father, back away sheepishly from his responsibility, and abandon a wife who carried his child. William Cleveland is a mystery, and you know how I love a good mystery."

"You hate a good mystery, remember? You've always hated mysteries."

"But I've never been directly and personally involved in one. That makes it different. Anyway, Mother, it's really not a mystery. I want to know my father."

"May I tell Flash, darling? I hate to hide what I'm doing from him."

"Tell him anything you wish to share, and tell him he'll soon be richer than he is now. Give him my love. I don't imagine he's around at the moment."

"He went to the office. Some of the cuts from the Major League camps were announced today and he wants to start planning."

"Oh Lord. I can't believe I forgot roster cuts are today. I'd better hang up and call the office. I love you, Mom, and I'll talk with you Monday."

"I love you too."

CC sat on the bed and sipped her wine, then frowned and looked at her watch. It was seven forty-five. *I need to call Jim*

Oats, but that call will have to wait, she thought. *It's dinner time for me and Jim is probably out to lunch. Maybe that's best. Talking to that idiot is sure to ruin my meal, literally this time.* She smiled, got up from the bed, took another sip of wine, and dressed for dinner.

CHAPTER NINE

Once again, dinner was both delicious and lonely. James must have been off because Richard served. "You do have a multitude of duties to fulfill," CC said when he came to refill her wine glass.

"I suppose I do, my lady, though when the earl was alive my only responsibility was to serve him."

CC wasn't sure but it didn't appear that Richard was pleased to be doing menial tasks. "Well, I want you to know I appreciate your willingness to stay on and help Hastings while I'm here," she said.

Richard nodded but he didn't smile. "My pleasure, Your Ladyship."

When the last dishes had been cleared away, Richard announced that he would be serving coffee in the White Drawing Room. "If it wouldn't inconvenience the staff too much," CC said, "I would prefer having coffee outside at the table under the tree, and Richard, please tell Hastings that I'll pull the bell when I am ready to start the tour of the house and then meet him in the library."

"I'll tell him. If you'll just give me a few minutes to wipe off the seat and the table for you, I'll bring your coffee."

"I can clean the table if you'll just get me a rag."

"I would be glad to do it for you, Your Ladyship, if you don't mind waiting a moment."

Reprimanded again, CC mused. *I'm certainly not behaving like a countess.*

The night was cool and lovely, and even though it was nine-fifteen, it was still light. CC remembered Alex saying that by July it would remain light well past ten o'clock. She would think of this beautiful evening when she was sitting at the stadium about the eighth inning of a ballgame during a hot, sticky summer day.

She strolled down the front walk and onto the lawn. A cool breeze blew her hair and her skirt and she put out her arms to embrace the freshness. When she reached the table, the coffee and sweets were waiting. She added as much cream as possible to the larger cup, pleased that Hastings had remembered, and took a skip. She couldn't believe she was eating again, but she picked up one of the sweets, a pink concoction, and took a bite. "Mmmm," she murmured, "delicious!" She leaned back to enjoy the coffee in the idyllic setting.

Despite the fact that the coffee was diluted, CC was afraid if she drank too much she wouldn't sleep, so she didn't pour a second cup. She pushed aside the other tempting sweets and went back into the house to her room. Her first inclination was to bypass Leslie and call Susan directly, but she thought better of it. She would find out what Leslie knew first and then deal with Jim when she was fully armed. She dialed. "Good afternoon, or as it is over here, good evening," she greeted Leslie.

"Hi. How was your day?"

"Interesting, full, and not over yet. What's new at the office? I got a message to call Jim. He says he needs to talk with me as soon as possible."

"I knew he planned to call you, but I have no idea why. Wes doesn't know either. I guess you'll have to be surprised when you reach him. Lucky you."

"I consider myself privileged, but before I listen to his latest ridiculous scheme, anything else?"

"Fortunately no. Everything's running smoothly. Spring training is going well and we're all looking forward to opening day."

"Remember there's a road trip first. Let's make a good showing against the Mets and the Pirates."

"*Sports Illustrated* picked us to win it all."

"The kiss of death," CC groaned. "Right now, all I want is to open at home with more wins than losses."

"Any idea when you're coming home?"

"Not next week, that's for sure. You know I hoped to spend a couple of weeks in Florida, but right now I'm shooting for the home opener. Cross your fingers."

"I will, but don't worry. Everything's fine here."

"Let everyone know how much I appreciate all of their efforts, will you?"

"Absolutely. Want me to transfer you to Jim?"

"Yes, and have a great weekend. It's one of your last peaceful ones before the season starts."

"And I plan to relax. Anyway, here's Jim."

Leslie evidently bypassed Susan because Jim answered. "Hi, CC. How are things in England?"

"Under control. Are they under control there, Jim?"

"They are, but I want to run something by you."

What now? CC wondered. "What's on your mind?" she asked, wondering if Jim could hear the exasperation she was feeling.

"I have a great new sponsorship idea. The White Sox have used it and I think it would really bring in the crowds. I hope you approve, because when you weren't here I had to place the order."

"Oh my God, Jim. Tell me this isn't another crazy promotion."

"You'll love this. I've ordered fifty thousand squeeze bottles. You know, the plastic kind that people can take to picnics or bring to the ballpark."

CC groaned. "Jim, for God's sake. You know the city won't let people bring containers into the stadium."

"But this is different, CC. This is a container with our logo on it."

"It's still a container, Jim. It can hold beer or an alcoholic beverage, and the city won't permit anyone to bring them into the park. You can ask George since that's his department, but I would bet they'll have a fit if you hand fans bottles before the game. Jim, why don't you check things out before you jump on every advertiser's bandwagon?"

"I checked with the White Sox, and they don't have problems at spring training."

"Spring training? You mean they give these bottles away at spring training and not during the regular season?"

"That's right, but they're thinking of ordering some for the regular season."

"The operative word here is 'thinking.' They haven't done it, and I'm sure they'll be checking with their stadium authority before they do. Am I right?"

CC could almost hear Jim squirm. "We could give them away as the fans exit. They could use them other places besides the ballpark."

CC knew the containers didn't have a place at the ballpark, not when the commissioner's office had just reiterated the new liquor policy and the desire to try to cut down on consumption of alcoholic beverages. There were fan groups fighting against the score board advertisements for alcohol as well as cigarettes, and all of the ballparks were now smoke-free. This was an invitation to trouble.

"Cancel the order, Jim. Do it now! There will be no excuses that it can't be done. I doubt George has sent a check, since he can't do so without my authorization, so no money has been exchanged. Do I make myself clear? Cancel! Since we get part of the refreshment revenues from spring training, I'll consider the containers for next year in Florida, but not at the ballpark. Cancel!"

"I'll try, CC."

"I didn't say try, I said do it, and Jim, we will most assuredly have a meeting when I get back. I don't think you've heard what I've been telling you about checking with me before you act. I am accessible, even in England. My e-mail is not up and running yet, and my cell phone won't be charged for a few days, but you have my number at the house. There is no excuse for this latest fiasco. Let me repeat once more so that you are quite clear on the matter. Cancel the order!"

"Oh, I'm quite clear. Thank you, CC!"

"Good. I'll speak with you on Monday morning and I'll want to hear that the matter has been cleared up; that no plastic bottles will be delivered."

"Fine!" Jim slammed the phone down.

"Stupid son of a bitch," CC fumed, but she wondered if he really was that asinine. *Maybe he's just sly,* she considered. *Maybe he's trying to undermine me and cause problems for me with ownership. I'll have to watch the idiot. He could be dangerous.* "My God," she groaned. "Does every damn aspect of my life have to be filled with intrigue?" She sat for a few minutes, trying to cool down before pulling the cord for Hastings. The time had come to forget work and go to the chapel and get those papers, papers that might tell her something about her mysterious father.

Hastings met her at the foot of the stairs. "If you're ready to proceed, my lady, I will take you to the chapel."

"Thank you, Hastings. I can't wait to see it. It's so unbelievable to me that a house would have its own place of worship."

"It's really not unusual, my lady. Many nobles built chapels during the English Reformation. The country went back and forth between Catholicism and the English church established by Henry VIII. The religion changed each time a new monarch assumed the throne. Henry's sickly son, Edward, preserved the new religion, but the king was not actually a ruler in his own right and was influenced to do so by his Protestant advisors. His successor, Lady Jane Grey, died to maintain the Protestant faith. Her parents and in-laws maneuvered to have her placed on the throne to gain personal power as well as to prevent the return of Catholicism which, if reinstated, would have meant their downfall. The next queen, Henry's daughter Mary, like her mother, Katherine of Aragon, was a devout Catholic. When she came to the throne, she executed many nobles who refused to embrace the pope and her faith, including Queen Jane's family."

"And then Elizabeth re-established the Anglican church."

"Very good, my lady. And meanwhile the noblemen built their own chapels so that they could worship as they pleased, hidden from the public eye."

"But didn't you say this house was built in 1720? By then the Reformation was over."

"True. The Puritans had recently lost power, but they were still a force. People were unsure if they would be allowed to worship as they chose, so they continued the practice of building their own chapels."

"But you say that this particular chapel isn't used anymore?"

"It was not used for worship during your father or your grandfather's lifetime. In fact, I'm almost ashamed to say we utilize it to store some of the things your father didn't wish to display in the house, works by Chinese artists, for example."

"I'm eager to see the place, if you'll lead the way." She followed Hastings through the formal rooms of the west wing until they reached a closed double door. Hastings stepped aside for CC to enter a dark chapel, which smelled musty from being closed up and from lack of use.

"I'm very much afraid there is no electricity connected in here, my lady. Had I known you were so interested in the chapel, I would have asked our handyman, Henry Green, to repair the wires. All the light we have now is what little remains of the natural light those dirty stained glass windows admit and this flashlight. If you truly wish it, I would be pleased to show you around the chapel despite these constraints, but I recommend you allow the staff to do some cleaning and give Henry time to install electricity before you spend any time in here. I assure you, all will be in readiness for you when you return from Scotland after your holiday. You will be able to see the chapel much better then."

CC was disappointed. She wouldn't have an opportunity to move the altar and extract her father's papers, but she realized that there was no way she would be able to get rid of Hastings, who would most likely refuse to leave her in the dim, dirty chapel and who would undoubtedly become suspicious of her motives if she insisted on being alone.

One obstacle she hadn't considered when she first made her plans was the lack of light. In the unlit room she would never be able to see what was hidden behind the altar. She decided not to press her luck and agreed to leave, so that Hastings wouldn't suspect her actual reason for being there. "You're right, Hastings. I'll follow your very good advice, and since

I've been here once, I'm sure I'll be able to find the chapel on my own when I get back."

"Very good, my lady, and when you do enter the chapel next time, I assure you the room will be sparkling."

"Please don't go to any trouble, but thank you." CC looked at her watch. "I imagine it's getting late for you. I've kept you up entirely too long with my curiosity about Litchfield Manor."

"It is my pleasure to show you your home anytime you ask, my lady. Anyway, I'm used to retiring late. Your father often stayed up into the morning hours working in his study. Neither Richard nor I retired before he did in case he needed something."

"His study? Did I see that room?"

"I didn't show it to you when you first arrived primarily because we only had time to see the lower floors. The study is adjacent to your father's bedroom suite. Except for the police, it hasn't been touched since his death; that is, except for Austen, who tidied up the room, and or course I've been in. Unless the earl was present no one else was ever allowed in his office; not even Richard."

"But I thought Richard found my father's body.'

"He did, my lady. When your father's bed hadn't been slept in and there was no answer when Richard knocked on the office door, he went inside and found your father slumped over his desk. He called me and I called the number the earl gave me several months ago."

"My father gave you a number to call if he was found dead? Didn't you think it strange that he wanted you to notify someone other than the coroner?"

"Not at all, my lady. Your father was a very organized man. I'm sure he had his reasons. But about the study."

"CC wanted to ask for more information about the mysterious number Hastings called, but it wasn't the time. "Yes, please go on," she said. "I apologize for interrupting."

Hastings smiled and continued. "Before your father became the earl, the room was a large guest suite. He had the entry from the hall sealed, though the door is still visible, and a new doorway cut from his bedroom. As I told you, his father used the reading room downstairs as his study, so this was quite a change. I only entered the room when your father was present, and Austen only dusted and vacuumed when he was there. Your father kept the only key to the room. Since his death, I have had the key, and no one has been in to look around, though I must admit, many staff members are curious about the 'secret room' as they call it. I put the key in the safe, which is where I will take you now. I believe you requested the papers and letters I told you about as well as a piece of jewelry. I would also like to show you how to open the safe."

As CC followed Hastings away from the chapel toward the main house, she thought about her father's bedroom, the room off her sitting room. She hadn't really explored it the night before. She hadn't looked into the closet or the bathroom. She remembered there were three doors but had not been particularly interested in opening any of them. Tonight she would take a closer look before going to bed.

Hastings opened one of the doors they passed before arriving at the chapel. The room was bare of furniture. Bookcases filled with ledgers lined the wall. "The household accounts and estate papers for the past two hundred and seventy years are kept in this room, my lady. There's a fascinating look at history in here. Though you didn't ask to see the archives, I thought you might like to know where you could go if you have questions about your ancestors or the history of the house."

"Thank you, Hastings. I hope I'll have time to delve into those files before I go home."

Hastings didn't respond. He shut the door to the storage room and walked a few paces to what was obviously a reinforced steel door with a keypad beside it. He punched in a five digit number, pulled opened the heavy door, and stood aside for CC to enter.

The room contained only one piece of furniture, a heavy unadorned table. It was incredibly stark in contrast to the opulence of the décor in the rest of the house. Straight ahead of her was a massive safe containing two keypads, one on top of the other.

"If you will observe, I will show you how to open the safe," Hastings said. "You must be careful to enter the numbers in order. If you deviate from the pattern or punch in an incorrect sequence, the safe will not open for several hours."

CC was surprised at the complexity of the system, but she didn't comment.

Hastings handed her a laminated card that contained four rows of numbers. "You must first enter these numbers on the top keypad." He pointed to the top line on CC's card. "Then punch in the second row of numbers on the lower keypad. Go back to the top keypad and enter the next sequence, and then complete the final series on the lower pad."

"This is certainly sophisticated," CC said.

"But necessary to ensure the safety of your jewels, the large amount of cash we keep on the premises, and your father's personal papers. I might add that the room itself has an alarm system as well as a very modern fire system, though the safe itself is completely fireproof." CC looked at the sprinklers in the ceiling as Hastings pointed upward.

"The door alarm is on at all times. It de-activates when the code on the keypad is entered correctly. If there is an error, the alarm will go off, signaling that there has been an attempt to breach security. When we leave, it will automatically reset."

"What if some technically challenged person makes an error trying to get in here?" CC asked. "I must tell you, Hastings, I don't think I'll try to enter this room, let alone try to open the safe without you."

Hastings smiled. "I felt that way when your father first explained the system to me, but eventually the process became routine."

"Did Lady Anne remove her jewels by herself?"

"No, my lady, she felt exactly as you do. Your father always retrieved them for her."

Once again CC looked at the card Hastings had given her. There were only four rows of numbers. The sequence necessary to gain access to the safe was not there. "How do I get into the room if I decide to be brave and not bother you to bring me my jewelry?" she asked. "I don't see the combination to the outside door."

The sequence is not written down, so you'll have to memorize it. Again, Mr. Caulfield has the combination should you forget it, though I don't imagine you will."

CC looked puzzled.

"The sequence is 62279."

"My birth date?"

"That's right. Your father informed me that you were born on June 22, 1979. You will find that your father used that sequence of numbers quite often. They will open the smaller safe at Knockie, in case you need to put your jewelry or any other valuables away. He trusted me with the information in case something happened to him, but except for using the combination to turn off this alarm, I have never used it."

To say the least, CC was stunned. Had she really meant so much to her father that he would remember her birthday in this way?

Hastings opened the safe, shut it, and watched CC as she followed his instructions. She breathed a sigh of relief when the safe opened for her. Inside were several shelves filled with papers, bundles of cash, and the jewelry. She took out the box, opened it, and removed a pearl ring surrounded by diamonds, matching earrings, and a pearl necklace with a diamond clasp. She also removed a thick gold bracelet and the gold necklace with the pear-shaped diamond at the tip. *I might as well enjoy these for the short time they will be mine,* she thought, a bit envious of the wife of whatever cousin would inherit the title.

She stepped aside and Hastings removed a bundle of letters. "These are the letters and papers your father asked me to give you, my lady. I do hope you enjoy reading them."

"I'm sure I will, Hastings, and thank you for all of your assistance tonight. Since I have to get up early, I'll go to bed and allow you to do the same."

"Very good, but if I may say one thing?"

"Of course."

"I served your father for many years, my lady. Despite the differences in our stations, I came to believe that we were friends. As I said before, your father trusted me, and I'm very proud. Some of his secrets will go to the grave with me. Others, when time permits, I will share with you. I only wanted to say that I hope that you will be able to trust me too. I will be here for you as your father asked me to be. If you need me for anything, please do not hesitate to ask."

CC was touched. "I appreciate it, Hastings. I'll certainly keep what you've said in mind, and I look forward to talking with you about my father when I return from Scotland."

"Very good, my lady. " All sentimentality disappeared as Hastings became the efficient butler again. "I failed to ask you the time you would be leaving with Sir Anthony and Lady Alexandra in the morning."

"They'll be here to pick me up at seven-thirty, so I would like breakfast in my room at seven."

"I'll see to it. Would you like a real English breakfast before your trip or would you prefer a breakfast similar to the one you had today?"

"I'm afraid I don't know what a real English breakfast is, but it sounds like a lot of food." Hastings nodded. "In that case, I'll have coffee, fruit, and wheat toast. I'll try your English breakfast when I get back from Scotland, after I've jogged a few mornings to get off the pounds I'm sure I've already gained from eating the excellent food John Claude and Charles serve. Good night, Hastings, and again, thank you."

"You are most welcome, my lady. I'll see you in the morning before you leave for Scotland."

CC clutched the jewelry and the bundle of papers Hastings had given her and went upstairs, not to go to bed as she said, but rather to take a look at the letters and explore her father's secret study.

CHAPTER TEN

CC wasted no time in her own rooms. Her first priority was to see her father's study. She set the bundle of papers on the lamp table by the bed, passed through her sitting room and her father's bedroom, and took out the key that led to his private world; a world that Hastings said could only be visited when the earl was present.

She inserted the key in the lock and then hesitated. This was also the room where her father died of a heart attack. Or was it a heart attack? There had been no autopsy. In his letter William said he was in excellent health? She decided to arrange an appointment with the physician who attended her father when Richard found him. Without an autopsy, how could he be sure the cause of death was a coronary? And then there was the phone number William gave Hastings. Did her father realize he was in imminent danger? Again she had a suspicion that William was so much more than simply a country gentleman with a title, and she intended to find out who he was and what happened to him.

She turned the key and pushed open the study door. The room was dark, and CC groped for a wall switch. She felt one near the door and turned on the light. Despite the glow from the chandelier, the room was still shadowy. She looked around and discovered the reason for the dimness. The great western windows that stretched from floor to ceiling had been partially blocked to provide additional shelf room for hundreds of leather-bound books. There were more books in this room than in the library. CC walked to the windows. It was stuffy and she wanted to let in some air, but the windows were sealed.

She turned back to the middle of the room toward a lovely table surrounded by four matching chairs. Several large leather-bound volumes and a marble statue of a horse and rider rested on the polished mahogany surface. CC picked up each volume. *So my father liked Hardy,* she thought as she placed *Far From The Madding Crowd* and *Jude The Obscure* back on the pile. She was unfamiliar with the authors or titles of the other books, but they appeared to be works of nonfiction, several on the topic of Northern Ireland and a few on events occurring in the Middle East.

CC turned and surveyed the rest of the room from this central vantage point. On either side of the window were large globes. CC walked over to take a closer look, wondering why anyone would have two globes in the same room. As she studied each one, she saw they were, in fact, very different. The globe to the right of the desk presented the world as it was in 1945, and the other showed the new countries in 2009.

In front of the bookcases that extended from the window was her father's desk, where he was working when he died. On it were additional stacks of books, an antique brass desk set, and a small brass reading lamp with a green shade.

Opposite the entrance to the room there were two other doors. She walked over to one and turned the knob. Nothing happened. *This must be the sealed door to the hall that Hastings mentioned*, she thought as she moved on to the second door. She turned the knob and the door opened. The ceiling light automatically switched on filling a huge windowless closet with bright light. "Oh my," she said as she began a cursory inspection of the area.

To her immediate left was an up-to-date computer station with every gadget imaginable including a desktop computer, a laptop, an external storage drive, a scanner, two printers, and a fax machine. CC was puzzled. *Why would all this equipment be locked away in a closet rather than near the earl's desk in his study?* She continued to look around.

Beside one of the printer desks was a locked five-drawer file cabinet. CC tried her desk key, but the cabinet wouldn't open. *I'll have to look for the key in the desk when I'm finished in here,* she thought. To her right was a small safe. CC was puzzled. With the huge safe downstairs, why would William need a second safe in his study? She bent down and tried the combination Hastings told her William always used, her birth date, 62279. Sure enough, the door opened. Inside were several packages of twenty-pound notes, numerous bundles of letters, and a small photo album.

CC picked up the album and opened it. "My God," she said aloud. "Where did William get all these pictures?" She sat on the floor and flipped through pages that chronicled her life. Staring back at her were baby pictures, photos of her in grammar school and as a high school cheerleader. These were not merely shots taken from a distance. They included copies of portraits hanging in the Arizona house, school class pictures, and a photo from the country club newsletter showing her after she won the Junior's Tennis Tournament. There were four sorority pictures; one for each year she attended Northwestern; a graduation picture of her in her cap and gown outside the Tri Delta House, and still another graduation picture, this one from Arizona when she received her master's degree.

The album also contained newspaper clippings announcing her appointments to different baseball positions. The latest photo was of her with the owners of the Knights when she was named CEO. She was astonished. "I can't believe this!" she exclaimed. "How could my father have all of this?"

CC was shaking when she put the album back in the safe and closed the door. Her father knew everything about her and she knew nothing about him. Who had provided the information?

Suddenly she felt exhausted. The letters would wait. When she read them, she wanted to be well-rested and have all her wits about her. Maybe they would provide a clue or, even better, an explanation as to how her father had kept track of her and who had provided the details of her life over the years. She was relatively sure her mother had played no part in the spying. Mary had said she had no contact with William and CC believed her.

Before leaving the vault-like room and the pictures behind, CC looked around the closet again. Strangely, the back wall was paneled. By itself this would not have seemed unusual, but the side walls were bare of paneling, and she wondered about the discrepancy. Why would her father panel one wall of the closet and not the others? *Good Lord,* she chided herself. *I have to stop this ridiculousness. I'm beginning to sound like Jessica Fletcher, an amateur trying to solve a crime that probably wasn't even a crime. I'm looking for clues that would prove a man to be other than what he probably was: a nobleman who lived in the country and tended to his own affairs.* She shut the closet door and went back into the study.

Hastings had given her the key to her father's desk, so she crossed the room and sat down in the straight cane-backed chair. She longed to feel some sense of her father by sitting in his chair, a seat that only he used; but nothing came to her. She was sitting at a desk not unlike her own, except that in Indianapolis she had a comfortable leather chair and this one certainly wouldn't lend itself to hours of sitting. Her key opened the top desk drawer. She looked inside, half expecting to find more pictures, but there was no album and nothing unusual that she could see. The silver ruler, Mont Blanc pens, initialed writing paper, and a brass-initialed letter opener were arranged neatly and precisely in order.

CC closed the top drawer and opened the locked side drawer on the right. Again she didn't notice anything unusual. Several leather containers held paper clips, postage stamps, and rubber bands. A stamp with the family crest carved on it fit neatly in a wooden box that also contained an inked stamp pad. CC hated herself for giving in to her curiosity, but she removed all of the containers and tapped the bottom and back of the drawer. *Here I go again*, she scoffed, *I'm Jessica, looking for a false back or bottom of a drawer that will hold the answers to all my questions, and of course that's ridiculous.*

She examined the contents of the two lower drawers on the right side and found nothing curious, but when she unlocked and opened the top drawer on the left side, she drew back quickly. The drawer contained only one item, a gun. She knew nothing about guns and had no idea what caliber it was. Guns had always frightened her, so she quickly shut the drawer and locked it again. Why would her father keep a gun in his desk? The study was upstairs; there was only one entry and that was through his bedroom. The windows were sealed and Hastings said the door was always locked. In addition, the house was swarming with servants, so there was little danger of someone sneaking into William's inner sanctum. Yet he felt he needed a gun. For what? For protection? If so, from whom? She opened the remaining desk drawers, hoping to find the key to the file cabinet in the closet. Still no luck.

Reluctantly deciding that if she was going to be ready to go in the morning she should pack and get to bed, she turned off the light, locked the door, and reentered her father's bedroom. Much as she wanted to continue exploring, the study and its contents would wait until she got back from Scotland.

When CC's breakfast arrived at seven, she was ready to go. Millie saw the packed suitcase by the door. "I would be glad to take your suitcase down, my lady," she said.

"Thank you, Millie. I have to add a makeup bag, so I'll bring it down with me in a while."

"Would you like for me to come back for it, or should I send Hastings?"

"Really, I can manage just fine, but I would appreciate it if you would tell Hastings I need a word with him before I leave. I'll be down in about twenty minutes."

"I'll tell him, my lady. Enjoy your breakfast."

CC ate her fruit, nibbled at her scone, and drank two cups of coffee. The caffeine did its work and she felt much more alert. She packed the small case with the jewelry she had taken from the safe the night before; put her father's letters and papers into her purse so she would have easy access to them in the car if the opportunity arose for her to read; picked up her luggage, and went downstairs.

Hastings was in the entry hall waiting for her. "You asked to see me, my lady?"

"I did. Thank you, Hastings. Last night you gave me keys to my father's desk and his room. The room key also opened his closet, which contained a locked file cabinet. Do you know where I can find the key to the file? I looked in the desk, but couldn't find one."

"I have absolutely no idea. I've never been in your father's closet. The door was always locked, and it was not my place to open it without instructions to do so."

"Is there any chance it's in the large safe?"

"Not to my knowledge." Hastings thought for a moment. "There are keys in there, but they are keys to the house, the stables, and the garage. You may certainly look when you return."

"Thank you. And while I'm thinking of it, there's also a small safe in the study closet. I opened it using the combination you gave me. In it I found a photo album that's filled with pictures of me. Do you have any idea who sent them? Did my father regularly receive mail from the United States?"

"My lady, the earl received mail from all over the world on a regular basis. I have no way to know if any of the parcels contained pictures of you."

"Can you recall packages postmarked in Arizona?"

"I'm sure I couldn't say. Most of your father's mail lacked a return address. I do know it came from different countries, because I'm a philatelist. The earl allowed me to keep all of the stamps from his letters and packages. I would be glad to go through my collection with you upon your return. Perhaps you'll see a particular stamp which will provide an answer to your question."

"That's a good idea, Hastings. If you remember anything else, please let me know."

"I'll do so, my lady."

"Thank you. As I mentioned, I'll be at Lady Alexandra's brother's lodge in Glencoe tonight, and tomorrow I'll be traveling to Knockie. I assume there are phones at the lodge."

Hastings smiled. "I'm confident you'll find all the modern conveniences at Knockie, my lady. Your father completely renovated the lodge five years ago. Because Knockie was his favorite place to entertain business associates, he was constantly improving the house."

"Business associates? What kind of business?"

"I'm afraid I can't say, my lady. Perhaps you'll find the answers you seek among your father's papers and letters."

Can't or won't say, CC mused. "Perhaps I will," she said smiling. "I certainly hope so."

Tony and Alex arrived at seven-thirty. While Hastings opened the car door for CC, Tony put her bag in the trunk, and after last minute instructions, the three were on the road to Scotland.

The air was damp and cool and smelled of rain. As they turned off the narrow road onto the A34 north toward Scotland, CC sat back in the comfortable leather seat to enjoy the ride through the English countryside. This time it was Alex who acted as a guide. As they passed a sign pointing to Stratford-upon-Avon, she talked of the amazing emotions she felt when she first saw Shakespeare's grave in front of the altar of Holy Trinity Church. CC made a mental note to see the famous burial site as well as Shakespeare's birthplace before returning home.

She added two more future sightseeing excursions to her list when they passed signs for Kenilworth Castle and Coventry Cathedral. Alex explained that Kenilworth was a magnificent red ruined castle that was once home to John of Gaunt and Katherine Swynford." Since CC had never heard of John or

Katherine, Alex offered to lend her *Katherine*, a novel by Anya Seton, "my very favorite book in the world!" she exclaimed. She also talked about how moved she was when she and Tony visited the unrestored ruins of Coventry, the only cathedral destroyed by German bombs during the war, and how much she admired the beautiful new cathedral that abutted the old ruins.

When Tony turned onto the M42 toward Birmingham, as when she made the initial trip from Heathrow to Litchfield, CC felt she could be back home. The motorway was bumper-to-bumper with rush hour traffic and Tony closed the sunroof to keep out the noxious diesel fumes. Without much scenery to enjoy, CC dozed.

In what seemed like no time, Alex's voice awakened her. "CC, I hate to disturb you, but Tony and I decided to take a slight detour on the way. We're going to drive through the Lake District and have lunch outside Grasmere at Michael's Nook, one of our favorite holiday spots. Tony called ahead and told the owner, Reg Gifford, to expect us."

The Lake District was lush and lovely, and as they drove alongside Lake Windermere, CC suddenly understood why the Romantic poets were so taken with the sights and sounds of the area. "No wonder Wordsworth loved nature so much. I think even I could be a poet if I lived here," she said. The line from one of CC's favorite poems, Wordsworth's "The Pass of Kirkstone," perfectly described the scenery: "Who comes not hither, ne'er shall know/How beautiful the world below."

Suddenly CC experienced an epiphany. Before this trip, her view of the world had been limited. She never had a desire to travel outside of the United States. Her entire life revolved around baseball. Now she wondered how she could have been so narrow in her thinking. For the first time the phrase "it's a big world out there," however trite, made sense. For the first time the Indianapolis Knights seemed relatively insignificant in the context of the history of the world. She thought of the history of the Lake District in particular. She too, as Wordsworth had so many years before, felt close to nature and God in this lovely spot.

Whatever Alex was saying fell on deaf ears and sounded like a drone, as CC marveled at her own realization. She wondered if the Romantic poets, who rejected civilization and found solace in nature, had felt as she did at that moment. It all sounded quite dramatic, but her life had changed in a very short time. She had just become aware of the differences. *In fact*, she pondered, *it has been totally turned around in only three short days*. Life would never be the same when she returned to Indianapolis. She would never again stay at home during her infrequent vacations. She would definitely see more of the world.

Tony's voice brought CC back to the moment at hand. He turned into a narrow lane. "We're about three minutes from Michael's Nook, CC."

"Tell me about your favorite place, Tony," CC said.

"With pleasure. As Alex told you, we come to Grasmere several times a year. Sometimes we stop for an overnight on the way to see Charlie and sometimes we stay for an extended period to hike and enjoy the countryside. Reg Gifford is a friend as well as the proprietor. I believe the main house was built around 1859 and was named in remembrance of the humble dwelling of the shepherd of Wordsworth's poem 'Michael.' Wordsworth lived near here at Dove Cottage, where he wrote the poem in 1800, and Reg often quotes the line 'Upon a forest side at Grasmere Vale/There dwelt a shepherd, Michael was his name.' The Nook was once a summer home of a cotton industrialist from Lancaster. Reg transformed it into a hotel in 1969. Over the past forty years it has become one of Britain's leading Country House Hotels."

Pastures, where the now familiar black and white cows grazed, lined the approach to the house. When they arrived at the top of the driveway, Reg, a tall, thin, slightly balding Englishman, greeted them cheerfully. He gave Alex an affectionate kiss, hugged Tony, and shook CC's hand.

The group passed through a foyer filled with an abundance of flowers and plants and into an elegant drawing room, where a fire burned brightly in a massive stone fireplace. On either side of the mantle above the blaze, tall vases of purple, pink, and white flowers added to the already appealing ambience. CC smiled when she saw the mahogany table between two overstuffed couches that sat on either side of the hearth. On the shiny surface was a vase of vivid-yellow daffodils. *How appropriate,* she mused.

A Great Dane who lifted his head momentarily to glance casually at the visitors, rested peacefully on a rug in front of the fire. "Why, this is more like a private home than a hotel," CC said as she admired the pleasant room.

"We make a concerted effort to keep it homey, Your Ladyship," Reg responded with obvious pride at CC's compliment.

"Please, no formality. I would just as soon be called CC"

"Excellent. Would you like to see the house, CC?"

"I'd love to."

"Shall we begin in the dining room? I imagine you're all hungry after your morning drive. Fortunately the room is all ours. None of our guests made arrangements to have lunch here today. He turned to Tony. "We have two American couples and a French couple staying at the house. They left early to take in the sights. The French couple asked for directions to Ullswater." He spoke to CC: "That's where Wordsworth wrote his poem 'The Daffodils.' I wish you had more time to spend at Michael's Nook. The daffodils are just beginning to bloom and they're worth a look."

"I wish we did too," CC said. "Would you believe I remember Wordsworth's poem from my high school English class? Let me qualify that statement. I don't remember the entire poem, but I recall the last few words. Wordsworth said that when he was faced with problems of the world, he remembered the springtime scene and his heart 'danced with the daffodils.'"

Reg smiled. "You're absolutely correct." He ushered them over to a table by the front window and seated CC so she could look out onto the patio and down onto the lawns beyond.

The meal was delicious. It began with a salad of lobster with watercress. "Unbelievable!" was CC's reaction to her first bite. Next they enjoyed the entrée, which the printed menu described as "Steamed Fillet of Turbot on a bed of Leeks, topped with Wild Mushrooms and served with a Twist of Noodles and a light Fish Cream Sauce."

Throughout the meal, the four chatted about the history of the hotel and the Lake District poets. When she'd finished the last bite of the hot mango tart, CC sat back in her chair. "If all your meals are like this one, I would like to move into Michael's Nook permanently."

Reg was obviously pleased. "You're always welcome." He stood up and held CC's chair so she could rise more easily. "Now, shall we take the tour of the house? I believe you're on a tight schedule."

"I'd love to see it." She looked at Alex. "That is if we don't have to leave right away."

There's time to see the main house, but we really must go after that," Alex answered. "We have a long drive ahead of us."

When the short tour was over, the three said good-bye to Reg. As Tony pulled out of the driveway, CC looked back at the charming house with its beautiful grounds, which were just coming into bloom in the early spring. Spring, a time of rebirth, CC thought. She too had experienced a rebirth that day. She smiled, thinking about all of the places she planned to see in the world.

CHAPTER ELEVEN

As they turned onto the highway for the two-hour drive to Glasgow, Tony opened the sunroof so that the fresh air could circulate in the car. There was still a feel of dampness, and rain seemed even more inevitable. CC looked at the dark, foreboding clouds in front of them to the north.

By the time they reached Penrith, CC understood why the region was called the Lake District. As they twisted and turned on the single-track road, she marveled at the grandeur of the scores of lakes, some large, some small, but all equally captivating and beautiful. A plethora of wild flowers in varying shades of pink, white, orange, and yellow dotted the shores, while ancient arching trees provided natural tunnels for the car to pass through.

Forty-five minutes after leaving Michael's Nook, Tony turned off the scenic road onto the M6. CC watched closely for a sign to indicate they were "Entering Scotland," a placard similar to the one between the border of Arizona and California, but there was no marker to show they were leaving England. The only way she knew they had actually arrived in Scotland was a well-marked exit pointing to Gretna Green. CC had heard of the famous marriage locale primarily because there was an imitation Gretna Green on the Arizona and California border.

Alex was asleep, so CC decided to use the time to read some of her father's letters. She removed the rubber band from the packet. The first envelope was addressed to "Caroline Charlotte, on your first birthday, June 22, 1980."

Oh my God! CC thought as she looked through the other envelopes, reading the date on the front of each one. There were thirty, one for each year of her life prior to her last birthday. *I must have read the thirty-first in Caulfield's office,* she thought, *and that message sounded so final. Did my father expect that would be his last communication with me? If so, why?* She opened the letter and read.

> *My Darling One Year Old Caroline Charlotte,*
>
> *I have no idea when you might read these letters. I intend to write to you each year on your birthday. It may be many years into the future before you come to know me or to understand the reasons I left you and allowed you and your dear mother to return to America. I will not elaborate on these reasons in the series of letters that I intend to write, since it could be dangerous for me and quite possibly for you. I hope one day you will understand and forgive me for not being the father you needed while you were growing up. Perhaps in the future you will love me as I love you. I pray this will happen when we still have time to know one another.*
>
> *What a beautiful baby you are. I held you right after you were born. You smiled at me. I'm sure your nurse would have told me you had a tummy bubble, but I know it was a smile. I will always treasure that moment. At night in my room, I often think of your lovely round face and the dark circle of fuzzy incredibly soft hair on your little head. And those hands, how small they were. Your little fingers barely closed around my index finger. I hated to wash my hands, since I knew this was the only contact I would have with you for many years to come; perhaps forever.*
>
> *I'm at home now at Litchfield Manor. It's been a year since I stood behind the column at the airport and watched you and your mother*

*get on the plane that would take you away from me. I don't believe
I will ever cry like I did after I returned to my room and hid myself
from the world. How I could give up such a treasure is beyond my
comprehension, yet I had to let you go. It was and is my duty and my
responsibility. May God help you understand.*

*I saw you again last month at your lovely home in Arizona. I
can picture you out on your front door step. We don't have palm trees
in England, but you certainly have three huge palms in front of your
house. I know little about your life this past year, but soon I'll know
what you're doing. I have asked a dear friend, a gentleman I met
when I was in Los Angeles on business years ago, to keep an eye on
you and your mother for me. I don't know if you will ever meet him
personally. His name is Miles MacTandy, though his friends, and I
number myself among those individuals, call him "Flash."*

CC gasped and dropped the letter. She could hardly
breathe. Her father had solved the first mystery for her, but she
never would have guessed the solution. Her own stepfather had
been the one reporting to William all these year, and neither
she nor her mother knew. "My God, I never suspected," she
whispered, not knowing if she was angry, resentful, or appre-
ciative for what Flash had done. All she knew was that she was
stunned. Had Flash married her mother to keep an eye on the
earl's first wife and their child or did he really love Mary? Was
their entire life a lie? Was the money her father left in his will
for Flash a payoff for spying? *Oh my God! Why didn't I put two
and two together sooner?* She felt crushed and deceived.

She didn't want to continue reading. She didn't want to
know anything more about Flash and his relationship with
her father. She remembered Flash's words when she asked him
for advice about her impending trip to England. He told her
to accept her responsibility like her father would want her to.

When she asked him what he meant, he backpedaled, but he had known exactly what he was saying because he and William were friends.

CC closed the letter, put it in the envelope, and leaned back in her seat. She tried to make sense of what she had just learned, but her mind would not or could not sort out the information. After a few minutes, she could no longer stand not knowing what else was in the letter, so she opened the envelope. Perhaps she would understand if she read on.

Flash knows why I need to remain apart from you. In fact, when I saw you, it was because I came to Arizona to see him; to talk with him about keeping an eye on you and your mother. I wish I had been able to see Mary that day, even from afar, but she was working at the hospital. You were sitting in a blue stroller waiting patiently for your maid to take you for a walk. I had a plane to catch and a meeting in Washington, so I could not spare the time to wait for your mother to return home.

Next year I'll know when you first walked, how many teeth you have, and the first word you spoke. How I wish it could be Daddy. Do not consider this spying on you, my darling child. Rather think of it as a necessary arrangement, because a father who loves you dearly has no other possible means of being a part of your life. At least through Flash I will know you from afar.

And so, my dear Caroline Charlotte, I kiss you good night on your first birthday, however imaginary that kiss may be. Perhaps through magic you will feel my love.

Until next year, I remain your loving father, William Cleveland.

For the second time CC put the letter back into the envelope, and then for the third time she took it out and reread her father's words. *Oh, Flash,* she silently cried. *Why couldn't you have trusted me?* Tears fell down her cheeks, but she had no idea if they were tears of anger, despair, or hurt.

She opened the second envelope dated June 22, 1981 and read.

My Darling Caroline Charlotte, or CC, on Your Second Birthday,

You see, I do know about you. I know that you and your dear mother have met Flash and that there will soon be a wedding. I also know that Flash affectionately calls you CC and that you stubbornly refuse to be called anything else. So I will try to oblige you, my darling CC. You might wonder how I feel about you having a stepfather when I would so love to be a real father to you. Let me say that since I can never occupy that place in your life, I'm glad your mother and Flash will be together and they will provide a loving home for you. Because of the love I feel for Mary, it will be quite difficult for me to accept her in the arms of another man, but neither can I imagine you two living alone. So I'm paradoxically happy and sad at the same time.

I have no idea what the years ahead will bring, but I know your mother and Flash will be happy together. I could not have picked a better match for her had I been asked to find someone, and that's a point I wish to clarify. Never think I hired Flash to marry your mother. I asked him to become acquainted with her and to let me know about her needs and your growth, but I did not ask him to make her his wife. I would never want your mother to live in a marriage that lacked love on either side, a marriage similar to the one in which I find myself.

I envy Flash for the access he will have to you. He has recently sent me several pictures. What an incredibly beautiful child you are. The loveliest blond curls have replaced that fuzz on your head. When I last saw you in front of your home, you were dressed in a little cap, so I was unable to see the color of your hair. Now I know what a lovely blond you are. If I were asked to paint an angel I would paint your face. Flash also tells me you're a sweet child; that you have a disposition to match your looks. You must be like your mother, the sweetest woman I have ever known.

I look forward to more pictures from Flash and more news of your growth and development. Until next year, I remain your loving father...

This time CC shed tears of relief. Her father hadn't paid Flash to marry her mother and to care for her. It had been only a coincidence that Mary had come to love him; William had not willed it to happen. She still felt betrayed by Flash's deception, but at least their whole life together was not based on a lie.

CC opened the third letter, dated June 22, 1982. She read about how beautiful she was, about how proud her father was of her successes at nursery school, where she had already begun to read. William knew about her trip to the Grand Canyon with Flash and Mary, about Martha, the new housekeeper Flash had hired. "He really did get a full report," CC whispered, but a little too loudly. Alex woke up.

"Who reported what?" Alex said groggily.

"I'm sorry, Alex. I didn't mean to awaken you. I was reacting to a letter my father left for me. Hastings gave me a stack to bring with me. While you slept I read three."

"That must have been difficult."

"It was, but not just because the letters were from my father. It turns out that my stepfather, Miles MacTandy, I call him Flash, has been reporting to William for thirty years."

"And you had no inkling that your stepfather was acquainted with your father?" Tony asked.

"None whatsoever. Last night, when I found pictures of my mother and me in my father's safe, I wondered who might have sent them to him, but I didn't make the connection. In fact, I would never have dreamed it was Flash. Now I'm not sure whether I should be furious or feel betrayed!"

"Why do you have to decide what to feel or why to feel what you do?" Alex asked. "Just feel. Quite possibly you'll experience one emotion now and another one hours from now. After all, you've had quite a shock."

"You're absolutely right, Alex. I've often been told that I analyze situations too thoroughly, so I'll try to take your advice and let my feelings happen without over analyzing. At the moment I'm trying to decide if I should call Flash and tell him what I found or if I should wait until I return home to confront him. I'm leaning toward bringing every- thing out in the open as soon as possible. No more lies and deception."

"There might be a second reason for doing that," Tony said. "You told us that you wanted to know your father better. Perhaps your stepfather can fill in some missing pieces of the puzzle for you."

"I hadn't thought of that. Hopefully Flash will tell me about his business dealings with William. But I won't call tonight. I certainly don't want to lash out at him without thinking first, so I'll carefully plan what I'm going to say and see how I feel tomorrow."

"Good idea. Do you want Tony and me to be quiet so you can read more of your father's letters?"

"No need. I've read enough for now."

"Good. We're very near Glasgow, and even though our route only takes us through the outskirts of town, you'll get a glimpse of the surrounding area; that is, if you can see out of the windows."

Tony closed the sunroof just in time. The sky opened and the long expected rain came crashing down. It continued to pour, and as a result, CC saw little of Glasgow. However, by the time they reached the Great Western Road, which Tony said would take them to Loch Lomond, the rain had let up and only a light mist fell on the windshield.

When Tony pointed out the famous loch, CC responded by humming Burns' chorus *On the bonny, bonny banks of Loch Lomond*. Because she was so enthusiastic, he pulled into a tiny car park across from the small town of Luss so she could walk out onto the pier and take a closer look. As she stood out over the water, CC watched the windswept clouds creep over and obscure the tops of the surrounding hills that rose lush and green from the banks on the opposite shore. Once again, as they had so many times over the past hours, feelings of contentment and renewal flooded over her while she admired nature's splendor.

As the wind began to gust, small ripples on the lake's surface increased in size and became modest waves. The sky quickly darkened and light showers began to fall. CC inhaled a deep breath of the fresh air before scurrying back toward the car. Right before the car park she ducked into a small store and purchased a few postcards of the loch to send to people at the office. "A touristy thing to do," she said as she slid into the back seat of the car.

She dried herself with a towel Alex kept "for just such emergencies," and they continued on the narrow, winding road that often required a stoplight be placed in the middle of nowhere so both lanes of traffic could use a single-lane bridge. Sheep and cows grazed in the pastures. They were not the black and white cows of England, but rather huge, brown, shaggy, horned Highland cattle.

By the time they reached the Bridge of Orchy, the mist had let up, so they pulled off the road to stretch, to watch the rushing river, and to gaze at Ben Doran looming above them. "We're only twenty-four miles from Glencoe," Tony said as they pulled back onto the highway.

The climb into the Highlands was breathtaking. Tall grasses replaced the pine forests, and in the distance, mountains with cloud-covered tops rose skyward. Alex pointed out the heather that protruded from rocks. "Within a month the entire countryside will be a blanket of purple when the heather is in full bloom. Right now you can only see sprigs of blooms here and there."

"You will absolutely love this place in May," said Tony. "The hills are incredible. It's my favorite time to be up here."

"Sort of like 'The Heather on the Hill' from *Brigadoon?*" CC hummed a few bars, wondering if her companions would recognize the song from the romantic musical she loved so much.

"Actually most of the heather here is the short variety, and there is much more of it than was shown on the movie set, but you have the idea," Alex said.

They left the main highway at Glencoe, and CC was delighted when she spotted a ewe that had started to shed, dragging her coat behind her. "I didn't know sheep shed naturally," she said.

"Most of the time they're sheared," Alex said, "but sometimes they do slough off their coats without man's help."

The road to Charlie's lodge was narrow and winding. "I hope you don't have a problem with car sickness," Tony joked, though CC guessed he was half-serious. "We have about three and a half miles to go on this twisting road before we reach the turnoff to the house. It's on the other side of Loch Leven. There's great salmon fishing in the loch. Do you fish, CC?"

"I went fly-fishing with Flash in Colorado, but I'm not a serious fisherman, or fisherwoman, as the case may be. I prefer to eat the catch after it's been cleaned, cooked, and deboned."

"I totally agree," Alex said. "Charlie's chef does wonders with salmon. Perhaps we'll be lucky and have one of his delicacies this evening for dinner."

CC looked at her watch. It was already past six. She felt drained, both physically and emotionally. Several times Tony had to brake for sheep that were either walking down the middle of the narrow road or crossing slowly in front of the car. "Sheep clearly have the right of way around here," he said as he honked for a particularly slow ewe to get out of the way.

They rounded a bend, and almost directly in front of them was Charlie's lodge. Alex was right. The place didn't qualify as a lodge by any definition. The huge gray stone house sat on acres of cleared land on the banks of Loch Levin. Huge pine, beech, and oak trees, which Tony said dated from the seventeenth century, dotted the lawns.

"Charlie owns four thousand acres," Alex explained. "The house itself has eleven bedrooms. I find them rather dismal, since the paneling is so dark, but I love the brass beds and the antique furniture. When Charlie's father-in-law, Lord Dougall, had the house restored, he created absolutely grand bathrooms with deep tubs and antique brass fittings."

"And you said your brother lives alone out here?" CC asked.

"Just Charlie, little Charlie, and a house full of servants. I know Charlie gets lonely in that huge old house.

Tony pulled up in front of the stone steps, which led to the circular protruding entry. He honked the horn, and much to CC's delight, a man in a Scottish kilt, knee-high socks, a suit coat, and a tartan tie that matched his kilt rushed out of the massive doors and down the steps.

The Highlander greeted them warmly. "Sir Anthony, Lady Alexandra, we were beginning to worry about you, and this must be Lady Litchfield. Welcome to Scotland, Your Ladyship."

"Thank you, er..."

"This is Thomas," Alex said.

"I'm pleased to meet you, Thomas. I hope I'm not being rude by staring, but I'm so impressed with your clothes. Do you often wear traditional clothing?"

"Most of the time, Your Ladyship, though I admit not the formal attire I have on now. But then we were expecting company, and out here that's good reason to dress up."

"Well as I said, I'm impressed." CC turned to Alex. "I really want to go to Inverness and buy an authentic Scottish kilt."

"By all means. In fact, you have your own tartan, the Fraser, I believe, since Knockie was once a hunting lodge for the chief of the Fraser clan, but I'm sure Charlie will tell you about your colors."

CC didn't have time to hear more about Knockie or her family's tartan, because at that moment Alex's brother came out of the front door and dashed down the stairs to greet them. *What an incredible tartan!* CC thought as she watched the tall, muscular, dark-haired man approach. Charlie wore a kilt of MacDonald, black and red with matching red knee socks cuffed just below the knee. He sported a black sport coat with a vest and tie made of the same MacDonald plaid. CC quickly appraised his attire and decided the handsome Scotsman could pose for a travel magazine to advertise his country.

Charlie embraced his sister warmly and shook hands with Tony. When he turned to face CC he smiled, his clear blue eyes twinkling. "So this is Lady Litchfield. My sister has already told me so much about you." CC remembered what Tony said about Alex's matchmaking plans. Had she possibly told her brother too?

"She's told me about you too." She extended her hand. "You have such a lovely place here, though as Alex said, it doesn't exactly fit my definition of a lodge."

"The estate was once used exclusively for hunting when the powerful clans ruled in the Highlands before the Battle of Culloden that destroyed the clan system. However, I believe it would probably be called a country manor today. At any rate, it's home to me and my boy."

He turned to Alex. "Why don't we all go inside? Thomas will see to the luggage if you would give him the key to the boot, Tony."

Tony tossed the keys to Thomas, linked arms with both Alex and CC, and followed Charlie up the stairs into the house. They passed through a paneled reception hall and an elegant but obviously comfortable morning room before entering a library, which was beautifully and tastefully furnished with an eclectic mixture of antiques, comfortable traditional furniture, fine prints, and lovely oil paintings.

Charlie turned to his sister. "I thought we might have a cup of tea while your bags are delivered to your rooms," he said smiling. "I realize it's quite late, so we'll skip the sweets and sandwiches. Dinner will be quite informal, so dress comfortably."

Thomas brought tea, and CC watched Charlie as he chatted animatedly with his sister. She decided that if she had met Alex and Charlie together without knowing they were related, she would not have been able to tell by looking at them. Where Alex was short and petite, Charlie was tall and quite muscular. Alex had a rounded face with two darling dimples and small laugh lines at the corner of each eye. Charlie, on the other hand, had an extremely masculine face with a square jaw and prominent cheekbones. Though clean-shaven, it was apparent he had a heavy full beard, since a slight shadow showed on his face. His brows were full and dark like his hair. The only phrase CC could think of as she admired what Leslie would call a "hunk," was "man's man." Charlie was certainly that.

CC thought of Alex's plans for her brother's future and smiled. *If I weren't in love with Bud and if I planned to stay around here rather than return to Indianapolis, I could half imagine a relationship with this man.* Charlie exuded sex appeal and CC couldn't keep her eyes off him, though Charlie didn't seem to notice she was in the room beyond a casual glance now and then. *I'm glad I have no plans to land Charlie as a husband*, she reflected. *He doesn't have the time of day for me, and he shows no more interest than any polite host would show for his guest.* She finished her tea, and when Thomas came to announce that their rooms were ready, she followed him, Alex, and Tony upstairs, leaving Charlie to take a phone call in private.

CHAPTER TWELVE

Thomas led CC to the McGregor bedroom at the top of the polished oak staircase. "All of the guestrooms are named after Scottish clans," he explained. "Sir Anthony and Lady Alexandra will be just down the hall in the Cameron suite."

Because of its name, CC expected to see a room decorated in bold, dark McGregor colors. Instead the bedroom she stepped into was bright and inviting, *almost feminine*, she pondered. The gleaming brass bed was covered with a pale yellow chintz comforter that contained a dark-blue floral pattern. Curtains made from the same fabric hung from two large windows that had been opened to allow in the cool air. Vases of fresh yellow and white flowers on the dresser and bedside table complemented the décor and added charm to the room. "It's lovely," CC said as she looked around.

"I'm glad it meets with your approval," Charlie said cheerfully as he entered the room. "The McGregor is one of our best rooms and the one we keep for special ladies." He turned to Thomas. "That will be all. Thank you, Thomas," he said.

"Yes, thank you," CC added as the butler left the room.

"As I was saying, I'm pleased you like the room. As you can probably tell, my wife, Flora, applied her feminine touch when we decorated the guestrooms, though after a great deal of what was often heated conversation, I persuaded her to keep the clan names."

"Well, she did a lovely job. The room is perfect."

"Good, but don't get too comfortable. Dinner will be served in thirty minutes."

"I'll be ready. Where should I go?"

"I'll come to take you to the dining room. That way you won't get lost."

"Thank you." CC returned her host's friendly smile and shut the door behind him.

There was no time for a bath, which was what she actually needed after the long journey, but there was time to clean up and change. She walked into the bathroom. Like the bedroom, it was rather dark, but the modern fixtures combined with the antique hardware gave the room a charm all its own.

There was a tub and a separate shower, and CC decided she had enough time to rinse off in the shower. The hot, steamy water felt great and she wished she had time to linger. She got out, toweled vigorously, put on fresh makeup, and combed her hair. Charlie had said dinner would be informal, so she put on black slacks, a brown silk blouse, and a brown and black woolen cardigan that was actually more like a jacket than a sweater. She slipped into black pumps and added the gold bracelet to her wrist. Even though she would have loved to wear the gold necklace with its stunning diamond, she didn't remove it from the case. It was far too dressy for her casual attire.

CC's timing was perfect, because just as she turned off the bathroom light, Charlie knocked. She opened the door. Her heart raced as she looked at her host, who had replaced his jacket, vest, and tie with a white shirt and a tartan ribbon to match the kilt. "Are you ready, Your Ladyship?" He extended his arm.

"Only if you'll call me CC." She smiled and hooked her arm through his.

"With pleasure. Shall we join the others, CC? I believe I heard Tony and Alex go down a few minutes ago."

"I would love to." CC was dying to say, "Lay on, MacDuff," but she refrained. She didn't want Charlie to think she was a total idiot, so she didn't make a comment and went with him toward the dining room.

"Charlie, I hope it's all right to call you that," she said. Alex didn't tell me your full name."

"Charlie is fine."

I know you're a laird because of your marriage to Flora, but are you Laird MacDonald?"

"No. My son will inherit the MacDonald property and title when his grandfather dies. I'm a Scottish laird because Angus, Lord Dougall, gave Flora and me this house and land when we were married. But then little Charlie isn't a laird either, at least not yet. That's because in Scotland the word 'laird' isn't a title. It's a designation for a landowner."

"So it isn't used as a form of address the way 'lord' is used in England."

"No. That being said, it is appropriate to use the word as an expression of affection. I use my family name. When my father dies, heaven forbid anytime soon, I will become Earl Timperley. My father's title dates from the 1570s, from Thomas Timperley, the grandson of the third Duke of Norfolk. Here in Glencoe I'm addressed as Lord Charles, or more formally, Lord Timperley. Little Charlie is the MacDonald, and he will eventually become Earl Timperley as well."

"All of this is extremely confusing. So Alex was originally Lady Alexandra Timperley?"

"That's right. Now she's Lady Alexandra Elizabeth Anne Timperley Chadlington. Quite a name, isn't it?"

"Somehow it seems a bit much for that little ball of fire."

"You've described her well. Alex could always run circles around me when we were growing up. She's perpetual energy in motion."

"Who's energy in motion?" Alex asked as she greeted her brother and CC at the foot of the stairs.

"You are, my sweet." Charlie pinched her cheek. "I was just telling CC how you used to run me ragged when we were growing up at Hintlesham Hall."

"How close is your father's home to Chadlington?" CC asked.

Alex answered: "Suffolk is in East Anglia. Ispwich, the actual location of our family's ancestral estate, is about fifty miles from London and forty miles from Cambridge."

Before CC could ask another question they entered the candlelit dining room and the conversation came to an end. Charlie held out the chair for CC while Tony did the same for Alex. Though the table was long and, CC estimated, would seat at least twenty people with room to spare, the four gathered at one end in a less formal arrangement.

As at Litchfield, on a card in front of each place was a printed menu. "Doesn't anyone eat lightly over here?" CC asked as she studied the fare to follow, which would consist of cream of watercress and mushroom soup, medallions of veal fillet flambé with a white wine shallot and chive sauce and a selection of seasoned vegetables and potatoes. The meal would end with a gratin of apple with almond cream glaze served with its own sorbet.

Charlie looked worried. "The menu doesn't appeal to you?" he said to CC.

"That's the problem. It appeals to me too much. I'm used to a Weight Watcher's frozen dinner at home."

"A what?" Alex asked.

"A diet meal," said Tony. "You know, Alex, the brand that the Duchess of York talks about."

Alex nodded. "Of course. After her divorce from Andrew, poor Fergie resorted to making commercials for the American telly. How scandalous!"

CC smiled. *Pretty smart if you ask me,* she thought. *I'm sure Alex echoes the opinion of most of the British aristocracy.* "I believe she was their spokesperson," she continued, "though I don't think she has the job anymore. She turned to Charlie. "I didn't mean to give you the impression I don't appreciate the food and your hospitality. I've eaten more, and better I might add, in the last three days than in the three months before I crossed the pond."

"I seriously doubt it. You look like the athletic type. I'll bet you're a runner."

"I jog as often as my schedule permits."

"In that case, would you care to join me in the morning? I run every day and I would enjoy a companion. That way you can eat all you want tonight and not have to worry what food will do to your figure."

"I doubt I'll be able to keep up with you if you jog every day."

"Of course you will. If you want to slow down, I'll use it as an excuse to slow down with you."

"In that case, I accept your invitation. What time?"

"How about seven? Breakfast is served at eight-thirty. Leaving early will give us time to get back, shower, and change before we eat."

"Seven it is. Will you pick me up?"

"With pleasure." He turned to Alex. "I'll knock quietly so I don't awaken you and Tony. He smiled. "Or perhaps you'll join CC and me for a little early morning exercise."

"I certainly wouldn't want to intrude on your time together, and I know Tony would find it absolutely disgusting to get up at six-thirty, so you two just go off and run to your heart's content." Alex was positively beaming as she winked at CC. *Obviously she feels she's making progress in her quest to pair me with her brother*, CC mused. *Sorry to disappoint you, Alex, but this is a one-time run and I'll be off to Knockie.* She rolled her eyes in response to Alex's wink.

During the meal CC found herself the center of attention. She answered numerous questions about baseball in general and her job in particular. Charlie, Tony, and Alex laughed at the antics of Jim Oats as she told stories about the man who frustrated her so much.

CC could hardly believe it when the meal ended. It was eleven o'clock. "I'm terribly afraid I've bored you to tears," she said as they rose to have coffee in the library. "I didn't even ask about little Charlie. I'd love to meet him, though I imagine he's in bed by now."

"I'm sure he is, but not here. He and his nanny, Brenda, are with his grandfather. Angus would have him stay at Dunollie permanently if I'd let him, I suppose in part because Charlie looks so much like his mother. You'll meet him next time you're here." *If there is a next time,* CC thought.

Charlie stoked the fire and they settled on the couches in front of the fireplace. CC declined the coffee. "I'll never get to sleep if I have caffeine at this hour," she said, "but I'll sit and enjoy your company."

During the next half-hour Alex filled her brother in on family news. Several times CC drifted off as she gazed into the roaring fire and felt its warmth. When Alex allowed a lull in the conversation, Charlie sensed that CC was only staying up to be polite. He looked at his watch and stood.

"If CC and I are going to jog in the morning, we'd better get to bed."

As CC rose, Alex looked at her brother and grinned. "You two go on so you can be up and about early. Tony and I will stay here for a while. It's so pleasant in this room, and you know I like to stay up late."

"As you wish." Charlie leaned over and kissed his sister on the cheek. "But I expect to see you at breakfast. Eight-thirty, Alex."

"You mean I have to get up early two mornings in a row?"

"If you want to go with CC and me to Knockie, you do." Somehow the grin on Alex's face told CC that she would intentionally oversleep.

CC assumed Tony would be driving to Knockie. "You're going with us?" she asked Charlie.

"Try and leave me behind."

Charlie left CC at her door with a reminder that he would be by to pick her up "very early," and continued on to his own rooms.

CC closed the door behind her. Her bed had been turned down; the tall shutters were closed and the curtains were drawn. She crossed the room, removed her jacket, and sat on the edge of the bed. She was exhausted, but her mind was so full of the day's events that she knew sleep would elude her if she went straight to bed. She put out her jogging clothes, glad that she had decided to bring them, and took her father's letters from her purse. *Maybe reading will help me sleep,* she thought as she removed the fourth birthday letter and began to read.

My Darling CC, on Your Fourth Birthday, June 22, 1983
It hardly seems possible that a full year has passed since I last wrote to you. You are a great big four-year-old. Flash recently sent me

a picture of you riding your new red bicycle with the training wheels. Your mother was clapping and cheering you on. What a wonderful grin you have. It's obvious that you're a happy girl, and your mother appears to be happy too. Flash reports that he and Mary are quite proud of you. I'm proud also.

Your stepmother, Lady Anne, received bad news yesterday. The doctor told her she would not be able to have any brothers and sisters for you. Do you know this makes you the heir to the Litchfield title? Do not misunderstand me when you finally read this letter. Of course I would like to have another child, and though I do not love Anne in the same way I love your mother, I would like for her to be a mother also, since this is what she desires. But in some ways, her sad news also gives me great joy to know that I will be leaving all of my worldly goods and titles to you. Someday when you're told you're the Countess of Litchfield, I'm certain you'll be surprised. I imagine you'll immediately say you want nothing to do with an English title, but I ask you, my darling girl, to get to know England and me before you reject your inheritance. I am unable to show you the love I feel for you right now, but I can leave you the title that defines who I am and what I forever will be, an Englishman who is proud of his heritage and his country. I do so hope you will accept my gift to you.

Flash tells me that even at your young age, all you can talk about is playing baseball or maybe being the boss of a baseball team when you grow up. He says you love the sport. We don't play baseball in England, but I guess the game is similar to cricket. Maybe you would be satisfied running a cricket team instead. At any rate, the major decisions about what you will do with your life are, God willing, somewhere in the distant future. By then I'm sure you'll be sufficiently mature to make the right choices. I only hope and pray that you will accept the greatest legacy I can give you: my name. Perhaps your inheritance will, in some way, make up for the love I have only been able to give you from afar. In the meantime, my beautiful child, play, grow

strong, and be happy. I will write to you next year. Again, I give you
that magic birthday kiss. I wish I could hold you in my arms and tell
you how much your father loves you. I remain as always. . .

CC put the letter back in the envelope and rested it on her chest. She vaguely remembered asking her mother if she had half-brothers and sisters in England. She had been between three and four at the time. Strange that she'd asked about the time William was writing to tell her that there would be no siblings.

The letter left her even more uncertain about her future. The title obviously meant a great deal to him, and as he anticipated, she instantly rejected her inheritance. With each letter she read, she was more conflicted.

Instead of continuing to read, CC returned the letter to the stack, put the bundle into her bag, and turned off the light. Her thoughts turned to Flash. Had it bothered him to deceive her all these years? Was there ever a time when he wanted to tell her about his friendship with her father? And what exactly had brought an English nobleman and a gruff, unpolished former baseball player turned oilman together?

CC thought of two clichés that described her father and Flash. The two men were "like night and day" and "oil and water do not mix."' What business could these two men possibly have had in common? As far as she knew, the only two industries Flash had ever been involved with were oil and baseball. To her knowledge, William had nothing to do with oil, and by his own admission, he knew nothing about baseball. What was the common ground on which these two very different personalities met and became friends?

Her thoughts turned to her mother. How much did she know? Did she realize that William was privy to all of the events in her life? Had Flash taken her into his confidence? Perhaps her father's letters would provide answers, but there were so many to read. No, Flash would have to answer her questions. He owed her that much after all the years of deception.

CC was shaken. For the first time in her life she had a problem with Flash. Had her feelings for her beloved stepfather really changed so quickly? Yes, she was disappointed, but in truth, had Flash done anything really dreadful? "Damn it, he certainly did. He betrayed me," she said angrily as she reached up to turn on the light by her bed. She sat up and took a pad and pen from her purse. At the top she wrote: *Questions I Must Ask Flash*, and began to make a list.

1. Why didn't you tell me you were friends with my father when I was older and able to understand, or at least when William died?

2. Did Mother know about your friendship? Did she know you spied on us for over thirty years? If not, why didn't you tell her? Were you afraid of her reaction?

3. Despite his denial, did my father ask you to marry my mother?

4. What was William's business? How did he make his money?

5. Why would someone on the level of a prime minister visit him?

6. Why would he receive packages and letters from all over the world?

7. Did you see my father again after you met in Phoenix when I was just a baby?

There was so much CC wanted to know, but she only wrote a few of the many questions that were running through her head. These would guide her. When she heard one answer, another question would occur to her. She considered calling

Flash right away. She threw the comforter back and started to get out of bed to place the call from the desk across the room, but she changed her mind and snuggled back under the covers. Her call to Flash would wait until she was rested and could think clearly. She couldn't allow poorly chosen words to do irreparable damage to her relationship with her stepfather.

Unable to fall asleep, her thoughts turned to the letter she'd just read. William's words had proved he was quite a seer. He knew she would have difficulty accepting her title. Well, she was struggling alright, and she was clearly beginning to allow her emotions to cloud her judgment. *But why should I feel sentimental about William? Despite the information he provided in his letters, he's still a stranger.* She really didn't know enough about him to be sentimental. Yet at the moment she felt dreadful. She was going to refuse his request and reject her inheritance.

For the first time, CC wasn't certain what decision she would make about her future. The office and Major League Baseball seemed so far away, not only in terms of distance, but also in her thoughts. In fact, baseball hadn't crossed her mind all day. True, she rationalized, the office was closed on Saturday, so she wouldn't have been able to reach Leslie or Wes or—what a terrible thought—Jim. The Florida camp was underway so she could have called Spike to see how the team was doing. Yet instead of worrying about signing free agents and renewing current player contracts, all she could think of was the beauty of nature in England's Lake District and the loveliness of Scotland.

"My God," she said, and lay back on the pillow. "Will I ever be able to put this dilemma out of my mind and sleep again?"

At that moment there was a tap on the door. "Come in," she called as she pulled the covers up around her.

Alex breezed into the room and approached the bed. "I saw your light and wondered if you were all right."

"Actually I can't sleep, I suppose because I have so much on my mind."

"Would you like to talk? I may chatter away, but believe it or not, I'm quite a good listener."

"If you wouldn't mind, I could really use a sounding board."

Alex sat on the edge of the bed. "I've felt that something was bothering you all day. Will you tell me about it?"

Instead of answering, CC began to sob. She was not a crier, so her reaction to Alex's question was surprising. Alex moved closer and hugged her tightly until the tears stopped. "I'm so sorry," she whimpered as Alex handed her a tissue.

"No apology necessary. I would be a blubbering idiot if I had to make the choices you'll be called upon to make."

"Alex, I'm so confused. For the first time in my life, the answers to my problems aren't clear cut, and I have no idea what I'm going to do about my future."

"Why don't you talk about it? Maybe I can help you sort through your options and together we can figure out why you're so confused."

CC spent the next forty-five minutes pouring her heart out to Alex. From time to time throughout the conversation, she paused and the tears flowed. "Cathartic," Alex said. When she finished, Alex offered some advice. "I believe your immediate problem is that you're trying to force yourself to make an important decision according to a timetable. You say you have to be back in Indianapolis for the opening game. This is the self-imposed time when you believe you must decide what to do with the rest of your life—whether you choose to be the Countess of Litchfield or the president of your baseball team. Is there anything in your father's will that says you must make the decision to accept or reject the title before a certain date after his death?"

"Not to my knowledge, though there was a part of the will Mr. Caulfield decided not to read. At any rate, he didn't tell me I was operating on a deadline."

"Then why rush your decision? Why don't you enjoy your time in Scotland and England? See how you feel after you've met with Harrison Caulfield in two weeks. At that point if you're ready, to plan your future, do so. If not, go home to Indianapolis. Be the baseball executive again and see if the title of president fits you better than the title of countess. After all, you hardly had a basis for comparison of the two ways of life before you left for England. Perhaps your attitude toward what is in Indianapolis will change when you're back there after being here for a time."

CC felt relieved for the first time since arriving in London. "Why couldn't I have seen the situation as clearly as you see it? I'll try to take your advice and not push myself. While I'm at Knockie and when I return to Litchfield, I'll use my time to find out as much as I can about my father and his business dealings. Whether I've made a final decision or not, I'll go home. Oh my God, where is home? I'll go to Indianapolis for the ten-day opening home stand. After that I should have some idea which way I'm leaning. If not, as you said, there's no deadline."

"Good. Now if you're going to jog with Charlie at that ungodly hour in the morning, you'd better get some sleep." Alex stood up and smoothed CC's covers.

"Thank you so much, Alex."

"You have no reason to thank me for anything. Selfishly, I hope you'll remain in England forever, but you must be happy, and I'm certain you'll make the decision that's best for you."

"I wish I were as confident in me as you are."

"You will be as you begin to sort through your feelings. But enough for tonight. Sleep."

"I will." CC settled her head back into the pillow and, almost immediately after Alex shut the door, slept peacefully.

"Oh no," CC groaned when the alarm sounded. "I'll put a note on my door that says 'Sleeping, Do Not Disturb, Even for Jogging.'" She turned back over, but five minutes later the snooze alarm blared. "No use," she grumbled as she dragged herself from the bed, stumbled to the bathroom, brushed her teeth, and splashed cold water on her face. It did little good, because she was still lethargic as she pulled on her sweats and put on her socks and shoes. When she was ready, she fell back on the bed, hoping to get a few more minutes of sleep before the inevitable knock from Charlie. No luck. She had barely shut her eyes when she heard the rap.

"I'm coming, I'm coming," she said as she staggered to the door.

Charlie stood there in a black sweat suit, grinning. "Are you ready to run?"

"As ready as I'll ever be, I guess. Lead the way." CC shut the door behind her and followed him downstairs.

"I expected you would be livelier than this," Charlie said.

"Normally I am, but I sat up talking with your sister until all hours."

"Would you rather skip the run this morning?"

"Definitely not. I got this far. However, would you consider postponing our starting time for about fifteen minutes? I would be a much better companion if I had a cup of coffee."

"Of course. How rude of me not to remember that most Americans need coffee to get them started in the morning. I could have had a cup brought to you in your room earlier, but since I failed to do so, why don't we shock the staff by going into the kitchen ourselves? Can you brew your own?"

"Point the way. I make the best pot of coffee on the face of the earth; that is, the second best. My secretary makes the best coffee I've ever tasted. She could make a coffee aficionado out of a dyed-in-the-wool tea drinker like you."

"No chance, but I make a pretty good cup of tea, so I'll brew the tea while you make the coffee, and we'll wake up together, if you'll excuse the implication."

CC laughed. "No problem, but hurry because I'm fading fast."

Charlie led the way to his huge, modern kitchen. The only coffeepot CC could find made sixty cups. Charlie saw her eyeing the monstrosity. "Have no fear. I know where to find a small pot. I believe it's the English equivalent of your Mr. Coffee, that drip kind."

CC smiled. "I'm great at using the DiMaggio special."

"The what?"

"When it first came out many years ago, Joe DiMaggio, one of America's greatest baseball players, became the spokesman for a brand of coffee maker called Mr. Coffee. Most of the kids grew up thinking of him as Mr. Coffee rather than a Yankees hero."

Charlie reached into a cabinet and brought out a ten-cup coffeepot, some ground coffee, and a filter. CC sat on a stool by the center island to wait for the dripping to stop while Charlie boiled water for tea. Both brews were ready at about the same time, and Charlie joined CC at the island. "This is marvelous. I'm really glad you suggested we wake up before running. In the future I'll have to make brewing a cup of tea a regular practice before I jog each day."

"I can't get out the front door without my coffee." CC sipped the hot brew. "I already feel better."

"Good, now tell me why in the world would my sister keep you up so late?"

"Actually, it was the other way around. I was feeling confused and upset and your sister offered some very good advice."

"That hardly surprises me. Alex has helped me through many difficult times, especially after Flora died. So what did my wise sister say to you?"

"She listened while I talked about my dilemma."

"By dilemma you mean whether or not to accept your title."

"Exactly. Do I accept my inheritance and give up everything I've ever known in my life or return home and leave all that my father loved behind?"

"What did she suggest?"

"Nothing really, but she gave me sensible advice. She told me not to rush into a decision; to let things happen for me. She's right. I've been trying to push myself to decide my future on a self-imposed time line. I'm sure it will take some effort, but I'm going to try and relax and not push myself."

"My sister should have been a psychologist."

"She can be mine any day." CC took the last sip of coffee. "Okay, I'm as awake and ready as I'll ever be. Shall we jog?"

"After you." Charlie ushered her out the back door just as the startled chef came in to prepare breakfast.

"Lord Charles, if I had known—"

"Don't worry, Ian. Lady Litchfield and I decided to be brave and prepare our own tea and coffee. I must say, we did just fine." He turned to CC and grinned.

CC had never run in such a picturesque setting. They jogged down a dirt path alongside the crystal clear loch. The air was incredibly fresh and smelled of wet pine needles after the rain the day before. Hundreds of bright purple foxgloves complemented the blue water and green pines that lined the route. Occasionally they had to detour around a lazy ewe that made the trail her bed.

CC knew that Charlie was off his usual pace to make the run comfortable for her. When they reached the end of the two-mile trail, he turned back toward the house and led the way at a steady pace. CC kept up with him, but she was obviously tiring, and Charlie noticed. He stopped. "If you'd like, we can walk from here. There's something I'd like to show you."

"I guess I'm out of shape."

"Nonsense. The air here is thinner because we're up so high. You kept up with me very well."

CC smiled and caught her breath. "What was it you wanted me to see?"

"Follow me." Charlie reached out and took CC's hand. As he touched her, she felt an unexpected tingle. She sighed. *Yes, Lord Charlie is definitely sexy.*

"Where are we going?" she asked as he led her through a small stand of pine.

"Just wait."

They climbed upward on a narrow trail for about a hundred yards. When they reached a level spot, the lovely blue of Loch Levin in its entirety unfolded before them. "It's magnificent!" CC breathed in the cool, fresh air. The view was truly the most beautiful she'd ever seen.

"I'm glad you like it." No more words were necessary as the two stood and admired the panorama below.

CHAPTER THIRTEEN

Ian had his second surprise of the morning when CC and Charlie again invaded his domain. He poured a cup of coffee for CC and made a fresh cup of tea for Charlie, though it was evident that he didn't approve of the master of the house coming to the kitchen to help himself.

"I think I've offended your chef," CC said as they climbed the stairs to get ready for breakfast.

"Ian will get over it. He's from the old school and insists he's here to serve me."

"Maybe he'll blame an American unschooled in proper etiquette rather than an Englishman who should know better." CC laughed. "I don't mind being your scapegoat."

"Great, and since you offered, let me make a list of a few of my other indiscretions to blame on you."

"I don't believe I gave you carte blanche. I merely said I would take the blame for invading the kitchen. You're on your own with the rest of your issues."

"A man can try, can't he?" Charlie paused as they stopped outside CC's bedroom door. "Breakfast will be served in about fifteen minutes. Will that give you enough time?"

"Why don't you go ahead and I'll join you when I finish dressing. I should try to look like the Countess of Litchfield when I arrive at Knockie, and I'm not sure jeans and a fisherman's sweater is the answer. I brought a knit dress, and it shouldn't take me much more than a half-hour to get ready and pack for an overnight. I'm pretty sure I can find my own way to the dining room."

"Do you plan to stay at Knockie tonight? Alex thought you might remain here at Glencoe both nights."

"Would it be easier for you if I do stay here? I wouldn't want you to have to drive back for me in the morning, and I hate to ask someone from Knockie to run me back."

"It would be no problem for me to return for you. For that matter, I could stay in one of the Knockie guestrooms. I've done that several times in the past. But the decision is yours."

"Then why don't you pack what you need for the night in case we decide to stay? We can make the final decision whether to remain at Knockie or come back here at some point later in the day." CC paused. "But what about Alex and Tony? We can't just abandon them."

"Why don't I leave them a note telling them you're unde-cided as to what you'd like to do, and that I'll ring them up them later? If we decide to stay overnight, they might like to join us for the evening."

"Are there enough spare bedrooms for them to stay over? I have no idea about the size of the lodge, though Hastings said William often entertained foreign guests in Scotland."

"If I remember correctly there are eight guestrooms in the main house, so there's plenty of room for Alex and Tony if they should decide to stay. There is also a separate servants' cottage for those who choose to live on the estate. When your father bought the place, he added a bathroom for each guestroom and central heating throughout."

"Then instead of making a decision later, why don't you write a note and tell Tony and Alex we'll expect them at Knockie for dinner and an overnight stay. Perhaps I can repay your hospitality by having you as my guests."

Charles nodded. "Then the matter is settled. I'll ask Thomas to call ahead and let the Knockie staff know our plans."

"Actually it hadn't occurred to me that the servants might not be prepared for dinner guests or overnight visitors. Is it being presumptuous of me to impose upon them without more notice?"

"Of course not. I'm sure Mrs. Lauriston and Henry are prepared for anything. Your father probably made many last minute decisions to stay at Knockie, and I imagine he brought unannounced guests from time to time. So having the three of us for an overnight stay will be nothing out of the ordinary for them. Anyway, they're expecting you and know you were my guest last night, so I imagine they're ready for us."

"Then I'm looking forward to the day and evening."

"Speaking of the evening, do you play billiards?"

"Not well, though Flash has a pool table and we play every once in a while. I never took the time to practice. Why do you ask?"

"Because one of the last rooms your father added before he died was a new billiards room. I thought you might enjoy playing a game or two after dinner."

"I'm afraid I won't be much competition for you, but I would love to try. Does Tony play?"

"Quite well, and so does Alex."

"Then I guess we've planned our evening entertainment."

Charlie smiled and turned to leave. "Pack only what you need for tonight and tomorrow and your jogging clothes for an early run in the morning; that is, if you're game to go again. You can leave the rest of your things here. Alex and Tony will have to stop back in for their belongings before you all leave; that is if you do leave tomorrow. I'm going to convince you to stay another night. I've already devised a plan. I will appeal to that tremendous need that most women have to shop and offer to take you and Alex to Inverness on Monday. I know you'll have a hard time refusing my proposition." He smiled at the frown that formed on CC's face.

"What a chauvinistic thing to say about women. Shopping does nothing for me," she said, feigning irritation. It was Charlie's turn to frown and raise his eyebrows. When he realized CC was teasing, he laughed. "Gotcha," CC said. "Seriously, I would enjoy seeing more of the countryside. But whether we stay or not will be entirely up to Alex and Tony, since I'm only a passenger in their car."

"I doubt if Tony has a need to return home quickly and I know Alex is flexible."

"Do you think Alex and Tony will join us on the drive to Knockie this morning?"

"Not if she looked anything like you did when you got up. My darling sister is a night person. For her, mornings don't exist. I would bet she'll continue to sleep long after we leave. I'll ask my chauffeur to bring the two-seater around. So get ready and let's eat and be off."

CC took a hot shower, washed her hair, and dressed with care. She packed her clothes and cosmetics for the overnight and enough for the next day if they decided to stay over, put the case by the door, and checked her purse to be sure she had her father's letters and papers in case there was time to read after the others went to bed.

Charlie was nearly finished eating when CC reached the dining room. Thomas greeted her cordially and held the chair for her to sit beside Charlie. He poured her coffee and opened the lid of a silver warmer to display the toast.

"This is wonderful. Thank you," CC told him as she took a sip of coffee.

"You look absolutely wonderful," Charlie said after Thomas had left the room.

"I thank you, kind sir." CC smiled at the compliment. "My suitcase is packed, so as soon as we eat and you're ready to act as my chauffeur, I'm ready to go."

"Very good. Thomas already called Mrs. Lauriston. She's expecting us this morning and Alex and Tony for tea this afternoon."

"What about little Charlie? I know he was with his grandfather last night. If he's returning to Glencoe today, Alex and toy could bring him to Knockie with them."

Charlie smiled. "If he understood, I'm sure he'd appreciate your kind invitation, but to bring him would require a great deal of preparation, so he's better off at Dunollie."

CC ate a piece of toast and drank a second cup of coffee. When she finished, Charlie was ready to go. "I'll just run upstairs and get my bag and yours, and we'll be off," he said cheerfully. "It's a lovely day for a drive."

"How far is Knockie?"

"Fort William is about twelve miles, and Knockie is some fifteen to twenty miles beyond that. Since the roads are so narrow, we'll need close to an hour or an hour and fifteen minutes to get there."

A silver Mercedes was waiting for them outside in the drive. "Is it too chilly to put the top down?" Charlie asked as CC settled into the passenger seat.

"I don't imagine I'll be cold, but it may be a bit breezy."

Charlie handed her a tartan scarf. "If you use this, your hair won't become windblown. This is your own plaid. I mean it's the Fraser tartan. You know that Knockie was the hunting lodge of the Fraser clan approximately two hundred years ago."

CC examined the scarf. "It's lovely," she said, "and no, I didn't know until Alex mentioned it briefly when we first arrived." The plaid was also red and black, but there was more red in the tartan than in the MacDonald plaid Charlie had worn the night before. "How did you happen to have a Fraser tartan here at a MacDonald house?"

"When Alex called to say you would be visiting, I took a run into Fort William to buy you a welcoming gift in the Fraser plaid."

"It's wonderful, and I thank you." CC leaned over and kissed Charlie lightly on the cheek.

Charlie grinned. "If I had known I would receive that kind of thanks, I would have bought the store for you."

"Would you tell me something about the Frasers?"

"As much as I can. There are one or two Frasers who made it into the history books, though I'm afraid that most of your ancestors died without notice. The first recorded Fraser in the Highlands was Sir Andrew, who obtained his lands through marriage and then gained a reputation for hedging on his loyalties. Simon Fraser, Lord Lovat, the fourteenth clan chieftain, was outlawed for outrageous behavior, but was granted a pardon by William of Orange. The Old Fox, as they called him, helped initiate the 1715 uprising, and then when it was clearly doomed, helped put it down. In 1745, he declared himself a Jacobite when the Jacobites won at Prestonpans. Because of this, when he was eighty years of age, he became the last man to be beheaded in England. I guess his motto, *Je suis prest*, 'I am ready', fit him. He was certainly ready to go with whichever side was winning at the time."

"And what about the MacDonalds? Alex told me that Lord Dougall is chief of the clan."

"He is. That's a longer story best saved for another time. I want you to enjoy the scenery without needless chatter. That said, feel free to ask questions and I'll make an occasional comment."

Charlie was true to his word. He didn't speak again until they passed a turnoff to Fort William, which he said, "consists of one street of shops."

They passed Loch Locky and turned off the main road at Fort Augustus. Alex said that Knockie was located in a remote area, but as they drove, CC wondered if they were going in the right direction. They were way off the beaten track. Tall grasses grew right up to the edge of the road and the views of the mountains were spectacular. "This is the old military road which links Fort Augustus to the Highland capital of Inverness," said Charlie. "It was built in the early part of the eighteenth century to pacify the Highlands. In fact, General Wade and his red-coat army marched past Knockie after his victory over Bonnie Prince Charlie at Culloden."

CC didn't have time to respond. She spotted a Highlander in full dress regalia standing in a rest area playing his pipes. "Oh look," she said. "Could we stop for a minute and listen?"

"Of course. I was just going to suggest we stop and put the top up. It's rather chilly up here." He pulled into the rest area and CC got out to enjoy the sound of the pipes and the view of the mountains behind the player.

"He's fantastic," she said to Charlie when they were again on the road.

"In the summer there are bagpipers every few miles. They make a good living from tourists who pay to hear them."

"Oh Lord, I didn't think to give him anything."

"I gave him a few pounds, so he's happy."

"Thank you. Next time I'll know, though I should have realized this time. We have street entertainers at the ballpark in the summer. I've heard they do very well. Before we stopped you mentioned Culloden."

"Right. It was the last battle fought on British soil and lasted only an hour or so. It took place on April 16, 1746. Actually Culloden was only one battle in a civil war, but it ended any hopes the Stuart dynasty had of regaining the throne of Scotland. Have you heard of Bonnie Prince Charlie?" CC nodded. "When the fighting was over, a disarming act forced the Highlanders to surrender all their weapons. Strangely enough, even bagpipes were identified as weapons of war. The Highlanders were prohibited from wearing the tartan, the kilt, or any other types of traditional garb. Doing so meant six months in prison, and repeat offenders were deported for seven years. In 1747, the Heritable Jurisdictions Act removed the clan chiefs from their hereditary powers, and they became ordinary landlords. For all practical purposes, the clan system died at Culloden. I would be happy to take you there and to nearby Cawdor Castle."

"The Cawdor of Macbeth?"

"Shakespeare's Macbeth. In reality the castle wasn't built until long after King Macbeth died, but that's yet another story. And it will have to wait, because we're at Knockie." He turned onto a dirt road lined with tall grasses, clumps of heather just beginning to bloom, and huge, arching trees.

"How in the world do two cars pass on this narrow road?" CC asked.

"If two cars are traveling in opposite directions, one has to back up to a turn out. In some areas, particularly around Loch

Ness, there are turnouts about every hundred yards. The roads are so narrow that only one car can proceed at a time."

"We're near Loch Ness?"

"Knockie is six hundred feet above the loch. Walking there takes about twenty minutes. By car, it's about ten miles away. I'll be happy to jog over there with you in the morning. That is, if you promise not to make me talk about the Loch Ness Monster."

"Actually, I'd thought about asking for a full run-down."

"Then would you at least promise to refrain from buying one of those ridiculous 'I Saw Nessie' T-shirts."

CC laughed. "I promise. No T-shirts, just a glimpse of the loch. But who knows, Mr. Cynic. Nessie just may come out to greet me."

"I'm saved from having to respond because we're at Knockie." They rounded a bend and CC saw the large white house with gray turrets looming lonely in the secluded countryside.

"The view is breathtaking," she said. "What did you say my father's loch is called?"

"Loch Nan Lann, which translated means Loch of the Liver. It was given the name because it's shaped like a kidney."

"Nan Lann sounds much more romantic than Loch of the Liver, so if you don't mind, I'll forget you translated." Looking at the scene in front of her, CC knew that Knockie would provide a perfect break from the cares of the world. No wonder it had been an escape for her father.

As they drove into the dirt parking area in front of the house, an elderly woman followed by a man who appeared to be in his mid-fifties approached the car. "Mrs. Lauriston, Henry." Charlie greeted the two cheerfully.

"Welcome to Knockie, Lord Charles." Henry extended his hand.

"My lord, we've not had the pleasure of your company at Knockie in quite a while. Welcome." The woman turned to CC. "And you are Lady Litchfield. I must say, you're the spitting image of your father, my lady."

"This is Mrs. Lauriston, CC." Charlie introduced the woman who had stepped back, obviously embarrassed by her enthusiastic greeting.

"How do you do, Mrs. Lauriston? I'm so glad to meet you. Charlie and Hastings have said wonderful things about you." She turned to Henry, "And about you, Henry."

"Forgive my excitement, my lady," Mrs. Lauriston stammered. "I loved your father, and I'm so proud that his beautiful daughter is here with us now. The earl often spoke of you and about how he hoped to show you Knockie one day."

"I'm sorry he didn't have that chance," CC said, surprised at how sincerely she meant what she was saying.

"If you will follow me, my lady. You too, my lord. I will show you the downstairs and then take you to your rooms. After that we can discuss the dinner menu and your plans for the day."

"First we need to make some plans." Charlie looked at CC. "I have no idea what you want to do until Alex and Tony arrive."

"I'd like to look around William's favorite place. And maybe later we could walk around the loch. Hastings said it's a lovely stroll. But I'm open to suggestions. You're the expert."

"Your plan sounds perfect. As Mrs. Lauriston suggested, we'll get settled. After lunch we can look through your father's rooms together. Maybe you can find the answers you're searching for among his personal belongings. After that we'll do whatever feels right at the time. Since you didn't sleep well, you may want to take a nap or, if you're feeling like some exercise, we'll take a walk."

CC smiled. "Sounds like a plan." She and Charlie followed Mrs. Lauriston into the house.

CHAPTER FOURTEEN

CC walked into her father's lodge through an ancient massive door studded with hand-forged nails. She looked around the appealing pine-paneled hall. Prized salmon in glass cases, antlered stag heads, and fishing rods and reels attached to the walls confirmed that the primary purpose of the lodge was the hunt.

Mrs. Lauriston led CC through an open door into a large, comfortable sitting room. Several groupings of furniture faced an immense fireplace filled with brightly burning logs. An inviting burgundy and white-flowered, overstuffed eiderdown sofa sat under double windows that provided an incredible view of Loch Nan Lann. CC walked over to the couch and sank down into the soft cushions. "I've found my favorite place at Knockie," she said smiling.

"That was also your father's favorite piece of furniture," said Henry, who had just come in with the bags from the car. "He often sat there after dinner and smoked his pipe."

"He smoked a pipe?"

"Only after dinner, and from what Hastings told me, only here at Knockie. The lodge was his spot to relax."

"I can see why. This is an incredible room. It's so cozy."

"Would you like to see the rest of the house, my lady?" Mrs. Lauriston asked.

"If I can drag myself off this couch, I'd love to." CC rose and followed the housekeeper out the door, leaving Charlie and Henry conversing by the fire.

Mrs. Lauriston led her back through the entry hall and into the dining room where Fraser ancestors immortalized in oil seemed to gaze down from the walls onto five round mahogany tables. On each table, which CC imagined might seat four to six people, was a single silver candelabra and a silver flower bowl resting on a mirrored centerpiece. "What a lovely room," she said. "I love the informal arrangement of the tables."

"Here at Knockie the earl sought to avoid the formality of Litchfield. He believed his guests would be more at ease if they dined in small groupings. When he had formal dinners, he used a large, oblong table that we store in the building behind the servants' house."

"I can see why an arrangement like this would be appealing. It's lonely sitting by myself at that huge dining room table at Litchfield."

Mrs. Lauriston smiled. "Well, tonight you won't be lonely. With your permission, I'll set the table in front of the window for you and your guests. And speaking of dinner arrangements," Mrs. Lauriston added, "Sir Anthony and Lady Alexandra called a few minutes before you arrived. I'm to tell you they'll be at Knockie in time for afternoon tea."

"I hope I haven't inconvenienced any of the staff with my last minute plans."

"Certainly not. The guestrooms are kept ready to receive guests, and Freeman is always prepared for company.

"Freeman is the chef?"

"He is. Your father lured him away from a prominent London restaurant years ago. Everyone who eats at Knockie wants to steal him away. He's a genius, my lady."

"Then I look forward to dinner." CC smiled at the woman who was so eager to please her.

"Would you like to see the billiards room or would you prefer to change into something more casual? Henry has put your bags in your rooms and Freeman has prepared a light lunch for you and Lord Charles."

"If you'll show me the way, I'll change. Are jeans appropriate or are they too casual? You said my father liked to relax here, but Knockie seems too elegant for such informal attire."

"Denims are perfectly acceptable. We want you to feel that Knockie is your holiday home, so wear whatever's comfortable."

Mrs. Lauriston led CC up a wide, graceful staircase with wooden banisters to the first floor landing, which contained a massive, antique grandfather clock. Two hallways branched off in separate directions from the landing. "This floor contains the guest rooms," Mrs. Lauriston said. "Would you like to take a look at one or two before I take you to your suite?"

"I would, thank you." Mrs. Lauriston opened the first door at the top of the stairs. "Oh my," CC said as she entered a lovely bedroom attractively decorated in cafe-au-lait and different shades of blue. The bedspread was forget-me-not blue, faintly patterned with tiny butterflies. A plump gentian-blue velvet settee sat by the window, and placed beside it was a table with a floor-length cloth in the same fabric as the bedspread. As in the other rooms CC had seen on the first floor, freshly cut flowers added sparkle and charm to the space.

When CC finished admiring the charming room and its attached modern bathroom, Mrs. Lauriston took her next door. She stepped into a bedroom that was, though differently decorated, just as appealing as the one she had just seen. This suite's principal colors, pale yellow and white, were reflected in the heavy yellow brocade bedspread and matching draperies. An antique mirror hung over an ornate marble mantelpiece, and on either side of it, delicate watercolors of game birds were grouped in threes. A rocking chair was situated by the window so the rocker could enjoy the view of the loch.

"The rooms are lovely," CC said. "Who did the decorating?"

"Lady Anne supervised the selection of the fabrics and furniture. Her goal was to make each room unique and comfortable."

"Well, if the others are anything like the two I've seen, she certainly succeeded."

"Lord Charles will be down this hall in one of the two large guest rooms." Mrs. Lauriston pointed to her right. "There is another large guestroom at the end of the other hall, and there are also three smaller rooms down that way. We will give the large room on the left to Sir Anthony and Lady Alexandra; that is, if you approve. When your father entertained here, the more spacious rooms were reserved for distinguished guests."

"My father entertained well-known people here at Knockie?"

"That he did. We often had a household full of dignitaries. Several years ago the servant's quarters were enlarged so that his special guests would have a place for their staff."

"Really? Mrs. Lauriston, when you have a few minutes, would you tell me about my father's friends?"

"I can do much better than that. There's a photo album in your father's, I mean in your sitting room. It contains pictures of many of our guests. You might recognize a few."

"Thank you. I'll take a look." CC followed Mrs. Lauriston up another flight of stairs. When they reached the top, instead of several rooms off two hallways, there were only two doors visible from the hall.

"This side of the third floor contains your father's suite," said Mrs. Lauriston. "It consists of three rooms and a bath. The other door leads to Lady Anne's rooms."

"The earl and Lady Anne occupied the entire floor?"

"They did. As you'll see, your father's suite is quite grand. Henry and I decided you should stay in there. I hope you approve."

Mrs. Lauriston opened a door for CC to enter a spacious foyer. From there they went into a large, high-ceilinged sitting room decorated with rustic antiques, several groups of extremely comfortable-looking leather easy chairs, and paintings of the Scottish countryside. The curtains and window seats were made from the red and black Fraser tartan. On one wall, an enormous glass display case was packed with unusual fishing flies and large mounted salmon.

To the right of the window was a massive oak desk that held what looked like a very sophisticated computer and a twenty-inch LCD monitor. Two identical oak attachments, one holding a fax machine and ink-jet photo printer and the other a color laser printer and scanner, formed a very sophisticated and remarkably up-to-date U-shaped workspace.

As CC walked over to look at the set-up more closely, she wondered why her father would have such a high-tech computer here in the remote Highlands. She could hardly wait to log on and peruse his files; that is, if he hadn't used passwords that would make access impossible.

As she wandered around the room, CC realized this was a place her father uses for private conferences that he didn't want to hold downstairs in the main rooms. *Oh Lord*, she thought with irritation, *here I go again with the mystery business.*

Mrs. Lauriston motioned for CC to follow her into the bedroom. Unlike his sitting room, which exuded masculinity and power, William's bedroom had a softer and more traditional feel. The walls were pale green and the carpet a lovely, harmonizing apple-green. The bedspread, which integrated various tones of brown and forest green interspersed with splashes of sharp pink, looked stunning on the William IV four-poster bed. Draperies in matching fabric hung on either side of a large picture window that CC presumed looked out over the loch. Overstuffed wing-backed chairs covered in the room's dominant colors provided yet another contrast to the sitting room.

In one corner of the room, a wide-screen television and a DVD/VCR player were placed opposite a forest-green, overstuffed sofa accented with soft apple-green pillows, only a shade lighter than the carpet. CC recalled the massive cabinet that hid the TV in the Blue Parlor at Litchfield. *So my father didn't feel he had to hide his television here at Knockie.* She thought how difficult it must have been for William to live in the formal rooms at Litchfield. *In the Highlands of Scotland he could relax and be himself.*

From the attractive bedroom, CC followed Mrs. Lauriston into a large dressing room that contained a single bed and a dressing table with a fine antique mirror. Mirrored wardrobe closets lined two of the walls and a door to what appeared to be a walk-in closet opened on the opposite side. CC tried the door, but it was locked. "Do you have the key to this closet, Mrs. Lauriston?" she asked.

"I don't, my lady. I'm not even sure Henry has one. Your father always kept this closet locked. It's possible the key is in his safe."

"Where's that?"

"In the sitting room. Did you notice the large cabinet to the right of the desk?" CC nodded. "The safe is in the cabinet. I don't have the combination, but I assume that's where the earl kept the key."

"I believe I know the combination to the safe," said CC. "I'll give it a try it later."

Beyond the dressing room was an elegant gray marble bath-room decorated with eighteenth-century prints. There was an antique-style paneled bath with gilded taps and hand shower and a French bidet. Masses of fluffy white towels warmed on hot racks. There was even a built in hairdryer.

"Look out of the window behind the tub," Mrs. Lauriston suggested.

CC crossed the room. "Oh my," she said as she looked down at the magnificent scene below. "The view's incredible. I could literally spend hours soaking in the tub and staring out at the loch."

"Your father said the same thing when he had the bath-room remodeled and added the window. Now I'll leave you to change for lunch."

"I'll be down in thirty minutes. And thanks, Mrs. Lauriston."

When she was alone, CC sat down on the bed. Her mind was racing. For several minutes she considered skipping lunch and going straight to the computer in the sitting room to try and open her father's files, or to the safe to find the key to the locked closet. However, much as she wanted to begin the proc-ess of unraveling the mystery that was William Cleveland, she thought about Henry, Mrs. Lauriston, and Freeman. They had made special preparations so she'd feel at home. She hated to put off her search for answers, but rather than disappoint them, she'd wait until after lunch to begin her investigation.

CC changed and was ready to leave the room when she remembered that Mrs. Lauriston mentioned a photo album. She looked around, and failing to see one in the bedroom, she went into the sitting room. On a table between the two leather chairs was the old album. She sat down and opened the book. In it were pictures of her father fishing in the loch and donning hiking boots to take a walk. Other photos showed him meeting with guests in the various rooms throughout the house, eating at one of the small tables in the dining room or playing host in the drawing room downstairs. Several snapshots pictured him playing billiards in the new billiards room. In most of the pictures he was with men she didn't recognize. Everyone wore casual clothes appropriate for the relaxed atmosphere her father wished to maintain at Knockie.

CC was surprised to see pictures of several Arabs with traditional headdress and western clothes. She gasped as she turned the page to see her father standing by the fireplace in the drawing room with none other than Tony Blair. CC studied the picture more closely. Were Tony Blair and her father friends? Or was William, Earl of Litchfield, an important enough peer to have the British prime minister pay a social visit to Knockie? Had Blair been there for business or pleasure?

When she turned the page, CC was even more astounded to see her father standing with Donald Rumsfeld, Bush Forty-four's secretary of defense. Why would he be a guest at Knockie? A prime minister; a secretary of defense? What could her father possibly have to do with these people? What did they have in common that would bring them to the Highlands of Scotland?"

CC turned the pages, hoping for a clue that would help solve the mystery. There was a picture of her father and Margaret Thatcher. The information Stanley provided made the photo of her father and the famous "Iron Lady" less surprising.

None of the other individuals pictured with her father were familiar until CC neared the end of the collection. On the next-to-the-last page a familiar face stared back at her. He was wearing western boots and a cowboy hat as he stood smiling, his arm casually around her father's shoulders.

"My God! Flash!" CC said aloud. "What were you doing here in Scotland? When were you at Knockie?"

She looked closely at her stepfather's face. He looked about ten years younger. She removed the snapshot from the corner mountings, turned it over and read: "Flash MacTandy, May 2001. *"Flash was in Scotland? In May? During baseball season? How could that be?*

CC struggled to remember. Yes, Flash had gone on a business trip about that time. She knew because she'd worried he might not make her U of A graduation ceremonies. She remembered the team was on the road, and since he usually travelled when they were away, his trip wasn't a big deal. He hadn't said anything about leaving the country, but of course she hadn't asked where he was going. Over the years his trips had become routine. She frowned. *But evidently this one wasn't ordinary or typical.*

She had so many questions. *Did Mother know Flash had come to Scotland? If so, was she aware he was staying with William at Knockie? How were William and Flash connected? Could their common tie be oil?* "But Flash wasn't involved in the oil business in 2001," she whispered. "In 1993, he sold his wells and land in Texas for a small fortune and was running his ball club as a hobby."

As she reflected, there was a knock on the door.

"Come in," she called out.

Grinning, Charlie sauntered in. He was dressed in a plain brown kilt with brown knee socks cuffed at the knee. His shirt was tan and loose fitting. "Mrs. Lauriston said you were changing for lunch. Are you ready to go downstairs?"

"Not quite. I was looking at this photo album and discovered my stepfather was a guest at Knockie in May of 2001." She handed the album to Charlie.

"That wasn't the only time Flash was here," he said. I met him in 2008, right after I married Flora. Your father invited my new bride and me for a weekend with the Camerons and the MacBeans. Your stepfather was also a guest; though until now I had no idea the earl was entertaining his first wife's husband."

"So you know Flash?"

"I only met him that one weekend. Your father introduced him as an important business associate. I recall he was quite friendly and personable."

"That's Flash! Can you remember anything else?"

"Only that he seemed to be a part of your father's inner circle. He and four other men met here in this room several times over the weekend. I was only a social guest and spent my time hunting and fishing with Ian and Roy or walking with Flora."

"And you didn't it strange there were two separate groups here at the same time?"

"Not at all. I've often combined business with pleasure at Glencoe."

"Do you remember anything about the six businessmen who were here that weekend?"

"I don't recall their names, but I believe that besides your father and Flash, there was a Frenchman and a German. I don't recall the nationalities of the other two."

"But they were foreigners? I mean they weren't British."

"That's right. Come to think of it, one was Asian. Japanese, I believe, though I didn't see much of him."

"And you don't remember the nationality of the sixth man?"

"No. At the time it didn't seem very important."

"Were their wives with them?"

"No. It was obvious the Camerons, MacBeans, Flora, and I were here for a holiday. The others were at Knockie for business. Your stepfather stayed in the large suite I'm now occupying and the others were housed down the other hall."

"Flash stayed in the large guest room?" CC recalled Mrs. Lauriston mentioning that her father kept the two larger rooms for important guests.

"Right. And the rest of us stayed in the smaller rooms. The house was full."

"Can you remember anything else about the weekend?"

"Not really. I was doting on my new wife. When she was busy with the other women, I was off with the men. However, I do remember that everyone seemed quite relaxed and friendly at meals, and when they weren't meeting, they spent their time fishing. I believe your stepfather went hunting with your father once or twice, but beyond that I recall very little."

CC thought about the picture on her father's desk at Litchfield. *Was the picture taken at Knockie?* "After lunch would you look through the album to see if you recognize any of the other guests who were here?" she said.

"I'd be glad to. This all seems rather strange. You say you had no idea your stepfather was in Scotland?"

"Not an inkling."

"Well hopefully this album and your father's computer will help us find out what he was doing here."

"That and a safe in that cabinet." CC pointed to the library wall. "If there's a key, it might open the closet in my father's dressing room. Maybe we'll find what we're looking for in there. Suddenly she asked, "What about oil? Was my father involved in anything to do with oil?"

"CC, I knew the earl socially. I visited Knockie because I'm a local landowner."

CC smiled. "A laird."

"True. It's more likely I received the invitation because William knew my father, though I don't know how well. Beyond that I have nothing to offer, but why do you think oil's the connection?"

"It may explain why the American secretary of defense would be included in the party and, though it's stretching it, Margaret Thatcher. It might also explain the Japanese visitor since Japan depends so heavily on foreign oil imports. I don't know how a Frenchman and a German fit into my theory, though it may have something to do with rebuilding Europe after World War II. Of course Arabs and oil are synonymous, but what really convinces me oil is key is Flash. My father had nothing to do with professional baseball, and except for baseball, Flash's only other interest was oil. But again, why would he be here in 2001? That was eight years after he sold his wells."

"All of this seems rather strange to me, but I am curious. If you need help discovering information about your father and stepfather, I would be glad to volunteer."

"I appreciate your offer. I plan to call Flash, but God knows what I'll say to him. All I know is for him to tell me why he was here in 2001, again in 2008, and however many other times. I need for him to explain his connection to my father, and I have to know why he felt compelled to report to William about me."

CC looked at her watch. "About the time Alex and Tony arrive for tea this afternoon, it will be seven in Phoenix. Flash should be up having his morning coffee. I'll try to speak with him before he leaves for the office."

"It's Saturday. Will he still go to work?"

"Later than usual, but yes he will. For baseball people, every day of the year is a workday. After I talk with him, depending on what he tells me, I'll see what I can do about accessing the computer files. While I'm doing that, I have some assignments for you, that is if you still want to help."

"I told you I'm at your service. What can I do?"

"First, would you see if you find anything pertinent among these books and papers?"

"Of course. What next?"

"Call your father and see what you can learn about his friendship with William You said you and Flora were invited to Knockie, in part, because of your father, so perhaps he'll be able to tell us something we don't already know. And finally, look through this photo album and see if you recognize anyone? Maybe you could show it to Mrs. Lauriston or Henry and ask them to identify the guests my father entertained. I imagine they would feel more comfortable talking with you. They hardly know me. If we can identify the people who met here, I'll be one step closer to learning why my father left Mother and me."

"I'll be glad to do everything you ask, but if you expect me to work this hard, you'll have to feed me first. I'm starving, and in case Mrs. Lauriston hasn't told you, Freeman is an incredible chef."

"Lead the way. I'm right behind you. We'll have several hours to explore after lunch, and if we don't finish, we can work after Alex and Tony go to bed tonight. If need be, we can put off the return trip to Glencoe for another night."

"We can stay here if you'd like. Little Charlie is well cared for both at Glencoe and at Dunollie. If Alex and Tony need to get back to Chadlington, I'll drive you to Litchfield whenever you're ready to go. Do you have a pressing need to be back on a particular day?"

"I have a meeting with my father's lawyer, but that's not for two weeks. Until then, I'm free to do whatever needs to be done. However, there is one piece of unfinished business I need to attend to at Litchfield."

"What's that?"

CC told Charlie about her father's letter, the secret papers, and the diary behind the chapel altar. "I wish I'd been able to bring the papers with me to Knockie," she said, "especially in light of what we've already discovered."

"If we have to go to Litchfield and return to Knockie, we will. That is, if you'll be hospitable enough to feed a starving guest."

CC laughed at the distressed look on Charlie's face. "I suppose that's the least I can do for someone who volunteered to help me sort through clues that may solve this mystery." She put the photo album back on the table and followed Charlie downstairs for lunch.

CHAPTER FIFTEEN

Freeman had just left for the market, so Mrs. Lauriston served lunch. "If this is light, I'd love to see the heavy stuff," CC whispered as she finished the delicious tartar of smoked and fresh salmon with a mustard sauce and awaited lobster on a bed of summer vegetables accompanied by a warm orange butter sauce.

She read the now-familiar menu card. "It says that our 'light dessert' will be something easy like an 'Iced Banana Parfait with a Mille-Feuille of Chocolate and Banana Mousse served with a Caramel Sauce flavored with Galliano.' Gee, I whip that up whenever I want dessert after a 'light' lunch."

Charlie laughed. "By Freeman's standards, he is serving us a light lunch. Remember, he's used to feeding hungry fishermen and hunters."

While they ate, Charlie steered the conversation away from food and William. "Tell me more about your Indianapolis Knights," he said. "I gather from our conversation at dinner last night that it's quite unusual for a woman to be in a position such as yours."

"Unusual and difficult at times, but I love my job and can't imagine doing anything else." CC continued to talk about her job; telling stories about cleaning the stadium toilets when she worked in the minor leagues, saving a rookie umpire from angry fans and her meteoric rise to the presidency of the Knights. Despite everything she had on her mind, she enjoyed conversing with Charlie. However, when Mrs. Lauriston served dessert and there was a lull in the conversation, she realized how much she'd shared and how out of character it was for her to open up so quickly. In her father's suite, without hesitation, she had told him about her father, the picture album, the letters and diary behind the altar. She had trusted him when she really knew nothing about him. *Perhaps he can't be trusted,* she suddenly thought. *Maybe allowing him to help me with the search will cause additional problems, or worse, put me in harm's way.* CC laughed out loud, and her laugh didn't correspond with what she was saying.

"Did I miss something?" Charlie asked.

"I'm sorry. I was in my mystery/spy mode."

"What were you thinking?"

"That I've been doing all the talking. I'd like to hear about you."

Charlie was about to respond when Mrs. Lauriston interrupted. "My lady, there's a phone call for you. It's Mr. MacTandy."

"Oh my God!" CC looked at her watch. She hadn't expected her stepfather to call so early. She turned to Charlie. "I haven't even made a list of what I want to say. How do I talk about thirty years of deception and lies?"

"You'll think of a way, but CC, before you condemn your stepfather, stop and think about what he means to you. Also consider there could be a legitimate reason why he never told you about his friendship with your father."

"I can't imagine what it could be, but I'll try to take your advice. Mrs. Lauriston, would you ask Mr. MacTandy to wait? I'll take the call in my room."

"Very good, my lady."

Walking up the stairs was like wading through waist-deep water. CC couldn't figure out how she felt. She wanted to talk with Flash, yet she didn't want to talk with him. She wanted to ask him why he'd deceived her over the years, yet she was afraid to find out. She wanted him to make her understand, yet she would never understand. When she reached her father's sitting room, she paused by the door. "I suppose I have to take the call," she said. "I'm not sure I'll ever be fully prepared to talk with Flash, so now's as good a time as any." She shut the door behind her and went to the phone on her father's desk. "Flash," was the only greeting she could manage.

"Good morning, or rather good afternoon, honey. You all right?"

"Of course, I'm all right," she snapped.

"You've answered my question, CC. I hear it in your voice. Do you want to tell me what you know?"

"Why don't you tell me, Flash. Beginning with how you happen to know the phone number at Knockie. Did you call Litchfield and ask Hastings how to reach me, Flash?"

"Let's not play games, CC. We've always been pretty straight with each other."

CC let out a little cry. "How could you possibly say that to me? How could you suggest that you've been, to use your words, 'straight with me'? All of our life together has been one huge lie after another."

"By necessity, honey. By necessity."

"Maybe at first, Flash, but not after I was able to understand. I found the pictures you sent to my father. I've read a few of his letters. You started spying on me when I was a year old, a year old, Flash. That means for almost thirty-one years you've deceived me. And what about Mom?"

"What about her?" It was obvious that CC's accusations were bothering her stepfather.

"Was your life with Mom a lie? Did the Earl of Litchfield ask you to marry his ex-wife to keep an eye on her for him?"

Flash was incredulous. "How could you even suggest such a thing, CC; his tone a mix of anger and hurt.

"How could I not? I know you visited Knockie. I saw pictures of you with your arm around my father. I saw pictures of me that you sent to him every year. Who are you, Flash? Why have you deceived me all these years?" CC began to cry.

"Calm down, honey. I can explain. Please, CC, you know how I hate it when you cry."

CC choked out the words between sobs. "I can't stop, and I hate myself for being so weak."

"Don't be silly, honey. You have every reason to be shocked and hurt. It's true. Your father and I go way back. We met when I owned my oil wells. I can't tell you the exact circumstances of our meeting or why we got together. That's classified information."

CC stammered, "What do you mean classified?"

"I mean I can't tell you the nature of my business dealings with William, but that's not important because it doesn't concern you. I can only say that whatever you find out about your father, you'll do so without my help. I'm not at liberty to talk about anything but personal matters."

"At liberty?"

"That's right. I had to obtain permission to reveal what I'm telling you now."

"Permission from whom?"

"Again, I can't say, so please, honey, for both our sakes, let it go."

CC was no longer crying. She was struggling to make sense out of what her stepfather was telling her. "I can't promise I'll do that, Flash, but I do want to hear what you have to say."

"Well at least that's a beginning. I met your father before you were born. We became friends as well as business associates. Mary believed William was on leave when they met Mary in Paris, but that's not true. He was working."

"What was he doing?"

"Please, CC, I already told you, I'm not at—"

"I know. You're not at liberty. Go on. William was in France."

"That's right. His mission was nearly finished when he met a beautiful woman at a sidewalk café, and he became sidetracked. He fell in love, and you know the rest of the story."

"I know he left that woman and her child so that he could do his duty—or that's the excuse he gave her. And now I'm aware you helped him keep track of us."

"He left you and Mary out of necessity."

"Because his father insisted?"

"Partly, yes, but also because of his mission, which—"

"You're not at liberty to tell me about."

"That's right."

"And this so-called mission was so important that he would abandon us and never see us again?"

"Evidently he thought it was, though I can tell you he never stopped caring about you and hurting because he couldn't be with you."

"So where do you fit in all of this, Flash?"

"William learned that you and Mary had moved to Phoenix, he asked me to keep an eye on you for him."

"Really."

"Yes, really. He never wanted to abandon you, CC."

"But you're not—"

"CC, cut the damn sarcasm," Flash growled. "I don't need to hear that from you again."

CC realized how nasty she had been. "I'm sorry, Flash. You didn't deserve that, but there's so much I don't understand and I'm hurting."

"I know, baby, and I'm trying. Maybe there was a way I could have confided in you years ago. I never tried to find out how. It never occurred to me that you'd learn about what I was doing. But back to what I was saying. Your father asked me to keep an eye on you and your mother from a distance and then, by sheer coincidence, when I had my knee surgery at St. Joseph's, Mary was assigned to the case, and we fell in love."

"Please, Flash. Please don't lie to me. Did William ask you to marry my mother?"

Flash was incredulous. "My God, CC," he implored. Never! He was distraught when I told him your mom and I were getting married. At first he asked me to back off, but several days later he called and told me that he was happy for us. He knew I would take good care of you and Mary."

"And did you take care of us or did my father support us?"

"I never took a penny from William, at least not personally, though as I told you, there were business dealings. You have to believe that."

"Then why would he leave you two hundred and fifty thousand pounds in his will?"

"He did what?"

"You heard me. He left you almost three quarters of a million dollars. Why, if it wasn't to pay you back?"

"I have no idea, CC, but think, baby. I have all the money I'll ever need. I never did, nor do I now want, your father's money."

"And speaking of money, Flash, can you explain how William made his fortune? How could an earl accumulate so much wealth when most English noblemen are struggling to pay their taxes?"

"Again—"

"I know. Please don't say it, Flash. How much does my mother know?"

"As much as I've told you."

"You mean she's been part of this duplicity for all these years?"

"Certainly not. Do you think your mother would have been a part of any deception where you were involved?"

"But you just said she knows."

"I told her everything last evening. As soon as I heard about your father's death, I knew I couldn't keep my secret any longer."

"Now I understand what you meant when you said 'take care of your inheritance and responsibilities as your father would have wanted you to,' or something to that effect."

"You're right, but at that point I couldn't tell you about my relationship with your father. I had to tell Mary first and then fill you in."

"How is Mother? How did she take the news?"

"At first she was confused and hurt, but I think she finally understands. I'm certain she knows that my love for her has always been genuine and that William never asked me to develop a relationship with her."

"I imagine she feels deceived."

"Yes, as you do, she blames me for not telling her, but she loves and, as I hope you will, forgives me."

"What did you tell her about your business relationship with William?"

"The same thing I told you."

"And she accepted your explanation?"

"For the moment, at least, but she's here with me. When you and I finish talking, she wants to speak with you. You can ask her yourself. I hope you know how dreadful I feel."

"Because you mislead me or because I found out about it?"

"That's not fair."

CC sighed. "Maybe I was out of line, Flash, but needless to say, I'm in shock."

"I know, honey. I wish we were together so we could really talk. Should I fly over there?"

CC couldn't help herself. "I guess you know how to get here, right?" she said sarcastically.

This time Flash wasn't angry. "Please, CC," implored.

His apparent dejection did little to assuage CC's anger. "So, Flash," she said indignantly, "did you come to Knockie for one of those mysterious business meetings, or to give William an update about Mother and me?"

"For business and to see my old friend, but, I must admit, to tell him about you and your mother, though not to report in the way you think. William loved Mary and you, and it devastated him not to be a part of your lives. My reports, as you call them, gave him a great deal of pleasure. He was happy that you and your mother were comfortable with me, and he appreciated the fact that I was taking good care of you. Doesn't that make sense, CC? Can't you understand?"

"Maybe I will when I've had time to think, but for now I can't seem to make sense out of anything." CC backed off. "We'll talk later, Flash. And no, for the moment I don't think it would a good idea for you to come to Scotland. I don't know how long I'll be here and I may be between Litchfield and the Highlands. By the way, were you ever at Litchfield?"

Flash paused before answering. "Yes, CC. I have been to Litchfield."

"Oh my God. Why, Flash?"

"Just think about what I told you and maybe you'll understand. But know one thing for sure, CC. I couldn't have loved you more had you been my own daughter. Besides your mother, you're the most important person in my life. No matter how mad you are, please remember that."

"I'll try, but Flash, you should know I'm going to continue my search. I hope I don't hurt you in the process."

There was concern in Flash's voice. "CC, I'm warning you. Leave well enough alone. If you keep looking for answers, you could find yourself in a mess and I may not be able to help."

"Then I'll have to get out of the 'mess,' as you call it, on my own; that is, if I get into trouble. Bottom line; you're asking me to understand what you've told me, and I'm telling you to understand my need to know everything about my father."

"I wish I could stop you, honey, but I know you well enough to realize that, despite what I say, you won't give up. Please be careful and remember, if you need me, I can jump on the jet and be there in eight or nine hours."

"But you won't give me any more answers?"

"I can't. At least not now."

"Then let me talk to Mother, and Flash…"

"Yes, honey."

"I didn't mean to be so nasty, it's just that—"

"No need to explain. If anyone should apologize, it's me. Maybe you'll understand some day."

"And forgive you for deceiving me?"

"I certainly hope so. Give it time, and please try to keep an open mind?"

"I will. Let me speak to Mom."

It was obvious from the sound of Mary's voice. She'd been crying. "CC, darling, I didn't know! I never knew! What can I say?"

"Nothing, Mom, I'm okay. How are you? You're up early."

"Actually I haven't been to bed. I'm in a state of shock at the moment, but I do know one thing, CC. Flash never meant to hurt either of us, and he didn't marry me and raise you for William."

"I know. Despite the accusations I made, I don't doubt that Flash loves us both and always has."

"Then remember that, and don't judge him too harshly."

"I'll try, but Mom, this doesn't change anything. I still want you to go to the bank and get the diary."

"I plan to be there when the bank opens at nine."

"Will you have time to read it by tomorrow morning?"

"I hope so. I've made a list of the things you want to know. Does this mean you won't heed Flash's advice and stop trying to find out why your father was so wealthy?"

"I have to know, Mom. Don't you see? I came to England to refuse my inheritance. Now I'm beginning to see my father as a man who loved you and me throughout his entire life. But beyond that I know nothing about William Cleveland, so I need to keep on with what I'm doing."

"What about the Knights? What about your life in Indianapolis?"

"For now, I'll try to run the office from here. I have good people working for me. I plan to return for the first home stand, and after that, we'll see. In the long run, what I do will depend on what I discover here. I may come back again, or I may put all of this behind me."

"Are you seriously thinking about accepting your inheritance?"

"I told you, Mother. I'll be here for at least two weeks. After that I'll return to Indianapolis and stay for the first home stand. Beyond that, I have no idea what I'm doing."

"All right, then. I'll talk with you tomorrow, darling. I love you."

"I love you too, and Mom, despite what's happening between us, tell Flash I love him too."

"I will, CC. I'm sure knowing that will make him feel a little better."

CC felt drained as she hung up the phone. She stood up and crossed the room to the window seat. As she looked out at the beauty and calm of Loch Nan Lann, she wished that she could feel half as serene, but her entire life was in turmoil.

CHAPTER SIXTEEN

CC had no idea how long she'd been sitting and staring at Loch Nan Lann when she heard a knock on the door. "Come in," she called.

Charlie handed her a plate. I brought you some dessert. I couldn't let you starve."

"After what I ate for that 'light' lunch, you mean?" CC smiled.

Charlie put the plate down on the desk. "How was your discussion with Flash?"

"It was difficult, as you might imagine, but I've been sitting here thinking. I really don't believe he was acting for my father when he married Mom. I know he loves us both very deeply."

"Did he talk about his business dealings with William?"

"He steadfastly refused to tell me anything, but I told him that, with or without his help, I'd find out about my father. Of course he advised me not to keep investigating, but I think I made him understand that knowing William is important to me. He seemed to accept that as a valid reason for my persistence. At any rate, he doesn't seem to have a problem with my mother helping me. Oh, I don't think I mentioned my mother's diary." CC told Charlie about her mother and father and their relationship in Paris.

"And she plans to read the diary today?"

"Yes. She has to get it out of her safety deposit box at the bank. I'll speak with her tomorrow."

"Then if your mother's ready to help on her end, shall we get started here?"

"What, and skip my 'light' dessert?"

"Speaking of food, Mrs. Lauriston said Freeman is baking his special scones and biscuits for afternoon tea."

CC grimaced. "I'll have to run twice a day if I keep eating all this light food."

"Speaking of running, why don't we jog over to Loch Ness in the morning? Didn't you say you wanted to meet Nessie?"

"I did, but I seem to recall you said Nessie doesn't exist."

"Then we should see who's right."

"If I don't die from overeating first. I should meet Freeman and tell him to lighten up." She smiled at her double entendre. "How about a tasty chef's salad instead of all those fancy dishes with the incredible sauces?"

"I'll introduce you to Freeman after dinner. When you see him, you can decide what you want to say along those lines."

"What do you mean?"

"Just wait. In the meantime, shall we work or take a walk?"

CC looked at her watch. It was already two-fifteen. Her phone call had taken more time than she had expected it would. "Let's work. Alex and Tony will be here in about an hour and a half, and that doesn't give us much time."

"While you work, I'll call my father and see what he has to say. What do you plan to do first?"

"I'll try to open this safe and see if it contains a key to the closet in my father's dressing room." CC crossed the room to the closed cabinets. She opened the double doors and stared in at a large safe. "I wonder how this floor supports the weight of this thing."

"Your father was a smart man. I'm sure her had the floor reinforced when the safe was installed."

CC tried the birthday combination, but nothing happened. She tried again, but still to no avail. The third time she began by turning the dial to the left rather than to the right. She heard a click and the door opened. "Victory!" she cried, and then grimaced when she saw Charlie talking on the phone. "Sorry," she whispered.

She opened the safe and stared at row upon row of files with varying color-coded labels. *My God! I'll have to move in here permanently to go through all this material,* she reflected; astonished by what she saw in front of her. She opened a small drawer, found the key Mrs. Lauriston mentioned, put it in her pocket, and continued her search.

There were more bundles of cash. *Yes,* CC pondered with incredulity, *William was enormously wealthy.* She took out and then put back the stacks of British pounds and, oddly enough, American dollars. As she had so many times since her arrival in England, she wondered how her father could have possibly made all this money.

In addition to the cash, she found more pictures of visitors to Knockie, not in albums, but in a wooden box. *I guess William didn't have time to organize these snapshots,* she thought as she put the box aside. *I'll go through them when I have a little spare time.*

There was too much material to sort through before Alex and Tony were due to arrive, so rather than continuing, she shut the safe and the cabinet doors and went to the closet in the dressing room. As she passed Charlie, he gave her a thumbs-up sign. The key fit the lock and she opened the closet door. When she turned on the light, she nearly fainted. The key hadn't opened a closet; it had provided entry to some type of sophisticated communications room. The walls were thick and obviously soundproofed.

CC stepped inside. The room contained a built-in desk with connecting shelving along one side. On the desk were several telephones, and on the shelves, a computer, a laser printer, a fax machine, a television, and other sophisticated electronic devices she couldn't identify. Along the opposite wall were three five-drawer metal file cabinets. CC sighed. *Oh, William, what were you up to? Who were you?*

"Good Lord!" She heard Charlie behind her. "What's all this?"

"I have no idea, but I imagine the answer lies in those papers and the diary my father left for me at Litchfield. I'd like to go back as soon as possible. After seeing what's in the safe in the other room and in this closet, though I'm not sure I'd call it that, I realize there's no way we could possibly begin to find the answers among all these papers. There are too many. My father must have known that when he told me to get the diary and papers from the chapel."

"Of course, we'll go back whenever you're ready, but right now let me tell you what I found out when I called my father."

CC shut and locked the door to the room, followed Charlie back into the sitting room, and sat beside him on the settee. "So what did he say?"

"He believes your father was involved with the British Foreign Ministry, though he's not sure how. He mentioned something about foreign relations, but was vague on that point too. You should know my father had nothing but praise for William. Several times he mentioned what a great man he was and what a loss England suffered as a result of his death. He also said something rather mysterious. Apparently William's death came as a shock to him and others because they all believed the earl was in excellent health."

"My father's last letter to me said the same thing. He told me if anything happened to him, I should be suspicious, or something to that effect. Did your father think he might not have died of natural causes?"

"He didn't come right out and say it, but the implication was certainly there."

"There's another reason I think your father's right." CC told Charlie about the phone number William had given Hastings."

"If the local coroner didn't remove the body, who did?"

"I have no idea. That's one of the mysteries I'm trying to solve." CC grimaced. "Oh Lord. Now I'm involved not only in an examination of my father's business dealings, but also in a possible murder investigation. If William was so distinguished and ethical, who would want him dead? And wouldn't the killer destroy files and papers so no one would know with whom or what William was involved?"

"You mean files like the ones you found in the secret closet?"

"Exactly, that is if the person or persons who killed my father had knowledge of the secret room. Mrs. Lauriston knew nothing about what's in the closet." CC shook her head. "I can't believe I just said that. Now I'm taking it for granted that William didn't die of a heart attack."

"Maybe he didn't, which means we'd better be careful. We don't know who to trust."

CC looked at Charlie. "You're absolutely right!" she said, imagining that Charlie would be stunned if he knew she was including him among those she would be careful to trust with what she discovered. *After all*, she reasoned, *I've only known this man for a day, and I've probably shared too much with him already.*

He was at the lodge with William. Could he know more than he's letting on? This time CC didn't laugh.

"It's getting late," CC said. "Why don't we walk around Loch Nan Lann before Alex and Tony arrive. When they get here, we'll have tea, play some billiards, and later on, enjoy Freeman's superb cuisine."

"You don't want to keep looking through the files and albums?"

"Not really."

"What changed your mind?"

"Let's just say I've had enough sleuthing for one day. I want to enjoy the Highland scenery and spend a pleasant evening with my guests." CC hoped she was being convincing about the reasons for her change in plans. What she really wanted was for the afternoon and evening to be over so she could get rid of everyone and work with the computer in the closet. Charlie would play no role in her search. Now as she reflected on the time she'd spent with him, she wondered if it was her imagination or if he had seemed excessively eager to help her from the beginning? *Could he actually know more about my father and his business dealings than he's letting on? Was he at Knockie with Flash for more than the social visit? Have I been naive and premature by letting him into my confidence and accepting him as a friend so quickly?*

For a moment she wondered if she was being too cautious and suspicious, but Flash's refusal to divulge any information about his business arrangements with her father and the discovery of the hidden communications room confirmed her suspicions that William was involved in something mysterious and dangerous. Whatever she learned in the future, she'd keep to herself.

"Are you sure?" Charlie was saying.

CC realized that she'd been lost in thought and hadn't heard anything Charlie had said. "Sure about what?"

"Sure that you want to go for a walk instead of keeping with our original plan."

"Definitely. I'll meet you downstairs after I call the Knights' training camp in Florida. I do run a Major League ball club, and I haven't even talked to anyone in my real world in twenty-four hours or so."

"What do you mean your 'real world'?"

"I mean I should leave this place tomorrow, go back to Litchfield, pack my bags, forget this sleuthing business, and go home."

"And give up your inheritance?"

"Exactly!"

"And this is a possibility?"

"More than that; it's likely."

"I see." Charlie looked disappointed, and CC wondered if he appeared to be disheartened because he would miss a friend or if he was afraid that her departure might prevent him from uncovering any additional details about her father's business dealings. *Lord,* she thought. *Listen to me. I'm becoming absolutely paranoid and bitchy to boot. What's worse, I'm sounding like a weak, despicable character from one of those mystery novels I loathe so much.*

She looked at Charlie. She had absolutely no proof the man was misleading her, in fact, quite the opposite. He was an open and a willing ally in her search. *I have to end the charade and be as honest with him as possible,* she pondered. *I certainly can't keep this up. I'll tell him everything and see what happens.* "I'm sorry, Charlie" she said. "I was curt and rude and it's not like me. My only excuse is I've had several exhausting and difficult days that have turned my life upside down, and I've taken in all the information I can handle. I need time to understand what I'm feeling about my father, my inheritance, and myself, for that matter. I'm going to have to make so many life-altering decisions in the days and weeks ahead."

Charlie took her hand. "I understand, CC. Perhaps I pushed too hard. I hope you know I wasn't urging you to do anything I didn't think you wanted to do."

Once again, CC was surprised by the tingle she felt at Charlie's touch. She squeezed his hand. "I know that," she said apologetically, "and I feel terrible. I took out my frustrations on you, even though I know this isn't your problem. Maybe I'm feeling pressured because I haven't been able to take your sister's advice. For some unknown reason I've told myself I have to find answers to my questions and make decisions about my future in a matter of days, but that's not true. I'm on a self-imposed deadline and that makes me incredibly edgy. So for now, I need to be outdoors, stop with the sleuthing, and try to follow Alex's recommendation."

"And that's all?"

CC smiled. "Well, not exactly. To be completely honest, I want to get to know you better before I share anything more. I like you very much, I'm extremely comfortable with you, and I feel like I've known you for years rather than for less than twenty-four hours, but I really know so little about you beyond what Alex has told me," CC smiled, "and she's biased."

Charlie grinned. "You think Alex's partial to me?" He didn't wait for CC to respond. "Seriously, I took for granted that you'd accept me for what I appear to be without probing more deeply. I talked to you about trust, and you wonder if you should trust me."

"I guess that's it. Silly huh?"

"Not at all. You think I'm one of those abusive fellows who will take advantage of you, betray you and break your heart.

You're convinced I spend time with you not because you're beautiful and bright and incredibly sensuous, but to seduce you and when I've gained your trust, run off with your father's fortune."

CC was about to respond indignantly to Charlie's seemingly insensitive comment when she saw his blue eyes twinkle. Realizing he was teasing, she relaxed. "You're right," she said smiling. "Not long after we met I realized your true intent. You're a dangerous enemy, and I have to be very careful. After all, I'm a helpless, defenseless woman completely at your mercy."

"Due, of course, to my charm, intelligence, and mystery."

"Not to mention your strength and dashing good looks."

"So because you are a feeble woman who recognizes my admirable qualities, even if I am fabricating them, I must live up to your well-founded opinion of me and take care of you. I can't very well let you walk alone in so dangerous a place as Knockie, where all sorts of evil people lurk behind trees and where monsters jump out of the loch. You must allow me to escort you on your stroll so I can protect you from all things evil and at the same time fill your head with more specifics about fascinating me and my honorable intentions. I believe at lunch you asked me to reveal more about myself, and I'm now ready to confess all."

"And I'm certainly eager to hear everything you have to say, so if you'll just give me a minute to put on my running shoes and grab my pen and pad so I can take notes, I'll be ready."

"I'll wait for you downstairs."

When Charlie left, CC put on her shoes and thought about the conversation that had just taken place. She was clearly attracted to the handsome Englishman and that was bothersome. How could she find him so appealing when she was in love with Bud?

The sky was cloudless as CC and Charlie began their walk around Loch Nan Lann. They followed a grass-lined path from the house toward the water. Charlie opened a gate he said kept the sheep off the lawns, and they entered the pasture. Instantly, a large flock of sheep with several newborn lambs charged toward them, bleating loudly. The animals in the next field, alerted by the din, bunched by the gate to await their arrival. "How many of these pastures do we have to pass through before we're out of danger?" she asked only half-jokingly as she swatted a swarm of flies away from her face and hair.

"Only one more, and I would hardly call this a perilous situation. These sheep won't hurt you."

"But if I recall, you said you would take care of fragile little me, and I'm terribly frightened, so protect me, or at least explain why these sheep are so interested in us."

"Since I have no need to defend you from these plant-eating animals, I'll explain. Now please don't be offended. The sheep aren't charmed by your beauty, warmth, and allure as I am. You see, it's lambing time and the shepherd is feeding his flock extra rations. These guys probably think you're bringing them more food."

"Can't the sheep go away and take these flies with them?" CC swatted at a swarm that was attacking her head. They're horrible, and they seem to like my hair. Will you protect me from them too, Sir Galahad?"

"I don't blame them. I too like your hair. Charlie stroked the top of her head and CC quivered at his touch. "Seriously, if you're wearing any perfume or what you women call hair spray, the flies will swarm."

"Thanks for telling me now when the beasts are after me. It doesn't appear you have a great desire to protect me from the monsters lurking around the loch?"

"Oh, I have desire, all right." Charlie laughed and CC reddened.

He took her hand and they continued down the path toward the loch. White and purple foxgloves lined the shoreline in masses, creating a beautiful natural garden. Charlie guided her across a stone path to the other side of the loch, and with no sheep around, the flies became less exasperating.

Pine, ash, and hickory trees lined either side of the trail and sometimes hid the loch from view as they strolled in the coolness the arched branches afforded. When they reached a place on a bluff above the pines almost opposite the house, CC left the path and made her way through the thicket down to the water's edge. She sat on a huge log, which had fallen on a grassy, flower-strewn spot under a gigantic pine, and stared across the loch. She sighed. "What an incredible view. If I'd only thought to pack my camera when I came over here, but I hadn't planned to come to the Highlands or, for that matter, to stay in England long enough to take pictures."

"What had you planned?" Charlie asked as he joined her on the log.

"I expected to see my father's attorney, reject my title, fly home, and forget I ever came."

"And now?"

"I've discovered that there's an immense world out there that I know nothing about. My entire life has revolved around one professional objective. I achieved my goal, and I want to be a success in my career, but for some reason, baseball and professional sports are not all-consuming anymore. I've come to realize, as they say, that there is more to life than work."

"But will you go back to your job and give up all this?"

"I frankly don't know the answer to that question. Ideally I'd like to find a way to combine the two ways of life; be

Countess of Litchfield for my father's sake, since that seemed to mean so much to him, and at the same time be the president of the Indianapolis Knights. But deep within me I realize that life isn't that easy. I imagine I'll have to make a choice."

Charlie put his arm around CC, and she relaxed her head against his shoulder, thinking of the decisions she would be forced to make. As she turned to suggest they continue their walk, she found her face only inches from his. She felt a quivering sensation as she willed herself to turn away—to no avail. Charlie bent and kissed her gently and then more passionately.

Unable to resist the feelings building inside her, CC returned the kiss, first cautiously and then with abandon as she felt his arms wrap tightly around her. "Oh, Charlie," she murmured as he kissed her neck. He silenced her with more kisses, and she answered his ardor with an eagerness she hadn't felt since she and Bud had first become lovers.

But. . ." She thought of him and tried to move away. She was going to marry Bud. But immediately all thoughts of home and Bud disappeared as Charlie began to unbutton her blouse. Fire shot through her as he caressed her breasts and lowered his head to tease her with his tongue. "Oh, God, what are we doing?" she moaned as he eased her to the grass-carpeted ground. There was nothing more to say as he covered her mouth with his.

CC unbuttoned his shirt and caressed his muscular chest while Charlie unbuttoned her jeans and ran his hand over her smooth stomach. He kissed her belly button and down her stomach while he undid her jeans. As he kissed and explored, CC writhed in pleasure. When she thought she could stand the agony he was creating no longer, his tongue stopped teasing and his kisses traced their way back up to her breasts. As he caressed her with one hand, he deftly removed his kilt with the other. Everywhere his tongue and lips touched, CC burned with pleasure and desire, and when he entered her, she groaned and eagerly accepted him.

CC was oblivious to everything around her but the incredible sensations she was experiencing. Suddenly when she could stand the agony no longer, she exploded in extraordinary spasms of delight.

Charlie kept moving until her tensing eased. Then, as his rhythm increased, he kissed her neck and her ears. Much to her amazement, CC could feel her passion building again. She joined in the movements, raising her hips to meet his. Suddenly she shuddered again, not in the waves she experienced only moments before, but sharply and intensely. Moments later Charlie groaned and grasped her tightly to him. He signed deeply, rolled off and took her in his arms. He pushed her hair from her forehead, kissed her lightly, and held her tightly. "God, you're incredible," he murmured into her ear.

"You're not so bad yourself," she teased as she kissed his eyes and his nose.

"I've never felt like this," he whispered softly as he kissed her lightly on the lips.

"Oh, Charlie..." CC began.

"Don't say anything, please. Let's just enjoy the moment."

They lay together quietly, listening only to the sound of the breeze in the pines and the water lapping the shore. CC finally broke the silence. "What if someone comes by and sees us?"

"There's no one to interrupt us. Remember, this is private land; your land."

"And what a wonderful spot to make love. Did you plan this?" She stroked Charlie's chest.

"In my wildest dreams, I never even imagined this would happen, but maybe that's why it was so good. It was spur of the moment."

CC lay quietly cradled in Charlie's arm, her head on his shoulder. He nuzzled her neck and hugged her tightly. "I'd like to stay here forever, my love, but if we don't get back to the house right away, Alex will launch a full-scale search."

"Is it four already?"

"Close to it. If Alex and Tony aren't at Knockie by now, they soon will be."

CC got up reluctantly and put on her clothes as Charlie admired the view. "Have I told you how incredibly gorgeous you are?"

"Not really, but then we've hardly had time considering we've known each other less than twenty-four hours."

"But I feel like I've known you a lifetime."

"I feel that way too, Charlie, but honestly, I don't know what happened here. I know how I felt and how I feel, but I certainly didn't expect—"

"Shh." Charlie bent and kissed her lips. "No words."

"But—" He kissed her again, and she felt giddy from his touch.

"We're going to have to talk about this sometime."

"I know, but not now. Feel, don't think."

"I recall your sister saying something quite similar."

"Then if two brilliant people are giving you such good advice, why don't you take it?" Charlie fastened his kilt and straightened his socks.

"I'd love to stop thinking altogether, but you have to admit, this afternoon complicates matters even more."

Charlie grinned. "I certainly hope so. I'm serving notice. I plan to make life even more complicated after Alex and Tony go to bed."

CC thought of her own plans for the night, of her need to get into her father's files. Charlie had muddied the waters, but in a way he'd resolved some of her issues. She trusted him. There was no way a man who made love to her as he had would betray her. She had no idea where their relationship, if there was a relationship, would go, but she did know one thing: she would trust Charlie with her life. She responded to his comment with a chuckle. "Well, maybe we can combine a little pleasure with business. We'll explore my father's files and—"

"Then explore each other."

CC laughed and took Charlie's extended hand. "Do you think anyone will know what we've been doing?"

"I'm sure Alex will know immediately. She has a sixth sense when it comes to romance, but I imagine she'll be discreet, and I'm certain no one else will suspect. That is, if you can hide your overwhelming passion for me."

"I'll certainly try," CC said with a laugh.

CHAPTER SEVENTEEN

Alex and Tony were waiting in the drawing room when CC and Charlie returned. Alex put down the *Country Living* magazine she was reading and met them in the entry. "You both look like you enjoyed being outdoors," she said smiling.

CC was mortified. *She knows*, she thought. *I don't know how, but she does. I can see it on her face.* "The fresh air was invigorating," she said, hoping the heat she was feeling in her face hadn't translated to a blush.

Charlie came to her rescue and changed the subject. "How long have you and Tony been here?"

"Actually we came a little earlier than we had originally planned." She looked at her watch. "I guess we arrived about an hour ago."

"I'm sorry we kept you waiting," CC said. "If we'd known you were here, we would have hurried."

"And cut your walk short? I wouldn't hear of it. Tony and I have been just fine."

"You're settled in?" CC asked.

"Unpacked and ready for tea."

"Then I'll go tell Mrs. Lauriston to serve in the parlor. I have to make a business call, but I'll join you in a few minutes. While I'm gone, Charlie can bring you up to date on our plans."

"Plans? What plans?" Tony came in from the direction of the billiards room.

"Charlie will tell you. I'll be right down." CC started up the stairs.

Before she reached the first landing, Mrs. Lauriston stopped her. "My lady, while you were out you had two calls. I put the messages on your desk upstairs."

"Thank you," said CC.

The first message was from Bud, who had called Litchfield for the number at Knockie. He wanted her to know he was thinking of her, that he'd be out for most of the day and would try to reach her about two LA time. CC counted ahead. That would be eleven in Scotland. She smiled, feeling slightly guilty about what she planned to be doing at that hour.

In all the years she and Bud had been seeing one another, she hadn't been interested in anyone else. She tried to tell herself that Charlie meant nothing to her; that it was only Bud she cared about. The afternoon had been about trees, lovely water, purple and white flowers, and a need to trust. "That's asinine," she said aloud. "This afternoon was about passion and sex and love." She hesitated. She had said it, "love." *Am I in love with Charlie? Is he in love with me or is this just a passionate interlude? Oh, God, here I go again, analyzing one of the most incredible experiences I've ever had. And what about Bud? What in the world do I tell him when he asks me about my day? And what do I tell Charlie about Bud?* She groaned. "God, I've got to stop thinking."

She read the second message. It was from Flash, who just wanted to see if she was okay. "Oh, I'm okay, Flash," she answered. "I'm really okay."

She went into her bathroom to freshen up. As she brushed her hair, two pine needles fell into the sink. She frowned. "No wonder Alex knows. I'm a walking advertisement for a roll in the pine needles."

CC had no need to call Bud, and since the team would be on the field for the morning workout in Florida, she decided to forego the calls, take a quick shower, and dress more formally. Though the hand-held showerhead in the tub was rather awkward, she enjoyed the feel of the water cascading over her skin. She only wished she could wash away the confusion she was feeling.

She got out of the tub, fluffed her hair to be sure there were no more hidden pine needles, touched up her makeup, and put on her slacks and a silk blouse. She fastened gold loop earrings in her ears and tried on the gold necklace. "Still too much," she decided. "I wonder if I'll ever get to wear this thing." She looked in the mirror. The outfit was simple yet elegant, and it did wonders for her figure.

Charlie, Alex, and Tony were already sipping tea when she walked into the drawing room. The two men stood to greet her. "You look beautiful!" Charlie said, perhaps a bit too enthusiastically.

"Thank you very much," CC responded, hoping that no one in the room saw her heart pounding under her thin silk blouse. "I'm sorry it took me so long. I decided to take a quick shower."

"While you were upstairs, Charlie told us that the weekend plans have changed, though I'm not really certain what our new agenda will entail," Alex said.

"Are you two in a hurry to get back to Chadlington?" CC asked.

"I have a meeting in London on Wednesday," said Tony, "but beyond that, we're open to anything."

"Then if it's all right with you, we'll make final plans tomorrow," CC said. "It's really a matter of whether I can get my business at Knockie finished tonight or whether I'll need another day."

While enjoying the tea, they talked about mundane subjects. CC often felt Charlie looking at her and tried to avoid making eye contact. She didn't want to confirm Alex's suspicions. After Henry came to take the tray away, Alex turned to Tony. "Why don't you and Charlie go play a few games of billiards before dinner. CC and I will sit here and talk for a while and then we'll join you."

"Right. You two practice so we don't beat you too badly," CC teased.

"So go!" Alex shooed the men from the room.

"Would you like to take a walk before dinner?" CC asked Alex when the men were out of sight.

"Actually I'd rather talk than walk."

"About anything in particular?"

"About you and Charlie."

"I don't know what you mean."

"Please, CC. You two don't fool me for a minute. I'm not prying, but I wanted you to know I'm aware of your relationship with Charlie."

"Aren't you being a bit premature, Alex? Charlie and I don't have a relationship. We barely know one another."

"Yet Charlie can't keep his eyes off of you and you won't look at him for fear of showing your feelings. That's precisely why I wanted to have this conversation. You know I hoped you and my brother would, as you Americans say, hit it off. Though I'm usually quite cautious about forming an opinion of a person the moment I meet him or her, for some reason I liked you immediately, and it should be obvious that I adore my brother and want him to be happy."

"It's obvious you care about him," CC said.

"Charlie loved Flora, but my father and hers arranged their marriage, and I imagine she and Charlie were, in reality, content rather than happy. The union was an acceptable one for both families. Flora's father possessed a title and had no money and Charlie had a great deal of money. By marrying Flora, our family gained a Scottish title to accompany the English one and, through Flora's dowry, a great deal of land in Scotland. But about their relationship: With Flora, Charlie was always restrained and courteous, almost dutiful, and she returned his love in kind. This afternoon I saw him look at you with an expression I've never seen before."

"Oh, Alex." CC spent the next fifteen minutes telling Alex about Bud and their relationship, including the fact that when she arrived home from her walk with Charlie, a message from Bud was awaiting her.

"Do you remember I told you to stop thinking and feel?"

"I remember it all too well. Charlie said the same thing this afternoon."

"Then take our advice."

"But I don't want to hurt anyone. That seems to be my problem all around. I don't want to hurt my mother or Flash. I don't want to hurt my father, even though he's dead. I don't want to hurt Bud, and what's happening between Charlie and me—there, I admit it—will really affect him. I don't want to hurt Charlie when I leave him and go home to Bud; that is, if I can face Bud after what's happened here. I don't want to hurt the owners and staff members of the Knights, people who have put their trust in me, and—"

"Hold it. You talk about all of these people you don't want to hurt. What about you? You haven't once talked about what you want."

"That's because I have no idea."

"So if you could pick an ideal solution to your problem, what would it be right now?"

"I would like to find a way to combine my two separate lives; be the Countess of Litchfield and the president of the Knights."

"And Charlie and Bud?" CC hesitated," please, CC, talk to me as your friend and not Charlie's sister. I'm trying to help you feel your way through this."

"I feel things for Charlie I never thought possible. I love his sense of humor. I love how he cares for me. I love the way he makes me feel every minute I'm around him. I love the way I feel when he holds me."

"Then what's the problem?"

"Bud. Though it's not official, we're engaged. He shares my interests in baseball and understands my love of the game and my need to be the CEO of the Knights. He would never interfere with my career plans."

"And what else? What about your personal relationship?"

"It used to be wonderful. I mean it was exciting at first, but I'm afraid we both let our careers get in the way. I couldn't even see my way clear to plan a night with him in New York on the way back to Indianapolis from London. Despite both of our efforts to make changes, everything has become so predictable."

"And this is the way you want to spend your life?"

"I don't know. I thought so until this afternoon, and then Charlie awakened feelings in me I thought were dead. No, I take that back. He stirred feelings I never knew I had. I feel funny talking with you about this, but you're right, I need to talk about how I feel."

"And you can trust that what we say will go no farther. I want to help you." Alex grinned. "Of course I would like for you to end up with Charlie and live 'happily ever after' between your estates with those titles and all that money, but that's what I want. I'd also like for you happy."

"Why do you really care? I mean, I've only known you for a few days."

"I know, but it seems much longer for me. As I said before, from the minute I met you, I felt a closeness I can't explain."

"I felt that way too." CC got up off the couch, walked over, and hugged Alex.

"I want you to know that I'm always available to be your sounding board. I'll listen, and if you ask for advice, I'll be glad to give it, but I won't offer an opinion unless you ask."

"I couldn't ask for a better deal than that."

"I also want you to know that I intend to bring this relationship between you and Charlie out in the open in front of Tony. We can't have you tiptoeing around and trying to hide your feelings from us. If you start doing that, you'll feel uncomfortable and eventually try to get rid of us, and I'm not going anywhere. I'm having too much fun watching you two."

CC groaned. "I give up. It would be ludicrous for me to protest. Shall we join the men?"

"Sure. We might even beat them in billiards; that is, after I've made my announcement to Charlie and Tony."

"Announcement?"

"Let's just say I plan to give Charlie my blessing and tell him that I won't come looking for him early in the morning for a jog; that he can sleep wherever he chooses."

CC laughed. She hooked her arm through Alex's, and they went to the billiards room to join the men.

Alex's announcement was hardly subtle. She interrupted the billiards game with: "No more sneaking around, Charlie. The pine needles gave you away."

Charlie looked puzzled. "I beg your pardon."

"It's obvious how you and CC feel about one another. I want to clear the air so you can behave however you feel like behaving. You'll have no problem with Tony and me, right, Tony?"

Tony seemed confused. "Absolutely, my love. Whatever you say."

Charlie approached his sister and kissed her on the cheek. "You were never one to mince words, were you?"

"You know subtlety was never my forte."

"Well, I for one am glad," Charlie said, "and I'll do my part to see there are no secrets among us." He gathered CC in his arms and kissed her passionately. Though uncomfortable, she returned his kiss with equal ardor.

"My, my," Tony turned to Alex. "I see what you mean." All four laughed at the look of astonishment on his face.

The evening that followed was truly enjoyable. CC and Alex lost the billiards challenge, but being with her three energetic and affable guests made losing less painful. Dinner was scrumptious, and CC finally met Freeman. The burly man relished the praise the diners lavished on him, and CC finally understood what Charlie meant when he teased her about asking her chef to prepare a light salad instead of the usual fare.

Coffee was served in the sitting room. CC and Charlie sat on the huge down couch in front of the picture window. During the course of the evening, CC told Alex and Tony about William and Flash. She explained her plan to find out about her father's business dealings and why she needed to remain at Knockie. Once or twice she remembered her self-imposed warning not to trust anyone, but she was certain she could trust all three of her friends; that was, to a point. She didn't tell Alex or Tony about the communications room. She and Charlie would search through those files when they were alone. Alone! She could hardly wait.

Alex and Tony volunteered to spend the following day going through hardcopy files and pictures at the same time CC was trying to access her father's computer files. Alex seemed pleased when they made plans to go shopping in Inverness Monday morning. They'd return to Glencoe on Monday night, and drive to Litchfield and Chadlington on Tuesday.

When the arrangements were finalized, Alex stood up and stretched. "This country air is making me sleepy," she said, obviously faking a yawn.

"At eleven?" Tony said skeptically. "I've never known you to be tired this early."

"But I am," she said resolutely, and CC smiled at Alex's efforts to give her and Charlie time alone. "And I'm sure CC and Charlie need to get up early to run. Am I right?"

"In fact, we do," said Charlie. We're planning to jog to Loch Ness. CC believes Nessie will emerge to greet her."

"Will you join us?" CC asked.

Like a light bulb going off in his head, Tony realized why Alex wanted to go to bed so early. "I'm afraid not," he said smiling, "and like Alex, I too am tired. I agree, it must be the country air. So we'll say good night and meet you for breakfast."

"Do you know what time Freeman serves in the morning?" CC asked.

"I would imagine around eight-thirty," Charlie said.

"Then eight-thirty it is." Alex kissed her brother on the cheek and hugged CC. "Good night, you two. Sleep well." She grinned; "or not!"

CC rolled her eyes. "You too."

When Alex and Tony disappeared upstairs, Charlie took CC in his arms. "And will we sleep, my love?"

"Eventually, I imagine, but first…" She kissed him.

"I like the ideas you're giving me. Your room or mine?"

"I have a bigger bath tub."

CHAPTER EIGHTEEN

CC raced to her bathroom to freshen up and put on a dab of perfume before Charlie arrived. She was about to brush her teeth when the phone rang.

"CC, is that you sweetheart?" she heard before she had time to say hello.

Oh, damn, she silently groaned. "Hi, Bud. How are you? How's LA?"

"To answer both questions, I'm fine and LA is LA. I hate these freeways."

"And your meetings, how are they going?"

"Worthless, as usual. We could have done this whole thing by conference call."

CC laughed. "If I had a dime for every time I've heard you say that, I'd be a wealthy woman."

"I know, I know, but enough about me. What's going on with you? Are you in Scotland for business?"

"At first I wanted to come and see the property, but now I'm combining business with pleasure." CC frowned. Wouldn't Bud be shocked if he suspected her pleasure was Charlie?

"What kind of business?"

CC told Bud about seeing Flash in the photo, her conversation with her stepfather, her father's files, William's diary, and the letters. She was about to tell him about the communications room, when she heard a rap on the door. "Could you hold on for a minute, Bud? I think Mrs. Lauriston is here with the tea I asked her to bring up." CC hated to lie, but she had no choice. She could hardly tell one lover that her new lover was at the door.

CC opened the door for Charlie, who, without saying a word, enveloped her in his arms and kissed her tenderly. "Charlie, I'm on the phone to Los Angeles. Could you wait out here until I'm finished? I shouldn't be long."

CC went back into the bedroom and shut the door. "Bud, I'm sorry. Mrs. Lauriston wanted to tell me about the plans for breakfast."

"I miss you. Any idea when you'll be home?"

"I've made a tentative plan. Regardless of what's going on here, I'll be home for the opener, and if everything's settled here, I'll stay. I hope to go with the team on the second road trip, if I can possibly catch up on the work I've missed. If things here are still up in the air in William's regard, I'll likely come back to England and try to sort through my options."

"It doesn't sound like you'll be stopping in New York."

"I can't Bud. I'm really sorry, but please understand. This is a confusing and difficult time for me, and I'm trying to juggle my job and my personal life so I can be somewhat successful in each."

"I thought I was your personal life. I realize that sounds a bit childish, but—"

"You are!" CC tried to sound reassuring.

"But we're having problems, aren't we?"

"I have no idea what you mean, and Bud, if we are having difficulties, a long-distance call across the Atlantic Ocean is not the time to discuss them."

"Then you admit that our relationship is in trouble?"

"I didn't say that. I told you I'm struggling to deal with everything on my plate. In a very brief time I lost a father I didn't know and inherited a title I didn't want."

"Didn't want?" "Wrong tense, don't want."

I'm sorry if I've made you angry but I sense things aren't right between us."

"Bud, stop reading things into what I sound like or what I'm saying or not saying. What I need from you is understanding. We'll deal with any difficulties we might have when I figure out what I'm going to do with my life."

"It seems to you're using 'I' more often than 'we.'"

"Again, a poor choice of words, but please appreciate what I'm facing and stop analyzing our relationship. I don't want to fight long distance. In fact, I don't want to fight at all. When I get home, we'll spend time together and see if we can work out whatever problems our careers have caused."

"I'm counting on that. I love you too. That's why I want you to stop in New York."

"I know, and I love you too," *but platonically,* CC finally admitted

"Get some rest. You sound exhausted."

"I am, so I'm going to have the tea Mrs. Lauriston brought to me and go to bed." CC frowned as she told yet another lie.

"Good night, sweetheart. Pleasant dreams of me."

"Goodnight," CC said, a little too curtly and hung up the phone. "Oh God!" she said, "I can't deal with this deception." She waited a few minutes before going into the sitting room.

"You look upset, are you feeling all right?" Charlie asked.

"I'm fine, really."

"Honestly, you look pale."

"I'm tired. Charlie, would you sit with me for a minute?" Charlie crossed the room and sat next to her. "No, not beside me, across from me. I'm afraid if you sit too close, I'll lose all resolve."

"Resolve?"

"I can't stay with you tonight. Believe me, I want to, but I need time."

"You feel I'm pressuring you?"

"Not at all. I'd be fine if I could do what everyone keeps telling me to do, feel rather than think, but that's not my way and I need space. I have strong feelings for you, but I have some thinking to do."

"Does this have anything to do with the call you were on when I arrived?"

"To be honest, yes, but don't want to talk about it now. I just lied to a dear friend, and I'm not proud of myself."

"You didn't feel you could tell the truth?"

"Not yet, and certainly not on a telephone from across an ocean."

"This person you lied to is important to you?"

"Is and has been for many years. I don't want to lie to you as well. Bud and I have been unofficially engaged for years, but the timing was never right for marriage, and now it seems it never will be. Anyway, at the very least, I owe him enough to be honest with him, and I need to close the book on that part of my life before I open a new chapter."

"And you plan to do that when you get home?"

"I think so, but if I do, I don't want you to think I'm ending my relationship with Bud because of you. We shared a wonderful afternoon today, and the time we've spent together has shown me what's been missing in my life and what I could have. You might say it put me in tune with feelings I didn't know existed, but whatever decision I make will be because of me and only me. You're the catalyst that helped me see I want more from a relationship than what I have or, for that matter, ever had with Bud."

"Do I fit into your plans?"

"I hope so, but I don't have the right to encourage you. I do know that in an incredibly short time you've become very important to me, but I'll tell you the same thing I told Bud: I have to put my own life in order before I can deal with anything else, especially a relationship."

"So you want me to forget the incredible afternoon we shared and leave Knockie?"

"Not at all. I'm asking you, for the moment, to be my friend and confidant, to help me understand these mysteries in my life in that capacity rather than as my lover."

"So if I choose to remain, without your encouragement and with no guarantees, you can honestly tell me you're not closing the book on us?"

CC laughed. "Our book is definitely not closed, at least not without a bookmark that indicates the place so it can be opened again, but I think we've beaten this extended metaphor into the ground."

Her response broke the tension. Charlie walked over to her, put his hands on her arms, raised her up from the chair, and kissed her on the forehead. CC shut her eyes. She wanted more, and she knew Charlie did too, but she couldn't give in to her feelings. She had to be true to herself.

She walked Charlie to the door. "It's going to be difficult for me to keep my hands off you, Lady Litchfield," he said smiling, "but I'll comply with your request. As of now, I'm a friend who's helping you search for information about your father. I'm sorry I made your life more problematic by rushing our relationship, but you're so damn delicious."

CC grinned. "And you're incredibly sexy."

Charlie kissed her softly on the lips and then dropped his hands from her arms. "So go take that bath by yourself. I can honestly say I've never taken a cold shower to wash away my desires, but tonight I'll see if it works."

"And you'll pick me up in the morning? Remember, Nessie is waiting for me."

"Seven o'clock. I'll probably still be up thinking of you in that tub and in your lonely bed."

"Charlie!"

"Sorry, my friend. See you tomorrow."

"I'll be ready." CC closed the door and went to her bedroom. "I have done the right thing," she said, "I can't live a lie."

When the alarm blared, CC had already been up for thirty minutes. While she waited for Charlie, she turned on her father's computer. She was pleased to see that he used Windows 7. *But why wouldn't William have the latest version?* she reflected as she opened his list of documents and scrolled through the files. One file contained a list of wines stored in the wine cellar. There was an address list, and CC brought that file to the screen and read the names. This time she wasn't surprised to see Flash's name among her father's acquaintances, but when she saw her own Indianapolis address, she was astonished. Did her father mean to contact her? If not, why was her current address on his computer? There was a list of names of individuals of various nationalities: German, French, Japanese, Irish, Israeli, and Arab. Hoping these would jog Charlie's memory and help him recall the people who visited her father at Knockie the weekend he and Flora visited William, she ran a copy.

Another file contained information about the Highlands and walks in the area. There was a file for groceries and one containing Freeman's special recipes. "Nothing here seems to be important," CC said. She wondered if this particular computer was used strictly for household business. It was clear that significant information would be kept on the computer in the communications closet.

She'd barely finishing scrolling through the files when Charlie knocked softly. She shut down the computer and opened the door. She laughed to see him standing there. His hair was a mess and he'd smudged dark circles under his eyes. His shirt was untucked, and one of his socks was down around his ankles. "Have pity on a lovesick man who spent a miserable night alone?" he teased.

"Oh, do come in, wretched sir. I'm truly mortified by your apparent state."

"Then I have made an impression? You're ready to take me in your arms and comfort me?"

"You made an impression, but I'm not sure exactly what kind."

"Then my efforts haven't gone unnoticed?"

"They are duly noted. Now if you'll make yourself presentable, I'm ready to see Nessie. We wouldn't want your sister to think I mistreated you, and right now you look like a battered man."

Charlie pulled out a comb and fixed his hair. A tissue removed the black lines, which he said were made from the soot remaining in the fireplace in his room. He tucked in his shirt and pulled up his socks. "Now am I more presentable?" he asked; a twinkle in his eye.

"Now you're irresistible. I much prefer a man who 'has it together' as the teenagers in the United States say."

"Then I shall definitely 'have it together' in the future. Seriously though, did you sleep? I hated to leave you so troubled and bewildered last night."

"I wasn't confused, at least about what I wanted last night, and though I may not look as awful as you did a few minutes ago, I didn't get much sleep either. I'll admit that there were a few times when I thought about sneaking downstairs and slipping into your bed."

"Then why didn't you?"

"Because I can't and that's the hard part. I want you to make love to me. It's all I can think about, but before you do, I have to make things right."

"And that will be after you go home to Indianapolis to speak with Bud?"

"That's what I thought last night when you left, but today I'm not sure. I may have to tell him before I go home, though a telephone call seems the chicken's way out. I know I won't be able to fight my feelings for you for long."

"Then don't fight." Charlie took her in his arms.

"Charlie, we can't! I can't! I want to talk to Bud first, so help me do what I feel is right."

Charlie backed away. "As much as I hate for you to let go, I will, but I won't be able to stay away for long."

"Let's jog and let me clear my head. We'll talk later."

The run was wonderful. The fresh air; the lovely blue water; the gray-turreted white house lonely in the vast expanse becoming smaller and smaller as they ran farther from it; the masses of flowers, and the smell of wood burning in fireplaces made for an idyllic scene. CC put all thoughts of decisions she would have to make on hold and took in the scenery around her. Once again, as so often during the preceding days, she felt a fellowship with nature and sensed that the man running with her felt the same way.

It took them twenty-five minutes to reach a small bluff overlooking Loch Ness. Charlie stopped. "Here it is," he panted, "so start looking for Nessie."

They walked down the embankment along a flower-lined path. The shoreline was covered with large gray stones, worn smooth by the water lapping over them. A massive log extended out about two feet over the water, and CC climbed onto it and sat with her feet dangling. She gazed at the opposite shore with its cultivated fields topped by forests of pine, maple, and sycamore. The light blue sky with its few wispy white clouds and the greenish blue of the loch seemed appropriate for a picture postcard. "I don't see a monster, but this view is incredible," she said.

"It is beautiful, isn't it? But I admit, until this morning I had taken our Highland scenery for granted."

"Until this morning?"

"Until I saw how much you were enjoying its beauty."

"And it is truly splendid. Thank you for bringing me here."

"You're welcome. Would you like to stay here for a while or would you prefer to walk along the lake and return to Knockie by another path?"

"Let's walk." CC got up and extended her hand. Charlie took it, and they made their way over the water-polished stones back toward the house.

CHAPTER NINETEEN

C C finished her shower, and while she was waiting for her
guests to come down for breakfast, she made a "to do" list
for the morning.

1. Call Switzerland to find out about the bank account.
2. Make an appointment with the physician who signed William's death certificate.
3. Make an appointment with John Norris, William's accountant.
4. Tell Hastings of the change in plans for my return.
5. Call Bud!!??

She wasn't sure she'd included everything, but her list
making stopped when Alex, Tony, and Charlie came into the
dining room. CC was amazed that she was so hungry. Rarely a
breakfast eater, she enjoyed a huge English breakfast, consist-
ing of two eggs, slices of tomatoes, bacon, sausage, toast, juice,
and coffee. During the meal she told her companions about
what she planned to accomplish during the day.

When they finished eating, Charlie took charge. "I'll being
by going through the pictures to see if I recognize anyone.
Tony, you peruse the files and look for any information about
William's business dealings outside of England. Alex, you try
to uncover information about William's relationship with the
Duke of Marlborough and other notable people."

"I will," Alex said, "and if I don't find what I'm looking
for, I'll ring the duchess tomorrow. Her Grace is on a holiday

in Edinburgh, but her secretary will be able to put me in touch with her."

"Good. CC, you continue to read the letters and papers you brought with you from Litchfield. Perhaps they will provide additional clues."

"Sounds like a plan. Shall we get started?" CC asked.

"After you." Charlie and Alex stood aside, and the ladies led the way up the stairs.

Charlie had no luck with the pictures. He recognized a few of the local people, but none of the foreign guests. In a file marked "Marlborough," Alex discovered three appointment cards for meetings at Blenheim, but there was no regular pattern to the dates or the times of the visits, and the engagements could have been for any reason.

CC was becoming frustrated with her father's letters. The ones for years five through fifteen concerned events in her life and his feelings for her, but they said nothing about his business activities. She was learning a great deal about William, but not what she really needed to know.

There were several references to Flash in the letters. Apparently the two men met regularly during those years. Frustrated, CC decided to skip ahead. She would read the earlier letters another time. She went through the stack until she found the letter for her thirtieth birthday. She opened and read.

My Darling CC on Your Thirtieth Birthday.

Another year has passed, and it has been quite eventful for me. In this letter I will turn from personal matters for a while and begin to tell you something about my business dealings. This is prompted by the fact that your stepfather visited me at Knockie, my hunting lodge in Scotland, this past year.

"Pay dirt!" she said. "On my thirtieth birthday William mentioned Knockie and Flash in the same letter."

"You're that far along?" Tony asked.

"I skipped ahead. The letters through my fifteenth birthday were personal, not business related, so I went for those that were written after 2008, when I knew my stepfather was here."

"Good idea," said Charlie. "What does Williams say?"

CC read aloud:

Flash and I have not had the pleasure of meeting in since the Committee of Seven met in Paris six months ago.

"The Committee of Seven?" CC wrote the name on her pad. "Have you ever heard of the committee, Charlie?"

"Never, but there were only six men meeting here at Knockie that weekend, I'm certain of that. Remember I told you there was Flash, an American, your father, an Englishman, a German, a Frenchman, Japanese, and as I said, I can't remember the nationality of the other person."

"So this Committee of Seven, minus one, met that weekend at Knockie?" CC asked.

"It would certainly seem so. Read more of the letter, CC," Charlie urged.

CC continued:

I imagine you're wondering about the Committee of Seven. I'll explain as much as I can, though I will not name names except my own, of course, and Flash's. There was a Frenchman, a German, a Japanese gentleman, and a Swiss citizen.

Charlie interrupted. "Swiss. That's right."

Over the years, several committee members have died or retired. Their respective governments have subsequently replaced them, but we are still seven.

I imagine by now you are quite curious about our Committee of Seven. I repeat, I will tell you what I can. The committee was formed by the respective governments of the individuals involved. However, if you check with the members' state departments, they will disavow knowledge of our work or, for that matter, us. We were originally called together because of a fear of oil shortages in the world and, as a result, the increased use of nuclear power. Our purpose was to work behind the scenes to promote international peace as well as reduce the threat of nuclear disaster.

We originally planned to meet every two years, but after our meeting in France, the wonderful year I met your mother and we conceived you, we did not convene on a regular basis. You were too young to remember, but as I told you in one of my earlier letters, I was in Arizona and saw you from afar. The purpose of my trip to the States was to take Flash to Washington with me. At that time the committee decided to meet quarterly.

"And I thought Flash was in Japan scouting ballplayers," CC explained, "when in reality he was involved in some sort of international intrigue."

This past year, it was my privilege to host our group at Knockie. I invited some of the local families to spend the weekend so the gathering would not seem unusual. I was glad to see Flash and receive my bi-yearly supply of pictures, clippings, and news of you, my darling CC. I understand you are a rising star in the world of professional baseball.

CC stopped reading aloud but continued to read to herself. Her father wrote about the pride he took in her career. He mentioned Bud and his hope that she would find as much happiness with him as he had with Mary. He talked of Anne's illness, which had just been diagnosed.

We will try anything possible to save her, but the prognosis is grim. The doctors have given her six months to a year to live. The disease has already spread to the bone, and it promises to be a gruesome ending for a wonderful woman. I will stand by her as she has stood by me. It is in times like this that all the temporal power that a man holds means little or nothing. If only I could save her.

He did love her in his way. It was different from the love he felt for my mother, but he cared deeply, CC mused. William said little more about Anne or his work. He closed by telling CC he hoped what he'd revealed in the letter would help her understand that he had a tremendous responsibility in the world, a responsibility that had to take precedent over his personal feelings. The implication was that he had left her mother and her because of this Committee of Seven, but for CC that was not an acceptable explanation. After all, Flash had stayed with them, and he was on the infamous committee. No, William had partially satisfied her need to know, but he hadn't gone far enough. He had opened the door, but not wide enough. He had only given her clues about his business dealings. She doubted he would tell her more in the letters she had in her hands. The real answers would be in the diary and papers behind the altar in the chapel at Litchfield.

"Is there anything else worth knowing?" Charlie asked as CC finished reading.

"Not really, other than my father hints that he left my mother and me solely because of his work on the committee. Perhaps what he was trying to say was that his work was dangerous and he didn't want to put us in jeopardy, but that can't be the whole story. If William was in danger, Flash was also in harm's way, and he didn't abandon us because he feared for our safely. No, there has to be more to William than he reveals in these letters, more than his membership on this Committee of Seven."

"But you have to admit he was an incredibly powerful man," Alex said. "And he could be in danger if people knew about his activities, whatever they were."

"I'm not arguing with you. I'm merely saying, if my father feared for Mother and me because of his committee membership, then why did he ask Flash, another member of the same committee, to look after us?"

"I see your point," Tony said. "It doesn't make much sense."

"And another thing, what about the money? Could my father make so much money sitting on a committee like this, and who paid him? His letter said the various governments who appointed the members of the committee, if challenged, would deny its existence, so he wasn't being paid by the British government, though his membership might explain Margaret Thatcher's and later Tony Blair's visit to Knockie."

"I hate to suggest this, CC," Alex said reticently. "But since we're looking at all possibilities, could it be that your father profited illegally from his contacts with various developing nations?"

CC didn't hesitate. "Of course it's a possibility, but Harrison Caulfield, my father's attorney, said he'd never met a more honest man than William. I have every reason to believe him."

"And Father attested to William's integrity," Charlie said. "CC's right. The letter said that, except for the Frenchman and Flash, committee membership changed over the years. If an associate died or could no longer serve for one reason or another, his government found someone else to replace him, but we have no idea who appointed the new member. From the photos we found and the information William left in his files and letters, it's obvious that whatever he was involved with in 2010, transcended his oil interests, the initial purpose for forming the Committee of Seven."

"Then we have to find out what my father was doing." CC looked at her watch. "It's eleven at Knockie. That means it's two in the morning in Scottsdale, so I'll call after tea this afternoon. My mother planned to take her diary out of her safety deposit box today. I'm hoping she'll be able to tell us something we don't already know. I'll also tell Flash what we've found and see if he'll give me more information. He adamantly refused to talk before, but now that I know this much maybe he'll change his mind."

"And in the meantime?" Alex asked.

"I'll keep looking. If you want to take a break, it's really fine with me, but I'm going to stay behind and keep searching for answers."

"I'm with you!" Charlie said.

"So are we," said Tony.

There wasn't much more in the files. The remaining letters were personal in nature and weren't like the annual birthday missives. They told of Anne's death and William's pain when he buried his wife. They told of his desire to make contact with her and his reluctance to disrupt her life and possibly cause problems for Mary and Flash. They even told of his purchase of a Mercedes convertible, a car for her if he could find a way to make her a part of his life.

Among his other papers she read of bi-yearly meetings of the Committee of Seven and of her father's concern about increasing tensions in Afghanistan, Iraq and of course Iran and North Korea. Unfortunately there was no information about people on the committee or how the group functioned, and she wasn't able to discern her father's role. She went back and skimmed the letters she had skipped, the ones between her fifteenth and twenty-ninth birthdays, but for the most part they too were personal with few reference to William's business dealings.

Alex discovered several communications between the prime ministers and William. The notes were cryptic, but as the four studied the words, Charlie decided that, veiled though they were, they were business letters that brought William up to date about government alliances and requests for action "These are obviously in some kind of code," Charlie said.

"So that anyone reading them would think they were irrelevant," Tony added.

"Are you sure we aren't creating more of a mystery than necessary?" CC asked. "These might actually be insignificant notes."

Charlie nodded no. "I doubt it. I think we should separate this file from the others and see what we can figure out later."

"Good idea," said CC. "I think we're making a little progress."

"But it doesn't seem there's much more to do here at Knockie," Alex said.

CC frowned. "You're right. I hate to disappoint you, Alex, but would you mind if we skip the shopping trip tomorrow and return to Litchfield, via Glencoe, of course? I have questions that may be more easily answered at William's home rather than here at the lodge." CC paused when she saw Alex's frown. *She's obviously disappointed,* she reflected, *and she and Tony have been so good to me. I have to make this right.* She smiled. "And of course if you're still willing, there are things you might do to help me."

Alex's frown quickly became a smile. "Of course, CC. The shopping trip was for you anyway. There will be plenty of time to see Inverness in the future."

CC didn't want to argue the point by saying that instead of coming back to the Highlands, she'd likely return to Indianapolis. "You're right," she said. "I hope you know I appreciate your willingness to be flexible. What about you, Charlie?"

"I'm in on this project until the bitter end."

"I know you told your staff we'd spend tomorrow night at Glencoe," CC said to him. "I hope our decision doesn't inconvenience them."

"Not at all. I'll phone Thomas and tell him to pack what I need for a few days. That way we'll only have to stop and grab the bags before continuing on to Litchfield. Give me a minute to call Angus and see if he'll keep little Charlie for a few more days."

"Will there be a problem?" CC asked.

"I don't think so, but let's see." Charlie took out his cell phone and left the room. CC chatted with Alex until he returned. "It looks like you'll meet my son after all," he said.

"He can't stay with his grandfather?"

"He can, but Angus has a business meeting in Glasgow tomorrow morning. He'll drop Brenda and little Charlie at Glencoe and pick them up on the way back to Dunollie."

"So we're on," Alex said.

"We are." CC turned to Charlie. "Do you want to stay at Litchfield or would you be more comfortable at Chadlington?"

"I think I could be more help at Litchfield, but it's entirely up to you."

Alex looked surprised. "Has something changed since last evening? I assumed you'd stay at Litchfield. Of course, you know you're always welcome at Chadlington, but—"

CC interrupted. "Nothing has changed."

"Are you sure?"

"Yes. Charlie and I were moving too fast, and I need time to complete some unfinished business at home before we move ahead."

"Then you plan to 'move ahead,' as you call it?"

CC looked at Charlie, who was gazing at her intently, waiting for her answer. "I hope so, Alex, but first I have to decide whether I'll remain in England or go home to my job; whether I'll accept my English title or remain president of the Knights; whether I can disentangle myself from a relationship I've been in for years with a man who means a great deal to me."

"I see. I'm prying."

"You certainly are, my dear sister, but you have nothing to worry about," Charlie said grinning. "When all is said and done, I have no doubt that CC will be unable to resist my debonair charm, my irrepressible wit, and my relentless pursuit."

"And what about your abundance of humility?" CC teased.

"That too." Alex and Tony went downstairs while Charlie remained behind and put his arms around her. "I'll try everything possible to keep you in England with me," he whispered.

"I know, and humble though you aren't, you do have some wonderful qualities, but you have to remember, if I stay it has to be for me. I have to want this life. Right now I don't know if I can give up the job I've pursued for over twenty years. Saying good-bye to baseball would be difficult, to say the least. Saying good-bye to Bud won't be easy either, though ending it with him hardly ranks up there with giving up a position I've fought so hard to achieve."

"But I have the feeling the door on England hasn't closed."

"Definitely not, and five days ago, if you'd asked me whether I'd even consider being the Countess of Litchfield, my answer would have been a definite no."

"Good, then let me show you one of the benefits of remaining on British soil." Charlie kissed her gently. CC wrapped her arms around him and held him tightly to her as the kisses became more intense. It was Charlie who moved away and held her at arm's length. "Would you add a call to Bud to that list of calls you need to make this afternoon?"

"I suppose there's no need to put it off any longer, though it won't be pleasant for either of us. And Charlie, I'll say again; I'm going to call him because of the way I feel, not because you want me to."

"I know, and though I hate it, I admire you for closing the book on one part of your life before beginning another."

"There's that overused metaphor again, and though I can't promise, we might begin a new chapter tonight."

Charlie kissed her again. "I'll be ready when you're available."

"Maybe you'll feel better if you realize, that though I don't show it like you, I want you too." CC laughed. "Maybe tonight, but while we're planning the evening ahead, since we're leaving tomorrow and have no idea when we might return, I have to make some time to try to access those computer files in the closet. There are other files in the cabinets you could look through while I'm working."

"Fine, we'll get to work right after dinner."

"What about Alex and Tony? We can't just leave them downstairs?"

"As I see it, you have two alternatives. We can go it alone and search the closet, or you can confide in Alex and Tony and allow them to help us."

"You think I should tell them."

"It's not for me to say what you should or shouldn't do, but I assure you, both Alex and Tony are trustworthy."

"If you're sure, I'll tell them about the closet during lunch."

"If you do, why don't we cancel the walk and begin our investigation when we've finished eating. If we find what we're looking or, we'll have more time to relax this evening."

"Ah, all becomes clear," CC teased. "You want me to tell your sister and brother-in-law about the communications room and enlist their help so you and I don't have to waste time tonight."

Charlie grinned. "At last you understand. I want you in bed, not in a communications closet. I haven't had the pleasure of making love to you beneath satin sheets."

"The grass was a wonderful bed." CC shivered as she remembered her feelings the day before.

"Anywhere with you would be amazing, but remember you promised me a splash in your tub."

"You're incorrigible."

"And irresistible."

"And obnoxious."

"And hungry for you and for lunch, so let's go. I'd like to satisfy at least one hunger."

CHAPTER TWENTY

During lunch, CC told Tony and Alex about the communications room in her father's suite. She felt remiss for not trusting her friends earlier, but they didn't seem concerned that she'd kept information from them. When lunch was over, the four made a plan for the afternoon. Charlie would ask Mrs. Lauriston, Henry, and Freeman if they could identify William's guests at Knockie or if they knew why the earl was entertaining the well-known men and women who came to visit. CC would look for names of the members of the Committee of Seven. In the meantime, Alex, Tony, and CC would begin their work in the communications room.

Charlie remained downstairs while the rest went up to William's suite. Tony was astonished by the modern communications center in the middle of the isolated Highlands. "This sophisticated set-up is incredible," he said, "and I absolutely agree, CC, your father was involved in something important."

While Alex and Tony searched the files, CC tried to access the documents on the computer. This time there was no familiar Windows program. Each time she tried to gain access to a document, she was rejected. She tried every code word she could think of, including her birthday, but to no avail. Her father's files were inaccessible.

Alex and Tony were having an equally difficult time. The files were dated, but the contents were coded, and in each one of them was totally worthless information, or so it seemed. CC removed the files marked 1997–2010 and put them aside to take with her to Litchfield. Since she couldn't transport all of the folders, these seemed the appropriate place to begin.

When they had almost given up searching for answers in the secret room, Charlie joined them. He had learned very little from the servants, but was convinced they weren't hiding anything. They believed the earl was nothing more than an influential man who had important friends, and they served him without question.

"This has been a relatively unproductive afternoon," Alex said as the four gathered in CC's sitting room.

"Maybe so, but we're not finished yet," said CC. "I'm going to call Flash. Maybe he'll be more forthcoming this time."

"Then why don't we leave and let you do your work," Charlie suggested. He kissed CC lightly on the cheek."

"We'll see you later," said Alex as the three left the room. CC sat down by the phone. She'd call her mother and Flash first. After that, she'd find a way to tell Bud her feelings for him had changed. Preferring to tackle Flash last, she was thankful when Mary picked up the phone. "Hi, Mom," she said cheerfully.

"Morning, honey."

"Over here it's good evening. How are you?"

"I'm fine. Flash and I talked a good part of the night, and though I can't say I approve of his deception over the years, I believe I understand why he kept his relationship with your father from us."

"Well, I'm glad you get it. I'm not sure I'll ever be able to overlook that he reported to William for years."

"CC, I certainly can't control your feelings, and this matter is between you and Flash, but I do believe that when you have the time to sit and talk with him, you'll understand his motives."

"Then after I speak with you, I'll talk with him. I realize we can't spend hours on the phone, but maybe if he answers a few questions, it will be a start."

"That won't be a problem because Flash isn't here at the moment."

CC looked at her watch. "But it's only eight-thirty. Has he gone to the office already?"

"Not exactly."

"Then where is he?"

"I'm really not sure."

CC was annoyed. "Come on, Mother. I didn't expect you to keep things from me, and I can't believe you don't know where Flash is."

"Think about what you said, CC. Why would I know where Flash is? I haven't known where he was going for years. Every time I thought he was on a routine business trip having to do with the club, he was off on some international adventure."

CC realized her mother was right. "I know, and I apologize, Mom, but I need to talk with him. Do you have any idea when he'll be home?"

"None whatsoever. Like I told you, I don't know where he went. He called the airport to have the plane fueled last night and left this morning about six. He told me that recent developments necessitated the trip, and he also said that what he was doing was in everyone's best interest."

"That sounds familiar." CC frowned. "When you hear from him, would you please tell him I need to talk with him as soon as possible?"

"I will, dear. Is there an emergency I should know about?"

"No. I'm hoping he'll be able to fill in some missing pieces to the puzzle for me, and speaking of a puzzle, did you get the diary?"

"I did, and I spent the day reading. I must say, I've done quite a lot of crying. In fact, I'm rather astonished that your father and our relationship in Paris would affect me so deeply after all these years."

"I'm so sorry I had to ask you__"

"Don't be silly. Reading this diary was the best thing for me. I loved, no, I still do love your father very deeply, and the memories are beautiful. Over the years I tried so hard to forget William, when I should have forgiven him and remembered what we had together."

"What about Flash?"

"I can't explain it exactly, but the diary has also shown me how much I love Flash; not in the same way I loved your father, but very deeply. You and I couldn't have asked for a better man to care for us. I want you to remember that regardless of what happens between you and Flash over the next few weeks. He loves you as much as William loved you. So try to understand what happened and forgive him for deceiving you. At the very least, he deserves your compassion."

"Your point's well taken, Mom, and if I ever get the chance to talk with Flash, I assure you, I'll remember what you said."

"Are you being sarcastic, CC?"

"I suppose I am. I don't mean to sound cynical, it's just—"

"I understand, but remember what I told you. Flash never did anything to hurt you in his life. What he did was what he felt would be best for you and for me, and while we're on the subject, why don't you give up this investigation of yours and come home? Run the Knights and stop trying to dig into William and Flash's business."

"Are you telling me to give up my title and inheritance? Is that your advice?"

"I don't know, CC. I fluctuate from one hour to the next. All I know for sure is that I want you to be happy. Marry Bud and have grandchildren for me. Be a baseball executive, if that makes you happy. Or if you choose to be the Countess of Litchfield, accept your legacy and live in England."

"But I can't combine both lives? Is that what you're saying?"

"You know you can't, but then I shouldn't try to influence your decision. You must weigh all of your alternatives carefully and decide which way you want to go. Believe me, I realize how difficult this will be for you."

CC sighed. *If you only knew.* With Charlie's emergence on the scene, the waters had become even more muddied. However, she'd already made one determination among the many she would be called upon to make: she would never marry Bud, but her mother didn't need to know; at least not yet. "What about the diary?" she asked.

"Most of the entries were personal. When William and I met, I thought he was in France on a military assignment, but now I'm not so sure. Before I read the diary, I was under the impression we spent every minute of the day and night together, but that was obviously not the case. He left the room without me for several hours at least four different times. Once he referred to a committee meeting he had to attend, and on another occasion he spoke of six business acquaintances he needed to see. He told me the meetings were arranged long before we met. I suppose I wasn't concerned with what he was doing; I only cared that he wasn't with me."

"Do you have any idea who he met with?"

"I could only find one name, and he mentioned him before two different meetings. He was going to the house or office, I'm not sure which, of Andre Lurcat."

CC wondered if this was the Frenchman who was one of the original committee members. "Did William leave a number for an apartment or a location where he could be reached?"

"Not specifically, but he mentioned Quai d'Orsay. I remember because I asked if he was meeting anywhere near the Louvre. I thought I might walk over with him and visit the museum while he conducted business."

"Did you tag along?"

"No. William didn't know how long his meeting would last, so he thought I should wait for him in the room. It was too beautiful to say inside, so I took a long walk along the Seine."

"Any idea how long he was gone?"

"Just a minute, let me find the entry for that day." CC waited. "I found it," Mary said excitedly. "William was gone for exactly five hours and thirteen minutes."

"You can be that specific?"

"Absolutely. You see, I was in love and I missed your father every second he was away."

CC laughed. "I'm sure you did. Anything else, Mom?"

"I did find one other entry that might be important. William mentioned a German several times, but only by nationality. He said the man was from Munich."

"That fits. Did he say anything about Flash?"

"Not in the diary, but last night Flash told me that he was in Paris when I met your father for the first time."

"He didn't see you?

"He says he didn't know William had a girlfriend. I believe him. I think he was as honest as he could be, given the restrictions—"

"Restrictions?"

"He told me there are certain things he can't reveal because they're classified."

"Do you think his trip today might have something to do with this classified information?"

"Possibly, but I told you before, he didn't tell me where he was going or what he was planning to do."

CC knew her mother had told her all she could, so she changed the subject. "Are you and Flash still planning to come to Indianapolis for the opener?"

"As far as I know we are."

"Good. And Mom, please don't worry. Flash and I will work things out."

"I hope so. I love you, honey."

"I love you too. I'll talk with you tomorrow."

CC hung up and looked at the clock on the desk. She had to hurry if she wanted to catch Bud before his meeting began. With the nine-hour difference between Scotland and LA, there was no time to waste. She went to her bedroom and located the pad where she had jotted down Bud's hotel information. She thought about calling his cell, but if his meeting had begun earlier than usual, she didn't want to interrupt him.

For a few moments she hesitated, thinking that perhaps a call of this sort right before an important meeting might not be appropriate, but she couldn't procrastinate any longer, despite the butterflies in her stomach. She punched in the number. The phone rang four times and with each ring, she was more nervous. She was about to hang up when Bud answered. "Bud," she said breathlessly, "I was afraid you'd already left for breakfast. Am I disturbing you?"

"CC, what a pleasant way to start the day. I had just shut the door when I heard the phone. I rushed back in to answer."

"Would you rather I call back later so you don't miss breakfast?"

"Not at all. You're better than breakfast any day. What's up?"

CC wavered. *Do I really want to end their relationship on the phone?* She quickly answered her own question: *Yes, I have to be honest and there's no use procrastinating.* "I need to talk with you, Bud," she said.

"That sounds ominous."

"Since your call last night, I've done a great deal of thinking. I realize that it's not fair for me to let you believe we'll ever get married."

"Are you saying you don't want to marry me?"

"I'm saying that for several years our timing's been off, and now it's too late to go back to where we were and make our relationship permanent."

"Because of your career?"

"For many reasons, my career among them."

"What other reasons?"

"My feelings for one. This trip and my father's death have shown me I need some space and freedom to get to know myself better. In the past few days I've begun to realize there's more to life than baseball and the Knights. It may sound like a cliché, but I've discovered that the world's a big place, and I want to know more about what's out here."

"Haven't I been telling you for some time that your job is not everything?"

"You have, and didn't I tell you that same thing about your job just a few years ago? But I didn't call to argue with you. Saying this is very difficult for me, and I just want you to understand, or at least try to absorb what I'm telling you."

"So you want space to explore other possibilities in life? Is there another reason you don't want to marry me?"

CC couldn't lie. "There is, but I don't want you to consider this the primary reason for my actions. It's merely a catalyst that made me move more quickly than I might have otherwise."

"Another man?"

"I'm not really sure. I know I have strong feelings for a man I met over here, and I can't explore those emotions without being honest with you first. I can't lie to you and pretend that circumstances between you and me haven't changed. But Bud, our relationship has been deteriorating for months, maybe for years, but we didn't take the time to stop and look at what was happening. We were both so damn busy with our professional lives. Maybe that's why we're in trouble; why we haven't been able to get things right."

"And this man?"

"I just told you, he's only one factor among many, but he has shown me that what you and I share is no longer enough for me. I want more, and you deserve more than a part-time relationship when I can fit you into my busy schedule."

"So this is it? Four years plus, and a phone call ends our relationship for good?"

"I'm afraid so. I didn't want to tell you this over the phone, but heaven knows when we'll be able to talk in person."

"Are you absolutely sure this is what you want?"

"Bud, I'm not absolutely sure of anything. My life's upside down and I'm in a state of flux."

"Then why do this now? Are you thinking about staying in England?"

"I have no idea, but I haven't ruled out anything. I'm weighing my options and trying to survive from day to day, and you mean so much to me. I can't string you along."

Bud's bitterness gave way to despair. "Do you know how much I love you?"

"I love you too, Bud, but I'm not sure the way I love you is enough to make a relationship work for the rest of our lives. I'm truly sorry."

"So what do you want me to do?"

"I want you to go on and meet someone else, someone who will fit into your life and be everything to you that I can't be, for whatever reason. This may sound trite and corny, but I want you to be my friend. I'd hate to think of a life without you around in some capacity."

"But you want me around on your terms."

"Maybe it's selfish, but yes."

"And your decision's final?"

"It is." CC began to cry softly as she said the words.

"Are you leaving the door open?"

"No, at least not in the way you would like."

There was silence on the other end as Bud obviously tried to pull himself together. "I'll try to do what you want," he said quietly.

"Then I'll talk with you in a few weeks."

There was no response, so CC hung up. She lay back on the pillows and cried.

CHAPTER TWENTY-ONE

During tea CC did her best to retain her composure. She told Charlie, Tony, and Alex about her discussion with her mother and about Flash's sudden, mysterious trip. Throughout the conversation, she avoided Charlie's eyes. When tea was over, he took her hand and pulled her up from the couch. He turned to Alex and Tony. "If you two don't mind, CC and I are going for a walk."

"Of course," Alex said. "It will do you both good to get outside for a while. Tony and I will play billiards while you're gone."

CC and Charlie strolled hand and hand down the same path they had followed the day before. As they crossed the pasture, they saw fewer sheep, but the flies were just as bothersome. They walked across the footpath at the end of Loch Nan Lann and strolled quietly down the path toward the log where they had spent such a blissful interlude twenty-four hours before. Though neither talked of their destination, they both knew where they were headed. When they reached the spot where they had wandered off the trail the day before, Charlie led CC down to the shore. They sat on the log, and he put his arm around her protectively. She rested her head on his shoulder.

"Do you want to tell me about your talk with Bud? I can see how upset you are."

CC began to cry. "It was terribly difficult and I hurt him so much."

"Was your call premature? Do you feel you made a mistake?"

"No. When I hung up I was even more certain that what I did was right. There really isn't a future for Bud and me and he deserves to know it so he can get on with his life. It's not fair to keep him waiting in the wings."

"But it has to hurt you deeply. You two have been together for a long time."

"Almost five years, but I'm really all right. I'm just concerned about Bud."

"Did you tell him about us?"

"I was honest with him. He asked me if there was anyone else and I told him about you. I told him we'd made no commitment, but I needed to be able to explore my feelings for you without deceiving him. I also made it clear that you're not the reason for our breakup"

"Did he believe you?"

"I think he heard me, but I don't think he truly understood. My news obviously came as a shock."

"He had no idea you were having problems?"

"I don't know. Last night when we talked, he insinuated that all was not wonderful between us, but I don't think he wanted to believe to what extent."

"And you feel guilty?"

"I guess that's part of it."

"Is there anything I can do to help you get through this?"

"You're doing it right now. You're letting me talk without putting any pressure on me."

"And I have no intention of doing so. Take your time. If and when you're ready, I'll be waiting."

CC kissed Charlie on the cheek and nestled against him. "I appreciate that." They sat quietly and watched the water lap the shoreline.

"Are you ready to go back and get ready for dinner?" Charlie asked as the sun dipped behind the trees and the first vestiges of twilight emerged.

"Is it that late already?"

"It's nearly seven. By the time we get back to the lodge, it will be seven-thirty."

"Then let's go, and Charlie, thank you." As they walked back, CC felt a strange sensation that someone was watching them. She considered telling Charlie about her feelings, but decided that he would think she was paranoid. After all, as he had told her, they were out in nowhere on her own property. She put aside her fears and enjoyed his company as they walked back through the meadow.

✵ ✵ ✵

Dinner was relaxing and as Alex, Tony, and Charlie bantered, CC began to recover from the afternoon ordeal. They made plans to leave Knockie early, stop by Glencoe, and drive to Litchfield. After dinner Alex wanted to play bridge. CC hadn't played since college, but she read the bridge columns in the newspapers whenever she had a chance and was willing to be a fourth. She was surprised how quickly the game came back to her, and as they played, she relaxed even more.

The evening turned out to be enjoyable after all. It was almost midnight when Charlie suggested that they all get some sleep. She said good night to Alex and Tony, who went upstairs to pack before going to bed. Charlie walked her to her door and kissed her on the cheek. He held her close to him. "Sleep well, and I'll see you early."

"Thank you for a relaxing evening with no demands."

"I told you, I'm willing to proceed on your timetable."

Not knowing if there would be time before they left in the morning, she opened her father's safe and removed the bundles of money. *There's certainly no reason for me to keep all this cash around,* she reflected as she packed them in her suitcase. *Better it is deposited in the London account collecting interest.* Once again she was mystified. Why would her father need to keep such an enormous amount of money in the Highlands of Scotland or at Litchfield, for that matter?

She removed several files she thought might provide pertinent information in the days to come, took the box of loose photos she had set aside to go through at a later date, and removed the photo album and jewelry she had deposited there upon her arrival. She packed these with the file folders she had previously taken from the communications room in the suitcase with the cash.

She got into bed and turned off the light, but though she tried to turn off her thoughts, she continued to dwell on her conversation with Bud. She knew breaking up with him was the right thing for both of them, but she was painfully aware that she'd hurt him deeply. Over and over she relived the conversation in her mind and questioned the way she had broken the news. *Could I have made it any easier for him? Should I have waited and talked with him in person? Am I giving up a long-term relationship for an incredibly passionate short-term fling?* The thoughts and questions kept coming and sleep wouldn't come.

And then there was Charlie. She couldn't believe she'd actually made love with him after knowing him for less than a day. That wasn't like her, and she was embarrassed. Could

Charlie think she was easy? That thought made her laugh. This was 2011. Was the term "easy" even used anymore? She remembered Flash's warnings when she was a teenager and just beginning to date. They were having a father-daughter talk when he sternly counseled her that the last thing she would want was a reputation for being "easy." Still, she couldn't help but wonder if Charlie thought less of her for succumbing to his charms so soon after they were introduced.

Try though she might, sleep wouldn't come. Thoughts of Charlie once again gave way to concerns for Bud, and then anguish over Bud was replaced by strong feelings for Charlie and memories of their lovemaking by the loch.

At two, when sleep was still a distant hope, CC admitted defeat. She knew what she wanted. Why was she wasting time? She threw back the covers, got up, and donned her robe and slippers. Trying to make as little noise as possible, she stealthily stole out of her suite and tiptoed down the stairs, hoping that her servants wouldn't hear her stirring and come to see if she needed anything. When she arrived at Charlie's door, she hesitated. "It's too soon," she whispered and turned back toward the stairs. She was halfway there when she changed her mind once again. *What the hell am I doing?* she asked herself. *Why am I waiting? What difference could a couple of days mean? Am I punishing myself because I disappointed Bud so terribly? And if so, why?*

When she could come up with no logical reasons for not being with Charlie, she turned back to his door and knocked softly. She listened carefully. Hearing nothing, she knocked again. Thinking she heard movement in the room, she waited nervously. After several minutes, Charlie came to the door. "May I come in?" she asked.

"Sure, are you all right?"

"I am now," she answered as she put her arms around Charlie's neck and raised her lips to his.

"Are you sure?"

"Positive!" Charlie swept her into his arms and carried her to the bed. As he laid her on the satin sheets, her robe fell away. Charlie took off his own robe and lay down beside her. He kissed her hungrily, and she responded with equal ardor, kissing all the sensitive parts of his body as he sighed with pleasure. This time she was in charge and his enjoyment was her desire. She rolled on top of him, easing herself down, all the time kissing him and moving seductively until she erupted in pleasure that equaled the passion she had felt the afternoon before. As her body twisted in exquisite agony, she rolled over and pulled Charlie on top of her. She wrapped her legs around him and lifted her hips to meet his. Suddenly he moaned and shuddered. His body stiffened and he cried out her name. CC held him tightly and began to cry.

"Sweetheart, have I hurt you? Are you all right?" Charlie whispered.

"Wonderful," she sobbed, "wonderful." Charlie held her tightly as her tears subsided, and she fell asleep wrapped in his arms. As the sun came over the horizon, he kissed her awake. They made love again. Satisfied and happy, they lay quietly, savoring their intimacy. They had just drifted off to sleep when there was a knock on the door. "Oh my God!" CC whispered as she pulled the covers over her head.

"Who is it?" Charlie called out.

"It's your sister. Are you two going to get out of bed and get moving or am I going to have to come in and drag you to the car?" CC stuck her head out from under the covers and looked at the clock. It was seven, the time they had planned to leave.

"We'll be right there," Charlie answered.

"Did you have to say we?"

"I imagine she went to your room first, and when you were nowhere to be found, she figured things out for herself. She's hardly dense about these matters."

"Do you think the servants heard her tell us to get out of bed?"

"I'm sure servants knew where you were before Alex found out. It's hard keep a secret around here, but Alex is right, we should get moving."

"What if we ignore her and spend the entire day right here?" CC murmured.

"Marvelous as that sounds, we have a lot accomplish today. Why don't we call this time out of bed a short respite and you can resume your seduction tonight at Litchfield. Shall we say your room at eleven?"

CC laughed. "My seduction? What about you? Will you be up for another rendezvous?"

"I guarantee it." Charlie laughed at CC's double entendre.

"That sounds gratifying, but before we begin our little tryst, I want to go to the chapel and retrieve those papers."

"You mean another night of incredible passion must take a back seat to business?"

"Didn't you just put business before pleasure? And I wouldn't call it a back seat, merely a momentary postponement. I have several calls to make today and those papers are important."

"CC, I'm teasing. Of course they're important, but I can't keep my hands off you, and I seriously doubt if I can wait until eleven."

"You mean a quickie before dinner might be in order?"

"Absolutely, and now that you mention it, how about a quickie right now?"

"Oh Lord. I think you could do it again."

"Unfortunately we don't have time for me to prove my prowess. Get up, slug-a-bed."

CC got up, put on her robe and peeked out of Charlie's door. There was no one in sight, so she raced up the stairs. She took a quick shower and dressed in her freshly washed jeans and sweater. She beat Charlie downstairs where Alex, Tony, and Henry were waiting.

"Are your bags ready, my lady?" Henry asked.

"They're by the bedroom door." Hoping she wouldn't blush, CC turned to Alex. "I'll be ready to go as soon as I have a cup of coffee."

"Coffee's been waiting for an hour," Alex teased, and CC felt her face turn red.

"Will you join me for a quick cup?"

"I certainly will. Tony, why don't you help Henry load the car and see what you can do to get Charlie moving? He must have had a rough night to sleep this late." CC reddened again as she entered the dining room.

Freeman had prepared scones and pastries to accompany the tea and coffee. CC poured the steaming brew and took a Danish. She and Alex sat at the table by the window over-looking the loch. "What a lovely place, and how my life has changed in the short time I've been here," she said.

"I take it you and Charlie rekindled your relationship?"

"We have, and Alex, thanks for not pushing."

"You're welcome. It was obvious you were upset yesterday afternoon. I'm smart enough to know you needed to solve your problems without my interference. I hoped you and Charlie could work things out, but if and when you were able to do so, it couldn't be because I wanted it."

"Well now everything's wonderful."

"And your plans?"

"No plans beyond today. That's the way it has to be. I have to take things a day at a time and see what happens."

"Perhaps that's for the best. Anyway, you look radiant."

"She is, and incredible too." Charlie came into the room and poured himself a cup of tea. He took a scone and joined them at the table.

"I was telling CC I'm happy you two are enjoying each other's company again."

"And how extraordinarily luscious this lady is." He put his coffee on the table and kissed CC.

"You're kind of enticing yourself."

"And you two are too much. If you could take five minutes and finish your coffee and tea, we could be on our way. I believe we're already forty-five minutes behind schedule because of your bedroom antics."

"I thought you approved."

"Oh I do, but not right now, so hurry. I'll go check our room once more."

CC sipped her coffee. "I can't remember ever feeling so relaxed and happy."

"Nor I," Charlie responded quietly.

Tony sauntered into the room. "Are you two ready. We'd best be off if we want to be at Litchfield before dinner."

CC hugged Mrs. Lauriston and thanked Freeman and Henry for a wonderful stay. She promised to return in the near future and planned to do so. Whatever decision she made, she would come back to see these kind people.

Before leaving, Charlie made arrangements for one of the Knockie staff to drive his car to Glencoe later that day. At eight, Tony pulled the Mercedes onto the lane leading away from Knockie while Mrs. Lauriston stood in the driveway waving her handkerchief. "She's a lovely person," CC said as she waved back.

"She certainly is, and she was obviously delighted you'll be returning to see her," said Charlie.

"Then we'll have to keep our word, won't we?" She grinned. "Maybe we could take another walk around the loch."

"That's a given." Charlie winked at her.

As they drove along the dirt drive toward the highway, CC experienced the same sensation she had the day before. She looked out of the windows, trying to spot a parked car or a person lurking in the trees, but she saw nothing. She considered mentioning her fears to Charlie, but as before and for the same reasons, she decided not to say anything.

They passed Fort Augustus and were heading toward Glencoe when CC took out her "to do" list. She looked at Charlie who dozed beside her and had an idea. Maybe she could combine a meeting with Norris in London with a night in her suite at the Ritz.

It was Monday, so the office would be open about four her time. She felt guilty for not calling over the weekend, *but I was busy,* she rationalized. She dreaded what she might hear, but she had to check on Jim and wanted to ask Leslie to make her return reservations through Chicago. She also needed to tell the staff about her plans to be in Indianapolis for the first home stand. She thought about calling Bud, but decided that wasn't a good idea. She had to leave him alone to work through his feelings. As promised, she would phone him from

Indianapolis. Her final call would be to her mother to see if she'd heard from Flash.

When they arrived at Glencoe, they all greeted Thomas, followed Charlie into the house and went to pick up the things they hadn't taken to Knockie. Instead of going to his rooms to get his bags, Charlie followed her into the suite. "When you're finished, I'd like to introduce you to little Charlie," he said.

"I'd love to meet him. Give me two minutes."

"Take your time. Alex doesn't move as quickly as we do, so we have a few extra minutes."

CC finished packing and followed Charlie down the hall and into a brightly decorated nursery. Cut outs of circus animals covered the walls and toys were scattered everywhere. Sitting on a blanket amid a large conglomeration of stuffed animals was a darling red-haired, freckled-faced baby. Charlie walked over and lifted the child. "This is Lady Litchfield, Charlie. Can you say hello?"

Charlie looked back over his father's shoulder. "Hi, Charlie. I'm CC," CC crooned and tickled the baby's cheek. Charlie giggled. "He's gorgeous, Charlie. I can see why you're so proud of him."

"He takes after his mother. At least he has her looks."

"May I hold him? I haven't had much experience with babies, but I don't think he'll break, will he?"

"Hardly." He handed Charlie to CC. Not a bit shy, Charlie pulled on CC's earring. "Mama," he gurgled.

CC was obviously flustered. "CC," she said smiling.

"Mama," little Charlie persisted.

"CC," Charlie repeated.

"CC." Little Charlie finally seemed to get the idea.

"Well, that took a while, but I'm sure you'll be the best of friends after this." Charlie took little Charlie from CC and kissed him on the top of the head. "See you later, pal." He handed him to Brenda. "Say good-bye to Da."

"Bye bye." Little Charlie waved and as they left, he was back on his blanket and playing with his toys.

"He's precious, Charlie."

"He's a good boy."

"And he'll be okay here without you for a short time?"

"Of course. He's pampered here and even more at Dunollie. I doubt he'll know I'm away."

"In that case, let's go meet Tony and Alex."

"In a minute. First, would you come to my room while I take care of something?

"Sure." She followed Charlie into his suite. The sitting room was warm and comfortable, unmistakably a man's room with massive, dark furniture. Royal blue couches picked up the blue in the plaid curtains, and there were personal knick-knacks scattered about. The room was Charlie.

"Come on," he urged as she stood and surveyed her surroundings. She followed him into his gigantic bedroom. Her eyes focused on a brass bedstead with a crown-draped canopy in the MacDonald plaid. She had no time to see anything else. Charlie swept her up in his arms and carried her to the bed. He laid her down gently and lay beside her.

"Charlie, you know we don't have time—"

He silenced her protest with a kiss, and CC could feel her body responding to his. "I know we don't." He laughed as he rolled off the bed and pulled her to a standing position. "I just wanted to give you a little preview of what awaits you when we come back to Glencoe. That way, if you think about leaving me and England, I can remind you."

CC laughed. "You're terrible. I thought you were going to make love to me."

"Oh, I am." He looked at his watch. "In exactly thirteen hours and thirty minutes, that is, unless I can figure out a way to get you alone before then."

"I'll work on that." CC straightened her clothes and her hair. "But we'd better head downstairs or Alex will be after us again."

"After you," Charlie teased. "I like the view from behind."

CHAPTER TWENTY-TWO

When they left Glencoe, Tony handed CC the phone. "Feel free to make whatever calls you'd like," he said. "We have one of those unlimited minute plans, or so Alex tells me."

"Hardly unlimited, darling, but since you never turn on your cell, which I imagine CC and Charlie can tell irritates me tremendously, you have enough minutes for CC to talk for hours without being charged for overage."

"I'm hoping my cell will be charged by the time I get home," CC said. "I took your advice, Alex. I'm hoping Hastings sent one of the servants to buy a converter. I should have asked when I first arrived, but I'm not used to having people ready to jump at my beck and call."

"It's truly a wonderful thing," Alex said. "Trust me. You'll get used to it very soon."

"I'm sure I will." CC smiled. "But before I change hats and become the baseball executive, I wondered if you and Tony would join Charlie and me for dinner at Litchfield tonight?"

Alex answered. "We'd love to, wouldn't we, Tony?"

"Absolutely. Besides the pleasure of your company, I could never resist John Claude's cooking. Why don't we drop you and Charlie at Litchfield, go home, get cleaned up, and return for cocktails?"

"That's a plan, but I should call Hastings or there might not be a meal to enjoy." She took out her address book and called the number for the servants' quarters at Litchfield.

"Litchfield Manor," she heard Hastings say.

"Good morning, Hastings."

"Good morning, my lady. I talked with Mrs. Lauriston earlier. She said you're on your way to Glencoe.

"We left Charlie's house a few minutes ago. We're headed to Litchfield and there are several things I'd like for you to do before we get there. First, would you let John Claude and Charles know I've invited Sir Anthony, Lady Alexandra, and Lady Alexandra's brother, Lord Timperley, for dinner?"

"What time would you like to dine?"

"Why don't we make it eight-thirty? That will give Sir Anthony and Lady Alexandra time to go to Chadlington and return."

"I'll tell John Claude. What else may I do for you?"

"Would you make two appointments for me? I want to meet with father's personal physician, the one who signed his death certificate, tomorrow morning if possible."

"Are you ill, my lady?"

"No, Hastings. I'd like to talk with the doctor about my father's health."

"I'm not sure he'll be able to provide the information you seek, but I'll make the appointment. Is there anything else?"

"Yes, call John Norris, my father's accountant? I'd like to meet with him on Wednesday if possible."

"I'll phone him right away."

"Good, and please call the Ritz. I'll be using my father's suite Wednesday night. The final request might not be as easy as the others. Stanley told me you might be able to arrange tickets for a musical."

"Any time you'd like to go."

"How about Wednesday evening?"

"Shall I arrange for a box for four?"

"Perfect. I'm inviting Sir Anthony, Lady Alexandra, and Charles."

"Would they like for me to arrange for a suite at the Ritz?"

"I have no idea if they'll need one. Please hold on for a minute. "I didn't even ask, but would you all like to see a show in London Wednesday night? If so, Charlie, would you be my escort?"

"I would be honored," Charlie said, smiling.

"We would love to join you," said Alex.

"Shall I ask Hastings to arrange a room for you at the Ritz?"

Tony answered. "We have our own townhouse in Kensington, but thank Hastings for asking."

"We'll need the box for four, Hastings. The Chadlingtons have their own place in the city."

"Then I shall make all of your appointments and reservations. Do you have any idea what time you expect to arrive at Litchfield?

"Hold on, I'll ask. Tony. Any idea when we'll be home?"

"If we stop at the Cavendish Hotel for an early lunch, I'd say around five."

"About five, Hastings."

"I'll have tea waiting."

"And one more thing, could you please have a guest suite prepared? Lord Timperley is helping me with some of my father's business matters, so he'll be staying at Litchfield instead of Chadlington." CC winked at Charlie.

"Of course."

"I appreciate your help, Hastings. I'll see you later."

"Are you sure you want to use the suite at the Ritz?" Charlie asked. "I have my own townhouse in the city. It's in Mayfair very near the theater district, so if you'd prefer, we could stay there instead of in a rented suite at the Ritz."

"It's not rented. My father owns his rooms at the hotel."

"That's impossible," Tony said incredulously. "I realize it's different in the U.S., but in London I don't believe the Ritz sells suites."

"Apparently an exception was made in William's case. My father owned the suite, and for the moment, it's mine."

"This gets more interesting by the hour," Charlie said. "Under the circumstances, I agree, the Ritz is the place to stay."

"Before you make another call, CC, I want you to know we'll be stopping for lunch in about thirty minutes," Tony said. "I know it's barely noon, but the Cavendish is another of our favorite luncheon places. We thought you'd enjoy the food and a few minutes to stretch your legs."

"The Cavendish is right next to Chatsworth, home to the Duke and Duchess of Devonshire," Alex explained. "You'll meet them eventually, and the house is by far one of the loveliest in England. I wish we had time to stop in so you could see the fabulous art and antiques in the collection."

"Maybe next time. And early or not, I'm famished. However, if you don't mind, before we stop, I have one more call to make."

"Make all the calls you wish," said Tony. "As Alex told you, I never use the thing."

CC opened her wallet and took out the paper with the number of the bank in Switzerland. She also removed the code necessary to access the account. As she dialed, she wondered what question the banker would ask. Would she really be able to answer as easily as Caulfield said she would?"

An operator with a French accent answered. "Bank of Zurich. How may I serve you?"

"This is Caroline Cleveland, Countess of Litchfield. I would like to speak with the bank manager."

"Of course, Your Ladyship, one moment please."

Almost immediately, she heard a man's voice. "Lady Litchfield, I've been expecting your call. I am Max Amberg, manager of the bank."

"I'm pleased to speak with you, Mr. Amberg. Mr. Caulfield, my father's solicitor, instructed me to call to ascertain the balance in my father's account."

"There are in fact two accounts, Lady Litchfield. One is personal and the other is a business account."

Caulfield hadn't mentioned two accounts. "I only have numbers for one," she said.

"That is correct. If you provide that number and answer two questions, we will provide information about the second account. All of your father's personal fortune will be yours as soon as you sign the necessary papers. At that time we'll give you specific instructions regarding the funds in the business account. The earl assured us that you would abide by his desires."

"I'm certain there won't be a problem." CC was baffled and wondered how her father could be so sure she'd cooperate.

"If you'll provide the necessary numbers, I'll ask the questions," Amberg was saying. "If your answers verify your identity, we will proceed."

"Of course." CC read the numbers Caulfield had given her. She wondered if she should have waited until she was alone to make this call, but decided that there was no need. Charlie was napping again and Tony had closed the partition between the front and back seats.

"Very good, Amberg said. "Now the questions: Please tell me the name of the maid who first cared for you when you moved to Arizona?"

"Ethel Gazuba," CC said without hesitation.

"Thank you, and the final question: Please tell me your first telephone number, no area code required."

How would my father know that? CC wondered, but she said, "2539358."

"And you said you would like the balances in both accounts, my lady?" Amberg asked.

I guess I passed the test, CC thought as she answered, "that's correct."

"Of course. In the personal account, which contains funds that will be available to you as soon as you formally accept your title and inheritance, there is a total of—would you like this in dollar amounts?"

"Please."

"At the current rate of exchange, the account contains $232,374,382 dollars and forty-seven cents."

CC tried to sound composed, "And in the business account?"

"The balance in that account is $315,432,789 dollars and twenty-two cents. However, there are restrictions attached to that money."

CC could barely talk. She dealt with vast amounts of money in salaries and benefits on a daily basis, but that money wasn't hers. Even without the money in the Bank of England, she was an incredibly wealthy woman. "Restrictions?" she managed to choke out.

"Yes, but these will only be revealed when you have signed the necessary papers."

"And accepted my title."

"That's correct. If you reject your inheritance, the money reverts to the estate and will then be claimed by your father's next closest relative, the one who will inherit his title."

CC regained her composure. "I see. Well, Mr. Amberg, you can be sure I'll be in touch as soon as I've made my decision about my future plans. Thank you for your help."

"You're very welcome, my lady, and if you need anything more, please don't hesitate to call. We're here to serve you."

"I will, thank you." Charlie was still asleep, and she tapped him gently.

"Are we there?" he asked sleepily.

"Not yet, and I'm sorry to awaken you, but I need to tell you something rather startling."

"Startling? Does it have anything to do with your phone call?"

"Caulfield told me my father had a Swiss bank account. He suggested that I call to find out the balance. It turns out that he has two accounts, one personal and one for business. The money in the personal account becomes mine if I accept my entire inheritance, title, property, etc. The other account has restrictions placed on it, but I won't know those until or if I sign the acceptance papers."

"That not unusual, but you seem upset."

"Stunned is a better word. There's over $232 million in the personal account and nearly $316 million in the business account."

"You're not serious! How could William amass so much money? Is the business account connected to the Committee of Seven?"

"I have no idea on either account; pun intended. Maybe his diary and those papers behind the altar will give us a clue."

"I certainly hope so."

Before Charlie could respond, Alex opened the partition. "We're at the Cavendish."

"Good. I'm famished," CC said as Tony pulled off the highway into the gravel driveway in front of the hotel.

CC was glad to be out of the car and able to stretch, the four went into the lobby through doors framed by rose-covered trellises. The owner, Eric Marsh, greeted them at the top of the stairs. He obviously considered himself Tony's friend. While the men talked, Alex accompanied CC to the lady's lounge. As she combed her hair and touched up her makeup, CC continued to think about the enormous amount of money in her father's account. She had to know how he'd become so wealthy. She was so deep in thought that she heard nothing of what Alex was saying until she heard: "Are you coming?"

"I'm sorry, Alex. I was thinking."

"Obviously, is there anything wrong?"

"No, and I didn't mean to ignore you. I have a great deal on my mind."

"I know. Believe me, I didn't say anything important. Shall we join the men?"

CC ordered two first courses rather than an entrée, fresh salmon and scallop tartar flavored with chives, olive oil, and lime, followed by English asparagus with hollandaise. There was just enough food to fill her up and give her renewed energy. As she ate, she only half listened to the conversation taking place around her. While Alex and Tony talked with Eric and the excellent chef who came to greet two of his regulars, she tried to absorb and make some sense of all of her discoveries over the past several days.

A few times she tried to return to the conversation at hand, but she wasn't able to concentrate for long. All she could think of was William. She was driven to find out how he made all that money? She really needed to talk with Flash, but where was he?

When the meal was over, she realized she knew nothing of what had transpired. She followed Alex out of the dining room, more anxious than ever to get to Litchfield and to her father's diary. She had to have answers.

CC dozed off and on during the ride from Cavendish to Litchfield. At four, she assumed her staff would be in the office and asked Tony for the phone again. Leslie had nothing to report. "I haven't seen anyone yet," she said.

"Any mail?"

"Nothing urgent. There's an owner's meeting scheduled for the first week in June. The commissioner' secretary emailed a preliminary agenda."

"Where's the meeting?"

"Philadelphia. Not too far from Bud, huh?" CC ignored the comment. She had no intention of telling Leslie about her and Bud over the phone, and especially not in front of Charlie. "Have you talked with him?"

"Yesterday." CC quickly changed the subject. "If there's nothing pressing, would you transfer me to Wes?"

"Right away. Oh, there is one thing I forgot to tell you. We signed George Davis."

"Wonderful! Within the budget limits?"

"I guess so. All Bob said was 'mission accomplished, and you'll be pleased,' so I guess the news is good."

"Would you get in touch with him for me? Tell him I'll call get him around four o'clock his time. He should be off the field by then."

"Will do. Will you be calling me back?"

"I'll check in with you this afternoon. If you need me, call Litchfield and leave a message. We're en route there now. Beginning tomorrow you can reach me on my cell."

Leslie ignored the second part of CC's statement. Who's 'we'?" she asked.

"Never mind. Leave a message if anything comes up."

"Sounds very mysterious. I gather you can't talk."

"Not at the moment, so transfer me to Wes, will you?"

"Right away. Talk to you later."

"Is everything all right?" Charlie asked.

"So far." She heard Wes' voice. "Happy Monday," she responded to his gruff tone.

"If you say so!"

"My, aren't we cheery? Bad weekend?"

"Bad Monday."

"It's awfully early for to be a terrible day, and you sound miserable. Could the source of your problem be our friend Jim?"

"It is, but to tell you the truth, I have no idea what he's doing this time."

"Is he in the office?"

"That's the point. He called and told Susan he has a brunch appointment with the Taylors."

"You're kidding. Why? What's he up to?"

"I don't know, but whatever it is, I'm sure he's out to cause trouble."

"Trouble for me, you mean? He probably scheduled the meeting after I spoke with him late Friday afternoon. He must have given the Taylors a convincing reason for getting together; otherwise I can't imagine why they'd agree to see him. Where was the appointment? Do you know?"

"Susan wasn't sure. All he said was expect him in the office sometime early afternoon."

"Use your sources to find out what he's up to."

"I'm already working on it. I hope to know more later today. I hate to say it, CC, but the man is using the time you're away to undermine your authority."

"Don't worry, I can handle Jim Oats."

"I'm sure you can, but you don't need this kind of grief while you're trying to deal with personal matters."

"I don't need it at all, but then none of us does. Everything will be fine, you'll see. Anything else happening?"

"I suppose Leslie told you we signed Davis. We're working on a special article for the first issue of *The Lance*."

"Good. How did the press react to the signing?"

"So far, positively. They're saying our changes for finishing first improved considerably."

"I hope they're right. When I get to Litchfield, I'll call you with the fax number. Send me the columns if you would. There's a computer in my father's room. I'll see if I can long on and bring the articles up on line, but I can't use the laptop. I still don't have a converter to charge the battery, though I hope to get one soon."

"Okay. I'll also fax a copy of the report we received from Doc Markaman this morning."

"Report about whom?"

"Willy Norton. He has several cancerous lesions in his mouth."

"Oh, God! Is he a chewer?"

"Big time."

"What's the prognosis?

"I'm not sure Doc knows yet. Do you want me to call him this morning?"

"I'll catch up with him later. Do Bob and Spike know?"

"The memo from Doc indicates he copied both of them."

"But you don't know what kind of treatment he'll undergo."

"No, but we're trying to keep the news from the press until we can answer all their questions.'

"Good idea. Keep me posted."

"I will. Anyone else you want to talk with?"

"Walter. I want check on season ticket sales."

"Then I'll talk with you this afternoon. In the meantime, I'll put on my spy hat."

CC chuckled. "Sounds familiar."

"What does?"

"Nothing. Put me through to Walter, and thanks."

"No problem." The phone clicked.

"Walter, CC. How's everything? What are our current season ticket numbers?"

"We're currently at 28,381. There was a rush after the announcement of the Davis signing."

"Good. We'll need the extra attendance to pay his salary."

"I talked with Bob. He did a damn good job with the contract. We were afraid we might get caught up in deferred payments, but he managed to avoid complicated financing."

"Congratulate him for me. I'll call him later, but you'll probably talk to him first."

"He's supposed to call me in a few minutes. We have a few more incentive numbers to work through."

"Then he was able to use incentives?" CC had always been an advocate of incentives. She liked a player to earn his salary, and knowing he'd make more money if he succeeded was a good idea.

"The contract's loaded with them."

"Wonderful. Anything else?"

"Nothing important. Will you be calling back later?"

"Before the office closes."

"Then put me on your list of people to talk to."

"I will. Have a good day."

"I'm amazed!" Charlie said when CC hung up. "You handled yourself like an expert businesswoman."

"Funny thing, I am a businesswoman, but I've had quite enough business for one day, I'm going to take a nap."

CC dozed during the last part of the trip. It seemed like minutes rather than hours passed when Charlie whispered, "we're at Litchfield."

"Home at last," CC said when they pulled up to the house, and much to her surprise, she really did feel at home.

CHAPTER TWENTY-THREE

Hastings came rushing out of the front door as Tony stopped the car in the gravel driveway "Is he all right?" Alex asked. "He looks terribly upset."

"He certainly does, Hastings. What's wrong?" CC asked, feeling anxious when she saw the distress on her butler's face.

"My lady, I'm so glad you're here. We received a call from Knockie about twenty minutes ago. Henry tried Sir Anthony's phone, but—"

"It was busy," Alex said. "I'm afraid I was talking."

What's the matter? CC said; her apprehension growing."

"There's been a fire. Everyone's safe, but your father's suite was destroyed by the flames."

CC couldn't believe what she was hearing; a fire at Knockie? "What about the rest of the house?" she asked.

"Lady Anne's suite was badly damaged but the rest of the house only suffered smoke damage. It miraculously survived the inferno. Henry says your father had a reinforced, fireproof floor put in several years ago. That's what kept the rest of the house from being totally destroyed." CC remembered Charlie telling her that William likely added a reinforced floor to hold weight of her safe. *A premonition of things to come?* she wondered.

"Do they have any idea how the fire started?" Tony asked.

"When Henry called, the inspector had made a cursory inspection, but it seems it was deliberately set.

"Arson?" CC was stunned. "Who would burn a hunting lodge out in the middle of the Scottish Highland? Suddenly she remembered the strange sensations she'd experienced when returning from her walk the day before and when they were leaving Knockie that morning. Could there really have been someone watching them and waiting for them to leave so he could burn William's suite?"

"They have no idea, my lady," Hastings was saying.

"But all of the staff is safe?"

"Yes. Mrs. Lauriston is shaken, but she wasn't physically hurt."

"Were they able to save anything in my father's rooms?"

"Nothing, but if you'd like to hear firsthand, here's Henry's cell number."

"I can't call the house?"

"No, the fire knocked out the phones and the electricity.

"Then I'll call Henry on his cell right away."

"Why would anyone want to damage such a lovely house?" Hastings asked.

"Someone who knew about my father's business dealings, which means we should be extra careful at Litchfield. If someone tried to burn Knockie to destroy the information in William's files, he could strike here too."

"Then we'll take additional precautions, my lady. We'll bring on more staff and notify the constable."

"Do whatever you think's necessary and let me know your plans. I'll feel better with Charlie here." CC suddenly realized that in her confusion after hearing of the fire at Knockie, she hadn't introduced her guest. "Hastings, forgive me for being rude. I don't know if you've met Lord Charles Timperley."

"I've not had the pleasure. Welcome to Litchfield, my lord. We've prepared a suite for you."

"Thank you, Hastings."

"Would you like to come in for tea?" CC asked Tony and Alex.

"No thank you," Tony said. "I'm sure you want to call Henry, and if we're going to get back here on time, we'd better be off. That is, if you still want us for dinner."

"Of course I do." CC kissed Alex and thanked Tony for being her chauffeur for the weekend. Richard removed CC and Charlie's luggage from the trunk, and Alex and Tony left, but not before promising to be back by eight.

"What do you suppose was in those files that made someone so anxious to destroy them?" CC asked Charlie as they entered the foyer.

"I have no idea, and I don't image we'll never know, since all of the documents have been burned."

"Not all of them. I packed the ones I thought might help in our search. Now I wish I'd packed more."

"Even though you have the files, they're coded. How do we decipher the code?"

"I'm counting on the diary and papers to provide the key. If not, there's Flash. I'm hoping he'll finally cooperate, but now I need to call Henry. Hastings will introduce you to Austen, who will get you settled in your room. I'll meet you back here for tea in a little while"

CC went to her sitting room and called Knockie. Mrs. Lauriston answered Henry's cell. As Hastings reported, everyone was fine. However, there was additional news. The inspector confirmed the fire was deliberately set. "Henry has more of the details, my lady. He accompanied the inspector to your father's suite. He's just returning now. Would you like to speak with him?"

"Yes. Thank you."

Henry came on the line. "My lady, the fire inspector completed his preliminary inspection."

"Does he know anything definitive?"

"He said the fire began in a closet in your father's sitting room."

"Oh my God!" *Whoever set the blaze had to know about the communications room, so it must have been someone involved with the Committee of Seven.*

"What is it? Are you all right?" Henry asked.

"I'm sorry. I was thinking how lucky you all were to escape safely and how fortunate the lower floors of the house were saved."

"I agree. I'll begin to solicit bids for rebuilding the third floor whenever you're ready."

"Start right away. Does the inspector know how the fire started?"

"He discovered an incendiary device that caused an electrical fire. Apparently there was a great deal of electronic equipment stored in the closet."

"They were my father's business computers."

"I had no idea. Could that be what the arsonist wished to destroy?"

"I wish I knew." Suddenly she felt sick. Had Flash come to Knockie and set the fire? Was he that eager to hide the business of the Committee of Seven? It fit. He was off on another of his mysterious trips, he'd been to Knockie before, and he knew what secrets the communications room held. CC hated herself for entertaining the thought, but she had to face the facts. Flash or one of the other members of the Committee of Seven, was the arsonist. *God, don't let it be Flash, let this me a figment of my imagination,* she silently prayed as she said, "hopefully we'll find out who did this."

"The inspector will return tomorrow. After he sifts through the rubble, we can begin the cleaning process. I have already enlisted the help of several of the young men from Whitebridge."

"Good, and Henry, please let me know if the inspector tells you anything more."

"I certainly will, my lady, and good evening."

CC hung up and immediately dialed her mother in Arizona. "Mom, have you heard from Flash?"

"And hello to you also, dear."

"I'm sorry. I didn't mean to be rude, but I've received terrible news. An arsonist has burned the top floor of Knockie, the floor that contained William's suite and his files."

"But what does that have to do with—? CC, you can't be serious! Surely you don't think Flash would do something like that?"

"I don't know what to think. I know he didn't want me to find out about his business transactions with William."

"But there's a great deal of difference between wanting to keep business dealings confidential and burning your father's lodge to prevent you from knowing about them."

"But what if he's here in England? Have you heard from him?"

"No, but that certainly isn't an indictment. He goes on trips and doesn't contact me for days."

"Yesterday when we left Knockie, I felt I was being watched, and I had the same sensation again this morning."

"You thought Flash was watching you?"

"No, but—"

"But what? CC, this is ridiculous. Are you forgetting you're talking about Flash? He would never do anything to hurt you."

"But would he do something if he thought he was protecting me?"

"I'm sure he would, but I don't think that includes burning your father's hunting lodge."

"I hope you're right, but at the moment I have a sick feeling in the pit of my stomach, and I'm afraid it won't go away until I've talked with Flash. As soon as you hear from him, please let him know I need to speak with him, and Mom, don't tell him what I told you. If my suspicions are unfounded, I don't want to upset him."

"That's exactly why I won't tell him. Your suspicions are groundless, and I won't allow Flash to be hurt by your accusations."

"But you'll tell him to call me?"

"As soon as he phones or comes home."

"I love you, Mom."

"I love you too, and so does Flash. Remember that, honey."
She hung up.

CC remained by the phone. She hadn't meant to be so accusatory and so abrupt with her mother, and she hated thinking negative thoughts about Flash, but he was definitely a suspect, and he knew she was looking for answers.

CC wanted to tell Charlie everything she'd learned, but she decided to calm down and unpack first. She was upset about Knockie and torn about her feelings about Flash, but her dinner guests would soon arrive and she had to get ready. *How British stiff-upper-lip,* she thought as she opened her suitcase and removed the diamond pendant. *No matter the problem, we do our duty and lie goes on.* She shook her head and chided herself for being so glib.

Her thoughts turned from duty to the dinner party she was having. She quickly realized she didn't have appropriate clothes for a dressy evening. *How ironic,* she thought, *most women choose jewelry to complement their outfits, but I have the jewelry and no outfit.* On a whim, she looked around the room. There was a second closet she hadn't opened. Surely William had disposed of Anne's clothing, "but why not check, just in case," she said aloud. *If there's nothing there, I'll have to make dinner less formal and take time to visit the Burlington Arcade before our evening at the theater.*

She opened the closet door and was amazed. The racks were full. "It was meant to be," she said when she saw she and Anne wore the same size. She glanced at the numerous cocktail dresses and selected a peach silk with a V neckline and a flared skirt. "Unquestionably apropos. After a quick shower, she dressed, put on the diamond pendant and went downstairs to tell Charlie about her discoveries.

Charlie wore a conservative suit instead of the kilt and tartan. He stood as CC entered the library. "You look gorgeous," he said. "I won't be able to keep my eyes off you. "

"Thank you and you look fantastic." Charlie bowed and grinned.

Almost immediately Richard came in carrying a silver tea tray and a plate of biscuits and scones. He placed them on the table. "Would you like for me to stoke the fire and add a few more logs?" he asked.

"Yes please, Richard. Thank you.

"Will there be anything else, Your Ladyship?" Richard asked when the fry was blazing.

"Not at the moment. Would you close the doors as you leave, and please tell Hastings I'll ring if I need anything, otherwise, unless there's a call from Henry or Mrs. Lauriston, I don't wish to be disturbed."

"Very good, Your Ladyship."

"What a wonderful idea, privacy at last," Charlie said as Richard closed the door. He gathered CC in his arms and kissed her. "Do you know how long I have wanted to do that?"

"About as long as I've wanted you to, but I didn't ask for privacy so you could kiss me."

"You mean you want to make love here and now?"

"Be serious, will you?"

"Oh, I am being serious."

"I'm sure you are, but you're going to have to wait. I asked to be left alone so we could talk without anyone overhearing us."

Charlie backed away with a look of dejection on his face. "You mean you dressed in that incredibly sexy dress, you smell like a flower garden, and you dismissed the servant so we could talk?"

"Charlie, please be serious? Come sit with me and have some tea."

"I'll sit across from you. That way I can look at your beautiful face and gorgeous body, and I won't be tempted to do anything more than talk."

"You're incorrigible."

"That seems to be your favorite adjective for me, but maybe you're right. So pour the tea and tell me whatever it is that's more important than making love."

As they drank their tea, CC told Charlie about Henry's news, her suspicions concerning Flash, and the disagreement with her mother. "I believe your mother's right," Charlie said when she was finished. "It sounds like you're jumping to conclusions and condemning Flash without real proof."

"Maybe, but I just have this feeling—"

"CC, you can't convict the man of arson without talking to him, and just because he's away hardly means that he's in Scotland setting fires."

"Then what do you suggest?"

"Wait and talk with Flash. See what he has to say."

"Should I confront him with my suspicions?"

"That's up to you, but I suggest you have proof before you accuse him."

"You sound exactly like my mother. I'll try to do as you both suggest, but it won't be easy."

"I know, but you don't want to do anything to ruin your relationship with Flash. It's possible he's innocent. Now why don't you come over here? We can take up where we left off before all this serious talk."

"However tempting you are, I'm going to refuse you yet again."

"Rejected twice? What's your excuse this time?"

"Plans for the evening."

"That's exactly what I want to discuss, so come closer and let me give you a preview of the night ahead; that is, after Alex and Tony leave us alone."

"My amorous darling," CC teased, "if you'll wait a while longer, I have a few things to do before our frolic beneath the sheets."

"What could possibly be more important than amour?"

"How about explorations of—"

"Oh, that does sound delightful."

"Charlie, please be serious."

"I'm sorry, CC. Tell me what you want to do."

When the final plans had been made, CC asked Charlie to tell her about his life. "You know a great deal about me, but we didn't have time to talk about you when we were at Knockie, and you promised to tell me about the MacDonald clan."

"My life isn't as exciting as yours, but I'll be glad to tell you whatever you want to know." CC listened as Charlie told amusing stories of growing up with Alex at his family's estate, attending school at Eton and Oxford, and, after graduation, traveling throughout Europe. He talked of his marriage to Flora in 2008, the birth of little Charlie a year and a half later, and the sad and unexpected death of his wife a few days after the baby was born. His eyes sparkled when he spoke about his love of riding and hunting and his passion for soccer, football he called it, which he played in school and followed faithfully. When he said he wanted to do something meaningful in life and talked of his frustration at not knowing what he wanted to accomplish, he had a faraway look in his eyes.

The fire died down to embers and CC had no idea how much time had passed. Charlie had just begun to talk about the MacDonalds and the Glencoe Massacre when they heard a knock. "Come in," CC called.

"I'm sorry to disturb you, my lady. Richard said you weren't to be disturbed, but I thought you should know your guests are here."

CC looked at her watch. "I apologize, Hastings. I had no idea it was so late. Please show Sir Anthony and Lady Alexandra in and ask Richard to clear away the tea tray. I imagine our guests would enjoy a cocktail before dinner."

"Certainly." Apparently Richard was waiting just outside the door because she heard Hastings say "Please clear." While Richard removed the dishes, Hastings added a few more logs to the fire, and when it blazed anew, he went for Alex and Tony.

CC hugged Alex while Charlie shook hands with Tony. "Have you been here for long?" she asked. "I hope we didn't keep you waiting."

"I recall you asked that same question the other afternoon. So you two didn't want to be disturbed?"

"We wanted a little private time to talk, Alex," Charlie said.

"Give up, Alex," Tony said. "We just arrived. CC, Hastings said you were meeting over tea."

"It wasn't a meeting. We were talking about trivialities, which, considering what's been going on, was fine with me. Would you like a drink?" The men ordered scotch, and on Hastings's recommendation, CC and Alex asked for a bottle of M. Vincent et Fils Chateau de Fuisse. Hastings brought a tray of hors d'oeuvres with the drinks.

When he left, Alex turned to CC. "So tell us what you've learned since we left you earlier." They sat by the fire and CC talked about her conversation with Henry and what he told her about the fire at Knockie. When she spoke about Flash, both Alex and Tony urged her not to be too hasty and jump to conclusions without proof. With so many people saying the same thing, CC had to agree.

John Claude lived up to his reputation, or so Alex said. The meal began with salmon mousse followed by stilton, port, and sage soup. Roast lamb fillet with watercress and jacket potatoes with buttered chives accompanied herb timbale served with a tapenade sauce and courgettes with pea puree filling. For dessert, James brought a rich chocolate mousse.

"May I move in here permanently?" Tony asked as he folded his napkin and put it beside his plate. "If not, do you think I could lure John Claude and Charlie away from Litchfield?"

"I'd like to live here too," Charlie said. He winked at CC, "but not just because of the cuisine."

"I for one would move in and never be able to leave the house, because I'd be unable to fit through the front door," Alex said as she rose from the table. "What a scrumptious meal."

"I agree, and don't even think about luring Jean Claude and Charles to Chadlington," Tony. I plan to take them home to Indianapolis with me. When she saw the downcast looks on the faces of her guests, she backpedaled. "That is, if I go back for good. Shall we have coffee in the White Drawing Room?" She turned to James who was at his post by the door to the kitchen: "If you would please serve there, James."

"Of course, Your Ladyship."

CC led her guests back through the house. As she passed through the lovely rooms, she experienced another epiphany. She suddenly understood her father's pride in his home. It was truly a magnificent yet warm and homey estate. Yes, she felt completely at home and very much aware of her heritage. Leaving all this behind and returning to Indiana would be extremely difficult. For the first time, she wondered if she would ever be able to be anyone but the Countess of Litchfield.

CHAPTER TWENTY-FOUR

Tony and Alex were about to leave for Chadlington when Hastings came into the Great Hall. "Before your guests leave, my lady, I wanted to tell you that I've arranged box seats for the seven-thirty Wednesday evening performance of *Mamma Mia* at the Prince of Wales Theater."

"I haven't seen that show in years. Thank you, Hastings."

"You're quite welcome. I rang the Ritz and told them to expect you. Your rooms are being prepared. When you check in, you will receive your own elevator key and the keys to your suite. After that, if you should want to stay over or use the suite for a day, you'll be able to do so with no prior notice. The car will be ready for you whenever you wish to leave, and your appointment with Mr. Norris is scheduled for two o'clock."

"I'll let you know my specific plans in the morning. Were you able to make an appointment with my father's doctor?"

"He'll be here at Litchfield tomorrow morning at ten. It was the only time he was available, and I took the liberty of scheduling him then."

"I would have gone to his office."

"I told him that, but he said there would be more privacy here."

"Then it seems everything's in order, so Hastings, why don't you retire for the night. After Sir Anthony and Lady Alexandra leave, I'll show Charles the main floor of the house and then go to sleep myself."

"You're absolutely certain you'll not need me?"

"I am. So enjoy the rest of your evening."

"I shall. Good night."

"Good night, Hastings."

"It looks as if you two have the house to yourselves," Alex said.

"We will after you leave," Charlie joked.

"How very rude." Alex pretended to be offended and turned to her husband. "It's time to go, Tony. I know when our company is no longer desired."

"Good night, you two." Tony shook Charlie's hand and kissed CC on the cheek.

"We'll call you tomorrow to make arrangements for Wednesday," CC said.

After waving good-bye to Alex and Tony, they went back inside. "I'll just be a minute. I want to change clothes before our excursion to the chapel," CC said. "Why don't you do the same?"

"I will, and while I'm upstairs, I'll call and check on little Charlie."

"And I'll meet you down here in about twenty minutes. That should give me enough time to call the office. I told them I'd be in touch about this time."

"Shall I come to your rooms? Hastings put me just down the hall on the other side of your father's suite."

"No way! Having you in my room is too dangerous. Once you're inside, we might never get to the chapel."

"But—"

"No buts, I'll see you in a while." She kissed him and went upstairs, leaving him staring after her, his mouth open to protest.

CC put on slacks and a pullover sweater and went to her sitting room to call the office. Her phone was there and charged, but she decided to save it for away trips, and picked up the house phone. Leslie was not at her desk, so CC had Helen, the switchboard operator, put her through to Wes. "Hi, how did the investigation go?" she greeted him.

"Are you sitting down?"

"Is it that bad?"

"It depends on how you look at it. It seems our friend had a marvelous idea and. He said he wanted to surprise you, Bob, and Spike, so he decided to go to the Taylors and see what they thought."

"In other words, he made an end-run to avoid hearing me say no."

"You got it, and I guarantee you would have said no."

"Tell me the bad news."

"Let's just say that I'm glad I don't have to talk to Bob and Spike like you'll have to do in a few minutes. Remember you told them you'd be calling."

"Don't keep me waiting, what did Jim do?"

"He bought a golf cart."

"He did what?"

"He decided it would be cute if the relief pitchers rode to the mound in a decorated golf cart when they're called in to pitch, so he went the Taylors, got them excited about the idea, came back, and without talking with Bob or Spike, ordered the cart and huge Knights logos to go on both sides. Our relievers will soon be riding to the mound in style."

"Oh shit!"

"Why, CC. We rarely hear you talk like that."

"I'm seldom this angry. You mean the Taylors approved of this ridiculous idea?"

"That's right. You know what a salesman Jim can be."

"Doesn't he know that part of baseball psychology is for the reliever to come out of the bullpen running aggressively like he's ready and able to get out of the jam?"

"Apparently he thinks the jaunt from the outfield will tire our guy, so he's going to give him a ride and, at the same time, create some spirit."

"I give up! Do the Taylors think I had something to do with this harebrained idea?

"No, but they don't expect you to squelch the plan."

"Gee, thanks. I get to call them and to try and undo the damage."

"You're the president. I believe this comes under your job description."

"Right, and we're going to revise all the job descriptions when I get home, including Jim's."

"I'll bet. Would you like to talk to your marketing man?"

"He's not mine, and I really would like to keep my dinner from coming up, so not today. I'll think of something to say tomorrow. Maybe I'll have Bob call him and tell him he refuses to allow the pitchers to ride."

"That might work. I think Jim's afraid of both Bob and Spike, but what about the Taylors?"

"I'll talk with them tomorrow. Right now, I'll call Florida. Leslie wasn't at her desk. Could you try her for me?"

"I think she left early. Her dog was sick or something like that."

"Leave her a note and tell her I'll check in tomorrow morning, will you?"

"I will. Anything else?"

"Yes. I told George I'd call him, so please connect me."

"Okay, and good luck with your Florida call."

"Gee, thanks. You sure you don't want to handle it for me?"

"No way. I'll put you through to George."

George was away from his desk, so CC left a message saying she'd call the following morning and dialed the office in Florida.

"Did you hear what that idiot Oats did this time?" Bob greeted her.

"And hello to you too. To answer your question, I heard, and I'll take care of it with your help." She explained her plan of attack to Bob, who agreed to call Jim at nine the following morning. Next he explained the incentives on the Davis contract. "You did a great job," CC said.

"Thanks. I guess we're ready to go. Wes tells me you'll be back for the first home stand."

"That's the plan, and I'm hoping to join you on the second road trip. I'll have to let you know."

"Is your business in England almost finished?"

Don't I wish! CC thought, but she wasn't going to get into her Litchfield issues with Bob. "I'm making progress, but it may take some time and maybe a few trips over the pond."

"I'm sorry about that. I miss our daily meetings."

"They'll resume again soon. What else is new?" Bob told her about the team, the spring training record, and some of the trades around the league. As he talked, CC realized how much she missed her work. When she hung up, she was ready to see a game, or "get my fix" as she called it.

She phoned her mother. Martha answered and said Mary was at the neighbor's. When CC asked about Flash, Martha said as far as she knew, he hadn't called. CC left a message urging her mother to have Flash phone her as soon as possible. Her calls finished, she went downstairs to meet Charlie and retrieve her father's papers.

Charlie was waiting and they went directly to the chapel. The room, that had been so difficult to see when she first visited, was empty of clutter. CC switched on the newly installed light and looked around. Fourteen light gray Corinthian columns supported the hall, which she judged was about sixty feet long and forty feet wide. The walls were dull gold with gray paneling ornamented with stucco swags. Instead of pews, there were six open benches on either side of a central aisle. The communion rail was white marble, and the reredos behind the altar featured a painting by Rigaud, an artist CC didn't recognize, in a matching white marble frame. Newly cleaned windows contained diamond-shaped panes of clear crown glass interspersed with a few stained glass designs.

"What a beautiful room," Charlie said.

"It certainly is. When I came in here before, it was used for storage, but now—"

"I wonder why your father didn't keep the chapel in this condition when the rest of the house is so well maintained."

"I have no idea. From the moment Stanley told me about the chapel, I've wondered why William would leave it in such disrepair." She paused.

"What are you thinking?" Charlie asked.

"I'm wondering if my father left the chapel a mess so no one would come in and try to find whatever it was he was hiding. No one would want to look around a dirty, unlit room."

"It's possible. If so, shall we see what was so important that he tried to keep it from being discovered? You said the papers and diary are behind the altar. From the looks of it, I'm not sure the two of us will be able to move the heavy marble."

"My father said the altar only looks heavy. Supposedly it's hollow. He believed, with a little effort, I could move it myself."

"Then by all means, let's get on with it." Charlie led the way down the aisle to the front of the chapel. He moved to the right of the altar and pulled it toward him. "William was half right," he said. "The marble is thin and the altar's hollow, but it's not that light."

He pulled the stone aside enough so CC could look behind. "Here they are!" she said. On a shelf lay a brown leather diary and a file folder about an inch thick. CC removed both items, and Charlie pushed the altar back into the exact spot they had found it."

"Let's hope these give us some answers," she said as she clutched the book and papers. "Shall we go see what my father thought was important enough to hide?"

"I'm right behind you." Charlie turned off the lights, and they went to CC's sitting room.

"I'll start with the diary." CC opened the well-used book.

"Why don't you begin reading and I'll look through the papers; unless you want to read them yourself. There may be some personal references that you would rather keep private."

"There's nothing I wouldn't want you to know, so go ahead." Charlie opened the first file as CC began to read. "Are you finding anything?" she asked after reading several pages. "The entries in the diary aren't telling us anything we don't already know."

"So far there's nothing new in the papers either, but I'm just getting past the historical background."

CC continued to read. "It says here that that the earl and Lady Anne's father threw their considerable influence behind the committee," she said. "Do you think that's the reason William felt marrying Anne was his duty?"

"Probably so, and actually it makes sense. If he was afraid for your safety as he indicates in these papers, and if he needed his father's and future father-in-law's support to achieve his goals, he would in all probability, put his personal happiness aside for a greater good. That's the way of the English and always has been."

"But why wouldn't Flash be worried about us? He was a member of the committee."

"Flash lived in America. Europe had nearly been destroyed by war; twice, in fact. The United States fought, but until your infamous 9/11 attack in New York, its cities hadn't been bombed by treacherous governments and fanatical dictators. My father told me no one knew whom to trust. There were fears that a new Hitler could rise out of the rubble and a kind of paranoia existed. Governments were collapsing and the Communist menace was looming. Flash was isolated from much of this, and he lived in a country which allowed disagreements with the government. England permitted dissent, but there were more implied restrictions on freedom of speech right after the war when all of Europe was trying to rebuild."

"So you think my father refused to defy his own father so that he could pursue his fundamental objective in life?"

"I believe he did, but he must have had a difficult time making the decision. I can't imagine how he could have concentrated on business matters when he was in Paris with your mother."

"The diary says the Paris conference was for organizational purposes and few decisions were made during the meeting. The men got together again in Washington, and William went through Arizona to meet with Flash before going on to that meeting. That was when he saw me and our housekeeper going for our walk."

"Does it say what came out of the Washington meeting?"

"It says that each member of the committee added some of his personal money to a business account in a Swiss bank. My father was chosen leader of the group, a position that was to be his for life. It also appears that it was during this Washington meeting that the committee's purpose was expanded to include working in various ways for international peace. My father says that essentially they were supported by their respective governments, but the understanding was that they might have to work in direct opposition to the government's policies if it was for the advancement of world peace."

"You mean if Britain, for example, overtly supported Israel, but it was really in the world's best interest for them to support the Arabs, the Committee of Seven would work with the Arabs in Britain's behalf while, publicly, the PM was voicing anti-Arab policies?"

"It looks like that's the case, but I wonder how they managed to accomplish their goals without being exposed?"

"I have no idea. Maybe that's why someone burned Knockie. Now that my father's dead, the others may fear that my investigation will expose their activities."

"Could you have brought out any files with records of disbursement of funds? They might give us an idea what assignments, if you could call them that, the committee had been given."

"I don't think so. I didn't pack any files that chronicle the early years of the committee's existence. My interest was not so much in how the committee functioned, but rather how William's work affected my mother and me. Now I find out he feared for his safety. Do you really think he was murdered?"

"It seems likely. William and the other committee members were defying governments, even if their governments tacitly approved of what they were doing. The question is why was William murdered at this point in time, if in fact he didn't die of a heart attack?"

"And how was he killed? Whatever the killer used made it look like that William died a natural death. And then there's the matter of where he was killed. No one entered his office without his permission. Could he have let his killer in? Did someone he trusted betray him?"

Charlie looked pensive. "Unfortunately I can't answer any of your questions, though I know they were rhetorical in nature. Every question you ask brings to mind several more."

"I know. You can be sure I'm going to find the answers to all of them. First I'll meet with Dr. Grimsby. From what we've learned here and after what happened at Knockie, I'm convinced William didn't die of natural causes. I also think he and his committee were about to do something that necessitated immediate action on someone's part."

"I agree with you, but who did this? And was William the only one in danger? Could Flash be the next victim?"

"Lord, I hadn't thought of that. I've been so angry with Flash because he hasn't been available to answer my questions. I never considered that he, or for that matter the other members of the committee, might be in jeopardy. Charlie, I don't know where to begin or what to do next. This situation grows more complicated and the answers aren't coming."

"Hopefully you'll discover more during your morning meeting with the doctor and when you see Mr. Norris in London tomorrow afternoon."

"I hope so. As you said, I do have more to go on now, but I want to be sure I ask the right questions."

"Then I suggest we make a list of things you want to learn. That way, when you see the doctor, Mr. Norris, and Mr. Caulfield, you'll be well prepared."

"That's a good idea, but are you sure you can postpone your other plans for the evening long enough to help me?"

"It will be a tremendous struggle for me, my lady, but I suppose just this once I could sacrifice."

"I do appreciate it, my lord. What would I do without you?"

"That's exactly what I want you to keep asking yourself." CC grimaced and Charlie grinned. "Shall we get started?" He took out a pad and began to write.

CHAPTER TWENTY-FIVE

When CC and Charlie finished making lists of her questions and concerns, it was late, and Charlie, though he pretended to be hurt when she asked him to spend the night in his rooms, was really not upset. He knew she was concerned about the servants and had a great deal on her mind.

He was right. CC tossed and turned all night. When it was finally a decent time to get up, she showered and dressed in a business suit with a V-neck silk blouse. She selected a linked gold chain with matching bracelet and earrings. With one final look in the mirror, she was ready to face the day ahead—a day she hoped would provide some answers to her numerous questions.

When CC arrived in the breakfast room, Charlie was waiting. "Good morning, CC," he said, a sly smile on his face.

"Good morning, Charlie," CC said politely. "Did you sleep well?"

"Very well, thank you. Though I must say I enjoyed the country air and the sleeping conditions at Knockie more."

"Would you like for me to prepare a plate for you, my lady?" Hastings asked.

"No thank you. I'm not really hungry." She smiled when she saw that Charlie had helped himself from the buffet, "but it seems Lord Charles was starving." I'll have coffee and a wheat toast."

Hastings poured the coffee. "I'll return momentarily with your toast."

When Hastings left the room, CC turned to Charlie. "I want you to know how much I appreciate your consideration last night. It would have been difficult for me to focus on anything but my plans for today."

"You mean my irresistible charm wouldn't have made you forget everyone and everything?"

"Humble, aren't you, but I'd prefer a rendezvous when I don't have William and this mystery on my mind."

Charlie stopped joking. "Are you all set to meet with the doctor and Mr. Norris?"

"I'm as prepared as I can be. I'm sure I'll have more questions than answers after I talk with them."

When breakfast was over, Charlie left CC in the White Drawing Room to wait for the doctor to arrive, while he went to his room to call his father. CC reviewed her list one final time. At exactly ten, Hastings knocked. "Come in," she called, suddenly feeling extremely nervous.

"Your Ladyship, may I present Dr. Grimsby. Doctor, the Countess of Litchfield."

"Good morning, Doctor." CC extended her hand. "Welcome to Litchfield. Would you like coffee or tea?"

"Tea please, Your Ladyship."

"Hastings, would you please bring tea for the doctor, coffee for me and a selection of breakfast rolls."

"Right away." Hastings left the room, closing the door behind him.

"Please make yourself comfortable, Dr. Grimsby." CC gestured toward a winged-back chair by the fireplace. "I'm sure your time is limited, so I'll come right to the point. My father's attorney, Harrison Caulfield, gave me a letter in which William spoke of his excellent health and his expectations of living a long life. He suggested that if anything were to happen to him,

I should consider the possibility that he died of other than natural causes. That intimation, combined with information that has come to light over the past several days, makes me suspicious of the circumstances surrounding my father's death."

"I understand, my lady. How might I help you?"

Before she could answer, Hastings returned. He poured coffee for CC, tea for the doctor, and put the rolls on the table between them. When he had closed the doors, CC began. "I would like to know why there was no autopsy conducted on the earl. Certainly I should have been consulted. My father's attorney could have reached me for permission to perform the examination, but I was never contacted. My father was buried without my knowing the definitive cause of death."

"I assumed your attorney had spoken with you, my lady. I was prepared to perform an autopsy. Though I had no time to do more than a cursory examination, it appeared the earl died of cardiac arrest."

"No time to conduct an examination?"

"No, my lady. Two men brought the body to me. Minutes later I received a telephone call from Mr. Caulfield instructing me to release the body for cremation without further examination. The earl was immediately spirited away. I assumed he was taken to the crematorium."

"Cremate?" CC realized she hadn't asked to see her father's grave and had no idea where he was buried. Now the doctor was telling her that her father had been immediately cremated and on Caulfield's orders. *Was his number the one William gave to Hastings?* CC wondered. *No, I don't think so. If my father wanted Hastings to call Caulfield, he wouldn't have to provide the number. Hastings told me he had Caulfield's contact information. So who gave the order?*

Grimsby was obviously disturbed by CC's silence. "My lady," he said. "I assumed it was you who denied my request to perform an autopsy and gave the order for cremation."

"I was never consulted. Where are my father's ashes buried, Doctor?"

"I believe in London, my lady, but Mr. Caulfield will be able to tell you more about the specific burial details."

"And you have no idea who actually prohibited the autopsy?"

"None whatsoever."

"Was there much coverage of my father's death in the newspapers, Doctor?"

"Very little, which also seemed unusual. The earl was a Peer of the Realm and, from what I understand, a very important and influential man."

"He was," CC said. "Can you tell me anything more?"

"Absolutely nothing beyond what I've already told you. Richard, your father's valet found the body. People I had never seen before brought it to me and immediately took it away. The local coroner wasn't involved."

"Then you didn't know the men who took him from his study?"

"No, my lady, I only know that Richard reported his death to Hastings and shortly thereafter, the body was taken from the house."

"And this didn't seem strange? Under normal circumstances wouldn't the police scour the room for clues? Wouldn't your CSI unit, or whatever you call the crime scene investigators over here, want to be sure my father died of natural causes?"

"In most cases yes, but Mr. Caulfield said there was no need for an investigation. He suggested it would be better if

I didn't ask questions and go on about my business. Of course I did as he instructed. Perhaps he'll provide the answers to your questions."

"I hope he'll do that. Now perhaps you could tell me more about my father, his health, and your association with him."

During the next thirty minutes, Grimsby talked about William. The doctor said he routinely cared for the earl, not because he was ill, but for minor ailments that for the most part came about from sports injuries. CC learned that her father was an avid polo player. He also loved to ride to the hounds and hunt for pheasant. Throughout the conversation, Grimsby stressed William's athletic prowess, all the time insinuating that his patient did not die of cardiac arrest, though he never actually said the words.

As he talked, CC grew increasingly mystified. By the time Grimsby stood up to leave, she was thoroughly convinced that her father did not have a heart attack, but she had no idea how he died. *And since he was cremated, I may never know,* she reflected. "Thank you so much for your help, Doctor," she said at the door. "I appreciate your taking time out from your busy schedule to speak with me."

"You're quite welcome, my lady. If there's anything more I can do for you, please don't hesitate to call. Hastings has my number."

CC watched as the doctor drove away before returning to the library. She was confused. Why would Caulfield have insisted that William be cremated immediately? She needed to see her attorney right away. There would be no waiting two weeks for a meeting scheduled at his discretion.

She pulled the cord, and Hastings quickly appeared. "You rang for me, my lady?"

"Hastings, please call Mr. Caulfield. Tell him I'll be in London and would like to meet with him tomorrow morning. Make it clear he's to make time to see me."

"I'll do so right away."

"When Lord Charles comes downstairs, please tell him I'm in the library?"

"Certainly." Hastings bowed and left the room.

CC went to the library and sat at her desk. As she usually did after an important meeting, she made notes about her conversation with the doctor. When she finished, she once again reviewed her list for the meeting with Norris. She was about to go and look for Charlie when he walked into the room. "How was your meeting?" he asked cheerfully.

"Amazing!" CC told Charlie about her conversation with Grimsby.

When she finished, he echoed her sentiments. "Amazing!"

"What did you find out from your father?"

"Not a great deal. Father did say that many years ago in the House of Lords, the Duke of Marlborough, who also serves on the Foreign Relations Committee, argued against the development of nuclear power. He also knew that William was involved with the government in some capacity. However, he knew nothing about the Committee of Seven or any clandestine meetings at Litchfield or Knockie."

"So basically you didn't learn anything new?"

"Unfortunately, no. My father invited us to Hintlesham Hall. Alex phoned him this morning and told him how wonderful you are."

"I'll bet she told him about us."

"That she did, and he wants to meet you."

"Did he object? After all, you're involved with one of those ugly Americans."

Charlie grinned. "Hardly ugly. My father wants me to happy. He'll love you."

"In that case, I hope we'll have time to visit. I'd love to meet your father and see your home." CC looked at the clock. "But first things first, I'd better pack if we're going to be in London in time for my appointment with Norris."

"I'll do the same, and meet you in twenty minutes."

Hastings was in the foyer. "Please ask Stanley to bring the Jaguar around," CC said. "Lord Charles and I will be leaving for London in about twenty minutes."

"Of course."

"I'm on my way to the safe to select some jewelry for tonight. Would you go with me? I'm not comfortable with the intricacies of the combination."

"Gladly, my lady."

CC selected a V-shaped necklace with the large pear-shaped diamond, a diamond bracelet, diamond earrings, and a diamond ring with a similar pear-shaped stone. *I'll 'drip' tonight,* she thought, and smiled. She selected a gold necklace, bracelet, and earrings for her meeting with Caulfield. Satisfied that she had all the jewels she would need for the next two days, she closed the box and the safe, thanked Hastings, and went to pack.

From her stepmother's closet she selected a black crepe dress. *This is too weird,* she thought. *I don't know if Anne wold mind, but I think my father would be pleased to see me wearing Anne's clothes—or not.* Anne's feet were smaller so she'd ask Hastings to have a pair of black silk shoes in her size delivered to her suite. She packed the dress with her own clothes and put the bags by the door. She'd just finished freshening up when Charlie knocked. "Come in," she called.

"I've waited all morning to do this." He kissed her, pulled back, leaned in, and kissed her again. "Why don't you call Mr. Norris and tell him we'll be about an hour late."

CC gently shoved him away. "It's time to leave for London, Charlie," she said smiling, "and really, what would Hastings think?"

"He'd think I'm the most fortunate of men, but I'll abide by your wishes, my lady, even though my own needs are much greater." He laughed, picked up her bags, and they went downstairs.

At the front door, CC gave Hastings an overview of her plans and asked him to call Harrods or another department store and have two or three pairs of black evening shoes delivered to her suite. Richard put the bags in the trunk and held the door as she slid into the passenger's seat. Minutes later, she and Charlie were off to London.

During the ride CC reviewed her notes for the meeting with Norris while Charlie made reservations at one of his favorite restaurants for after the play. She asked, but he refused to tell her which one. It would be a surprise.

They pulled onto Piccadilly and parked in front of the gilded Louis XVI chateau. A liveried doorman opened CC's door and ushered her inside the Piccadilly entrance. CC looked around at the lobby that glittered with mirrors, chandeliers, ornate plasterwork, flowers, dark-pink velvet-covered chairs and matching draperies. She admired the elegant palm court with its gilded statuary, small tables, couches, and chairs. "What a lovely place. It's so full of life."

"It's my favorite hotel in the city." Charlie led CC across the lobby to the hotel offices. Mr. Miller, the manager, greeted her warmly, gave her keys to "her" suite, and led her across the lobby to a private elevator. After inserting a key into a slot, they rode upstairs to the top floor. The elevator opened into a magnificent living room.

"Is this the only room on the floor?" CC asked.

"There are actually two suites, my lady," said Miller. "If a key is inserted into this second slot, the opposite elevator door opens."

"This entire floor contains only two suites?"

"That's correct. There are sixteen suites on the floors below, but these suites are the only two in the hotel which are privately owned."

"I see." CC stepped into a huge room that contained a mixture of priceless antiques, comfortable chairs, fine china, and valuable art. She walked to the window.

"Your view is of Green Park, my lady," Miller said.

"It's lovely."

"Would you like to see the rest of the suite?"

"I would. Lord Charles, would you care to join us?"

"I have several calls to make," said Charlie. Why don't you go ahead and I'll take care of business here."

CC followed the manager through several painted anterooms, each magnificently decorated. One was furnished as an office with heavy leather furniture and a large desk. Behind the desk were shelves lined with books and knickknacks. The second room was obviously William's sitting room. It too was decorated in dark-colored leathers with comfortable-looking couches and chairs. At the far end of the two anterooms was an enormous bedroom. "This was the earl's bedroom, my lady. He had it redecorated just last year."

"It's exquisite." The room was decorated in browns and blues and the king-size Edwardian bed was topped with a dark blue canopy. A fireplace with a blue Delft tile mantle adorned one wall and on either side were magnificent wall sconces. Two comfortable couches that picked up the colors of the canopy faced one another in front of the fireplace. CC went into the ultra-modern bathroom with its marble floor and massive brass fittings on the bathtub, shower stall and sink. A telephone and a huge towel warmer struck CC as being the epitome of opulence.

Miller accompanied her back through the anterooms and living room and then through another door into a small paneled bar furnished with leather chairs. Through there she entered a mirrored dining room with its centerpiece, a large mahogany table that seated ten comfortably. On one wall was a matching buffet and built-in shelves lined with exquisite Royal Doulton china. "There's a small kitchen through those doors," Miller said, "but you can order whatever you'd like from the hotel kitchen. Your father preferred room service, and, like we did for him, we'll provide daily menus for your perusal."

"Thank you," CC said. "Are there other bedrooms in the suite?"

"Three, my lady. Each has its own private bath."

CC calculated the number of rooms. There were at least ten. She wondered what her father had paid for this in-town luxury. Miller left the key and withdrew. "Good Lord!" she said when the elevator door closed. "This place is fantastic!"

"Your father was definitely comfortable when he stayed in London," Charlie said. "So which of the many beds will we sleep in tonight?"

CC laughed. "I suggest we try them all."

"Shall we start right now?" He moved toward her.

CC looked at her watch. "Not and get me to my appointment on time."

"Thwarted again," Charlie said. "I had the car parked, so we'll have to take a taxi."

"Excellent. I've been dying to ride in one of your famous cabs. I'll be right with you." She went to her father's suite, and after looking around, found what she was searching for. Bolted to the closet floor was a large safe. She tried the now-familiar combination and the door popped open. As in the other safes, there was a bundle of cash. She removed her jewelry from her bag, put it inside, locked the door, and went to join Charlie for the taxi ride to her appointment with William's accountant.

CHAPTER TWENTY-SIX

At precisely two, CC and Charlie entered the office of Norris, Spencer and Dudley. A secretary immediately ushered her toward the senior partner's office while Charlie made himself comfortable in the outer office to wait for the meeting to end. A smiling secretary opened the double doors. CC faced a distinguished-looking man who appeared to be about sixty years old. He quickly rose to greet her.

"Good Afternoon, Lady Litchfield." He extended his hand.

"It's a pleasure to meet you, Mr. Norris."

Norris gestured toward a table, around which were placed eight burgundy leather chairs. "Won't you sit down?" CC sat in the chair he held out for her. Norris sat opposite her. "How may I help you?"

He gets right down to business, CC reflected. "Last week at Mr. Caulfield's suggestion—I assume you know Harrison Caulfield, my father's attorney?"

"I know him well, my lady."

"Mr. Caulfield urged me to see you. I was stunned to discover the earl had an enormous amount of money deposited in personal accounts in the Bank of England and in Switzerland; not to mention the balance in his Swiss business account."

"Your father was an extremely wealthy man, Your Ladyship."

CC decided to imitate her father's accountant and get right to the most pressing matters. "He certainly was," she said smiling. "What I want to know is how he made his money."

"Over the years your father made extremely wise investments, Lady Litchfield. His assets increased twenty times over
since his father's death."

"You're telling me all that money came from wise investments?" CC didn't wait for Norris to respond. "Could you give
me an idea of what's in his portfolio?"

"Of course, my lady. Your father initially invested heavily
in American oil stocks. Originally he owned Standard Oil, and
when that company split into several others, he continued to
purchase shares. He owns vast quantities of Chevron, which
is now BP Amoco, and Exxon, which is now Exxon-Mobil.
In addition, he possessed stock in other American companies
such as IBM, American Telephone and Telegraph, and several
drug companies. Recently he invested in Microsoft, Hewlett
Packard computer and numerous dot-com companies. I'm sure
you know those companies have done well. After making a
great deal of money, he sold the stock of the companies that
seemed to be in trouble. In addition, there are shares of smaller
companies; many which I imagine would be unfamiliar to
you. Besides stock market investments and bond holdings, he
owns a great deal of land in England and elsewhere. Many of
these properties are leased to major corporations on a long-
term basis."

"So his money was initially made in oil?" CC wasn't surprised. There again was the connection to Flash."

"Yes, though as I indicated, he had diversified greatly over
the years," Norris was saying. "His father was the one who
urged oil stock purchases."

"And you made these investments for him?"

"Your father instructed me what to buy and sell, my lady.
He was an extremely astute businessman. I merely made the
acquisitions he desired and handled his tax matters."

"Do you have copies of all his transactions over the years?"

"Your father kept his business papers in his safe at Litchfield, though both Mr. Caulfield and I have duplicates."

"Do you know of any other way my father made money?"

"My lady, if I understand your question, you're asking me if your father made this vast sum of money by illegal means."

"Please understand, Mr. Norris. I never met my father, so I know little about him above and beyond what others tell me. So far I have no reason to believe he was involved in anything illegal, but I'm unwilling to accept blindly. Therefore I'm asking if you believe my father was an honest man."

"The most honorable of men, I assure you, my lady. Your father was indisputably ethical. He would never be involved in anything that was not completely honest. His character was above reproach."

CC smiled. "I appreciate your glowing endorsement."

"I'm sorry I can't help you beyond what I've said this morning. My relationship with the earl, though lengthy and far-reaching, was not personal in nature. We never became friends, and I was never privy to anything occurring in his life beyond his investments and tax burdens, which I assure you, he accepted without complaint."

"Speaking of taxes, will you be handling my father's estate taxes?"

"When you accept your title and inheritance, my lady, I will be happy to explain the British death tax structure to you. However, you should know your father set aside enough money to cover all taxes, so you will have no burden."

"You mean the money will come from his personal English bank account?"

"No, my lady, that money is yours once you accept your title. The tax money is invested in tax free bonds which matured years ago. When the time comes to pay the British government, those accounts will be closed and the taxes will be paid. You will not spend a shilling of the money in your British or Swiss accounts on taxes."

"It sounds like my father planned well; almost as if he knew he might die."

"I don't think your father expected to die," my lady, but he wanted to be sure you were well cared for if he did pass on. His estate has been in order since his father's death. He modified some of his wishes after Lady Anne's demise, but except for what he left to care for her should he die first, the bulk of his estate was always left to you."

CC sat quietly. Her father had thought of everything. He had left her all of his worldly goods and no liabilities. Her esteem for William increased. He really had cared for her. Sensing that Norris had no more to say, she thanked him for his time and left the office, realizing that it was becoming more and more difficult for her to say no to William's legacy, and again wondering if there were a way to combine her two titles, countess and president.

Charlie stood to greet her when she entered the outer office. CC thanked the secretary and took Charlie's arm. They said little in the elevator to the ground floor. Charlie hailed a taxi and directed the driver to take them to the Ritz. While they drove she shared the details of her visit with Norris. He didn't seem surprised when she explained she'd be told nothing more until she accepted her title. "I'm sure your father believed that by the time you met with Norris, you'd want to accept your inheritance."

"He was a wise man."

"Then you're leaning toward signing the papers."

"At this point, yes, but I'm still trying to figure out a way to retain my title as president of the Knights as well."

"Do you think there's a way to do that?"

"I have no idea, but we'll see. Right now I have many more questions than answers."

Charlie took her hand. "The answers will come, I promise, and I'll help you find them."

"Thank you, but I'm tired of talking about William, money and titles. I'd like to relax before Alex and Tony arrive." She grinned, "and, my lord, I don't believe we've had an opportunity to enjoy each other's company in private for quite a long time."

"What a fabulous idea, my lady. I feel myself rising to the occasion."

When the door to the elevator closed behind them, Charlie took CC in his arms. Time no longer ticked for her. He led her to the bedroom and laid her gently on the bed. "God, you're incredible," he said as he slowly and seductively removed her clothing and then his own. He lay down beside her and began to caress her body. CC writhed in pleasure as his fingers created sensations of intense pleasure. She explored his body, seeking places that would give him delight. When he was not sure if she could stand any more of the exquisite agony, he entered her. She responded to his movements and their bodies joined in perfect rhythm. CC felt her passion build and then release in pulsing waves of ecstasy. The combined feeling of pain and pleasure intensified as Charlie groaned deeply.

"I love you," she murmured as Charlie's breathing quieted.

"And I love you." He brushed the hair from her forehead, kissed her lightly, and pulled her to him. They lay quietly, savoring the moment.

Safely tucked in Charlie's arms, CC dozed. The ring of the telephone jarred her to awareness. The phone was on Charlie's side of the bed, so she climbed over him to answer. "Hello. Where are you two?"

"I'm glad Charlie reached you, and how far is your flat from here? So you'll meet us here in an hour for a drink before we go to the theater? Fine, we'll see you then."

"I take it that was my sister. She always manages to interrupt."

"It was, and as you heard, we only have an hour before she and Tony get here. I hope my shoes are in the closet, because there's no time to go out and buy a pair. I should have checked before we became otherwise engaged."

"So that's what we're calling it now?" Charlie chuckled, "but you're right, Alex is never late, in fact, she's usually early."

"Then I suggest you go to your room, my lord. If you stay in here, I'll have to make a decision I'm not willing to make."

"I would never ask you to do that." Charlie patted her playfully on the bottom. As he gathered his clothes, CC admired his muscular body. She sighed, pulled the sheets over her head until he was out of sight, and then got up to remake the bed. She didn't want Alex and Tony to see an obviously romped-in bed if they wanted a tour of the suite.

Cc was relieved when she was several pairs of shoes in the closet. Any of the styles would have been fine, and she picked those with the lowest heels. She showered, washed her hair, and dressed. When she had fastened the last piece of jewelry, she looked in the mirror. Satisfied with what she saw, she went to join Charlie in the living room.

"You're by far the most beautiful woman I've ever seen!" he said as he rose to greet her. "I'll be the envy of every man at the theater."

"And you look incredibly handsome in your dark suit. I wondered if you'd wear Highland attire."

"Not here in London. I like to 'blend in' as you Americans say."

CC called room service and ordered champagne. She selected an assortment of canapés, including the chef's recommendation, quail eggs and salmon. In fifteen minutes, the kitchen phoned to have her insert her key in the slot by the elevator. Charlie did so, and minutes later a crisply starched server pushed a cart filled with silver dishes and two champagne buckets. He arranged the food and wine on a table opposite the couches, bowed, and departed. Charlie was uncorking the champagne when the telephone rang again. CC inserted the card so that Alex and Tony could take the elevator upstairs.

Alex swept into the room, looking stunning in a gold cocktail-length dress. CC was glad she'd thought to make the bed, because Alex wanted a tour of the suite. Both she and Tony raved about the place and Alex was extoling William's exquisite taste when they settled in the living room to enjoy the champagne and hors d'oeuvres.

"I've never seen a suite quite like this one," Tony said. "I agree with Alex, your father had superb taste."

"Am I the only one who finds all of this extraordinary?" CC asked.

"Absolutely not," said Alex. "Your father has one of the most magnificent collections of furniture, antiques, art, and china I have ever seen."

"I wonder how he found the time to do this serious collecting, though I imagine some of the items have been in the family for generations," Charlie said, "but he obviously added to the collection."

As the four sipped champagne, CC told Tony and Alex about her visit with Norris and the tax account in America. Once again, they all marveled at William's wealth. "My father was a remarkable man, CC said pensively. "I wish I knew more about him."

At seven, Charlie phoned the desk and asked to have the car brought around. He explained that, when he'd called the concierge to make arrangements for a limousine to take them to the play, he learned that William had a car at his disposal. *The trappings of the rich and famous*, CC thought, though she didn't comment.

The Rolls was waiting when they arrived in front of the hotel, and they headed to the theater. Aware of the stares of the other playgoers as she and her party took their seats in one of the special boxes, CC felt uncomfortable. But when the lights dimmed and the curtain rose, she relaxed and enjoyed the play. When the performance was over, she hated to see it end. Though embarrassed, she stood to receive the bow from the cast.

Dinner was equally phenomenal. Charlie took them to Morton's in Berkeley Square, a restaurant so famous that the owners had no need to advertise. CC saw a small plaque out front—the only evidence there was a restaurant inside.

Though CC wasn't particularly fond of lamb, she decided to try the English specialty, which the menu described as fillet of lamb on a bed of red onions with roasted garlic and a lamb sauce. It was fabulous. Charlie bragged about his guinea fowl, and Alex and Tony boasted about their sole and turbot. All three heaped praise on Charlie for selecting a perfect place to end an extraordinary evening. After coffee, Charlie and CC dropped Alex and Tony at their flat.

"I can't imagine sleeping," she said as she and Charlie took the elevator to the suite.

"In that case, I have a suggestion."

"I have no doubt how you want to spend your time." CC was laughing when she walked into the suite. "Flash!" she cried out and slammed the door behind her.

CHAPTER TWENTY-SEVEN

Sitting there on the couch was her stepfather. "Flash," she said again. "What are you doing here? How did you get into the suite? Have you talked with Mother? Why haven't you returned my calls?"

Flash crossed the room to greet her. "Hi, honey. My, you are full of questions. I didn't mean to startle you."

CC's surprise gave way to anger. "Why didn't you let me know you were coming to England?"

"If you'll calm down and come on over here, I'll explain everything to you." He extended his hand to Charlie. "I believe we met at Knockie several years ago," Lord Timperley."

Charlie took his hand. "That's right, Mr. MacTandy, and please call me Charlie. It's very nice to see you again."

"And you call me Flash. How's that pretty wife of yours? I believe you visited the lodge shortly after your marriage."

CC was embarrassed, but Charlie didn't seem disturbed. "I'm afraid I lost my wife when she gave birth to our son."

"I'm sorry to hear that." Flash looked at CC and immediately realized his beloved stepdaughter was in love with the young man. He smiled. "I'm awfully glad that CC has you to show her around London."

"I've enjoyed spending time with her here in England and in Scotland."

"Well, now that the niceties are behind us," CC said, "why don't you answer my questions, Flash."

"With pleasure, honey, if you'll sit down." CC and Charlie followed Flash across the room and sat on a couch opposite him. "So what is it you want to know? You rattled off those questions so quickly I don't know where to begin."

CC was even more annoyed. "Why don't you start with how you got in here? I thought I had the only key."

"CC, I've been coming to the Ritz to see your father for years. I've known Mr. Miller for years. When I told him I was your stepfather and had come to surprise you, he was more than happy to let me in."

"So you and my father met in London often? Mother and I thought you were off scouting ballplayers."

"I was. That is, most of the time. Contrary to what you might believe, I didn't deceive you every time I left town, and when I did, it was because I couldn't tell you where I was going.

"And where have you been this trip? Did Mother tell you I wanted to talk with you?"

"I spoke with Mary yesterday afternoon from Tokyo. She said you wanted to talk, so I came here instead of going to Arizona?"

"A little out of the way, isn't it?"

"You could say so. That is, if I didn't have a specific reason for being here."

"I hope your purpose for coming to London is to tell me everything I want to know about my father, your relationship with him, and your infamous committee."

"CC, I came because I wanted to check on you, to be sure you're doing okay. I'll answer as many of your questions as I can, but—"

"I don't want any buts, Flash."

Flash momentarily lost his composure. "I said I'll tell you what I can. Now I expect you to drop the attitude and listen.

I realize you're furious with me. You feel betrayed, but if you'll stop and think, you'll realize how much I love you. I've tried to protect you over the years and I don't deserve this kind of welcome."

CC was surprised because Flash rarely lost his temper. She backed off. "I'm sorry, Flash. This has been a tough week for me and I guess I needed a scapegoat; someone to blame for my shock."

"I know, honey, and I'm sorry I scolded you. Now will you give old Flash a hug?"

CC embraced her stepfather. "Where are you staying?" she asked. "And how long will you be in England?"

"Where I stay is up to you. I could get a suite here at the hotel, but I'd rather bunk with you."

"Of course, I'd love to have you stay here. There's plenty of room. I can't believe the size of this suite."

"It's mighty special!" Flash said. "Are you sure I won't be in your way?" He looked at Charlie.

"Absolutely not, Flash. There's an empty room right next to mine."

"Are you hungry? I can order something from room service?"

"I ate downstairs a while ago, honey. Right now I'm dog-tired. It's been a long day and it was a very long flight. Why don't I turn in for the night? We'll talk in the morning."

"Okay, but I have an appointment with Mr. Caulfield."

"I know you do, CC. Harrison phoned me. I'm asking you to put off the meeting for two days. In fact, I'd like to take your scheduled appointment. Let Charlie show you a little of the English countryside. I'll join you at Litchfield in two days. By then I should have some answers."

CC was irritated. "Flash, unless I have a valid reason for leaving Litchfield, I'll have to say no and keep my scheduled appointment. Here we go with the mystery business again, and frankly I'm tired of secrets and riddles."

"I know, CC, and I understand how you feel, but you'd be safer in the countryside with Charlie."

"You think I'm in danger?"

"Possibly, CC. I told you I was in Tokyo. I went there to attend the funeral of Taido Yamato."

CC recognized the name. "Wasn't he a member of the committee?"

"Yes, and he was a dear friend. He committed suicide last week."

"Suicide?"

"That's the official word."

"But you don't believe it?"

"Not any more than I believe William died of heart failure, but I have no way to prove my theory because he was cremated."

"Immediately, like William was?"

"That's right."

"And you think CC may be in danger?" Charlie asked.

"I don't know, Charlie. It may be that the people who killed William and Mr. Yamato will assume CC plans to pick up where William left off."

"And try to kill me too?"

"I don't want to alarm you, honey, but we have no way of knowing. That said, I'd feel a lot better if you're out sightseeing with Charlie."

"And you think you may know more in two days?"

"I believe so."

"Are you in danger, Flash? I couldn't stand it if anything happened to you because I was so stubborn."

"Don't worry about me, honey. Old Flash can take care of himself."

"And if I agree to your proposal, you promise to do some serious explaining in return?"

"As I said, I'll tell you as much as I possibly can."

"Then I have a condition. I'll go if you'll give me a general idea of what you and William were up to over the years and how he became so wealthy."

"CC—"

That's the deal, Flash, so you decide what you want to do."

"I guess you leave me no choice. Charlie, if you'll excuse us."

"Charlie knows everything, Flash. You can speak freely in front of him."

Flash turned to Charlie. "You know about the committee and CC's father's involvement?"

"I do, sir."

"Then, if you don't mind, I'd like to ask you a question or two?"

"Go right ahead."

Flash looked at CC. "I don't mean to pry, darling, but what we're going to discuss is top secret. I want to know about your relationship with Charlie, because if what we suspect turns out to be true, just by knowing, he could be in danger."

"I love Charlie, Flash, and I trust him."

"And what about Bud? You've been together for years. Can you forget him in a matter of days?'

"Come on, Flash. You had to know Bud and I had problems for the past year or so. We drifted apart. Charlie has nothing to do with my breakup with Bud. He was merely a catalyst to prompt quicker action on my part."

"Does Bud know you don't want to marry him?"

"He does. You know me, Flash. I could never begin another relationship behind Bud's back. You asked how two people could fall in love in two weeks. Think about Mom and William. I don't say this to hurt you, Flash. I know my mother loves you, but she and my father knew how they felt in only a few hours."

"Your point's well taken," Flash said, "and I'm not hurt. When I married Mary, I knew she was on the rebound." He turned to Charlie. "And you, young man, how do you feel about my stepdaughter?"

"I love her, sir."

"Have the two of you talked about getting married?"

CC was embarrassed. "I hardly think this is the time to discuss marriage," she said crossly.

"I don't mean to pry, honey, but I need to know about your relationship before I trust Charles with what I'm going to tell you."

"I haven't asked CC to marry me, Flash, though the thought has crossed my mind more than once. Your stepdaughter has many decisions to make over the next few weeks, and I felt it was unfair to ask her to make another decision. I didn't propose because I chose not to put any pressure on her beyond what she's already feeling. However, to answer your question, if CC decides to remain in England, I will ask your permission to marry her."

"And if she goes back to the States and gives up her title?" Flash asked.

"Then I won't be able to make her my wife. Of course I'll continue to love her, but I have a son who has ties to Scotland.

I will eventually inherit my father's title and estates and take my position in the House of Lords. My wife couldn't be a countess and an American citizen. I couldn't move to the United States, and even though I love CC deeply, it would be unfair to her to be involved in a long-distance relationship."

CC looked at Charlie. "My God, I never considered that giving up my title and moving home would mean giving you up as well, but you're right. You could never move to the States."

"So you're beginning to understand," Charlie said, "and if you realize my predicament, perhaps in some small way, you'll understand how your father felt when he sent you and your mother away."

CC nodded, but said nothing. "I've always believed CC is an astute judge of character," Flash said, "and I've prided myself on having the same gift. Young man, I'm impressed with your honesty and level headedness. I believe I can trust you."

"In that case, Flash, will you please stop beating around the bush and give me a good reason for taking a two-day excursion?"

"I'll try. As you know, the Committee of Seven was originally formed to oppose the use of nuclear power, but over the year's we've used our resources all over the world to bring about peace."

"How, Flash?"

"Let's just say we had help from our respective governments, and we worked behind the scenes, urging and cajoling."

"So you're a political group?" Charlie asked.

"Not exactly."

CC was puzzled. "But the scope of your power and mission changed from what it was in the beginning?"

"Let's not get ahead of ourselves. I want to take you through this step by step. After the end of World War II and the dropping of the bomb over Hiroshima and Nagasaki, individuals in power in the American government feared the proliferation of nuclear weapons or the use of nuclear energy for peaceful purposes. Their reasoning was with the unsettled world, any country with nuclear capability could bring about destruction of their enemies. A third world war would mean the end of life as we know it—"

"But—"

"Let me finish honey. Each individual country had a reason for employing our committee. The Japanese feared a repetition of the bombings that took so many lives and caused so much misery. The German government feared the rise of another Hitler. If the fuehrer with his total disregard for human life possessed the technology to drop the bomb, the result of the war might have been very different. With their people's history of military fanaticism, the German leaders couldn't take a chance. The American oil barons, me included, couldn't risk losing millions of dollars if oil was replaced by nuclear power. The Swiss, a neutral country during the war, wanted to make the world a safer place without fear of a European nuclear war. The French were still reeling from the Nazi occupation and worried that if another dictator were to come to power in Europe, they might suffer another occupation or, worse, be annihilated by an atomic bomb."

"And my father?" CC asked.

"William's father had invested most of his assets in American oil. Thought it was never publicized, he did a great deal to help his country rebuild economically after the war. The British government asked his son, your father, to represent them on the committee, and because of his connection to oil, he accepted. Of course, after his initial exposure to the committee, he wholeheartedly supported our cause, and not for personal gain."

"But he did gain financially, as you did. Is that right, Flash?"

"In a way, CC, but your father and I had profited from oil long before the formation of the committee. We didn't make our fortunes as a result of our work or through tips we might have received from other members. CC, your father was an ethical man."

"But he was incredibly wealthy, Flash. How could he not have profited?"

"You're saying that in order to be part of the committee, your father and I should have divested ourselves of our oil interests."

"I don't know, Flash. Mr. Norris told me my father diversified his portfolio."

"I did too; does that ease your mind?"

"Who appointed members of the committee," Charlie asked.

"Prime ministers and presidents at a high-level economic meeting. The countries were not called the G-8 at the time they decided a committee such as ours was necessary. However, when the committee was formed, the heads of government, for strictly political reasons, refused to acknowledge our appointments or publicly discuss our work. There would have been too much political backlash and too much explaining to do if our existence became public knowledge, so we worked behind the scenes at the beginning and we still do, though our role has changed considerably."

"Did Prime Minister Thatcher and later Tony Blair know of my father's membership? I've seen pictures of both of them with William at Knockie."

"They did, CC, as did several American presidents."

"And if a committee member died?" Charlie asked.

"The government in power appointed someone to take his place."

"So you believe my father's death and the questionable suicide of Mr. Yamato are because of their membership on the committee?"

"I suspect they are, though I have no proof and without autopsies we may never know how the either one of them died. That said, the investigation continues. All I can say for sure is that both men died under mysterious circumstances, and we're working to find out why."

"Is the committee involved in a dangerous project right now?" CC asked.

"That's something I can't talk about, but I will tell you, I'm in England to see you and to meet with other committee members."

"To do what?" CC asked.

"To regroup and investigate your father's death."

"You said you needed to meet with Harrison Caulfield? Why?"

"He kept papers for your father."

"The papers he wouldn't give me?"

"Not without the approval of the committee. After your father's death I was appointed chairman of the group. I need to see Caulfield to get your father's papers and notes."

"I'm not sure he has what you're looking for, Flash," CC said.

"What do you mean?"

"I mean I may be the one to provide the answers you're seeking."

"What makes you think so?"

"For now, let's leave it at that. After you see Harrison Caulfield, we'll talk again. If he doesn't have what you need, I may know where to find the information."

"But you're not going to tell me now?"

"No, Flash. I need leverage. I appreciate your sharing what you have tonight, but you stopped short of telling me everything. If I give the papers to you, or what I think are the papers you're searching for, I'll have nothing to convince you to tell me everything."

Flash laughed. "Your trump card?"

"You might call it that. Let's just say I know you, Flash. You're a wheeler-dealer, and you raised me right. I can be exactly like you."

"Disadvantaged by my own teachings." Flash laughed. "Okay, honey, you keep your secret for now. I assume this means you'll leave London tomorrow as I asked? After I meet with Caulfield and contact the other committee members, I'll see you at Litchfield. Shall we say around dinner time day after tomorrow?"

CC turned to Charlie. "Are you able to fit a two-day excursion into your plans?"

"Absolutely. You said you wanted to see Coventry and Kenilworth. They're on the way to Hintlesham. Would you like to meet my father?"

"I'd love it!" CC turned to Flash. "All right, I'll do what you ask, but when you get to Litchfield, I expect answers."

"And I hope to be able to give them to you, honey. But right now, I'm beat. If you don't mind, I'll go to bed."

"Of course. Let me show you to your room."

"I know where it is. I'll see you in the morning before you leave."

CC kissed Flash on the cheek. "I don't think I told you, but I'm glad you're here."

"It's wonderful to see you too, honey." He hugged CC and shook Charlie's hand. "I'll see you tomorrow."

"I look forward to it, sir," Charlie said.

After Flash closed the door to his suite, CC sat down on the couch. Charlie joined her. "Unbelievable! He's the last person on earth I expected to see tonight," she said.

"I believe he was trying to be honest and make things right between the two of you."

"I know, but I also think there's a great deal he's not telling me."

"That may be true. Perhaps he'll tell you more when he arrives at Litchfield."

"I hope so. Anyway, I'm sorry he put you on the spot with his questions about your feelings for me."

"He hardly brought up a topic I haven't considered over and over from the first moment I laid eyes on you. At least he broached the subject and let me explain my predicament. If and when I ask you to marry me, and I hope I'll be able to do so, it will be after you make your other decisions. What you decide will tell me if I can ask you to be my wife."

CC rested her head on Charlie's shoulder. "Knowing that doesn't make my choice any easier."

"I know, CC, and I'm not trying to put additional pressure on you. Now, we're both tired, and I think it would be best if I slept in my suite."

CC frowned. "I agree. I'd rather not flaunt our relationship in front of Flash."

"This afternoon makes it a little easier for me to leave you at the bedroom door."

"Ditto. Come to think of it, we won't even have tomorrow night. I can't very well arrive at Hintlesham Hall and move into your room. What would your father think?"

"He too would agree I'm an incredibly lucky man, but I understand. Propriety."

"A word I could do without." She kissed Charlie. "I'll see you in the morning."

He kissed her again. "On second thought, maybe I'll go with you."

"Propriety!" CC hugged him and went to her suite.

CHAPTER TWENTY-EIGHT

Charlie was eager to get an early start. Because neither he nor CC had appropriate clothes for a country excursion, they decided to go to Chadlington where Charlie kept a wardrobe so he wouldn't have to transport clothing each time he came to visit. They would then drive to Litchfield so CC could pack what she'd need at Hintlesham.

It began to drizzle as they pulled away from the hotel. "I was wondering if it would ever rain around here," CC said. "I've always heard about England's rainy weather."

"We've had an unusually dry spring."

By the time Charlie exited the M25, the drizzle had stopped and he cracked the window so CC could enjoy the fresh air and fragrant smells. They turned off the A40 at Burford to take the back roads to Chadlington.

CC hadn't approached Chadlington Manor from that direction, so she was seeing the quaint towns for the first time. "I love it here," she said. "What a wonderful place to live."

When they pulled into the driveway at Chadlington, CC remembered she hadn't called Alex. "I almost forgot. Alex and Tony are still in the city and we forgot to let them know we were leaving. With Flash's unexpected arrival, my plans with your sister completely slipped my mind."

"We'll call them right away so they won't worry when they try to reach us and we're nowhere to be found."

"Why don't I do that while you get your clothes? I don't want to hang around here or at Litchfield. I want to see more of your glorious countryside."

"I'll only be a few minutes."

Charlie went upstairs to pack while CC phoned Alex. Tony answered and told her Alex was still asleep. He was surprised that CC was calling from Chadlington. She explained that Flash was in her suite when they arrived at the hotel the evening before, and at her stepfather's urging, she and Charlie were going to Hintlesham. She promised to explain everything when they got together.

When she hung up, Charlie was ready and waiting. "After we stop by Litchfield, would you like to see more of Cotswold country?" he asked as they drove away from the house.

"If it won't put us at Hintlesham too late, yes."

Packing for the overnight trip took CC very little time, and soon they were off. As they drove through Stow-on-the-Wold, Chipping Campden, and Broadway, CC ran out of adjectives to describe the charming scenery. Sheep grazed in the meadows and on the hills, and once again she compared the countryside to a bright patchwork quilt. The dampness of the morning gave way to bright sunshine, and Charlie opened the windows as they headed for Shakespeare country.

They passed Warwick Castle, drove through the charming town of Stratford, made a short detour to see Trinity Church, and savored the glorious countryside they were passing through.

When they arrived at Kenilworth, Charlie parked in the car park and they walked toward what he said was "one of the finest and most extensive ruins in England." Hand in hand, they wandered through the Strong Tower, the Saint Lowe Tower, the Great Chamber, and Gaunt's Tower. They climbed the rickety stairs to the castle's second and third levels and looked over the remains of the Great Hall, a magnificent room even in its ruined state. "I feel a strange connection here," CC said. "I don't know why, but I'm fascinated with this place."

"I believe your father was related to Katherine Swynford, John of Gaunt's third duchess and the mother of the Beaufort line. They were the ancestors of Richard III, Edward IV, and the Tudors."

"Really? Did Kathryn and John live here?"

"I believe they did, but I'm not certain."

"I'd love to know more about my family tree. I wonder if there's information at Litchfield."

"I'm sure there is. There will also be extensive peerage records available in London."

"Would you help me do some research?"

"Gladly, and I hope this means you're considering remaining in England."

"I'm closer to it than I ever thought possible. After all, how else could I get that proposal I so much want to hear?"

"As soon as you decide to stay, you'll have it." Charlie took her hand.

"In the meantime, I've made one very important decision," CC said. "I want an ice cream cone from that stand over there. Let's eat it on that bench under the tree. I have something to tell you."

"Ice cream sounds wonderful, but should I be worried about what you plan to say?"

"Maybe. After all, it could affect your life."

Charlie bought two toffee ice cream cones and they walked over to the bench. "Now what's this momentous announcement you have to make that you say will transform my life?"

"I didn't say it would alter it immediately, but this is an enormous step for me."

"Then by all means, share it with me."

"I've decided to ask the Turners for a leave of absence from the Knights. I want to stay in England, at least until the mystery of my father's death is solved. After that, I'll make my final decision whether to extend the leave, go home, or resign. What I do know is I can't do an adequate job running a baseball team from thousands of miles away. It's not fair to the Turners or the people in the office, and it's not fair to me either."

"Are you sure that no one, including me, has pressured you to do this?"

"No one."

"And you feel you can't possibly combine your job as president of the Knights with your responsibilities as the Countess of Litchfield?"

"Realistically, there's no way. I hate to admit it, but I can't handle both jobs the way I would want to. I don't do anything halfway."

"Can you give up baseball for your English title or vice versa?"

"I really don't know, but I can't make a decision until I hear what Flash has to say tomorrow night. After that, I'll know what I have to do. I'm sure of one thing, however. It would be terribly difficult for me to say good-bye to you."

"CC, I didn't tell Flash about my intended proposal to put undue pressure on you. I wanted him to understand how I feel."

"I know that, and I want you to know how I feel." She leaned over and gave him an ice cream-flavored kiss.

"When do you plan to ask for the leave of absence?"

"If it's okay with you, I'll call the Turners from Hintlesham. With the home opener just weeks away, I want them to know that our baseball people will do a great job even though I'm not there."

"Does it bother you to know that the Knights can function without you?"

"Not at all. It makes me proud. It says I've worked hard to bring competent people on board."

"Good. And of course you may call from Hintlesham. But first we have to get there. Shall we go over to Coventry and then head to my father's house?"

"Absolutely!" They drove the seven miles to Coventry, parked the car, and walked to the cathedral. CC was unimpressed with the city, but the cathedral was another matter. The old and the new; the gothic and the modern, the destroyed and the recreated combined in the two vast structures.

Charlie reiterated what Alex had said during the ride to Knockie. The old gothic building was the only cathedral destroyed by German bombs during the war, and the new, modern cathedral naturally emerged from the ruins of the old. As they walked through the ruins, CC experienced an extraordinary understanding of man's inhumanity to man and the effects of war. She stood in front of the stone altar in the sanctuary, with the charred wood cross behind. She had chills as she read the two words inscribed on the wall behind the powerful symbol: *Father Forgive.*

They explored the rest of the ruins until there was no more to see. "Are you ready to look at the new cathedral?" Charlie asked.

"I am." They walked to the front of the ruins and crossed the street to the Cathedral of the Reconciliation. CC looked up at the gigantic sculpture of Saint Michael casting out the devil emerging militantly from the facade of the building. "This is rather outrageous," she said.

"You don't like the piece?"

"It's not that I don't like it. I suppose I didn't expect to see such a modernistic grotesque sculpture in an English cathedral. This place really is ultra-modern."

"But you have to admit it's beautiful. The altar tapestry designed by Graham Sutherland is entitled *Christ in Glory*. See the cross on the altar? After the destruction of the cathedral in 1940, the Reverend A.P. Wale took three fourteenth-century nails which had once secured the roof beams from the rubble and shaped them in the form of a cross as a symbol of hope."

CC again had goose bumps. "What a remarkable experience!" she said as they left the church. "I love it here."

"I hope going to my ancestral home is equally as marvelous and that you love it there too. After all, if I have my way it will be your home someday." CC smiled, but didn't respond. Charlie took her hand, and as they walked to the car, CC looked back at the symbolic ruins.

Industrialization had crept in to mar the scenery in the countryside they traveled through on the way to Hintlesham. Tired from her encounter with Flash and little sleep the night before, CC napped while Charlie drove toward Suffolk. After what seemed like no time, she was awakened by his touch on her arm. "You are at Hintlesham, my lady."

"Have I slept that long? Are we at the house?"

"We're just entering the property. I thought you might enjoy the scenery on the drive to the hall."

"I would, and will you be my tour guide?"

"Gladly. Hintlesham is set in a wooded park of approximately four thousand acres. The house, though some would call it a small castle, was built between 1815 and 1820." As if on cue, they rounded a corner and the gray stone building came into view, perched proudly amid a springtime sea of bright pink rhododendrons, head-high azaleas, snowdrops, daffodils, bluebells, and yellow irises.

"What an incredible picture," CC said admiringly. "Once again I wish I had my camera. My cell phone camera won't do the house justice."

"You'll be able to take many pictures as you want in the years to come." Charles didn't give CC time to respond. "And I'm glad you approve. You're in good company. Queen Victoria visited Hintlesham several times during her reign. My father said she wrote in her diary that she had never seen a lovelier or more romantic spot."

"I would have to agree. It's beautiful."

"And I hope to make it romantic too." Charlie put his hand on CC's leg.

"And shock your father?"

Charlie groaned. "Oh yes, I almost forgot. Are you ready to greet the lion in his den?"

"Should I be nervous?"

"Not at all. He'll love you."

"I hope so. It would be horrible if he forbade you from seeing me."

"He would never do that, especially when he sees how much I love you. So let's go." Charlie pulled the car up to the front door. A liveried servant came down the stairs to greet them. "Good afternoon, Spence," Charlie said.

"Good evening, Your Lordship. It's wonderful to have you home."

"Thank you. May I present Lady Litchfield?"

"Welcome to Hintlesham, my lady."

"Thank you, Spence. I'm glad to be here."

"Your father is in his study, my lord. Would you like for me to announce you?"

"That won't be necessary. I'll show Lady Litchfield some of the house on the way to see him."

"Then I'll put your bags in your room and Lady Litchfield's in the green suite."

Charlie led CC into the house. She looked up at the crystal chandeliers hanging from the lofty ceiling of the entry. In the drawing room she admired the elaborate plasterwork and the floor-to-ceiling windows that let in the sunlight and made the immense, formal room seem paradoxically warm and cozy.

They walked through Charlie's "favorite room," the billiards room that contained an impressive collection of horned trophies of the chase. "I'm totally lost," CC said. "If you were to leave me here, I would never find my way back to the front door."

"It's really not that difficult. I probably should have taken you on an organized tour, but I wanted to show you some of my favorite places before we meet my father."

"It's an extraordinary house. I imagine you and Alex had a fantastic time growing up here."

"I had a very happy childhood, and now you'll meet one of the reasons why." He stepped aside to allow CC to enter his father's study.

A tall, distinguished, older-looking Charlie rose to greet her. "Welcome to Hintlesham Hall, Lady Litchfield. It's a pleasure to meet you."

"Thank you very much," CC said. She had no idea what to call the earl. "It's wonderful to be here. Charlie has told me a great deal about you and his home."

"Did he speak well of both?"

"He certainly did."

"I'm glad to hear that." He gave Charlie a hug. "And Lady Litchfield is as lovely as you said she is."

"Would you mind calling me CC, sir? That is, if it's not highly improper. I have a great deal to learn when it comes to proper British etiquette. In fact, I have no idea how I should address you."

"Would 'Richard' be acceptable to you?"

"That would be perfect if it's truly all right with you."

"It is. Now, my dear, come and sit down. Charles, would you ring for John? I imagine you and CC would like some tea. I waited for you."

Charlie pulled the cord. After several minutes, a young man appeared with a silver tray containing a teapot, three cups, and a plate of finger sandwiches. "It looks delicious," CC said. "I didn't realize how hungry I was."

"There was no time to stop for lunch," said Charlie. "We had to make do with only an ice cream cone."

"That's right. You covered a great deal of ground today. Forgive me." He turned to CC. "Would you like to wash up before tea?"

"If there's time, and I'd like call to my office. If you'd like to go ahead without me, please feel free."

"We'll wait for you," Richard said. He turned to John. "Would you show Lady Litchfield to her rooms and wait for her outside the door. When she's ready, please bring her back here."

"Certainly, Your Lordship. My lady, if you will follow me." Charlie and Richard stood as CC left the room.

CC was glad Richard had told John to wait. She knew she'd be lost forever in the huge house if left to her own recognizance. She saw rooms Charlie had failed to take her through on her initial tour, including the huge dining room that looked as if it would hold fifty people. The house was much larger than Litchfield. As Charlie had said, it was really a small castle.

The Green Suite was lovely. The ceiling was high and the room shimmered with reflected light from the many mirrors. As expected, the walls were green. There were stunning antiques everywhere, including the bed with a green canopy.

"The sitting room and bath are through that door, my lady." John gestured across the room.

"Thank you, John. The room's beautiful."

"It's my favorite suite, my lady. I'm glad you like it. The maids have hung your clothes in the closet. I'll wait outside for you." John left the room, closing the door behind him.

CC decided to change her clothes and chose a simple silk print dress, another from Lady Anne's wardrobe. She touched up her makeup and sat at the desk to make the all-important call to Indianapolis.

"CC's office," Leslie answered.

"Hi, Leslie."

"CC, it's great to hear your voice. It seems like forever since we heard from you."

"I know, and I'm sorry. Life's been crazy."

"Here too with the opener right around the corner. Are you okay?"

"I'm fine. What's happening there?"

"Same old, same old."

"Jim?"

"Bingo!"

"What about his meeting with the Turners?"

"I have no idea, but I know he's grinning a lot."

"Oh Lord." CC paused. How could she possibly ask for a leave of absence under the circumstances? But how could she not? There was no way to deal with Jim Oats from thousands of miles away. Bob could handle him if the Turners were warned about his antics. She had to let go, at least for now.

"CC?"

"I'm here."

"Do you want me to transfer you to Jim?"

"Not right now. Are the Turners available?"

"I know they're in the building. They came in for a pre-season booster club luncheon. I think they're with Bob right now."

"Excellent. Could you please put me through? I'll get back to you after I speak with them."

"Okay. CC, are you sure everything is all right? You sound upset."

"I'll explain after I speak with the Turners. Would you connect me?"

"Will do!"

"CC, this is Bob. How are you?"

"I'm fine, how about you? Is everything under control?"

"For the most part, everything's great with the team. I'm a few days away from heading out for the season opener. Are you still planning to be here for the first home stand?"

"At this point, I can't really say. Bob, are the Turners there with you?"

"They're sitting right across from me."

"Could you close the door and put me on the speaker phone? I need to speak to all three of you."

"Right away." CC heard a click. "We're all here."

"Hello, Peter, Janice. How are you?"

"We're wonderful, CC," Peter said. "How are you doing?"

"I'm holding my own."

"We missed you in Florida. You and Bob put together a great team. We think we can take it all," Janice said.

"I wish I could be there to start the season." CC suddenly realized how torn she was."

"You won't be back by then?" Peter asked.

"I don't think so. In fact, I'm glad you're both there with Bob. Unfortunately, Peter, I need to ask for an indefinite leave of absence from the team. My family matters in England require all my concentration, and I can't run the club from a distance."

"CC, how long do you expect to be away?" Bob asked.

"I really can't say for sure. At first, I thought I'd be back for the first home stand, but now I really doubt I will be. Peter, I believe this is the best move for the Knights. Bob has a great office staff, and I have no doubt he'll do a great job running the team without me. Of course I'll be available to consult if the need arises. I'm not dropping out of sight, but I need to put my personal life in order before I can assume the reins of the ball club on a full-time basis."

"Of course, CC. We understand," Janice said with concern in her voice. "Can Peter and I do anything to help? You sound so distressed."

"I'm really fine, Janice, but I feel dreadful about letting you down. As I said, Bob will do an outstanding job. However, there is one thing I need to tell you."

"What is it, CC?" Peter asked.

"Bob, are you listening?"

"I'm here, CC."

"You must tell the Turners about Jim Oats and his shenanigans. I know we agreed that you and I could handle him, but from what I've been told, he's gone over both our heads. Has he met with you Peter?"

"He has, CC, but we thought he had your blessing."

"Quite the contrary. Jim's playing another one of his games. Peter, you and Janice need to hear the entire story. If I were home, Jim would be gone, kaput. I believe Bob has to fire him right away. He'll be a thorn in his side as long as he works for the Knights."

"But CC, he seems to have some excellent ideas," Janice said.

"Janice, it would take hours to tell you about the times we've rescued the Knights from Jim's so-called good ideas. Please listen to Bob. And Bob, tell them everything. Janice, I know you and Peter will be in absolute agreement when Bob is finished."

"I'll fill them in just as soon as we hang up." Bob sounded pleased that he would be the catalyst for Jim's downfall.

"We'll miss you, CC," Peter said. "You know your job is here for you when you're ready to return to Indianapolis. We have no intention of losing the best president in Major League Baseball."

"I appreciate it, Peter. At this point, I don't know when and, to be honest, if I'll be back. I want to be totally up-front with you; I'm seriously considering accepting my inheritance, which would mean a permanent move to England."

"You're not serious, CC," Bob said incredulously. "After your struggle to become the first woman chief executive in baseball and with all the respect you've earned in the industry?"

"Damn we'd hate to lose you," Peter said glumly. "That being said, we appreciate your forthrightness, CC. But there's still hope for the Knights. You haven't made a definitive decision?"

"That's right, Peter. I'm still very much up in the air. For now I hope you'll accept my leave of absence for exactly what it is: time away to make some very important choices."

"Of course, but please remember what I said. We don't want to lose our CEO. Your position is secure until you decide otherwise. You certainly don't need to add apprehension about your job to your list of concerns."

"I appreciate your understanding, Peter. I'll keep you posted. Bob?"

"Yes, CC."

"I'll talk with you tomorrow. Let Leslie know where I can reach you. I'll want to know what you and the Turners decide regarding Jim, and I want to fill you in on a few projects I have in the early planning stages. I would also appreciate it if you could get Wesley to put out an inter-office memo announcing my leave. Be as general as possible, and please keep everyone believing this is strictly a short-term proposition. I don't want any speculation about the possibility of my not returning until I make a decision one way or another."

"Wesley will get out the memo today and I'll call Spike. He can tell the team."

"Good, and please give Spike and the players my best wishes for a fantastic season. Tell them I expect to hear about a record-breaking winning streak."

"I'll pass on the word. Do you want me to fax or e-mail game reports?"

"We get CNN, so I'll see game highlights. I think it would be more difficult for me to concentrate on what I'm doing here if I'm directly involved. I need to distance myself until I decide what I'm going to do. You understand, don't you?"

"Perfectly, and good luck, CC. I hope you decide to come back to Indianapolis."

"Thank you, Bob. Will you transfer me to Leslie? I don't want her to read about my leave of absence in an office email."

"Sure. Keep in touch."

Even though she made it clear her leave of absence was temporary, Leslie was crying when the call ended. "I wish

I could make her feel better," CC said as she put her phone in her purse. She looked at her watch. She looked at her watch. She'd been upstairs for thirty minutes. "Poor John," she groaned, "he must be tired of waiting, and the tea must be very cold."

John stood patiently by the door, seemingly unfazed that she had kept him waiting so long. He led CC back to the study and, at Charlie's request, went to get a pot of hot tea. "I'm very much afraid we started without you," Richard said.

"I apologize. My telephone call took longer than I expected."

"Did you accomplish what you set out to do?" Charlie asked.

"I did. As of five minutes ago, I am on an official leave of absence from the Indianapolis Knights."

"Did the Turners understand?" Charlie asked.

"They did, but they vowed not to give me up without a fight."

"In that case, I welcome the challenge. I also refuse to let you go."

"My, my, you are a popular young woman," Richard smiled. "Please join us for tea." John brought the hot brew, and during the next hour CC had a wonderful time hearing stories about Charlie and Alex's youth. After a few minutes, the Knights were worlds away and out of her mind.

At Charlie's urging, CC shared particulars about her father and the Committee of Seven. Richard didn't seem particularly surprised about William's involvement with the committee and apologized that he couldn't answer her questions. His relationship with William existed only in the House of Lords and occasionally on social occasions. However, like all the others who had spoken of her father, he praised the man's integrity.

When teatime ended, Charlie walked CC back to her suite so she could change for dinner. "Your father's extraordinary," she said.

"He obviously likes you."

"I'm glad, and again I apologize for taking so long calling Indianapolis. That didn't make for a very favorable first impression."

"We understood. While you were out of the room, I explained some of your predicament. Father understands your dilemma."

"I must admit I feel much less pressure after calling the Turners. With the Knights in Bob's hands, I can concentrate on solving the mysteries here."

"And on me?"

"If I have time in my busy schedule." CC turned and went into her room to change for dinner, leaving Charlie in the hall, his mouth open to make another comment.

The entire evening was wonderful. CC shared stories of Flash and growing up in the baseball world. Richard was shocked she didn't mind cleaning the bathrooms at the minor league ballpark where she began her career. Richard talked of Charlie's mother and the pain he felt when she died after a lengthy illness. By the end of the evening, CC felt extremely comfortable in Charlie's house and wondered if this magnificent place would someday be her home.

At midnight, Richard rose to retire. "I believe I'll say good night," he said. "I want to be up early." He turned to CC. "Do you ride?"

"In my youth I rode quite a bit, but as I told Charlie, I rode western quarter horses. I did some riding on an English saddle in college, but that was quite a few years ago."

"I have a wonderful mare that would be perfect for you. Would you care to join me in the morning?"

"I'd love to, but I don't have riding clothes."

"Alex always leaves several riding outfits here, and though you're taller, I believe you're about her size. If not, anything you wish to wear is permissible. And what about you, Charlie, will you join us?"

"Do you really think I'd let this lovely woman ride off into the countryside alone with you?"

"You do flatter me, son. So I take it that's a yes?"

"Tell me what time."

"I suggest we gather for breakfast at eight and proceed to the stables when we're finished. Would that be acceptable to you, CC?"

"Perfect." Richard kissed her on the cheek and said good night.

"You've obviously won his heart," Charlie said.

"He's great. I'm already very fond of him."

"Another check in my plus column. You see, I planned it all. I decided to make you adore my father so you'd find it even more difficult to leave me and return to America."

"It sounds like you thought of everything."

"Shall I tell you what I'm thinking right now?"

"I can imagine, but forget it. There's no way I would do anything to make your father think less of me. Anyway, don't you want him to believe you're a gentleman?"

"And change his already-formed opinion? But you're right, we should get some sleep. We're going to have a busy day tomorrow, and tomorrow night will be quite an important one for you."

"If Flash maintains his end of the bargain."

"I really believe he will, CC. Flash wants to help you understand your father."

"I hope so."

"Come on, I'll walk you to your room, though I have no idea how I'll be able to leave you at the door."

,

CHAPTER TWENTY-NINE

CC felt exhilarated after the ride through the countryside. "That was amazing, she said. "I didn't remember how much I enjoyed riding. I even liked the English saddle."

"Join me anytime," Richard said.

"I'll take you up on the invitation." CC smiled at Charlie who grinned in response

"Will you be able to stay for lunch?"

Charlie shook his head. "Not if we're going to get back to Litchfield before Flash returns. I think we'd better clean up and be on our way."

"Then by all means, let's get back to the house. I'll have the chef prepare a box lunch for you. That way you won't have to stop along the way."

"That would be wonderful," CC said.

They left the stable area and walked back to the house. CC admired the flowers blooming profusely in the well-manicured beds. "You have such lovely gardens."

"Thank you, CC. I do a little gardening from time to time. It's one of my hobbies, though I don't interfere too much with the gardeners who watch over their domain quite jealously."

After CC and Charlie had changed clothes and packed for the return to Litchfield, Richard walked them to the car. "It was wonderful meeting you, CC. I hope you'll come to Hintlesham Hall often." He hugged her and handed her the box lunches he had promised.

"And I enjoyed meeting you. I'll see you very soon. I'd love it if you would come to Litchfield. You would be welcome."

"I accept." He gave Charlie a bear hug and waved as they drove off.

"You certainly made a good impression on my father." Charlie squeezed CC's hand. "It seems like all the men in my family are quite taken with the Countess of Litchfield."

"And I'm impressed with the men in your family."

During the trip back to Litchfield, Charlie pointed out the sights, and when they pulled up in front of the manor, Hastings came down to greet them. "Is my stepfather here?" CC asked.

"No, my lady, but I do have a surprise for you."

"A surprise?"

"Yes, in the White Drawing Room."

CC had no idea what to expect. When she walked into the room, her mother got up from the couch to greet her.

To say the least, CC was shocked. "Mother, what a surprise."

"I hope a pleasant one, darling." Mary crossed the room and embraced her daughter.

"Absolutely. It's great to see you." She looked around to see Charlie standing quietly. "Mom, may I present Lord Charles Timperley. Charlie, this is my mother."

Charlie crossed the room and shook Mary's hand. "I've heard so much about you."

Mary smiled. "I hope it's all been good."

"Now, Mother, what could I possibly have told him that wasn't wonderful? When did you get here? I had no idea you were coming."

"Neither did I, dear. Flash called me yesterday. He said you might need me, so he sent the plane, and here I am."

"Do you have any idea why Flash might think I would need you?"

"None whatsoever. He was quite mysterious. But why don't we forget Flash for the time being? It's been so long since you and I've spent quality time together without you having to rush out and deal with some office or team issue."

CC didn't want to push. "I'd like that," she said, trying to hide the exasperation she was feeling. "I'll go change, and when I come back, we'll have tea."

"Tea? You've already adopted English habits."

"You'd be surprised." CC winked at Charlie.

Mary laughed when she saw CC blush. "Oh, I don't think so."

While she changed, CC's mind raced. *Where is Flash? Has he duped me again?* "Damn you, Flash," she whispered as she closed her bedroom door and went downstairs to join her mother.

During the next hour CC and Charlie filled her mother in on everything they knew about William and Flash. Mary sat quietly, but CC could tell she was shocked by what she was hearing. Before they knew it, Hasting announced dinner. Still Flash was nowhere to be seen. CC was worried but didn't want to alarm her mother, who still held out hope that her husband would arrive. CC thought about waiting. *But what good will that do? Flash won't show up. He's using my mother like he obviously has all these years.* Suddenly her anger gave way to sadness. Had her entire life been a lie?

Convincing her mother that she and Charlie were starving after their meager box lunch, they went to the dining room for dinner. CC deliberately turned the discussion away from Flash and instead told her mother about Knockie and her visit to Hintlesham. When the delicious meal was over, Flash still hadn't arrived and Hasting reported that there were no messages for any of them.

CC's sadness turned to concern. Where was Flash? Why wasn't he here with them? *Never mind deceiving me,* she mused, her worry once again reverting to anger. *He's misleading me and he sent Mom to appease me while he runs off to do God knows what.*

When CC looked at Charlie, his unease was unmistakable. *Obviously he shares my fears.*

Mary saw CC periodically check her watch. "I know you're concerned about Flash, but don't worry, darling. You know your stepfather. He's always late."

"I'm sure you're right, Mom."

"Would you like coffee in the Blue Parlor, my lady?" Hastings asked.

Mary answered. "I'm afraid I'm going to pass." She turned to CC. "If you don't mind, I'll go to bed. Despite the nap I took on the plane, I'm terribly jet lagged."

CC realized her mother wasn't driven by exhaustion. She too was worried about Flash. CC quickly decided not to belabor the point. "Of course you are, Mom," she said as she got up from the table. "How rude of me not to realize you'd be tired. We could have eaten earlier. She hugged her mother. "Get a good night's sleep."

"It is wonderful to meet you, Charlie," Mary said, though with a little less enthusiasm than she had shown when they were first introduced. *She really is worried,* CC mused.

Charlie smiled. "I've enjoyed our evening. Sleep well."

"I will." Mary looked at CC and spoke hesitantly. "Are you two staying up to wait for Flash?"

"For a little longer," CC answered. "It's still early for us. Shall I call Hastings and have him take you to your room?"

"No, dear, I can find my way. I believe Hastings put me in the room next to yours."

"Then let me know if there's anything you need or want."

"This visit must be hard on your mother," Charlie said after Mary left for bed. "Litchfield is one of the reasons William left her."

"You know, in all my anxiety over Flash not showing, I didn't even think of how Mom would be feeling. It must be terribly difficult for her to sit here in William's home, a home that could have been hers. If you don't mind, I'll go up and talk with her for a few minutes before she goes to sleep. I've been insensitive."

"Preoccupied, not insensitive, but I believe your mother would appreciate a visit without me intruding."

"Thanks for understanding." CC leaned over and kissed Charlie lightly on the lips. "I'll be right back."

"Take your time. I'll call and check on little Charlie."

"Tell him hello for me."

"I'll do that."

CC went upstairs and knocked on her mother's door.

"Come in," Mary called.

Mary was sitting on the bed when CC entered the room. "Mom, I want to apologize for being insensitive." CC sat down on the bed beside her mother. "All I could think of were the questions I wanted to ask Flash and his promise to clarify things for me. I never thought of what you might be feeling being here in William's home."

"There's no need to apologize, CC. It's strange being here in William's home. I thought I'd feel so much closer to him here, but I don't."

"Maybe you will when I show you his rooms tomorrow, but Mom, it was so long ago and you never came here. Your life with William was in Paris."

"I know it was. But I still thought I'd feel a connection."

"Do you feel any resentment?"

"I don't think so. Not toward William anyway. I don't know if I'll ever understand why he chose his father over me."

"Maybe you will when I tell you what I know. Most importantly, I know William loved you very much. If you'd like, I'll share some of his letters with you. He constantly talks about his feelings for you, even after her married Anne."

"But if he loved me as much as you say he did, why didn't he break his engagement to Anne? He certainly wasn't marrying for money, and if it wasn't love—"

"It's that English sense of duty that I would never have understood had I not come here." CC spent the next half-hour telling her mother everything she knew about William, the Committee of Seven, William's role in trying to curb nuclear proliferation and his efforts to achieve peace in the world. Throughout the conversation, Mary cried as she realized, perhaps for the first time, what William's duty had entailed. The tears seemed to be cathartic. "Thank you so much, darling," she said when CC was finished.

"I hope what I've said helps a little, Mom.'

"It does, CC. Now tell me about Charlie. It's obvious you care a great deal about him."

"I do, Mother. I love him." CC described her breakup with Bud and her relationship with Charlie.

"And what about the future?"

"Flash asked me the same thing when we met in London. I'll tell you what I told him. Right now I'm taking it a day at a time. But enough of this for one night. You look exhausted. I'll go down to wait for Flash and you get some sleep. I'll see you at breakfast." She kissed her mother good night, went by her room to pick up her father's diary and papers, and went downstairs to join Charlie, who was sipping a brandy. "No sign of Flash?"

"Not yet. How long do you want to wait for him?"

She looked at her watch. It was already eleven. "Another hour or so, but you go on to bed if you want. I'll just sit and go through these papers. Who knows what I'll find."

"Would you like to be alone?"

"You know, I think I would. I haven't had much time to collect my thoughts, and after talking with my mother, I could use some space."

"Then I'll say good night."

"How about a jog in the morning?"

"I'll meet you in the kitchen for coffee. We can make ourselves."

After Charlie kissed her and left the room, CC poured a glass of wine and lay down on the couch to peruse the papers. Troubling thoughts impeded her concentration: Where was Flash? Was he in danger? She thought of her father's death, the mysterious fire at Knockie, and her recurrent feelings of being watched. "Oh, Flash. What's going on?" Maybe the papers would give her an idea. She started to read...

CC wasn't sure if she actually read anything. She woke up and looked at the clock. It was four-thirty. Her untouched glass of wine sat on the table beside her and the lights were still on. She started to get up, but when she reached down to remove the papers so they wouldn't fall on the floor when she stood, they weren't there.

Suddenly she was wide awake. She got up quickly and looked around the room. The papers were nowhere to be seen and neither was the diary. She searched the room and the adjoining rooms, thinking that possibly Charlie or Hastings had put them aside while she slept. They were nowhere in sight. There was no doubt. The papers were missing.

Though she hated to awaken him, she rang the bell for Hastings. A few minutes later, the obviously startled butler arrived in a bathrobe. "Forgive my appearance, my lady, but I didn't know if you needed me quickly. I didn't take the time to dress."

"I apologize for awakening you, Hastings. Did you come in here while I was asleep and remove some papers and a diary?"

"No, my lady. I met Lord Charles on his way upstairs. He said you wanted to be left alone and told me to retire for the night. I didn't stop in to say good night because I didn't want to disturb you."

"Then you didn't come in here at all?"

"No. Is there a problem?"

"I don't know yet. I was reading some of my father's papers when I fell asleep. They're gone. Hastings, did Mr. MacTandy arrive last night?" CC wondered if her stepfather had taken the papers, her "trump card" he called them.

"No, my lady. He didn't come, though we were expecting him."

"And you're sure he couldn't have gotten in without you knowing?"

"Definitely not! I would know if anyone came in or went out of the house. I haven't discussed the sophisticated alarm system at Litchfield with you. I had no need, beyond telling you about the alarm on the safe, but I assure you, if someone tried to get into this house, I would have been alerted."

"Thank you, Hastings. Let me check with Charles. Maybe he took the papers while I slept. After all, he was helping me with them."

"Is there anything else I can do for you, my lady?"

"Not at the moment. Again, I apologize for awakening you, Hastings."

"As I said, I'm at your service whenever you need me."

After Hastings left, CC searched the room again, wondering if maybe she'd put the papers somewhere before falling asleep and didn't remember, but the papers were nowhere to be found. She looked at her watch. It was nearly five, but she couldn't wait. She had to wake up Charlie and find out if he had the papers.

CC paused outside Charlie's room, wondering if she should wait until a decent hour. "No," she said, "I can't." She knocked.

After several minutes Charlie opened the door. He looked at his watch. "It's awfully early to run," he said sleepily. "Or did you come to enjoy my pleasures, my lady? I'll always get up for that."

CC ignored the comment and pushed her way past Charlie into the room. "I need to talk with you."

"CC, what's the matter? Haven't you been to bed?" He looked at the rumpled clothes she had been wearing the night before. "I was teasing. Sit down and tell me. Did Flash come home? Did he say something to upset you?"

"No, he didn't come home, but that's not the problem." She told Charlie about falling asleep with the papers and diary beside her and waking up to find them missing. "Did you come in and take them?"

"Of course not, CC. Why would I do that?"

CC knew she had been rude and accusatory, and she backpedaled. "I didn't mean that like it sounds, Charlie. I wasn't accusing you. I wondered if you had taken the papers to look them over while I slept."

"I would never do that, CC. Those are your papers. I would help you look through them, but only if you're with me. I would never be so presumptuous."

"Once again, you didn't understand what I was trying to say. I wanted you to have the papers. If you don't have them, who does? What happened to them?"

"Perhaps Hastings put them away."

"I thought of that and woke him up to ask, but he hasn't seen them. He said you sent him to bed."

"I did. I thought you might like some time alone. Is it possible that Flash came in and took them? After all, you bragged about their importance."

"Hastings said Flash couldn't have gotten in without his knowledge."

"Well, CC, if Flash couldn't get in, then no one else could. Perhaps it's one of the servants."

"Maybe you're right. I'll ask Hastings later this morning. Maybe the servant also killed my father. Maybe he's working for a foreign government."

"That's a lot of speculation, CC, and this from a woman who doesn't like mysteries."

"I know I sound ridiculous, but Charlie, what other answer could there be for the papers disappearing? I know my mother wouldn't take them, and that leaves only the servants."

"I have no idea, but we aren't going to solve anything standing here. I'll get dressed and we'll do some snooping around, starting in the chapel."

"Good idea. I'll meet you back here in ten minutes."

Charlie took CC's hand. "Don't worry, sweetheart. There must be a logical explanation."

"I hope you're right, but Charlie, I don't have a good feeling about this. All I can think about is that person, if there really was one, who watched me at Knockie. And what about Flash? He promised he'd be here last evening."

"One thing at a time, CC. We'll figure it out."

CHAPTER THIRTY

The minute CC pushed open the chapel door, she knew something wasn't right, but she couldn't quite tell what was amiss. She preceded Charlie up the center aisle. As they neared the altar, she suddenly knew the problem. "Look!" she said, alarm in her voice.

"What is it?"

"Someone moved this altar since we were in here."

Charlie looked more closely. "Are you sure? I know I tried to put it back the way it was, but maybe I was a little off."

CC was adamant. "Oh, yes you did! I checked it again as you walked back to the chapel door. I didn't want anyone who might have come in to look at the newly cleaned chapel to know about the hiding place. Who could have known about the altar besides us?"

"I can't imagine. And you say Flash didn't come in last night?"

"Not according to Hastings, but could Flash have known about the altar?"

"If he went to see Caulfield, perhaps he learned what you did."

"But I read about the chapel in a letter my father left for me. Supposedly Caulfield hasn't read any of my father's personal letters."

"Maybe he actually did, CC. Flash said your father's attorney was privy to a great deal of information."

"You may be right, but even if you are, Hastings said the house is so sophistically alarmed that no one could get in."

"Maybe Flash has the codes? Perhaps your father trusted him to come and go as he wished."

"I think Hastings would have known if my father had given the codes to anyone, and he didn't mention that to me this morning. No, I don't believe Flash could have gotten in here without someone seeing him or knowing he was in the house."

"Then who? Those papers didn't just get up and walk away."

"Do you think it's possible that someone posing as a servant killed my father and watched us to see where the papers were hidden? After we retrieved them, that same person took them when the opportunity presented itself?"

"It's a remote possibility. Why don't you ask Hastings for background information on all the staff? Maybe someone was hired recently, though it's common for the same people and their offspring to work for one family for generations."

"I've already asked. Except for Richard, my father's valet, all of the servants have been here for years, and Hastings said William knew Richard when he was valet to one of his friends. Supposedly he came highly recommended. There's also Charles, one of our chefs. He's been at Litchfield for three years. Could the killer possibly be a long-time employee, someone from a sleeper cell of sorts? Could it be that my father had an adversary in the house? If so, Hastings wouldn't know, so what good would it do to alert him?"

"I'm not sure it would do any good, but I still believe we should talk with him. Come on, let's ask him to join us for tea, but first, let's put this altar back where it belongs." He and CC pushed the altar back into place and left the chapel.

Hastings was in the dining room when they arrived. "I'm sorry I awakened you so early this morning, Hastings," CC said, "but I was upset when those papers and my father's diary were missing."

"As I told you before, there's no need to apologize, my lady. I understand your concern. Have you managed to locate the missing items?"

"Not yet. I'd like to ask you a few questions. I realize it's highly irregular, but would you have a cup of tea with Lord Charles and me in the breakfast room? We can talk more informally in there."

"Of course, my lady, I would be glad to have tea with you. This practice is not totally irregular. I often joined your father to discuss estate business in the morning or during afternoon tea. I'll have some scones and fruit brought in."

"Thank you." CC turned to Charlie. "Or would you like one of your English breakfasts instead? I don't eat much in the morning, but you shouldn't be deprived."

"Scones and fruit are fine for me, and perhaps several slices of cold ham."

"That sounds good to me too," CC said.

"I shall put in your orders and join you in the breakfast room." Hastings left while CC led Charlie to the smaller, more intimate room.

During breakfast, CC talked with Hastings about her father's servants. As Charlie had predicted, except for Richard and the several young men who worked part time, all of the earl's employees had been with him for years. Hastings was sure none of them could be involved in a theft, much less in the murder of their employer. CC sensed that Hastings was slightly offended that she could even suggest such a thing. By the end of the meal, she was certain they were on the wrong track thinking that a servant could have taken the papers and diary while she slept

When Hastings rang to have the dishes cleared, Charlie excused himself to call Glencoe. "I think I'd better check on little Charlie," he said. "I'll be back in a few minutes."

CC's frustration at reaching a dead end with Hastings was evident as she turned back to the butler once again. "Were there any incoming phone calls last night?"

"Only one, my lady. Lord Charles received a call right after he went upstairs to dress for dinner. The caller said he was from Glencoe. He wanted to report that all was fine with His Lordship's son."

Hastings excused himself to take some of the dishes to the kitchen. All of a sudden CC felt a queasy feeling in the pit of her stomach. Little Charlie wasn't at Glencoe. He was with Angus at Dunollie, and if plans changed and Lord Dougall hadn't picked the little boy up after the meeting in Glasgow; if someone from Glencoe had called, why would Charlie need to excuse himself and call for an update this early in the morning? "Oh, God," she said, "how could I suspect the man I love?"

Moments later, Charlie returned to the breakfast room. "Everything's fine at Glencoe, I'm pleased to say."

"Were you worried about anything in particular regarding Charlie?"

"No, why do you ask?"

"Hastings told me you spoke with the Glencoe staff last evening. I was concerned there might be something wrong, especially if little Charlie was at your house and not with your father-in-law."

Charlie hesitated and CC could see he was agitated. "Hastings is mistaken. Angus was taking Charlie to Cara's for the day. He left word with Thomas. When I talked with him from Knockie, he told me what he'd planned so. . ."

"You called Knockie," CC said. "I guess I misunderstood." Her hands turned cold and clammy, a sure sign that she was stressed. Something was different. She could sense it, and she didn't know why. For the first time since meeting Charlie, she felt a distance between them. He was lying to her.

"I guess so." Charlie quickly changed the subject. "So what's our plan now?"

"I'm going to make an appointment with Caulfield. If he can't see me, maybe he'll answer some of my questions over the phone. I want to know if Flash saw him and if Flash or anyone else but us knew about the secret compartment behind the altar."

"That sounds like a plan. I'll drive you to London if you can get an appointment."

"I'd like that, but I'm sure you have other things to do. I'll ask Stanley to drive."

"If that's what you prefer." CC noticed coolness in Charles's response.

She tried to sound cheerful. "Come on, don't take this personally. During the drive I'll try to gather my thoughts, and I have calls to make. You know I'm trying to turn over the reins of power to my staff." CC hoped she sounded convincing.

"CC, you don't have to make excuses," Charlie responded curtly, "but are you sure I can't do anything for you while you're away?"

"Nothing until I know where those papers are, who took them, and why Flash didn't show up here."

"Then I'll go over and see Alex and Tony. That is, if I could use one of your cars."

"Certainly, take the little Mercedes." CC brightened slightly. "And why don't you invite them for dinner. I know my mother would love to meet them."

Charlie smiled weakly. "I'll do that. What time?"

"About eight, though you certainly don't have to stay away that long."

"So the lady will miss me?"

"Of course, so give me a hug." As they embraced, CC felt the same familiar thrill. *I've been ridiculous,* she thought. *Charlie would never betray me. Maybe he didn't take that call. I have to give him the benefit of the doubt until I know better.* "And how about a kiss for the road?"

Charlie kissed her. "I'll miss you," he whispered.

CC laughed. "You'll only be gone a few hours. That's hardly enough time to miss me."

"You're so wrong. I think of you every waking minute."

"Only when you're awake?"

Charlie's blue eyes twinkled. "Okay, I dream of you when I'm asleep too. Does that satisfy you?"

CC laughed. "I don't know if that does, but you certainly do."

"Then how about a brief respite from the cares of the world before I go?"

"It's tempting, Charlie, but the servants and my mother..."

"I know, I know. Will you say good morning to your mother for me? I'm sure she'll enjoy a day with you."

"I'm looking forward to being with her. It's been so long since we've had quality time together, and I do want to give her a tour of the house."

"Then have a good day."

CC rang for Hastings and asked him to have Stanley bring the Mercedes around. She also told him to expect dinner guests. She walked Charlie to the front door and waved as he drove away; relieved she would have some space to see if her doubts were justified.

"Is there anything more, my lady?" Hastings asked as she walked back inside.

"Not until my mother gets up. Thank you."

"Then I'll attend to my other duties." He turned to leave.

"Oh, Hastings."

"Yes, my lady."

"You told me that the only call into the house last evening was for Lord Charles."

"That's right."

"Was the call from a male or female?"

"A gentleman, my lady."

"Did he take the call?"

"He did. I put it through myself and heard him answer."

"Thank you, Hastings. That's all." Hastings bowed and left the room. As she nibbled on a scone, questions raced through her mind. *Why would Charlie lie to me? What difference could a call from Glencoe possibly make to me? Unless the call really wasn't from Glencoe.* "Oh my God! Jessica Fletcher's back at work. What reason could there possibly be for me to think Charlie's call wasn't from home? I'm losing it." She took a sip of cold tea and continued to ponder the events of the past few hours. Unfortunately, she couldn't shake her suspicions.

Mary interrupted CC's musings. "Good morning, darling. Did you sleep well?" She didn't wait for CC to answer. "I must admit I slept wonderfully after our conversation." She walked over to the table. "CC, what's wrong? I can always tell when you're upset."

"Let me ring Hastings and have him bring coffee and breakfast for you, and then I'll tell you everything."

A few minutes later her mother was served and they were alone. "Now tell me what's going on, darling."

CC explained that Flash hadn't kept his promise to meet her at Litchfield, that her papers were missing, and that Charlie had lied to her about receiving a call from Glencoe. "CC, you're jumping to conclusions," Mary said sternly," and that's not like you. Flash didn't show up, but he probably has a valid reason for not keeping his promise. Hastings said Flash couldn't get into the house without setting off the alarms. You know he didn't take your papers and flee the scene, so you suspect the man you love because he didn't tell you about a phone call?"

"You mean he lied to me."

"He may have had a valid reason, I don't know, but I do know that this misunderstanding doesn't make him a thief or your enemy."

"I know that, Mom, but where are the papers and the diary? Flash knew about them."

"But CC, Flash wasn't here."

"You're right, I'm not thinking straight, so why don't we talk about something else while you eat breakfast, and then I'll show you the house."

After breakfast CC took her mother through all the downstairs rooms, including the chapel, and then upstairs to the portrait gallery. Mary paused in front of William's picture, and CC left her alone with her thoughts. After a few minutes she joined CC in William's bedroom. She walked around touching many pieces of furniture as if trying to make a connection with her dead love. "This room is so William," she whispered.

"Let me show you a few special things." CC walked over to her father's desk, removed the photo album and handed it to her mother, who sat down on the bed and opened it to CC's cheerleading picture.

"Oh my," she said quietly as she leafed through the other photographs.

"And I have the letters he wrote to me during the first few years we were in Arizona. They're all bundled up so you can read them. They will tell you so much more than I can."

"Thank you, darling." Her mother closed the album and held it to her breast. "This means a great deal to me."

"Shall we look at the rest of the suite?" She took her mother through William's sitting room and office.

In each room her mother paused to look around. "Being in William's rooms makes me feel so close to him," she said quietly.

"I'm glad. Would you like to see my—or rather Lady Anne's rooms?"

"Not right now. I'd like to spend some time alone in your father's rooms. That is, if it's all right with you."

"Of course it is. Look around all you want. Maybe you'll find something I overlooked. I have a few things to do anyway. I'll come back in an hour or so to check on you. Would you like something to drink? More coffee or some tea?"

"Nothing, darling. I want to sit here and think."

"Then enjoy yourself." CC kissed her mother on the forehead and left her alone. Now she would go and commence an unpleasant but necessary task. Instead of going to her rooms or back downstairs, she went toward the guest suites. She paused in front of Charlie's door. "What am I thinking?" she said. She considered turning around and leaving, but quickly reconsidered. She had to find out for herself. She opened the door.

The maids had already been in and the bed was made. CC went across the room to Charlie's dresser and opened the drawers. Only two had anything in them. She carefully went through the clothes, putting each piece back exactly as she found it. When she discovered nothing, she opened the closet. She was relieved that her search again produced no results. Perhaps she was wrong in suspecting Charlie. She was about to leave the room and give up on what was beginning to seem like a ridiculous mission when she saw the corner of Charlie's suitcase protruding from under the bed. She pulled it out and opened the lid.

The suitcase was empty. Just as she was about to close it, a thought came to her. "Jessica's at it again," she said. She knocked on the bottom of the case. The rap produced a hollow sound. She knocked again and then tried to pry open what seemed to be a false bottom. After several tries, the bottom popped out. Lying in the case were her father's papers and his diary. "Oh my God!" CC exclaimed. "Charlie, what have you done? Has everything between us been a lie?"

She sat on the floor and rested her head in her hands. Thoughts and questions raced through her mind. *What am I going to do? I can't confront him with what I know. I have to get away from Charlie and Litchfield, but there's no time before dinner with Alex and Tony. I'll have to wait until tonight. But what if Charlie should come home and look for the papers? He'll know I found out he took them and that could put mother and me in danger.*

Suddenly a frightening thought came to her. What if Charlie murdered her father? What if he was working for a group that opposed the Committee of Seven? "He can't be! I would know. Or would I? He swept me off my feet so quickly that I had no time to think or question his real motives. Oh God, what am I going to do?" she cried frantically.

She put the papers back into the case, secured the false bottom, and pushed the bag under the bed with one corner protruding exactly as she'd found it. She opened the room door a crack and peeked out to be sure no one was in the hall.

When she saw it was clear, she left the room and went to her own suite.

She lay down on the bed to think. Slowly a plan formed in her mind. First and foremost, she knew she could no longer trust Charlie. She also knew she had to get those papers and leave Litchfield. But when? She decided to wait until after dinner. When they were having coffee, she would excuse herself to freshen up, asking Charlie to entertain her guests. She would retrieve the papers from the suitcase, put them in her room, and return to the group downstairs. When Alex and Tony got ready to leave, she would ask Charlie to accompany them, to give her one more night of much needed time with her mother. While he packed his suitcase, she would be right there with him so he couldn't check the secret compartment. When he was gone, she'd get the papers from her room and she and her mother would leave Litchfield.

But how can I possibly pull this off, especially with ever alert Alex sitting there? She pondered. *She's bound to sense a problem between her brother and me. If she asks, I'll tell her I'm worried about so many things, including the decisions I'll have to make in the near future. Surely she'll understand.*

CC got up. "This plan has to work," she said adamantly, "but first I have to tell Mother what I found so she can call and have the plane fueled and ready to go." CC started to cry, but she wasn't sure if she was angry or hurting. "Maybe I'm both," she said, and went to see her mother.

CHAPTER THIRTY-ONE

CC found her mother sitting at William's desk. "I'm sorry to interrupt you, Mom, but this is important."

"You're not interrupting. I'm through here." Mary took a closer look at her daughter's face. "CC, you've been crying. Come tell me what's the matter."

CC began to sob. Mary held her tightly, and like so many times when she was a child, her mother made the pain hurt a little less. She let CC weep until she seemed to be cried out. When the tears had subsided, Mary asked again, "What's the matter, darling?"

Between periods of crying, CC told her mother about Charlie's dishonesty. "What do you want to do, CC?" she asked.

"I want to leave here as soon as possible." CC explained her plan.

"And you want me to call and have the plane fueled and ready at Gatwick?"

"Please."

"What time do you want to leave? I have to let the pilot and co-pilot know so they can file a flight plan."

CC thought for a few moments. "I'd like to leave London at noon tomorrow. I'll call Mr. Caulfield right now and ask if can see me at ten. As soon as Charlie, Alex, and Tony leave tonight, I'll have Stanley drive us to London."

"Tonight?"

"Yes. The sooner the better. I have the key to William's suite at the Ritz. We can stay there tonight without the hotel staff knowing. I wouldn't want Charlie to start looking for me in the morning and track us down there."

"Won't he call Litchfield and ask to talk with you?"

"He might, but I'm sure Hastings will tell him I'm asleep and asked not to be disturbed. I know Charlie well, or I thought I did. He won't ask Hastings to wake me up. He knows I need some private time and want to spend part of the day with you. By the time he suspects anything, we'll be in the air."

"If this is what you want to do, I'll make the arrangements, but CC, maybe you should talk with Charlie. There's probably a logical explanation for all that's happened."

"A logical explanation for lying to me, for stealing my father's papers and then helping me look for them, for obviously deceiving me all along, and maybe for killing my father?"

"There you go jumping to conclusions again. CC, I like this man. I also trust him and think you should too. I don't know what happened here, but whatever it is, I believe you owe him a chance to explain, especially if you love him as you say you do."

CC wouldn't budge. "Mother, it's all been a lie. From the time I arrived here at Litchfield everything's been wrong for me. I should never have thought about accepting the title and remaining in England. President of the Knights is all the title I want."

"Are you sure you're not running away from your problems by leaving without talking with Charlie?"

"I'm running away, but not from my problems with Charlie, rather from possible danger for you and me. My father is dead and so is a Japanese businessman who was part of this infamous Committee of Seven. I don't plan to be the next one to die because someone thinks I know too much. No. I've had it with Litchfield, with being a countess, and with Lord Charles

Timperley. I'm going home to deal with what I can control and with what I know."

"That was some speech. Are you trying to convince me or yourself?"

CC was irritated. "I don't really care what you think I'm trying to do. I just want out of here. I'm tired of the Jessica Fletcher persona I've assumed."

"Jessica Fletcher—"

"I'm tired of sleuthing. At this moment even Jim's antics would be welcome."

"Well, I guess if you can say that, you are ready to go home I'll make the arrangements while you call Mr. Caulfield."

"Good." CC moved toward the door between her father's suite and Anne's bedroom. She turned. "Oh, and Mother, I want you to tell the pilots that they're to tell no one beyond those they have to inform about the trip. If they know how to reach him, I don't want Flash contacted. Tell them you want to surprise Flash. Will they go along with that?"

"If I make it sound like a surprise, they will. They know how excited Flash would be if you and I flew home."

"Then please make this work."

"I will, darling. Now you go do what you have to do, and CC, would it be all right with you if I took a few personal things from this room? They would have no meaning to the next Earl of Litchfield, whoever he may be."

"Take whatever you want. You certainly deserve a few mementos." CC smiled sadly and went into her own rooms. *I'd like to take some of this jewelry*, she mused, knowing she would take nothing from Litchfield but bitter memories.

CC called Caulfield's office from her sitting room. His secretary said he was booked with appointments the following morning and would be unable to see her. CC persisted, and after putting her on hold for a few minutes, the secretary came back and said that Mr. Caulfield would be able to fit her in for a few minutes at ten. CC asked that Caulfield be immediately told the appointment would come under attorney-client privilege; that she wanted no one to know of their upcoming meeting. The obviously irritated woman promised to relay her message."

"Step one accomplished," CC said. She went back to her father's room to see if her mother had made the flight arrangements. Mary was on the phone when CC entered the room, but it was obvious she wasn't talking to one of the pilots. CC started to leave so her mother could have some privacy, but Mary motioned her back into the room. CC waited until she hung up. "Were you able to make the arrangements?"

"We're all set, though for some reason I got the impression the plane has left England. Anyway, they think they're part of a conspiracy to surprise Flash, so I know they'll keep quiet."

"Good. Were you just talking to them?"

"No, I was speaking with Martha."

"You didn't tell her about our plans."

"Of course not, CC. Give me some credit."

"I do, and I'm sorry, Mom, I guess I'm nervous."

"I know, darling, but relax. Everything will work out."

"I hope so." CC looked at her watch. "It's already three. I imagine Charlie will be back for tea at four, so we should get dressed."

"Do you really think you can fool him?"

"I'll have to. So much depends on how good I am."

"I'm going to try one more time, darling. Please trust him and see if you can't end this misunderstanding. There has to be a rational explanation—"

"For finding my father's papers in his suitcase? Gee, Mother, maybe he was just keeping them safe for me."

"That's enough sarcasm for now."

"I'm sorry. Shall we get ready for the big show? CC smiled, thinking about the term "big show." It was what the minor league players call the big leagues. *Well I'm in the big leagues now,* she mused

Mary went to her room while CC remained behind in her father's suite. She looked around. *This is probably the last time I'll be in here,* she reflected. *I can't believe I'm feeling sentimental.* She walked over to her father's desk and sat down. *And to think I was about to accept all of this as mine.* She thought of Charlie. *But it couldn't be. It wasn't a fairy tale and no one will live happily ever after.* She got up and went to her rooms to get dressed.

Charlie arrived at four. Hastings escorted him to the library where tea was waiting. "Lady Litchfield and her mother will join you in a few moments, my lord."

"Very good, Hastings. Did they have a good day?"

"They spent a great deal of time together in the earl's room. They didn't need me to interfere."

"Interfere with what?" CC asked as she entered the room.

"I was just telling Lord Charles that you and your mother spent the day without need of my services."

"We did and enjoyed every minute of our time together, didn't we, Mother?"

"We certainly did, darling. Hi, Charlie." Mary walked over and extended her hand.

"I think we're beyond handshakes," Charlie said. He hugged Mary and turned to CC. "And how about one for my favorite lady?"

"I can't think of anything I'd enjoy more."

"Oh, I can," Charlie whispered in his ear while he hugged her.

"I believe my mother's in the room," she whispered. "Are Alex and Tony joining us?"

"They'll be here for cocktails at seven, if that's all right."

"Great." CC turned to her mother. "I'm eager for you to meet my friends." As she spoke the word "friends," CC suddenly wondered if Alex and Tony were part of Charlie's deception. *Oh God! How will I make it through this evening?* she wondered.

Actually, tea went better than CC imagined. Her mother and Charlie dominated the conversation, and despite herself, CC enjoyed their banter. The primary topic was Mary's life in Arizona, though she talked a little bit about her time in Paris with William. While they conversed, CC realized that her mother truly did like Charlie. There was no reluctance to share intimate moments of her life.

When Alex and Tony arrived, the remainder of the evening went just as well. Alex and Mary quickly found they had similar interests, and the two talked nonstop. CC was relieved that she didn't have to act. Despite the problems facing her, she enjoyed her last evening at Litchfield.

When they entered the White Drawing Room for coffee, CC pulled Charlie aside. "I need to freshen up. Would you act as host while I'm gone?"

"With pleasure. CC, are you okay?"

"Of course, why do you ask?"

"You were so quiet this evening."

CC smiled. "How could I get a word in edgewise? You and my mom talked nonstop."

"She's almost as wonderful as you are. I'm crazy about her."

"I think I can safely say she returns your sentiments, so keep her company, would you? I'll only be a minute."

"Hurry back."

CC paused at the head of the stairs to make sure no one was following her. "God, I'm paranoid," she whispered. When she heard no footsteps on the stairs, she moved quickly to Charlie's room, opened the door, and closed it quietly behind her. It took only minutes to pull out the suitcase, pop out the false bottom, and retrieve her father's papers and diary. She tucked them inside her jacket, went to the door, and peeked outside. "So far so good!" she said as she opened it wider.

Just as she was about to go out in the hall, one of the upstairs maids headed toward her. Now what? CC ducked back into the room. *She's obviously here to turn down the beds and change the bathroom towels. How can I explain what I'm doing in here?*

The maid opened the door and stopped in her tracks when she saw her mistress. "Your Ladyship," she stammered, "I didn't expect to find you here. I was going to turn down His Lordship's bed."

CC thought of a response and realized she didn't owe her maid an explanation. "There will be no need to do that, thank you. I don't believe Lord Charles will be staying here tonight."

"Very good, my lady." The maid turned and left the room.

Rank does have its privilege, CC reflected. Whatever the mistress says goes. No explanation needed, though she wondered if she would be a topic of conversation in the servant's dining room that night.

CC took the papers and diary to her room, tucked them in her underwear drawer, and went to rejoin the others. "Welcome back," Charlie said. "I was beginning to think you'd forgotten about us."

"I made a quick call home." CC couldn't believe she was lying so easily.

"Everything all right, darling?" her mother asked.

"It is, but I have a splitting headache, and I think I'm going to be a very rude hostess and bring this delightful evening to a premature close."

"Why didn't you tell me?" Charlie asked. "Is there anything I can do for you?"

"I took two Tylenol, so I should be okay, but I wonder if you would consider leaving Mother and me alone for one more night. I want to get some rest and we've made plans for an early morning excursion."

"You can stay with us, Charlie," said Alex. "We'll drive you back tomorrow afternoon."

Charlie looked disappointed but accepted CC's excuse and his sister's invitation. "Let me go up and get a few things."

"I'll go with you," CC said. *So far everything's going according to plans*, she thought.

"There's no need. If your head's bothering you, why don't you wait here?"

"And sacrifice a few minutes of being alone with you?"

Charlie smiled, but it was obvious he wasn't too pleased. "Then let's go so you can get to bed."

"Are you sure you're going to be okay?" Charlie said when he finished packing his suitcase.

"Charlie, it's just a headache. To be honest, this has more to do with Mother than me." *Lying again*, CC thought. "She had a rather difficult time this afternoon. We went through William's rooms and she was very emotional. I want her to be alone with me and her memories for one more day."

"I understand, CC, but we've been together so little over the past few days."

"I know. Everything will change very soon. I promise. *But you can't imagine how*, CC thought sadly. *In fact, this is good-bye.* She regained her composure and continued, "My mother won't be here for long, and when she leaves, you and I will continue to look for clues to solve the mystery of the missing papers. Maybe Flash will show up after all."

"Come to think of it, you haven't seemed very concerned about those papers today. You haven't mentioned them since this morning."

God, he's right! CC thought. She tried to cover. "My mother's feelings and well-being have taken precedence for the time being. There will be plenty of time to play sleuth when she goes home."

Charlie seemed to accept her explanation. "How long does she plan to remain at Litchfield?"

"I expect she'll go home the day after tomorrow. We can't figure out why Flash brought her here in the first place, but we're glad he did. As I said before, it's been a long time since Mother and I have spent quality time alone together."

"Then I should go and let you enjoy each other's company. But know this, my lady, as soon as your mother leaves, you're mine. To hell with what the servants think."

"I'm shocked, my lord." CC hugged him, hoping he wouldn't notice the tears in her eyes. "Maybe we'll go to Knockie for a few days. I think the countryside would do us both some good."

"Sounds like a plan. Why don't we stop by Glencoe for a night on the way? I would like for you to become better acquainted with little Charlie."

"I'd like that," CC said, knowing that the trip to Scotland would never be.

Charlie closed his suitcase and, hand in hand, he and CC went downstairs. Alex and Tony were waiting with Mary in the entry hall. While Charlie said good-bye to Mary, Alex pulled CC aside. "You can't fool me," she whispered.

"I don't know what you mean."

"I think you do. Something has changed between you and Charlie. I don't know what it is, but I intend to find out."

"Alex, my mother is here. She's very emotional about being in William's house, and I'm trying to help her. If I sound annoyed at your insinuation, I apologize, but I can't take much more right now. That's why I asked you to take Charlie home with you. I need some space."

Alex backed off. "I'm sorry, dear. I assumed your silence this evening had to do with my brother and I was worried."

"Not at all, Alex. Give me some time and everything will be as it should be." *Yes*, she reflected. *I'll be gone and all of this will be behind me.*

"I'll try to do that, and CC, I apologize for interfering. Is there anything I can do?"

"Yes, as a matter of fact. Please, Alex, don't talk about this with Charlie. If he thinks there's something wrong, I'll have more problems to deal with, and I certainly don't need any more than I already have."

"I won't say a word. I wouldn't want to upset Charlie like I upset you. You're sure you accept my apology?"

"Absolutely. We're going to forget this conversation ever happened."

"Fine by me."

CC and her mother finished their good-byes. It took all CC could do not to cry as she waved to her departing guests. "It's been quite a fling," she said as she put her arm around her mother's shoulder and guided her inside.

"Are you sure you want to leave it all behind?"

"Right away, so let's get started. You get your things and I'll call Stanley."

CHAPTER THIRTY-TWO

"I'm so sorry to awaken you at this hour," CC said when Stanley answered the phone.

"It's no problem, my lady. What can I do for you?"

"Would you please bring the Jaguar around and drive my mother and me to the Ritz?" There was a pause on the other end of the line. *Can he refuse me?* she wondered.

"Of course, my lady. Give me fifteen minutes and I'll be there."

"Thank you, Stanley." CC was relieved. She turned to her mother. "Let's go, Mom. We have fifteen minutes."

"I'll be ready."

Before CC could ring, Hastings appeared. "My lady, Stanley just phoned me. He says you and your mother are leaving for London tonight. Is everything all right?"

"It is with me, but Mother decided to fly out tomorrow and I want to take her to London tonight so she can get an early start." CC congratulated herself for her quick thinking. She hadn't planned an excuse for Hastings.

"Is this a sudden decision?"

"You could say so. Since Flash didn't come here last night as planned, Mother felt there was no reason for her to stay any longer. It's been a very emotional time for her."

"I understand. Will you be returning tomorrow, my lady?"

CC hated to lie, but she had no choice. "I don't know. I may stay in London for a few days. I'll let you know."

"Then I'll wait to hear what you decide."

CC went to pack. She made it halfway up the stairs when she turned back. "There is one more thing, Hastings. Lord Charles went home with Lady Alexandra for the night. If he calls in the morning, I would prefer he not be told I'm in London. I want these last few hours with my mother to be private and he would probably want to join us. It would hurt his feelings if I told him not to come."

"As you wish."

For some reason, CC felt that she had to explain in more detail: "And I have a few business appointments tomorrow, so please wait until tomorrow evening before telling Lord Charles where I am. By then if he decides to drive in to see me, I'll be ready for social activities."

"I'll keep your secret until tea time tomorrow. I too would hate to have Lord Charles's feelings hurt."

Because of her conversation with Hastings, CC had very little time left to pack. She tossed her clothes and her father's files from Knockie into her suitcase and packed her makeup case. There would be no time to return her jewelry to the large safe, so she put them in the small safe in her father's room. She would tell Hastings where to find them when she called from Indianapolis. She looked around the room for the last time. "I can't think of what might have been," she said and turned out the light behind her.

Her mother was waiting at the foot of the stairs. CC was relieved that Hastings was nowhere to be seen. She hadn't had time to tell her mother her excuse for going to London in the middle of the night and didn't want her to give Hastings a conflicting story. "Did you get the things you wanted from William's suite?"

"I did. Thank you, darling."

CC looked around the Great Hall. "I could have really grown to love this place," she said.

"There's still time for you to change your mind. Talk with Charlie."

"No, Mother. Time ran out when I found those papers and the diary in Charlie's suitcase. I could never trust him again."

"I'm sorry, dear."

"So am I." CC picked up her suitcase. "Shall we go?"

Hastings and Stanley were waiting by the car. They put the bags in the trunk. "I'll call you later tomorrow and tell you what I plan to do," CC said to Hastings.

"Very good, my lady, and please come to see us again very soon, Mrs. MacTandy."

"I hope to be able to do that, perhaps next time with Flash."

"I would enjoy seeing Mr. MacTandy again. When you see him, please give him my regards."

"I'll be glad to. Thank you for your hospitality, Hastings."

"You're quite welcome." Hastings opened the back door for the women while Stanley got behind the wheel. "I'll talk with you tomorrow, my lady."

"You certainly will." CC smiled. She knew Hastings would be shocked if he knew the call would be from Indianapolis; that she wouldn't be coming back to Litchfield. Hastings shut the door and Stanley drove away from the house.

Neither CC nor her mother felt like talking during the trip. Each was deeply involved in her own thoughts. Though she tried, CC couldn't stop thinking about Charlie, and each time he crossed her mind, the anguish she felt at his betrayal was intense.

Stanley pulled up in front of the Ritz and jumped out to open the trunk while the hotel's doorman opened the door for the ladies. "Thank you so much for driving us to town, Stanley.

Rather than returning to Litchfield tonight, would you like for me to arrange a room for you here at the hotel?"

"That won't be necessary, my lady. I have a friend who has a flat nearby."

"Does he know you're coming?"

"He does. I phoned him from the road. Would you like for me to remain in town and drive you back to Litchfield after your appointments tomorrow?"

"No, but thank you very much. I'm not sure how long I'll remain at the Ritz. You go on back. I'll phone you when I want you to come for me."

"I'll be back at Litchfield by noon tomorrow and, my lady, if Lord Charles should want to use a car to come and join you in the city, would that be acceptable?"

"Certainly, but not until after four. If he asks before then, please tell him I want to finish my business before I enjoy myself."

Stanley smiled. "I'll try to stop him, but I don't think it will be easy keeping a man from the woman he loves."

CC's frown put Stanley in his place. "I am sorry, my lady. I've overstepped my bounds."

"No, I apologize for my reaction. I'm just tired."

"Then if you don't need me..."

"I'm fine. Go on and thank you, Stanley."

The bellman arrived to pick up the bags. "Shall I take these to the desk?"

"No thank you. We can manage them." CC picked up her suitcase and makeup bag and Mary took hers. The bellman seemed surprised. "I guess he's not used to guests fending for themselves," CC whispered to her mother, "but I don't want the hotel management to know we're here."

"In case Charlie calls?"

"Exactly. He would probably try to stop me from leaving."

"Well, doesn't that tell you something?"

"It does, but not what you're imagining, so let's drop it and lug these bags upstairs." CC went to the private elevator and inserted her key.

When the door opened into the suite, her mother gasped. "Oh my! This is quite a place!" she exclaimed. "And you said William owned these rooms?"

"He did, and that was exactly my reaction when I first came here, but come on, let me show you around."

CC took her mother through the suite. "Which bedroom would you like to sleep in tonight?" she asked when they had finished looking at all the rooms.

"It doesn't matter. You choose for me."

"Why don't I put you next door to me?"

"Fine, but let's settle in quickly. I'm exhausted."

"I'm tired too. I hope I can sleep."

"Maybe knowing you'll be home tomorrow and away from all these problems will help you relax."

"I hope so." CC put her arm around her mother and they walked toward the bedrooms. "I'll wake you up before I leave for Mr. Caulfield's office. While I'm gone, you can look around here, take any mementos you want, and confirm our departure with the pilots. I should be back by noon and we can be off."

"CC—"

"Not now, Mother. I know what you're going to say. And yes, I'm sure!"

"Have you called the Turners to let them know you're returning?"

"Not yet. I'll call from the plane tomorrow."

"Good." She kissed CC on the cheek. "Try to get some sleep, darling."

CC didn't sleep well. Though she was worn out, she couldn't relax enough to drift off. Her mind was filled with thoughts of Charlie. Finally, when any thought of sleep was merely a dream, she got up and sat at her father's desk. "I have to end it once and for all with Charlie," she said aloud as she took out stationery to write a letter. She looked at the monogram at the top of the page. It was the crest of the Earls of Litchfield. *It could have been mine*, she mused as she started to write:

Dear Charlie,

You must know from my dealings with Bud that I'm reluctant to confront personal issues by phone or letter, but in this instance, I have no other option. I know during dinner last evening you sensed I had a problem. Though I denied it, you were correct. I doubt you could have imagined what was really bothering me. In fact I can hardly believe it myself. Let me enlighten you.

I know you took my father's papers and diary. My need to follow up on my suspicions got the best of me, and while you were at Alex's I searched your room and found the suitcase. Later in the evening while you thought I was freshening up, I went to your room and took my property from its hiding place, but I imagine you know that by now. You probably checked on your stolen goods when you arrived at Alex's. Need I tell you I'm devastated? I trusted you with everything I knew about my father's death and the committee. I allowed you into my life. I considered giving up everything I ever wanted to be with you. Yes, you were the primary reason I decided to remain in England. It wasn't just because my father's love his land and his heritage. But now it seems we'll never get beyond our brief encounter. I'm sure you know there can't be love when there isn't trust, and how could I possibly trust a man who betrayed me or perhaps worse?

My mother continues to urge me to talk with you. She wants to believe there's a logical explanation for your having the papers, but for me, there can't be. So I'm going home to a life I love and understand. I don't want to know what happened to my father! I don't want to know what the committee was doing! I'm tired of sleuthing. In fact, I don't ever want to think of Litchfield or an English title ever again. As I told you when I first met you, being president of the Knights is the only title I want. Though my resolve to remain in baseball waffled for a brief time, I am once again on the right track.

In moments of weakness, I wish things could have turned out differently for us. I believed we had a unique relationship. Now I know why you wanted to be with me.

Please don't try to contact me. It will be hard enough for me to forget you. I certainly don't need to hear your voice.

CC read the letter again. "I said what I had to," she said. She put the letter in an envelope, addressed it to Charlie in care of Alex, and sealed it. She had no idea where Charlie would be and she didn't know the address at Glencoe. Alex would be sure her brother received the communication. She looked at the clock. It was eight. She would get dressed, go out for a bite to eat, and mail the letter from the nearest mailbox.

After she finished dressing and packing, CC popped her head into her mother's room. "Time to get up, Mother."

"I'm awake, darling." Mary looked at the clock. "Aren't you leaving rather early? It's only nine."

"I'm going to get some breakfast before going to Caulfield's. If you're hungry, go down and eat in the hotel dining room. No one will recognize you. I'm leaving the spare key to the elevator on the table by the door."

"I'll do that after I make my calls. I'll be sure we have a hot meal on the plane."

"Good. I imagine we'll both be hungry, though all I really want to do is sleep."

"You didn't sleep well?"

"I didn't sleep at all, so I welcome some quiet time as soon as we're out of here. See you soon, Mom."

"I hope your meeting is successful."

CC avoided the hotel lobby and went to a small restaurant around the corner. The coffee was terrible, but the caffeine helped her wake up. *How long has it been since I've had a good night's sleep?* She couldn't remember.

While she ate wheat toast and fruit, she perused the *London Times,* amazed by how little she had kept up with the news of the world during her stay at Litchfield. "I guess I've been living a fairy tale in more ways than one," she whispered softly. "It's time for me to get back to reality."

She paid the bill and walked over to the mailbox on the corner. She hesitated momentarily before mailing the letter, wondering if she really was doing the right thing by not confronting Charlie with what she knew. Was her mother right? Was there an explanation for his actions? "No, I could never trust him again," she said as she dropped the letter into the slot. She felt miserable as she walked back to the Ritz to hail a cab.

At nine-fifty CC walked into Caulfield's office. The same rigid secretary looked at her and the clock. *I wonder if it's gauche to be early,* she mused. "I'm here to see Mr. Caulfield."

"He's expecting you, Your Ladyship. If you'll take a seat, I'll tell him you're here."

"Thank you," CC said. She didn't even have time to pick up a magazine when her attorney came out to greet her.

"CC, I was surprised to hear from you. Won't you come back to my office?"

CC rose. "It's nice to see you, Mr. Caulfield. I appreciate your fitting me into your busy schedule. I assure you, this matter will only take a few minutes of your time."

When they entered the luxurious office, Caulfield motioned to the chair across from his desk and CC sat down. "Now what can I do for you?" he asked as he sat at his desk facing her.

"Actually several things. First, I'd like to ask you about your meeting with my stepfather, Miles MacTandy."

"CC, I'm sure you realize that, like American law, whatever Mr. MacTandy and I discussed is privileged information."

"I realize that a conversation between an attorney and client is privileged. Is Flash your client?"

"He is and has been for years. Because of all the work he does in Europe, he decided early on that it would be beneficial to have an attorney who's familiar with international law. Your father recommended me and we've had an association ever since."

"Then you won't tell me anything about his visit?"

"I'm afraid not."

"Can you tell me if he planned to go to Litchfield when he left here? He promised to meet me at the house, but he never came. He even flew my mother over, but he failed to join us."

"I'm sorry, CC. I can't tell you anything about Flash's plans. I hope you understand."

"Perfectly!" CC was exasperated. "Then I should get on to the second reason I asked to see you. I've decided to reject my title and all that goes with it."

Caulfield didn't look particularly surprised. "I thought that might be the reason for our meeting. Are you sure this is what you want to do? Flash believed you had decided to accept your inheritance and remain in England."

"I was leaning toward doing so when I saw Flash in London, but circumstances have changed. I'm going home to Indianapolis where I belong."

"May I ask you what caused you to change your mind?"

"If I could ask you a question first." Caulfield nodded. "Who else knew about my father's hiding place behind the altar at Litchfield?'

"I don't know what you're talking about, CC. What hiding place?"

"Then you didn't read my father's letters and he never told you where he kept important papers at Litchfield?"

"No, I wasn't privy to that information."

"In that case, I believe I'll keep my reasons for leaving to myself." CC stood and extended her hand. "If you would please have the appropriate papers drawn up and overnighted to me, I'll sign in front of a notary and send them back to you."

"I'm not sure that will be possible. You may have to make one more trip over here to sign in front of a British notary. But I shall look into the matter."

"I would appreciate it, as I have no intentions of returning to England anytime soon."

"Was your visit really that unpleasant?"

"That and more, but enough said. Here's my card. It also has my e-mail address and fax number, and I've put my home phone number on the back. It's unlisted. And I would appreciate it if you would not give it to anyone."

"I will respect your privacy."

CC walked toward the door. "I will expect to hear from you very soon. Thank you for seeing me. Would you be so kind and call a cab for me? And oh, I almost forgot, until I've signed those papers renouncing the title, the attorney-client privilege extends to me. Please tell no one about our visit today."

"You can be sure I'll keep your confidence. Good-bye."

"Good-bye." CC couldn't even manage a smile. Her frustration with Caulfield for not telling her about Flash coupled with exhaustion had put her in a terrible mood.

CHAPTER THIRTY-THREE

Charlie got up early and jogged around the grounds at Chadlington. After a cup of tea and a shower, he called CC. "Is Lady Litchfield awake?" he asked Hastings.

"No, my lord. She and Mrs. MacTandy stayed up quite late last night. She left a note saying she was fatigued and asked that neither she nor her mother be disturbed."

"Will you ask her to ring me at Chadlington when she gets up?"

"When I speak with her, I shall give her the message."

After a late breakfast with Alex and Tony, Charlie called Litchfield again. "They're still not awake?" he asked.

"I'm afraid not, my lord."

"Are you sure everything's all right?"

"As far as I know."

"Then please ask her to phone me."

"I'll tell her when I speak with her."

Alex saw Charlie's puzzled look as he hung up the phone. "Is something wrong?"

"I don't know, but I think so. I'll be certain in just a minute."

"What do you mean?"

"I have to check on something in my room. Then I'll be able to tell you if there's a problem."

Charlie raced up the stairs. He was tired and upset when they arrived at Chadlington so he hadn't checked the suitcase to see if the papers and diary were still there. He removed the bag from the closet and pried open the false bottom. "Oh my God!" he said as he stared at the empty space. "Now what?"

He raced back downstairs. "What's the matter?" Alex asked. "From the look on your face, I would say something terrible has happened."

"More than you could imagine!" Charlie responded. "Alex, I need to borrow a car. I have to get to Litchfield."

"Of course. I'll have it brought around."

"I'll go to the garage myself."

"Do you have time to tell me what's bothering you?"

"Not a second. I'll speak with you later."

"Good luck!" was all Alex could say as she watched her brother race toward the garage.

It was after one when Charlie pulled up to the house. Coincidentally, Stanley drove in right behind him. "My lord," Stanley said. "Are you here to get the little Mercedes? Lady Litchfield thought you might drive it to London and meet her at the Ritz."

"She's at the Ritz? Did you take her in this morning?"

"No, I drove her and Mrs. MacTandy to town last night after you left. I believe she had a meeting with Mr. Caulfield this morning and wanted to be sure she would be there on time. I believe her mother was flying home today."

"And are you supposed to pick her up?" Charlie had a nauseating feeling in the pit of his stomach. He already knew the answer.

"No, my lord. She said she would ring the house when I'm to come for her, though she didn't indicate it would be today."

"And you took her to the Ritz?"

"I did."

Charlie raced up the stairs and into the house. "Hastings," he called. "Hastings!"

"My lord, what is it?" Hastings saw that Charlie was extremely agitated.

"You told me Lady Litchfield was sleeping in this morning. Was she here?"

"I'm afraid I can't say, my lord."

"Can't or won't?"

"My lord."

"Oh, never mind. May I use the phone?"

"Of course."

Charlie hurried to the library and dialed the number at the Ritz. When the manager answered, he said that Lady Litchfield had occupied her father's suite the night before, but that he hadn't known she was at the hotel until she turned in the key."

"When did she leave?" Charlie asked, wondering if there was a chance to catch her before the plane left.

"A little over an hour ago."

"Did she say when she'd be back?" Charlie shook his head. *Why did I ask the question? I already know the answer?*

"All she said was that she wouldn't be returning anytime soon."

"Oh my God!" Charlie said as he hung up. "She's gone!"

At that moment Hastings entered the library. "I beg your pardon, my Lord," he said, a puzzled look on his face.

"I said I don't think I would wait for Lady Litchfield to return to Litchfield. I believe she went home to America."

Hastings looked puzzled. "Are you sure, my lord?"

"I'm afraid I am, but I'm going to try and confirm my suspicions."

Charlie called the private plane terminal at Gatwick. "Could you please tell me if Mr. Miles MacTandy filed a flight plan from London to Indianapolis, Indiana, USA?"

Charlie waited for the answer he dreaded hearing. After a few minutes, the operations director came on the line. "I understand you are inquiring about Mr. MacTandy's jet?"

"I am. I'm Mr. MacTandy's assistant, and I need to know if the plane has left Gatwick."

"About thirty minutes ago, sir. The flight was to Indianapolis, Indiana, with a stop in New York City to refuel and clear customs. There were two passengers and three crew members aboard."

"Thank you very much." Charlie hung up.

"Then it's true?" Hastings asked.

"It is. She went home."

"I'm so sorry, my lord. Do you have any idea why she would leave?"

"I do. It's because of me, but I'm afraid I can't go into it. I'm going back to Lady Alexandra's. If Lady Litchfield should phone, please ask her to get in touch with me."

"I certainly will, My Lord. And again, I'm sorry."

"So am I, Hastings. So am I." Charlie went to the car and drove off toward Chadlington.

✵ ✵ ✵

When the wheels of the plane lifted off the ground, CC relaxed. "We're really going home!" I can't wait." She spent the next fifteen minutes telling her mother about the appointment with Caulfield.

"So you actually gave up your title? I wondered if you would be able to refuse everything your father left you."

"I did, and I'm eager to leave it all behind. I'm also worn out, so if it's okay with you, I'll try to get some sleep."

"I brought your father's letters to read. I'll be perfectly content."

The flight attendant brought a blanket and pillow and CC adjusted her comfortable leather seat to a full recline. Her mother moved to the rear of the plane so her reading light wouldn't bother her daughter. In no time, CC was sound asleep.

✦ ✦ ✦

Alex met Charlie at the front door. "I can tell from your expression that you're upset."

"She's gone, Alex!"

"What do you mean gone?"

"Her plane left for Indianapolis at little after noon today."

"But why, Charlie? Do you know of any reason why she would leave Litchfield and you?"

"Unfortunately I do, Alex, but I can't explain."

"Don't be ridiculous. Of course you can. You can tell me anything."

"Except what happened."

"But I'm convinced CC loves you."

"Did love me until last night. No, it's over, and CC has a valid reason for leaving. I can't blame her." Charlie went into the library and sat down on the couch.

Alex followed, unwilling to accept her brother's vague explanation. "Are you telling me CC will reject her inheritance, that she's returning home and not coming back?"

"Exactly! And that's what I have to do right away—go home."

"And give her up without a fight?"

"Nothing I do would make a difference. CC believes I betrayed her, and frankly all the evidence is stacked against me. There's nothing I could say if she gave me give a chance to explain, and I don't believe she will."

"It can't be that bad."

"It is. So if you would ask Jenkins to drive me to Glencoe, I'd appreciate it. I've been away from little Charlie too long. It's time I spent time with my son."

"Charlie, this isn't like you. I've never seen you abandon anything you care about without a fight."

"Well, what's that cliché? There's a first time for everything. So will you please call Jenkins while I go up and pack?"

Alex knew this wasn't the time to press for answers. "Of course," she said. "But I intend to bring up this subject again. If you won't tell me what transpired with CC, I'll find out somehow."

"Leave it alone, Alex. If you interfere, you'll only make matters worse. That is, if they could be any worse than they already are."

✧ ✧ ✧

A firm hand on her shoulder awakened CC. "We're almost ready to land in New York, darling."

CC looked at her watch. "Oh Lord! I slept for almost six hours."

"You obviously needed the rest."

"I guess." CC pushed her chair back upright. "Do I have time to wash up before we have to be in our seats?" she asked Susan, the flight attendant.

"You have about thirty minutes."

"Good." CC was stiff when she stood. "Will you bring me some juice and water, please?"

"Of course. Are you hungry? I could give you a sandwich or a piece of toast."

"Toast would be great. Any coffee?"

"A fresh pot. I'll have it ready for you when you return to your seat."

CC returned to the smell of hot coffee. She sat down and took a sip. "This is exactly what I need. I'm starving."

"You slept through dinner, and I must say the filet was great."

"I think I ate enough for a lifetime while I was in England and Scotland." CC couldn't believe the despair she felt when she thought of Knockie and Charlie. She quickly changed the subject. "How long is our layover in New York?" she asked Susan.

"About forty-five minutes. That will give us time to clear customs and have the plane refueled and restocked."

"Good, and it will give me time to call the Turners and the office. And I should phone Hastings. It's not fair to leave him wondering when I'll be returning to Litchfield."

They had no difficulty clearing customs. While Mary met with the caterers, CC went to the private lounge. Her first call was to the Turners, who were both surprised and thrilled that she'd made her decision and was returning home to run the team. "And we have some good news for you," said Peter.

"Don't tell me. You did my dirty work for me?"

"Bob did. Jim's moving out of his office as we speak. You'll have no more problems with him."

"Then you figured out my real motive in taking the leave. I wanted all of you to handle Jim." CC laughed. "Actually, despite the fact that he drove me crazy and kept me perpetually frustrated, he did keep me entertained."

"So you want us to rehire him before you get back to the office?"

"Sanity before entertainment has just become my motto. Let's let Jim be on his way. I imagine there will be an audible sigh of relief from everyone in the office when he closes his door for the last time."

When she hung up with the Turners, CC was excited and even more eager to get back to work. She called the office. When Leslie heard the news that her boss was no longer on a leave of absence, CC was sure her squeals of delight could be heard all over the building. Bob was also pleased that his boss was returning for the first home stand. "When will you be in?" he asked. "We need to meet with Spike and make a few decisions about the pitching staff."

"I should be in the office tomorrow morning. I'll probably have jetlag and be behind on what's going on with the team and the league, but I'll make up for it with my enthusiasm."

"I'm sure you'll be up to speed in no time. Why don't you come in after noon? Spike won't be in the visitor's clubhouse before two, so sleep and get over the jetlag. Otherwise you'll never make it through the game."

"We'll see. If I can sleep, I will. If I can't, I'll see you much earlier. Peter told me about Jim. How'd he take it?"

"As expected, he played the victim. You and I are the ogres and he's misunderstood."

"Did the Turners waver?"

"Not after I finished telling them what I knew. To say the least, they were shocked."

"Any idea who you'd like to fill the spot?"

"As a matter of fact, yes. There's an assistant marketing director with the Padres. Her name is Denise Porter. I think she would fit in perfectly, and from what I hear, she's great."

"A woman? Aren't you afraid we're driving you men out of the office?"

"Well…" Bob stammered.

"I'm teasing, Bob. Call the Padres and ask for permission to talk with her?"

"I already have. When we weren't sure when you would be back, the Turners told me to go ahead and do whatever I thought was best for the club. We have a luncheon meeting with her day after tomorrow at noon."

"Are you sure you want me along? You can handle this without me. I hate to steal your thunder."

"CC, you know I'm a team player. I'm glad you'll be here to meet Denise."

"In that case, I'll be happy to join you. Is there anything I need to do before tomorrow?"

"Nope. Everything's under control."

"In that case, I'll hang up. They're refueling the plane and we'll soon be in the air heading home."

"You didn't fly commercial?"

"No. My mother's with me. We're on Flash's plane."

"Is Flash with you?"

"No, why do you ask?"

"I've been trying to reach him about two of his players Spike's interested in bringing up to the big leagues. He hasn't returned my calls and his secretary said she has no idea when he'll be home or where he is."

"Neither do I, but I'll fill you in when we have a few minutes to spend on a topic other than baseball."

"Is Flash all right?"

"I really can't answer that question. I hope so, but he failed to keep an appointment with me. If we don't hear from him in the next day or so, I'll contact the police."

"Why aren't you sounding panicky?"

"Because this behavior seems to be normal for Flash, or so I've learned over the past few weeks. Anyway, as I said, I'll tell you all about it tomorrow."

"See you soon!"

After Bob hung up, CC held the phone and composed her thoughts before calling Litchfield. "I guess I can't put this off," she said and punched in the number.

"Litchfield Manor."

"Hastings, how are you?" *Now that's an inane question,* CC thought.

"My lady, it's good to hear your voice. Where are you? Lord Charles said you were returning to America."

"He was right; I'm in New York heading for Indianapolis. I'm sorry I had to deceive you, Hastings. I also apologize for asking you to lie for me. However, circumstances necessitated drastic measures on my part."

"Do you intend to remain in Indianapolis for long?"

"I'm not coming back, Hastings. I spoke with Mr. Caulfield. I won't be accepting the title."

"Then Lord Charles was right?"

CC felt a pang when she heard Charlie's name "When did you talk with him?"

"He came racing in here yesterday about one. He must have known I wasn't telling him the truth and he wanted to see you. When he realized you were gone, he said it was his fault; that he had let you down. Is that true? Is that why you left?"

"It's far more complicated than that, Hastings. That's part of it, but I believe you knew from the beginning that I would most likely return home to my career."

"But I assumed that changed when you became good friends with Lord Charles and then when your mother came to visit."

CC smiled at his use of the word "friend" as a euphemism for her relationship with Charlie. "Perhaps I did reconsider for a short time, but this is where I belong, Hastings. I want to concentrate on baseball. I can't do that and be Lady Litchfield, though I must say, the service and care you and the staff provided while I was with you almost caused me to change my mind. I thank you for everything."

"There's no need to thank me, my lady. I served your father and considered him a friend. I hoped to be able to serve his daughter."

CC felt tears form in her eyes. "I wish things could have been different, but we can't always have what we want. I had to choose the path that's best for me."

"Will we see you again?"

"Possibly. Mr. Caulfield said I might need to return to London to sign papers. If that happens, I'll call. Perhaps Stanley would pick me up and drive me out for a visit."

"I'm sure he would be delighted. We would all enjoy seeing you."

"In that case, I hope I do come back, if only for a few hours."

"Until then, my lady, if there's anything I can do, please don't hesitate to let me know. As far as I'm concerned, you are the Countess of Litchfield until someone comes through these doors and tells me differently."

"Thank you, Hastings. There is one thing you could do for me."

"Anything."

"If Lord Charles should call and ask if you've spoken with me, please tell him you haven't. Again, I hate to ask you to lie, but this is important to me."

"I will keep your confidence."

"I'll be in touch." CC was surprised that she felt so sad when she hung up. "It's more of that 'might have been,'" she said and went to join her mother on the plane.

CHAPTER THIRTY-FOUR

After a light meal, CC slept the remainder of the way to Indianapolis. When her mother woke her to prepare for landing, CC apologized. "Mom, I've been a terrible traveling companion. I'm so sorry."

"Don't give it another thought, darling. I know how tired you were."

"It's wonderful to be home," CC said as she stepped off the plane. "It feels like I've been gone forever."

"So now what?" her mother asked when they had settled into the back seat of the limousine that was waiting for them on the tarmac. "Do you just go about your business and pretend the last few weeks never happened?"

"I'm going to try and do just that."

"What about Flash?

"Mother, I have no idea where Flash is, what he's doing, or if he'll ever come back."

"Don't be absurd. Of course Flash will come home. He's probably in Arizona right now, and if he is, how are you going to treat him? Are you going to let matters drop or continue to demand answers?"

"I haven't given it much thought, Mom, but right now I don't want to talk about Litchfield or Charlie or his connection to Flash. And I could care less about William's infamous Committee of Seven. All I want to do is get on with my life and forget the time I spent in England. Can you understand that?"

"Yes, dear. I understand what you want to do, but I don't think you're going to be able to put all of your questions aside and continue on. You must find some closure."

"You mean I have to close the book on this chapter of my life?" CC remembered her metaphoric conversation with Charlie and the subsequent phone call with Bud.

"That's exactly what I'm telling you."

"Well, consider the book slammed shut. It's that easy."

"I see. And the testiness in your voice tells me how comfortable you are with your decision."

"Mom, just drop it. I'm home. All I want to do is to resume my duties as the president of the Knights." As the driver turned into CC's circular driveway, she pointed to her house. "This is all I want."

The housekeeper greeted CC cheerfully. "I'm so glad you're home, CC."

"And I'm thrilled to be here and pleased to hear someone call me CC instead of 'my lady' or 'Your Ladyship.' Any messages, Hannah?"

"No phone calls, but there's a huge bouquet of flowers in the living room."

"From whom?"

"From the Taylors and your staff. They're glad you're home."

"How nice of them to be so thoughtful." CC was pleased and yet slightly disappointed, and she was annoyed with herself for her feelings.

"I'll take your bags upstairs." Hannah turned. "Will you be staying with us, Mrs. MacTandy?"

"Just tonight, Hannah. I'm flying home tomorrow."

"Are you sure I can't convince you to stay, Mom?"

"No, darling, I want to get home and wait for Flash." CC frowned at the mention of her stepfather's name. "CC, stop this right now. You're not being fair to Flash. At least give him a chance to explain. And if you can't do that, please be courteous enough to keep your thoughts and comments to yourself when I'm around. I hope you know that if you and Flash remain estranged, I'll be put in a position where I have to choose between you. Believe me, that's not a pleasant thought."

Her mother was rarely angry, and CC couldn't remember the last time she'd lectured her in the tone of voice she was using. "I'm sorry, Mother, and I seem to be saying that quite often lately. You know I love Flash and would never put you in a position where you have to choose one of us over the other. I'm angry and hurt, and I don't know how to deal with these feelings right now. Please give me some time, and in the meantime I'll try to be more sensitive to your feelings."

"That's a beginning, darling. At least you're admitting you have an emotional attachment to Flash, and if I heard you right, to Charlie and Litchfield. I realize you're trying to deny that connection, but if you are able to put it behind you, it will take some time. You have to heal, and as you so cynically put it, you have to put that chapter of your life behind you."

"Mom, I was being sarcastic because the metaphor about the book of life was one Charlie and I used when I broke off my engagement to Bud. I told him he was the new chapter, and now I'm using the same metaphor again, this time to end a relationship with Charlie. It hurts, Mom. It really does." CC started to cry. Her mother held her tightly and let her sob.

✣ ✣ ✣

CC slept uninterrupted until the sun coming in through the curtains awakened her. She looked at the clock. *I can almost be at the office on time,* she thought, *and I certainly don't need any more sleep. I think that's all I've done for the past two days.*

When she stood, she felt groggy. "What I need is a hot jolt of caffeine," she said, and she frowned as she remembered the coffee and tea she and Charlie had made before their jog on her first morning in Scotland. "Oh God! How long will I connect him with every event in my life?"

Her mother was reading the paper when CC entered the kitchen. "Morning, darling. Did you sleep well?"

"Like a log. That coffee smells good."

"I just made a fresh pot. Help yourself."

Hannah came into the room carrying a load of laundry. "Good morning, CC. Can I get you some breakfast?"

"Nothing right now, thanks. I'll have a bagel on the run. I can't wait to get to the office. What are your plans, Mom?"

"I'm headed home at noon. The plane is standing by." She hesitated before continuing. "And Flash is waiting for me."

"Flash is in Phoenix? How long has he been there? When did you talk with him? Is he okay?"

"I spoke with him last night after you went to bed. I called the house to tell Martha I would be home today and Flash answered."

"Did he tell you why he didn't meet us at Litchfield? Why he sent you instead?"

"No, all he said is he misses me and loves us both."

"But did you ask any questions?"

"No, I didn't. A phone call is not the time to get into a serious discussion. I'll talk with him when I get home. He asked if you were coming with me."

"And you said?"

"I told him you were going to work; that you had rejected your title and inheritance and were headed home for good."

"How did he react?"

"He merely said, 'we'll see.'"

"Yes, we will!" CC said angrily.

"CC!"

"I know mother. I'm trying, but I don't like Flash's attitude. I'm through with everything to do with William, the mystery surrounding his death, Charlie, and England, and the sooner Flash understands that, the sooner we'll be able to reestablish a relationship."

✳ ✳ ✳

The ride to Knockie was miserable for Charlie. How could such joy dissipate in only hours? How did things go awry? He pondered the events that led to CC's discovery of the papers and diary and her subsequent departure for home.

He had received a call that Hastings said was from Glencoe. Worried that there was a problem with little Charlie; that for some reason Angus had brought him home, he took the call. However no one from Glencoe was calling. It was Flash, who urgently asked for Charlie's help. He explained that the papers and diary in CC's possession contained information that could be dangerous or even deadly for her if she continued with her plans to find out what the committee was doing or tried to solve the mystery of her father's death. He urged Charlie to retrieve the papers, hide them, and as soon as possible take them to Caulfield in London. He pleaded with him to work quickly.

As instructed, Charlie took the papers while CC was sleeping and, to cover his tracks, deceived her by helping discover the thief when, in fact, it was he. What he hadn't counted on was CC's suspicions getting the best of her and her subsequent discovery of the papers and diary in his suitcase. Now she'd made it clear. She would never trust him again, and ironically, it was only because he had been trying to help her.

"Why didn't I just tell her what Flash told me and ask her to give me the papers?" he asked and quickly answered his own question: "Because I know how obstinate and headstrong she is." *She would never give up until she discovered what her father and the committee were up to. What choice did I have? And what choice do I have now? She's gone back to her world, and I'm returning to mine. Maybe that's for the best.* He knew it would take a long time for him to believe his last thought.

✵ ✵ ✵

CC's first day at the office was everything she could have wanted. She had a morning staff meeting and a conference call with her manager and coaches at three. It was easy to get back into the swing of things, and she only thought of Charlie a dozen times throughout the day. For her, that was pretty good. Burying herself in her work was what she needed.

The most difficult part of the day was the grilling she received from Leslie, who finally got the idea that her boss wasn't going to tell her anything; that the subject of England and what occurred there were off limits. CC thought about calling Flash, but decided to wait until she could talk to him without attacking. She needed some time.

She watched the game in her pajamas in her own family room and ate a simple dinner on a TV tray. Though she didn't want to think of England, she couldn't help but wonder what Hastings would have thought about her dining arrangements or how her chefs would have felt about the cuisine she was enjoying so much.

The Knights won and the game was a "fix," as CC called it. As she went up to bed, she couldn't believe she'd considered giving up baseball. She was back and happy—or at least content to be home.

CHAPTER THIRTY-FIVE

Three months passed like three days. CC buried herself in her work, and without Jim around to haunt her, life seemed relatively normal. The team was in first place at the all-star break, and three Knights players had been selected to the team. In fact, one of their aces had been chosen as the starting pitcher and appeared to be a shoo-in for the Cy Young Award.

Over the months she had talked with Flash numerous times, but by tacit agreement, they spoke about baseball. The first time he called the office she begged him to tell her why he had broken his promise to meet her and Mary at Litchfield, but he refused to explain and wouldn't tell her where he'd been. Her anger and frustration grew with each "I'm not at liberty." After several more pleas that fell on deaf ears, she told herself she no longer wanted to know and gave up. She was trying to heal. Why rub salt in old wounds. She often thought of Charlie, but time made vivid memories slightly less painful.

On the Saturday before the all-star game in July, CC flew to Phoenix with the Turners on their jet. The closer she got to the desert city, the more apprehensive she was. How ironic that this year's game would be played at the Diamondback ballpark. There would be no avoiding Flash and her mother, as they would be part of the festivities. They invited her to stay with them, but she made the excuse that it was essential she stay near the Turners at the headquarters hotel. CC doubted that Flash believed her reason for refusing the invitation, but he didn't argue with her. She had reluctantly agreed to spend Sunday with the family and was bringing the Turners with her for an afternoon barbecue. Beyond that, the gala, the receptions, and the game would prevent her from seeing Flash except in crowds. She was relieved.

On Sunday at one, she and the Turners arrived at the MacTandys'. After greeting Martha, CC sought out her mother, who seemed tense. CC tried to hide her apprehension with a smile and a warm greeting. Her response to Flash was considerably cooler, but he scarcely seemed to notice and gathered her in a bear hug. "CC, it's good to see you," he growled.

"It's been a long time."

Flash ignored her cool response. "It certainly has." He greeted the Turners: "Peter, Janice, come on in and meet our other guests."

"Who else is here?" CC asked her mother as the two women joined arms. There was no answer, and CC felt increasingly anxious. "Mother?" They walked into the huge living room. CC looked around at the familiar place she'd loved her entire life. All of a sudden she spotted Charlie standing by the fireplace. In a split second she experienced a myriad of emotions. She was incensed that her mother and Flash had invited Charlie without telling her. She was delighted to see the handsome man, yet she didn't want to see him. She wanted to throw herself into his arms, yet she wanted nothing to do with him.

Before she could figure out what to do, Charlie approached her and the Turners. Though she was shaking, CC forced herself to be cool and calm as she made the introductions. "Mr. and Mrs. Turner, may I present Lord Charles Timperley. Lord Timperley and I were friends while I was in England."

"Happy to meet you, Lord Timperley." Peter extended his hand.

"Charlie, please."

"You and CC met while she was in England?" Janice asked.

"We did. My sister and her husband have an estate near hers."

CC corrected him coolly. "An estate that was mine for a short time, you mean."

"Then you've decided to remain in Indianapolis?" Charlie asked tentatively.

"I'll only return to London to sign the papers Mr. Caulfield is preparing."

"I'm sorry to hear that," Charlie said sadly. "You'll be sorely missed

"Thank you, but there's nothing for me in England," CC said a little too adamantly. "My great love is my career. Though I vacillated from time to time during my stay at Litchfield and even more when I was in Scotland, I eventually realized what's important."

Flash sensed the mounting tensions. "And I know the Turners are glad to have you back."

"We certainly are," said Peter, "though I gather you miss this wonderful woman, Charlie."

"We all do. She left so abruptly that none of her friends had the opportunity to say good-bye, and that's unfortunate, because all of us had something important to say."

CC looked directly at Charlie. "I'm sorry I disappointed you, Lord Timperley, but once I make a decision, there's no turning back."

Mary frowned at her daughter. "I've never known you to be so rigid, CC."

"Perhaps I've never felt so strongly about anything." She glared at her mother and turned to the Turners. "Let me show you the house where I grew up. Lord Timperley, if you'll excuse me. I hope you enjoy your stay in the States."

"CC!" Flash tried to intercede.

"Not now, Flash, I said I'm going to show the Turners the house."

Flash knew it wasn't the time to try and make peace between CC and Charlie, so he backed off. "In that case, come with me, Charlie. We'll have a good old American beer."

As CC led the Turners from the room, Peter took her arm. "I don't know what just happened in there, but I've never seem you so uncomfortable. It's none of my business, but—"

"Please, Peter, with all due respect, it isn't. I'd appreciate it if you'd leave this one alone. The story you're asking me to tell is personal and very complex. Someday I'll fill you in on all my English experiences, but not now. I've tried to put this part of my life behind me and concentrate on baseball, but it seems Flash has other ideas." CC smiled a fake smile. "I'll deal with him later."

"I respect your feelings," Peter said, "but as your friend, I must say that, despite the fantastic job you're doing with the team on a daily basis, I believe you're unhappy. This afternoon I realized why. If you ever want to discuss this with us, our door is always open. We're not only your bosses; we're your friends."

"I know that, and I'm sorry I was rude. Charlie represents a part of my life I want and need to forget. That explanation will have to do for now."

"Then I won't broach the subject again, and this really is a marvelous house."

When CC and the Turners returned to the living room, Charlie was nowhere to be seen but Flash was and he obviously wasn't happy as he walked toward her. "May I borrow CC for a few minutes," he asked Peter.

"She's all yours, Flash. Janice and I are going out and take a whiff of whatever it is that smells so good."

Flash grinned. "That would be my world famous ribs. They're being taken off the barbecue as we speak, so grab a plate."

"I hope you know what you're doing, CC," Flash said as he led her away from the crowd."

"This is not the time, Flash. I hope you know what you did. Where's your guest?"

"He realized he wasn't welcomed here, at least by one family member. He's gone."

CC was startled. "Gone where?"

"I assume home. I sent the plane to bring him over, and he asked me to make arrangements for him to return to Glasgow. I called the pilots and he's on his way to the airport. Don't you think you should go after him? Talk with him about what happened at Litchfield. If you can't do that, at least apologize for your obnoxious behavior."

"Absolutely not! And Flash, bringing him here is unpardonable."

"If I had known how rude you could be, I certainly wouldn't have exposed that fine young man to your wrath."

"Did you really expect me to act any differently?"

"I expected you to act courteously and at least give the man his fair hearing."

"Why should I?"

"Because he isn't guilty of stealing your papers."

CC scowled. "Give it up, Flash," she said coldly.

"So you don't want to hear what I have to say?"

"There's nothing to say, and I'll thank you to stay out of my business. Are we clear?"

"Perfectly. I won't interfere again, except to say you're making a mistake, and this isn't one of old Flash's hunches. Do you think you and I could find some time to sit down and talk this over when you're not so angry with me?"

"I don't see how. I'm tied up every minute until we leave on Wednesday morning."

"You can't make time to have breakfast?"

"Sorry, Flash. You know what it's like to run a ball club. I'm always on call."

"I see. Well, honey, I never thought it would come to this—"

CC cut him off. "Neither did I, Flash. Neither did I." She walked away.

Though CC and Flash tried to be civil during the meal, their displeasure with one another was apparent to everyone around them. When the meal was over, there was general relief. Anxious to be away from the tension-filled house, CC hugged her mother and bid Flash a curt goodbye. Back at the hotel she returned phone calls and picked up her credentials for the events. She was standing in the lobby talking with a group from the Red Sox when she heard a familiar voice. "May I steal this lady from you gentlemen for a moment?"

"Bud!" CC was surprised, though she had no idea why she should be, she knew he'd be at the game. "It's good to see you," she said smiling. Realizing he wasn't sure how to act, she stepped up and gave him a kiss on the cheek. "How are you?"

"Doing fine, though I would say I'm better now that this awkward moment has passed. "I have a meeting in ten minutes, but would you like to have a drink before the gala?" CC hesitated, and he continued, "to talk as old friends, nothing more."

CC smiled. "Of course. I have a few things to do and I have to change. Why don't we meet in the lounge at seven? We can have a drink and catch the shuttle to the gala."

"Sounds great to me. I'll see you in a while."

Now why did I agree to do that? CC pondered as she rode the elevator upstairs. Seeing Bud hadn't rekindled old feelings. On the contrary, the encounter made her think of Charlie. She finished making her calls and changed for the gala. Bud was waiting when she arrived at seven-fifteen. "I'm sorry," she said breathlessly, "the damn phone never stops ringing. She held up her cell. "I've turned it off, so I'm all yours."

"Tell me about it. I'm glad you're here. As punctual as you usually are, I was beginning to think you'd changed your mind about meeting me."

"I wouldn't stand you up. You know that. Anyway, I'm here now, so why don't we have that drink?"

Though the conversation was strained at first, CC and Bud soon relaxed and spent the next hour talking about his job with the commissioner and the goings-on with the Knights. CC shared the "Jim stories" that resulted in Bob's firing the wayward market director. Now that Jim was no longer a perpetual thorn in her side, CC could laugh about his ridiculous antics. When it was almost time to catch the shuttle, Bud steered the conversation from work to personal matters. "You've clearly avoided talking about your stay in England. Because you're here, I assume you decided not to accept your title."

"I really don't want to go into any detail, but you're right. I opted for a life in baseball, and here I am."

"And your Scottish friend, the one you wanted to get to know better?"

"I guess you could say I learned more than I wanted to know. Anyway, it's over. Needless to say, I was shocked when I arrived at the house this afternoon. Charlie was standing in front of the fireplace in the living room. Thinking we could solve our differences, Flash flew him in from Scotland.

"And were you able to work things out?"

"No. We're beyond that."

"So does that leave the door open even slightly for me? You know how I feel about you."

CC figured Bud would ask about getting back together, so she was ready. She took his hand. "Bud, I'll always care for you. You're one of my closest friends."

"Friends?"

"Exactly. I didn't break off our relationship because of someone else. I told you that on the phone. I ended it because we weren't going anywhere. Our lives were, and still are, for that matter, totally separate."

"But if we lived in the same town—"

"It still wouldn't work. My unfortunate experience in England showed me we don't have what it takes to live happily ever after, so to speak. I hope we'll always be close friends and spend time together at all of these fabulous events, but beyond that—"

"There's nothing."

"I'm afraid you're right. Looking at your handsome face tempts me to say let's give it a try, but I know better. The end result would be the same. So could we go to this gala together and do so as dear friends?"

"Do I have a choice?"

"You don't, and I'm sorry."

"Then I'll have to settle for what I can get." He stood and held out his hand. "Come on, friend, let's go to the party."

The rest of the three-day all-star experience was a blur. CC was constantly running around between league meetings, the fan fest, receptions, the pre-game party, and finally, the game itself. The Knights' pitcher threw for three innings, striking out six of the first nine batters he faced. When he was relieved in the fourth, the National League was ahead five to nothing, and when it was all over, they had won eight to three.

During those hectic few days, CC didn't see Bud except from a distance. The same was true of Flash, though she talked with her mother on the phone and at one of the hotel brunches. Even then, Bob, Spike, and the Turners were around, so there was no time for a private talk.

Finally it was time to return to Indianapolis. "I'm glad the all-star game is over for another year," CC told the Turners as they got back on the jet for the flight home, "but I wish we had a few more days before we open the longest home stand of the year."

"Too much partying?" Peter teased.

"Too much of everything. I remember when the mid-year classic was for baseball people. Now it's for sponsors, politicians, and just about anyone who can bring in money."

"I thought about that yesterday. There must have been over five thousand people at the gala."

"At least, and by the time we host the game two years from now, we'll probably have ten thousand." CC grimaced when she thought of the work that would soon begin for the 2013 all-star game.

There was no time to rest up before the second half of the season resumed. The Knights beat the Giants two out of three and then swept the Phillies. During the first game of a day/ night doubleheader with Cincinnati, CC received a call from the switchboard. "CC, there's a Mr. Caulfield on the phone. He says he's phoning from England."

CC's heart raced. "Put him through to the box please, Helen, and thank you."

Seconds later, CC heard a familiar voice. "Mr. Caulfield, how are you?" she said. "I apologize for the background noise. We're in the middle of a ballgame."

"I'm doing well, thank you. Since you're busy, I'll get right to the reason for my call. I've done some investigating as I indicated I would. I've determined you'll have to return to England to sign the final documents renouncing your title and inheritance."

"Oh Lord!" CC groaned. "It won't be easy, but I suppose I can make time for an overnight trip. When will the papers be ready?"

"They're waiting for your signature right now. However, I'm very much afraid you'll have to remain in England for seventy-two hours after you've sign the documents. This is the right of rescission period."

"And I can't decide to change my mind at home?"

"I'm afraid not. The law is quite clear."

"Then I suppose I have no choice. I'll have my secretary make arrangements and let you know when to expect me. Will I be able to use the suite at the Ritz while I'm in town or should I make other arrangements?"

"The suite is still yours. It will be until the seventy-two-hour period is over. Would you like for me to call the hotel when I know your arrival time?"

"Yes, please let them know I'll be staying overnight. The rest of the time, I'd prefer to stay at Litchfield. Would you please call Hastings and have Stanley pick me up so I can say a proper goodbye to the staff."

"Hastings will be pleased. Let me know when you're arriving. I'll have a car waiting at the airport."

"Thank you, Mr. Caulfield." CC hung up, left the box and went to the office. Leslie called the travel agency to make reservations and CC went to find the Turners and Bob. Neither seemed particularly bothered by her travel plans. After all, the team was winning consistently and in first place by seven and a half games.

When she returned to her office, Leslie confirmed a first-class seat on the flight leaving Indianapolis for London at seven-thirty p.m. the following day. CC had her call Caulfield with the itinerary while she went to watch the Knights win the first game and lose the second.

CHAPTER THIRTY-SIX

The bellman put CC's bags in the living room of her suite at the Ritz. When he left, she looked at her watch. It was eight-thirty and she had to be at Mr. Caulfield's office by ten. There wouldn't be time to take a nap. She'd tried to sleep on the plane, but thoughts of returning to Litchfield kept intruding. Foremost on her mind was whether or not to contact Alex and Tony? Finally, after much consideration, she decided to call them just before returning home. That way they wouldn't have time to reach Charlie before she flew home, though she doubted Charlie would want to see her after the way she treated him in Arizona.

As Caulfield promised, the papers were ready for her signature. CC didn't know if it was her imagination or possibly the guilt she felt at refusing the title, but she thought Caulfield seemed distant and more formal than during her past visits. Once again, he asked if she was sure that renouncing her title was what she wanted to do. Without hesitation, she answered "yes."

"Then in seventy-two hours, you'll return here and sign the papers," said Caulfield. "At that time, your connection to William, his title, and estates will no longer exist. However if you should change your mind, call me, come in, sign the acceptance document and you'll officially become the Countess of Litchfield."

"I assure you, that won't happen." CC extended her hand. "I'll see you in seventy-two hours, and thank you, Mr. Caulfield."

"I'll show you out." He walked her to the elevator, and CC caught a cab back to the Ritz to take a nap before calling Stanley.

When she opened the door to the suite, she was startled by a familiar voice. "Hi, darling," Flash bellowed, a grin on his face.

"Déjà vu," CC said sarcastically. "We can't keep meeting like this," Flash. What are you doing here, though I doubt you'll tell me anything that comes close to the truth?"

"CC!" Flash said sternly. "Get over here and sit down. I've had enough of your sarcasm and endured your disrespect for too long. It was one thing to treat me like you did in Arizona. Maybe it was warranted, but your mother's feelings were hurt and she doesn't deserve your wrath. And then there was Charlie—"

"Don't go there, Flash. You invited Charlie to Arizona and meddled where you had no business. What happened because of your interference was predictable."

"Maybe so, but that's in the past. I came here to have that talk I've wanted to have for months, and this time you're going to listen to what I have to say. You didn't have time in Arizona, or so you said, but now you do. I have seventy-two hours to make my case."

"So you're familiar with my schedule. I assume your good friend Caulfield keeps you informed."

"He does. I knew you had to return to sign the papers, and I asked him to tell me when you'd arrive. I flew over to have a discussion that's long overdue."

CC sighed. "Flash why don't we agree to put everything that's happened behind us and move on?"

"We might move on independently, but we won't be moving ahead. There's too much animosity between us, and there's too much I need to tell you. I wanted you to hear me out when you were in Arizona, but you're so damn stubborn," so come over here and sit down."

"Do I have a choice?"

"You know you don't."

"Then if we're going to have a long, drawn-out conversation, I'm going to change clothes." Without further comment, CC left the room. She returned a few minutes later dressed in jeans and a Knights sweatshirt. "If this discussion has to happen, let's have it out and get on with our lives." She sat down on the sofa.

Flash sat in the chair opposite her and leaned forward. "When I came the first time, I told you I'd been in Japan. That was true, but not for the time period I specified. When I realized there was a connection between your father's death and that of Mr. Yamato, I was nervous, but when I found out you were at Knockie, I was scared. I flew over immediately."

"You were in Scotland when I was at Knockie." Flash started to respond, but CC held up her hand. You were stalking me, weren't you? Why the hell didn't you come to the house? At the very least you could have answered some of my questions?"

"I couldn't, CC. Not until I knew what happened to your father."

"And now you do?"

"Let's just say we're close."

CC didn't hear what Flash said, next. "My God!" she exclaimed as she stood up and walked over to the window. After several minutes, she turned back toward Flash. "You were the one who burned Knockie," she said, thinking as she spoke. "That's why William's suite was the only area. . ." She didn't finish the sentence. "Why, Flash," she pleaded. "Make me understand. When I told Mom and Charlie I suspected you, they told me I was crazy, but I wasn't was I?"

Flash didn't immediately respond. He appeared to be choosing his words carefully. Finally he joined CC at the window. "You're right, darling. I set fire to your father's suite. I didn't have a choice."

In a split second, CC's despair gave way to furor. "On whose orders?" she barked. "You're the leader of the Committee of Seven. You're the one who's making the decisions."

"We make the decisions together, CC. The members of the committee decided the documents and files in the Knockie office as well as the information on your father's computer had to be destroyed before the bad guys hacked through the firewalls William was always updating or, God forbid, before they broke into Knockie looking for hard copy files. That wouldn't bode well for Henry or Mrs. Lauriston."

CC frowned. "Dammit, Flash," she said angrily. "There was another way to destroy the files. You've been to Knockie numerous times. The staff knows you and William were friends. You could have come to the lodge, told Henry one of your lies making him think you had a right to be there, gone upstairs, wiped off my father's hard drives and removed the hard copies yourself?" CC shook her head. "Better yet, why couldn't you trust me? If you'd been open and honest, I would have given you anything you asked for. You stalked me for two days. How about knocking on the door? Ya don't think burning the office was a little over the top?"

"I understand your anger, honey—"

"I'm not sure you do, Flash. It's not just Knockie. It's everything. For starters, make me understand what was in those files that gave you no other option than to destroy my father's suite, a place, I might add, that contained personal items I'd like to have."

"I'll explain everything, if you'll stop talking and give me a chance."

"Will I get a full account or only what you're at liberty to tell me?"

Now it was Flash who was furious. "I've been listening to your tirade and putting up with your sarcasm and hostility," he growled, "but the party's over and you'll listen to me. I understand why you're upset, but there's a hell of a lot you don't know——."

"Then for God's sake, tell me. Hasn't that been what I've asked all along?

Flash shook his head and took a deep breath. "I'm trying, CC," he said, struggling to regain some semblance of calm. "First, you should know that with a few exceptions, Knockie has been restored to the way it was before the fire."

"What exceptions?"

"Your father's sitting room is larger because there's no longer a communications room. The only computer in the house is downstairs in the small sitting room off of the lounge, but I've had a wireless system installed so you'll be able to use your laptop from your suite."

"Not my suite, Flash. I'm going home, or have you forgotten."

"I'm not going to tell you again, CC. I can take a lot from you because I love you, but frankly I'm sick of your attitude. So cut the crap. If you want to hear what I have to say, show me some respect. If not, I'm leaving and there won't be another chance for us to make amends and sort all this out. Once I'm out of here, I'll never answer another question about

William or the Committee of Seven, so decide now. How this conversation continues is up to you."

CC walked over to the couch and sat down. Tears ran down her cheeks as she spoke. "I know I'm being a bitch, Flash and I apologize, but I'm so angry; angry about my father's death, angry about Charlie—I could go on, but I'm sure you understand. I suppose for the first time in my life I have no control and I'm frightened."

Flash sat beside her and put his arm around her shoulder. "I do understand, honey. I'm doing the best I can. I won't say the words you hate to hear, but—"

"You're not at liberty." This time there was no anger when CC said the words. She continued to cry quietly. I know you're trying Flash. And yes, I do want to know what you can tell me, so please. . ."

Flash removed his arm from CC's shoulders and took her hand. "First let me finish telling you about Knockie. Mrs. Lauriston and Henry are no longer in danger nor are you if you decide to visit. I'm hoping you'll want to take a look at the restorations before you fly off forever. I think you'll approve."

"I'm sure I will, but you're going to have to send pictures. I'm not going to Knockie. Now will you tell me what happened to my father and why? And where were you when you were supposed to meet me at Litchfield, Flash. I ask you once and you refused to answer my question. You promised to be there and it's not like you to break your word."

"I'll answer all your questions as best I can, but first I need to provide a little background. I don't know what your father wrote in those letters he left for you, so if I repeat what he said, bear with me. The Committee of Seven was formed to deal with the question of nuclear power and the use of oil." CC nodded. "Well, in February 1967, all that changed. We became involved in the Northern Ireland Campaign for Social Justice and the Northern Ireland Civil Rights Association. Working under-cover, our goal was to stop the violence and promote peace. Since then we've operated in other parts of the world, places like the Middle East and Eastern Europe, but Northern Ireland has always been our primary focus." Flash produced a folder of papers. "This is a chronology of our work, if you should care to read it." He handed the papers to CC, who said nothing.

"Our efforts came to fruition on May 22, 1998, when the citizens of Northern Ireland and the Irish Republic voted overwhelmingly for a referendum approving the Stormont Agreement, a peace accord we worked behind the scenes to implement. It brought an end to a hundred years of conflict between Roman Catholics and Protestants in Northern Ireland. Those papers you're holding will explain the entire conflict to you. More than seventy percent of the voters in Northern Ireland and ninety-four percent of voters in the Irish Republic supported the accord.

"What was so perilous about the negotiations?"

"To achieve our goals we had to infiltrate the IRA, not down in the trenches, but in the upper echelons of power. Our missions were dangerous and William, because he was English and bet-ter looked the part, often took the lead." Flash grinned. "I wish you could have heard your proper-speaking English father's Irish brogue. There were times when I thought he was the real thing. Your father and the rest of us were agents of U.K, so we were the enemy. If we'd been discovered, we would have been killed."

"I understand, Flash, but I don't. You're telling me the visits from the Duke of Marlborough, Margaret Thatcher, Tony Blair and Donald Rumsfeld were to discuss your work in Northern Ireland?"

"That and much more."

"Then it must have been more about the 'much more' than about Ireland." CC laughed. "That didn't come out the way I meant for it to."

"Believe it or not, I understood," Flash said smiling.

"You said the peace agreement was reached in 1998. In my father's photo albums I found pictures of you at Knockie in 2001 and I know you were here in 2008 when Charlie and Flora came for the weekend. Were you also William's guest in the 1990s?"

"I was, and we met in other isolated places throughout the world."

CC sighed. "The peace agreement was only the beginning, wasn't it Flash? You didn't stop there, and now you're involved in something that's extremely dangerous. Was one of your new projects, for want of a better word, the reason my father was murdered? And why didn't you order an autopsy to be sure he didn't die of natural causes?"

"First, our latest projects, as you put it, are not as dangerous as they once were, but we're going strong. I've been appointed to fill your father's spot and we already have a new Japanese member appointed by the prime minister. We're dealing with terrorism and the fight for freedom in Libya, Egypt, Syria and other countries where ordinary citizens are demanding basic human rights. We're also monitoring the nuclear programs in Iran and North Korea. I said what we're doing isn't as dangerous. That's because this time, we're working behind the scenes to coordinate financial support for freedom fighters throughout the world."

"You're drawing on the Swiss business account?"

"We have accounts all over the world, CC. The Swiss account was your father's primary source of income for his particular assignments. That money will be used by his successor as soon as someone is appointed to fill his place."

"Will that be soon?"

"I honestly can't say and not because—"

CC smiled and finished the sentence, "you're not at liberty, so back to my initial question: who killed William and Mr. Yamato?"

"If you read the British papers when you were at Litchfield, you know that peace in Northern Ireland is tenuous, to say the least—"

"Are you trying to tell an IRA agent murdered my father and if so, what makes you think so?"

"Let's just say I have a hunch."

CC rolled her eyes. "How many times have I heard you say that over the past thirty-one years?"

Flash grinned. "I suppose too many to count."

"But you don't know for sure. Has anyone actually taken responsibility for William's death? I mean isn't that what terrorists do? They brag about their successes."

"Maybe because they're not through. We believe their goal is to eliminate the entire committee."

"Then you're still in danger."

"As are you."

"Why would I be? I'm an American baseball executive."

"And the Countess of Litchfield. I'm sure whoever's behind your father's death knows you've been snooping around and asking a lot of questions."

"I'll admit I've been relentless. As soon as I arrived I began my Jessica Fletcher routine." Flash looked puzzled. "You remember, Jessica, the super-sleuth in the TV series *Murder She Wrote?*"

"Ah yes. Years ago that was of your mother's favorites shows. I rarely watched the program with her, but I should have understood the reference. So, Miss Jessica, because you started asking questions you became a target. Are you through snooping?"

"Not yet because you haven't answered all my questions. Why no autopsy on William?"

"Because if what we suspect is true, if your father, an earl and the leader of the Committee of Seven was, in fact, murdered by a member of the IRA and word got out, our efforts to maintain the fragile peace would be jeopardized and an additional strain would be put on both sides. For that reason, the committee decided to allow the public to believe your father died of natural causes. We couldn't risk a leak of autopsy results.'

"I know I'm repeating myself, but I still don't understand why a member of the IRA would be trying to kill off the committee. The agreement was signed thirteen years ago."

"Who knows? Maybe someone holds a grudge. We don't have the answer nor are we sure we're right. We could be off base."

CC grinned. "A baseball reference and that famous Flash hunch again. What more could I ask for?"

Flash let out a belly laugh. "It's not that old Flash feeling, honey. This time it's more like an educated guess."

Suddenly the implication of what Flash said hit home and CC was frightened. "Do you think my father's killer is still at Litchfield, and if so, could Hastings, Stanley, Richard or any of the other servants be in danger?"

"Anything's possible, CC."

CC gasped. "You're not thinking one of the servants could be the killer?" She paused and answered her own question. "No, it's not possible."

"We're running background checks right now. So have I satisfactorily answered your questions?"

"Not all of them. Not the one that for me is the most important, because I've trusted you all my life and I know your word is your oath."

"It is."

"Then why didn't you come to Litchfield and meet with me, Flash. You promised you would. I can't remember a time in my life when you promised something and didn't follow through. Though I didn't want to go, I did what you asked. I went with Charlie to Hintlesham, and in turn, you sent Mother to Litchfield and then you didn't show up to be with us and to answer the questions you promised to answer. Where were you?"

"I was in Paris meeting with the French member of the committee. He was the only one of us left unprotected. I picked him up in the jet and flew him to safety."

"Where and why couldn't you tell me that when I first asked?"

"Out of harm's way, and I couldn't say anything because we were in the middle of our investigation and I wasn't—"

"At liberty. . .I know."

"Does it help to you know I had every intention of meeting you. That's why I flew your mother in from Arizona, but at the last minute, saving my colleague's life took precedent. I'm sorry, honey."

Suddenly CC remembered what Flash had said at the all-star barbecue. He'd tried to tell her she needed to listen to Charlie's reason for stealing the papers and the diary. He said Charlie wasn't guilty, but she'd been too angry and stubborn to listen to what he had to say. She turned to look Flash squarely in the face. "Please tell me you didn't ask Charlie to steal from me and then pretend to help me find the thief?"

"I had to, CC. I was scared. I tried to tell you—"

"But why? You knew how I felt about Charlie."

"Why? Because I couldn't be there to protect you, so Charlie became my pawn. I figured you'd search for your father's papers and diary in Charlie's room. I also knew when you found them, you'd be furious. You'd think Charlie betrayed you and instead of confronting him, you'd leave Litchfield immediately."

CC's despair quickly turned to anger. "And you were right. You realize your actions made my decision for me. I don't know whether to scream or cry."

"You're wrong, CC. My actions didn't make you decide to go home. If you'd been honest with Charlie, if you'd talked with him about your suspicions—"

"Don't go there Flash. Don't you talk to me about honesty! If you'd been honest with me from the beginning—"

"It seems we both have a lot to be sorry for, CC. Shall we keep on accusing one another, or shall I continue with my explanation?"

"By all means, go ahead."

I had to get you out of England until I could be sure that friends and enemies alike knew you weren't involved in committee business. I couldn't have you meet the same fate as your father because someone knew you had his papers. At the time we believed your father's murderer was in the house. We still do and when he's exposed he'll be dealt with."

"Dealt with? What does that mean?"

"It means he'll be arrested. We don't go around murdering people, CC."

"Well that's certainly a relief, but you don't know the identity of the killer."

"Not for certain, but we're close. We're waiting from news from two of our investigators."

"News"

"Information that will verify what we believe to be true. I'm hoping we'll be able to take action later tonight or tomorrow morning, but we got off track. Let me finish telling you about Charlie. I called him and, without providing specific details, told him you were in grave danger. Of course he was eager to help me do anything possible to keep you safe. I asked him to get the papers and the diary, I didn't care how. At that point we had just begun to suspect your father's murderer was a member of his staff. We believed he watched you and Charlie go to the chapel, move the altar, and remove what was hidden."

CC was incredulous. "I'm so confused, Flash," she said, her voice a mixture of anger and frustration. You had a suspect, someone who was living and working at Litchfield and yet you sent the plane for mother. You subjected her to the same danger I was facing."

"I brought Mary to England to keep both of you safe. Yamato died in his home. I didn't want your mother to be alone in Scottsdale. We all figured I was the IRA's next target. What if someone came for me and found your mother there instead? I hate to think about what could have happened. Would they have killed her to warn me off or to cause me unbearable pain? I thought the two of you would better off together at Litchfield. Your mom wanted to see you and I didn't think either of you was in danger because I planned to join you and keep you safe."

"I know I'm skipping from topic to topic, Flash, but I have so many questions."

Flashed smiled. "Ask away, honey."

"When Charlie and I went back to the chapel, the altar wasn't back where we had placed it. Do you think my father's killer moved it?"

"Probably, but I can't say for sure. If so, he was likely looking for additional information about the committee members. Now, do you want me to finish telling you about Charlie?"

"I guess I need to hear it all, so go on."

"When I called, I told Charlie that your life could very well depend on whether or not he took immediate action. I asked him to get the papers and put them in the hidden compartment of the suitcase that he'd find under the bed in his room. I called Hastings and had him get the bag from your father's closet. We often used this and others like it for transporting sensitive papers. I also told him that once Charlie put the papers inside, to go to the room and be certain the edge of the suitcase protruded out from the corner of the bed and was clearly visible to anyone searching the room."

"So I would find it and believe that Charlie had lied to me."

"That was the plan. As I said, I was pretty sure once you suspected Charlie of deceiving you, you'd leave Litchfield immediately."

"Well, you were right, I left. Was Hastings always a part of the plan?"

"Not at first. When I realized I had to be in France, I called, explained the situation and asked for his help."

"Well he's a damn good actor. He played along until the bitter end. Sounds like he might have done something like this before."

Flash grinned. "No comment, I'm not. . ."

CC groaned. "Spare me from hearing your mantra yet again. So Charlie didn't know what you were up to? He didn't realize you and Hastings were setting him up, so to speak?"

"He had no idea—that is until I sent for him and flew him to Arizona. I told him everything right before you arrived. I planned to tell you too, but as you know, you wouldn't have any part of it."

"So if Charlie knew everything, why didn't he stay and try to explain? That is, if he still cared for me?"

"He saw how angry you were with him and knew you were going to remain in the States. After all, in his mind, whether he was my pawn or not, he deceived you. You had a right to be furious with him."

"But if he'd persisted."

"CC, one look at your face and everyone knew further discussion would be futile. No, I believe Charles saw the writing on the wall and went home. Anyway, he knew there could be no relationship between the two of you if you were going to continue working for the Knights. Didn't he say if you left England, he'd have to do his duty and remain behind?"

"He did say that."

"And you made it quite clear that your 'love,' I think you said, was for the Knights. The implication was that you no longer loved him."

CC sat quietly. "Well, I hate what happened, but in the end everything turned out for the best," she finally said. "I'm where I should be and Charlie's back in Scotland where he should be. I don't want to be lady anything. I want to be CC."

Flash smiled. "Now where have I heard that before? Could it be when you were a year old? I think you stomped your feet at the time, but whether you remain CC or become Lady Litchfield is a decision only you can make."

"I have made. I signed the papers."

"I realize that. I certainly won't try to change your mind, but I felt you needed to know how your father died and why Charlie and I did what we did."

"Did Mother know what was going on?"

"If you mean was she a part of the plan form the beginning, no. She wouldn't have been a party to deception. I told her when I told Charlie. She knows everything except that I'm still involved with the committee. I didn't tell her and I hope you won't either. I don't want her to worry every time I leave home."

"Secrets are what got us into trouble in the first place," Flash

"Yes, honey, they did, but like your father, I have a purpose in life and I'm going to continue my work whether or not Mary knows. I would like for you to help me out, but it's entirely up to you."

"I'll think about it. That's all I can promise right now."

"That's good enough for the moment. So now you see why your father left Mary and you? At first it was his duty to the anti-nuclear movement, and then his role in the attainment of world peace. When Lady Anne died, we had recently become involved in the stabilization of Iraq. William was unable to do what he wanted most to do, get in touch with you and try to develop a relationship. Before he could find a way, he was murdered. So you see, his entire life, right up to the end, was one sacrifice after another for his country and for what he believed in. He never put his own wishes and desires above his duty. I suppose that could be said for Charlie as swell. He did his duty as he saw it. He was trying to protect the woman he loved."

"But if that's the case, why hasn't he tried to contact me to explain."

"You need to ask him that question."

Though she tried to hold back the tears, CC began to cry. Flash put his arm around her and she rested her head on his shoulder. "It's okay, honey. Get it out."

Throughout the afternoon, CC and Flash continued to talk. When they were hungry, CC ordered dinner from the hotel dining room. By the time the meal was over she understood why Flash did what he did, and she finally felt she knew the man who had left her mother and her behind to serve a higher cause. More importantly, she and Flash had gone a long way in their effort to rebuild a relationship that had been so strained over the previous months.

When CC could hardly keep her eyes open, Flash suggested she go to bed. She asked him to stay at the suite and accompany her to Litchfield to say good-bye to Hastings and the staff. He seemed pleased to be invited and promised to awaken her by eight so they could get an early start.

CHAPTER THIRTY-SEVEN

When CC woke up, Flash was already dressed and ready to go. "Morning, honey, I hope you slept well."

"Better than I have in a long time. Something smells good."

"I ordered breakfast. It was just delivered, so the coffee's hot."

"Wonderful. I'm starving."

"And when we're finished, Stanley's ready to drive us to Litchfield."

"He's here already? You have been busy."

"You know me. I'm always up early and raring to go."

Breakfast was pleasant. Flash had a phone call to make so he remained upstairs while CC went to meet Stanley. "My lady, it's good to have you home," he said as he opened her door.

"Thank you, Stanley, though I'm afraid this will be a short visit." She had learned the lesson Stanley taught her during the first ride from London to Litchfield. She wouldn't share her plans with a servant, even one she liked as much as her chauffeur. She wouldn't tell him that she had returned to reject her title and say good-bye. Stanley would know soon enough, but he wouldn't hear it from her.

"I'm so sorry about Richard," Stanley said.

CC was puzzled. "Richard? What about him?"

Flash came up from behind her. "Before he came to England fifteen years ago, Richard was a fighter for the IRA. Apparently he was still fighting against those he believed destroyed his dream. "I just got word, but what do you know, Stanley?"

"Only that Richard was arrested early this morning, Mr. MacTandy. The constable said he murdered the earl."

CC gasped. "Richard killed my father? I don't believe it."

"Believe it honey," Flash said. "Right after he was arrested, Richard took full responsibility for your father's death. Another member of his IRA group killed Yamato and made it look like a suicide. Come on back in the lobby and I'll tell you everything. If you'll excuse us, Stanley."

"Of course, Mr. MacTandy, my lady."

Flash led CC back into the hotel. They sat on a couch away from the guests who were mingling in the lobby. "So tell me everything," CC pleaded. "Did you always suspect Richard? How did he kill my father?"

"If you'll let me get a word in edgewise, I'll try to explain. To answer your first question, yes. When we figured out William was murdered by someone in the house, Richard became our primary suspect. We did a little digging and discovered that he had inquired about several open positions on your father's staff over the past few years. He never applied, we think, because none of the jobs would have given him access to the earl. When William's valet retired, he applied for the position on the pretense that he had advanced as far as he could in his current employment and aspired to be the butler when Hastings retired. He came highly recommend and William trusted him from the beginning. He had the means and the opportunity to carry out the crime. Until recently, we didn't know why. We discovered his IRA connection the night I asked Charles to steal your father's paper and diary."

"Why didn't you have him arrested immediately?"

"Because we didn't have the proof we needed to prosecute. The night he died your father rang for tea. Richard brought a tray and your father buzzed him into the study."

"He could do that?"

"He had a button on his desk that unlocked and opened the door automatically. Richard gave him tea laced with an undetectable poison. William drank it and died. Instead of sounding the alarm right away, Richard left William slumped over his desk and returned to 'find' him in the morning."

"If that's true, why did he remain in the house? Why didn't he use William's death as an excuse to leave? There was no longer a need for a valet on the staff? If he'd gone, maybe no one would have suspected him."

"He began to work part time, probably to see if anyone suspected foul play or to be sure no one picked up where William left off. You came to England and when he realized you were snooping around, he rejoined the permanent staff, supposedly to pick up the slack wherever he was needed, but in truth, to keep his eye on you and maybe because he thought I'd come over to visit you."

"So he could kill you like he did William."

"Possibly. We hope to learn more about his motives. He's still being questioned."

CC paused for a moment and Flash waited, letting her gather her thoughts. "And the number William gave Hastings?" she finally said.

"It was my cell number. As soon as I knew William was dead, I had to act. I called two of his bodyguards."

"Bodyguards?"

"Yes. Though he didn't have personal protection at Litchfield, William always traveled with bodyguards. All of us do."

"You too?"

"Of course, honey. You never know who might be out to get you. For a while there I thought I might need protection from you."

CC laughed, glad for a momentary respite from the dreary news she was hearing. "Believe me, there was a time when you did. So William's bodyguards took his body, and you gave the order for him to be cremated."

"I did, for reasons I've already explained. Your father's buried at St. Paul's in London. If you want, I'll take you to see his niche."

"I'd like that. And Richard, do you really think he would have tried to kill you?

"I do, you too if he thought there was a reason. We're hoping he'll identify Yamato's murderer as well as the names of other members of his cell." Flash stood and helped CC off the couch. "Frankly, I'm talked out, honey. Shall we let Stanley drive us to Litchfield? I for one would like to see Hastings and be sure everyone's alright. I'm sure Richard's arrest shocked all the members of the household."

"I'm ready. We'll talk more later?"

"Of course, honey," if you'd like."

Stanley was waiting by the car when CC and Flash left the hotel. During the ride to Litchfield, CC tried not to think of Richard and what Flash had told her. She enjoyed the beauty of the Cotswolds, sorry that this would be her last ride through the English countryside. She said very little, and Flash left her alone with her thoughts. As they neared Litchfield, he closed the window between them and Stanley and spoke. "Have you given any more thought to Charlie since our talk last night?"

CC thought Flash would broach the subject, so she was ready. "I have. I was furious with you when you told me what you did. I'm still not happy, but I understand why you enlisted Charlie's help. Yes, I realize Charlie was an innocent pawn and I'm no longer angry with him, but I know I've done what's best for both of us."

"Now what does that mean? You're telling me that it's better to live by yourself and work in Indianapolis than to be over here married to the man you love, enjoying a privileged life of a wealthy and happy woman?"

"You know how hard I've struggled to get where I am, Flash. Baseball is my whole world. Charlie's world is Scotland and England. He made it clear that unless I remain here, there can be no relationship. So you see, it won't work, and Flash, I want your word that you won't contact Charlie while I'm in England. It would be too difficult for both of us."

"Then you're not going to tell him you understand why he did what he did?"

"I'll call him from Indianapolis."

"Isn't that the chicken way out? You did that once and look where it got you."

CC frowned. "It may be," she said with annoyance, "but that's the way I'm going to handle it."

She was relieved that there was no more opportunity to talk. Stanley pulled up to the house and Hastings hurried out to greet them. "Welcome, Your Ladyship, Mr. MacTandy. It's so good to see you both."

"It's great to see you, Hastings. How are you?"

"I'm doing well now that Richard's been arrested. We're all relieved." He turned to CC. "I would like you to know how sorry I am about your father, my lady. If I'd only known—"

"Neither William nor Flash knew either, Hastings. Richard fit in well."

"None of us had any idea there was someone dangerous working in the house," Flash added. "The earl's death isn't your fault any more than it's mine," Hastings.

Hastings looked relieved. "Thank you, sir. Now if you'll both follow me into the house, Stanley will see to your bags."

CC looked around as she entered the foyer. "I can't believe it but this place almost feels like home."

"Maybe you ought to listen to what you're saying," said Flash, a wily smile on his face.

Hastings didn't give CC time to respond to Flash's admonition. "Once again I've put you in Lady Anne's rooms, my lady. Mr. MacTandy, you're in a guest suite down the hall. After you unpack, would you like a light lunch?"

"Another one of Jean Claude and Charles's simple repasts?" CC laughed and turned to Flash. "Are you hungry?"

"I'm always hungry, but for something substantial, not one of those fancy meals your chefs make." He turned to Hastings. "How about one of those huge English breakfasts?"

"For lunch?"

"A good breakfast works for me anytime of the day."

"I'll see to it, and you, my lady?"

"Whatever John Claude prepares will be fine, and Hastings, we'll eat in the breakfast room, not in the dining room."

"Would you like to go with me to Knockie?" Flash asked when they were finishing their coffee. "Like I told you, I want to take a look at the renovations and I believe you promised Mrs. Lauriston and Henry you'd come back to see them."

"It's such a long drive, Flash."

Flash grinned. "But promises are promises. Didn't you say something to that affect not too long ago?" He grinned when he saw CC's frown. "And who said anything about driving?

I'll have the plane ready first thing in the morning and we'll fly to Inverness. There's an airport there that can handle my jet."

"Ah, yes. You flew in there recently, didn't you?"

Flash ignored the remark. "A car will be waiting for us. It's a short flight."

"I'll go, but on one condition."

"Why do I know what you're going to say?'

"Because you know how I feel, but in case we're not on the same wavelength, let me make it crystal clear. You're not to call Charlie to tell him I'm around the corner from Glencoe. You promised, Flash."

"I did. You can be sure I won't contact him."

"In that case, I'd love to see the lodge, Mrs. Lauriston, and Henry one more time."

"Good, we'll leave first thing in the morning, but what about this afternoon? What do you want to do? Would you like to ride with me?"

"I don't think so, Flash. I'd like to go through my father's personal possessions. There are a few things I want to take home, especially now that you've told me so much about him. I can't imagine I'd be taking anything the next Earl of Litchfield would want or need."

"Whoever he is, I'm certain he won't mind, so I'll leave you to yourself." He turned to Hastings. "Will you please call the stables and have Crooks saddle a horse for me? Tell him I'll use the western gear William kept around for his cowboy friend." CC grimaced. "No comment please, Flash said. CC smiled and nodded.

"Shall I tell Crooks you want to ride your favorite stallion?" Hastings asked.

"Absolutely. I'm sure we both could use the exercise." He bent and kissed CC on the forehead. "Enjoy your afternoon, honey. We'll head back to London after an early dinner. I'll call and have the plane ready to leave at nine in the morning, if that's not too early for you."

"You know I'm at the office by seven-thirty every morning. Nine will be fine." She turned to Hastings. "We'll dine at six-thirty tonight. I realize that's early, but I'd like to be on the road around eight."

"My lady, may I ask if you plan to contact Sir Anthony and Lady Alexandra while you're here? They called several times after you left and I know they would want to see you. Perhaps you could invite them to dinner?"

"Thank you for the suggestion, Hastings. I'll call them when I return to London from Knockie. Hopefully they'll be able to join me for dinner at the Ritz."

"Then I'll let Jean Claude know there will be only you and Mr. MacTandy dining this evening. Would you prefer to eat in the dining room or shall we serve in breakfast room?"

"The breakfast room, please, though I imagine flaunting traditions around here doesn't make me too popular."

"This place is yours to begin your new traditions, my lady. Whatever you wish is fine with all of us."

"Thank you, Hastings. Right now, I'm going to my father's suite, and I don't want to be disturbed."

CC spent the afternoon going through William's things. She packed the brush that held his silver hair, the picture of him with the Japanese gentleman, and other photos of him taken at Litchfield. She made a mental note to take additional pictures from Knockie. *That is if any of the albums survived the fire,* she thought sadly. When her task was finished, she roamed through her father's suite for the last time, but unlike the first visit, she felt William's essence in the room.

During dinner Flash raved about his ride through the countryside. "I can't believe you're going to give all this up just to go back to work," he said, but when he saw CC's scowl, he didn't continue.

When the meal was over, CC went to the kitchen to thank her talented chefs. At the door she said good-bye to Hastings and once again thanked him for everything he'd done to make her stay memorable. "How long will you in America this time?" he asked. "We enjoy having you at Litchfield."

"I'm afraid I'm not coming back, Hastings. I've already signed the papers. Very soon there will be a new earl in residence here."

"My lady, I had no idea. I'm so sorry. I expected—"

"Expected me to remain here as the Countess of Litchfield."

"That's right. I mean, it's what your father would have wished."

"I know, but Hastings, I'm an American baseball executive. Running a ball club is all I know how to do, and actually, all I want to know. I wouldn't fit in here."

"I hope I'm not being too bold by saying that you're half-British, my lady. All of us at Litchfield Manor would have been proud to serve you."

CC felt tears well up in her eyes. "Thank you, Hastings." She realized her next action would shock the old man, but she didn't care. She hugged him warmly and thought she saw a glint of tears in his eyes as she stepped back. "Good-bye, Hastings."

"Good-bye, my lady."

"From now on, it's CC." She smiled and got into the car.

Stanley too seemed upset when he left his passengers at the Ritz. "It was a pleasure driving you, my lady. We shall miss you at Litchfield."

"Thank you, Stanley, and thank you for being such a fabulous tour guide"

"You're welcome. I hope you have a wonderful trip to Scotland and then home."

"I'm sure I will," CC said pensively.

✧ ✧ ✧

Though they had to fight rush hour traffic, CC and Flash got to Gatwick in time to take off at nine. The flight was uneventful and CC alternated between dozing and reading several current magazines that had been brought on board in London. "I rarely have the opportunity to indulge myself like this," she said as she leafed through *Elle.*

"Well, maybe you ought to make time," Flash said, once again dropping the subject when he saw his stepdaughter's glare.

A car was waiting when they landed at Inverness. During the drive to Knockie, both Flash and CC admired the countryside they were passing through. "I never get tired of coming here," Flash said. "Now if you were to become Lady Litchfield, I could visit as much as I'd like."

"Flash, this discussion is becoming repetitive. Please let it go. You know what my plans are, and you also remember what you promised."

"I do on both accounts, but you can't blame a man for trying."

"If you try much more, I'm afraid I will blame you. Now let's look at the house and have no more talk about a possible future for me here or in England. Once and for all, I'm going home."

Mrs. Lauriston and Henry greeted CC and Flash warmly. "Come and let me show you your father's suite, my lady. You would never know we had a fire."

CC looked sideways at Flash. "Lead the way, Mrs. Lauriston."

The housekeeper was right. Had CC not been aware there was a fire, she wouldn't have known. The furnishings, carpet, and draperies were the same as they were when she first arrived months before. "The room looks wonderful, Mrs. Lauriston."

"It certainly does, my lady."

"Were you able to save any of my father's pictures?"

"We were, and largely because of you. If you'll recall, the photo albums were brought downstairs when you were last here. I never took them back up after you left."

"Then I'd like to go through them and take some of the pictures with me."

"Henry will bring them to your room."

"Thank you, but I won't get to them until later this afternoon. I'm going to change clothes and go for a walk around the loch. After that, Mr. MacTandy and I will have a late lunch."

"Very good, my lady. Will you be staying overnight?"

CC turned to Flash. "It's up to you, honey," he said. "We can go back later or first thing in the morning."

"Then we'll stay and leave early tomorrow. Do you want to walk with me?"

"No thanks. I have some phone calls to make. Might as well see who's up and working this early, and I think I should call your mother. I'm sure she's wondering what's up."

"Give her my love and tell her I'll talk with her this evening."

"I'll do that. Enjoy your walk."

CC changed into a jogging suit and put on a Knights cap. As she crossed the sheep pasture, fewer flies attacked her. "Probably because they can't smell my hairspray," she said. She smiled when she thought of Charlie's promise to protect her from the savage sheep. This time even the sheep avoided her. *Either they're angry with me for rejecting my title or they're not lambing.* She shook her head. "I have to stop thinking about Charlie and what might have been."

The cool air was pleasant, and CC compared the glorious weather at Knockie to the hot, humid summer they were having in Indianapolis. When she approached the inlet where she and Charlie first made love, she felt an overwhelming sadness. She walked toward the water and sat on the log they had shared. "We had such a wonderful time," she said pensively.

"We certainly did!" came a response from behind her.

She turned to face Charlie, resplendent in a kilt, a loose-fitting shirt, knee socks and hiking boots. It took tremendous restraint on CC's part not to fly into his arms. She smiled and hoped he couldn't see her heart beating. "And how did you know I was here? Though I think the answer to that question is obvious."

"Flash told me to tell you he didn't phone me. He had Mrs. Lauriston do it for him. Therefore he didn't break his promise to you."

"Flash has always been good at rationalizing his actions. It's good to see you, Charlie. I was going to call you when I got back to Indianapolis. Flash told me everything. I apologize for doubting you and for my behavior in Arizona. Even if you had betrayed me, as I thought you did at the time, I shouldn't have been so rude in my parents' home."

"I accept your apology, but I'm also at fault. I shouldn't have burst in on you without warning. My only excuse is I wanted to see you, to find out if we had a chance."

"Charlie, let's not go there."

"Then you are going home? You're going to give up your title and inheritance?"

"I am. I've done a great deal of thinking over the past months, and I think it would be best me, for both of us actually. These last few months have been difficult. Thank God for my work. Forcing myself to think only of the Knights in order to forget you has shown me how important being a baseball executive is to me.

Charlie sat beside her on the log. "And I'm not as important?"

"It's not that you aren't important. It's that you can't be, and believe me, it would be very easy for me to throw myself into your arms and let you make love to me right here and now.

"Then why don't you?"

"Because I don't belong over here, I belong in Indianapolis running a baseball team. Obviously you can't live there with me. If you could, I wouldn't be sitting here at arms distance, but as you said, you have little Charlie, your family in England, and an English title. You told me you would never shirk your responsibility. A few months ago, I might have questioned anyone who put duty before love, but that's not the case anymore. Since I've come to know my father, I've begun to understand what duty means to an Englishman. I've tried to figure a way to make us work. I even considered a long-distance romance, but we both know that's impossible and it would be unfair to you and your son. Little Charlie needs a mother to help raise him and hopefully, for his sake, brothers and sisters. I couldn't provide the stability he needs if I'm living thousands of miles away."

"Then we're at an impasse."

"Actually we're not. Our future's decided, and as much as I wish it were different, we're not going to be together."

"So this is good-bye? I can't even keep in touch?"

"You know how painful that would be. We both have to get on with our lives, and I certainly can't do that if you're constantly in my thoughts."

"Then you do think of me?"

"Just ten or twelve times a day, but that's down from the couple of dozen thoughts a day when I first got home. At that point I couldn't get you off my mind."

"Do you hope to forget me entirely?"

"Charlie, you know I could never do that. You'll always have a special place in my heart."

"I just wish circumstances could be different."

"So do I, but—"

"I know, but I'm glad we had this talk, and in person. I love you, you know?"

"And I love you." Charlie kissed her lightly on the lips. "I believe you'll always be the love of my life."

"This may sound like a trite phrase out of a romance novel, but I hope not. I want you to be happy. So walk me back to the house. Would you like to stay for lunch? Your being there might save Flash's life. I'm considering murder."

"If Flash is in danger, yes, I'll stay, but are you sure that's best for you?"

"Actually I'm not, but I hate to say good-bye for the last time. At least I'll be able to see you for a while longer. And I'd like for you to see the repairs that have been made to the house."

"I've seen them because I've been overseeing the construction for Flash."

"You've done a wonderful job and I, or rather the next Earl of Litchfield, thank you." They walked back toward the house arm in arm.

CHAPTER THIRTY-EIGHT

Flash was both pleased and surprised when he saw CC and Charlie come into the lodge. "Well, this is a sight for sore eyes!"

"You're lucky you're alive to see the sight," said CC. "I believe you promised—"

"Didn't Charlie tell you that Mrs. Lauriston called him?"

"Merely a matter of semantics, Flash. Charlie has agreed to join us for lunch, and then he'll be on his way home."

Flash looked disappointed. "Then this is not the happy occasion I'd hoped it would be?"

"No, sir," Charlie said. "What you have here is two very good friends enjoying lunch together before they go their separate ways."

"I'm sorry to hear that."

"No more of this, let's have that lunch, shall we?" CC took Flash's arm and they walked toward the dining room.

During the meal, by tacit agreement, they avoided sensitive topics. Flash could sense the strain between his stepdaughter and Charlie. *So what am I going to do about this?* he said to himself. Unfortunately he had no opportunity to play matchmaker.

When lunch was over, Charlie made his excuses. Without argument and ready for their final meeting to end, CC walked him to the door. Her heart ached as she hugged him for the last time. "You take care of yourself," he said quietly.

"I will. You too." CC lowered her eyes so he wouldn't see her tears.

Flash shook Charlie's hand and went back inside, leaving the two on the porch alone. "I love you, CC," Charlie whispered.

"And I love you. Be happy."

"Without you that won't be easy, but I'll try." He turned toward his car without looking back.

Flash met CC when she walked back into the house. "Oh, Flash," she sobbed. She ran past him and up the stairs. She spent the next hour going through her father's photo albums, hoping she wouldn't ruin the pictures with her tears. When she was through, she went down to the lounge. Flash was sitting on her favorite couch under the window. "I want to go back to London tonight, Flash. Can you have the plane ready to leave in an hour or so?"

"I can, but I thought you wanted to stay at Knockie."

"I've done what I wanted to do here. I've seen Mrs. Lauriston and Henry, and I have William's personal belongings, or what's left of them. There's no reason to remain."

"Not even the misery you're feeling right now? Not even the fact that you love Charles?"

"Not even that. Charlie and I agreed this is best for both of us."

"So you say, but how do you feel?"

"Like hell actually, so I want to finish what I have to in London, and go home."

"Whatever you want, darling. I'll call Inverness and make the arrangements."

"Good, but there's one more thing I need to do. I'm going to call Alex and Tony, Charlie's sister and brother-in-law, and invite them to eat with us tonight, that is, if you don't mind.

I left last time without saying good-bye and they deserve better. They were, or should I say, are good friends."

"By all means call them, but let me contact the pilots first."

After Flash made the arrangements to fly back to Gatwick, CC called Alex. "Maybe she won't be home," CC murmured as she heard the first ring. However, Alex was in. "Alex. It's good to hear your voice," CC said as cheerfully as possible.

"CC! Charlie told me you were at Knockie. How are you?'

"I imagine if you talked with him you know."

"I spoke with him before he drove over to see you. I gather things didn't go well for the two of you?"

"They went as I expected they would. Alex, I'm leaving England for good tomorrow afternoon and I hoped you and Tony could join my stepfather and me for dinner at the Ritz tonight."

"We'd love to. I'd hoped we'd be able to get together before you left for good. You know despite your differences with Charlie, you and I are good friends."

"That we are, and I'm pleased you're willing to drive to town. Shall we say cocktails in the suite at eight?"

"We'll be there."

CC said good-bye to Mrs. Lauriston and Henry. This time there were no promises to return for another visit. As they drove away, she felt a pang of nostalgic for the wonderful place where she and Charlie first made love. *Will I ever feel indifferent as Mother says I must?* she asked herself as she turned around to look at the beautiful white house one last time.

☼ ☼ ☼

CC and Flash barely had time to shower and change before Tony and Alex arrived. She greeted her friends with hugs and introduced them to Flash. "So you're the two fine people who took such good care of CC when she was first here," Flash said. He shook Tony's hand and kissed Alex on the cheek.

"We loved every minute we spent with her," Alex said. During cocktails and over dinner, the four talked of mundane matters. CC told them about the Knights and how the team was doing and Flash talked about life in Arizona. They all laughed when Alex asked Flash about the dangerous Indians who lived in the West.

Over coffee they reminisced about the enjoyable times they had when CC first came to England. Near the end of the pleasant evening, CC and Alex excused themselves and went to the ladies' room. "I didn't want to bring up the subject of Charlie in front of the others," Alex began.

"Alex, please, let's not talk about this. It's painful enough for me as it is."

"Then you love my brother? I know he loves you."

"Yes, I love him, and I'm going home. We decided that's the right thing for both of us."

"You both decided?"

"Let's say Charlie agreed with me, so I'm going back to Indianapolis where I belong. "Lately all I've done is cry," she wiped her eyes, "and I'm not a crier, so please, Alex, don't try to give me advice. I've heard it all."

"I'm sorry, CC. I didn't mean to upset you. I had hoped—"

"Whatever you hoped for, it can't possibly be. I would like for us to be friends, but for a while I won't call you. I have to put England and everyone here behind me."

"And there's nothing I can say to change your mind?"

"If Charlie and Flash couldn't—"

Alex completed the thought. "I can't."

"Right. Please know how much I appreciate your kindness while I was at Litchfield. I hope you'll let me return the hospitality sometime in Indianapolis."

"I hope we will be able to come see you, maybe sometime next year during baseball season. It would be fun to be a part of your world, if only for a few days."

"I'd like that too."

"Will you give me your email address you're your home and office numbers?"

"Why don't you let me call you when I'm ready?"

"And you'll do that?"

"I promise. Now, before I start bawling all over again, let's go say good night."

After Tony and Alex left for their flat, CC and Flash went back upstairs. "They're mighty wonderful people, CC."

"They certainly are, and I'll miss them."

"I'm sure you will, honey."

Though CC fell right to sleep, she didn't rest for long. She couldn't stop thinking of Charlie, her father, Litchfield, Knockie, and her legacy. William had believed she would eventually renounce her American citizenship and accept her English heritage and title. *I'm sure he'd be disappointed if he knew I've done the opposite of what he wanted me to do.*

She tossed and turned much as she had the night at Knockie when she had given up and gone to Charlie's bedroom. That was the only way she could sleep, safely in his arms. "Oh God! I love him so much," she moaned. "How can I go home and leave him behind?"

She looked at the clock. It was only four. She lay down again, hoping she could fall asleep for a few hours, but once again thoughts of Charlie kept her awake. "I don't want to be without him for the rest of my life," she moaned. The minutes crawled by. At six she opened her phone book, found Charlie's number at Glencoe, and picked up the phone. "I love him!" she said as she heard the phone ring.

She didn't recognize the voice of the man who answered, but she could tell she woke him up. He groggily informed her that that Lord Charles was out for a run. CC's heart raced as she left a message asking Charlie to phone her at the Ritz. She lay back down to wait for his call, wondering if she really could tell him she wanted to stay in England and become Lady Litchfield.

When Flash knocked on her door at nine, Charlie still hadn't called and CC was miserable. She told Flash about her call to Glencoe, and he was obviously elated when he heard the news. "But he hasn't called," CC said; feeling as nervous as a teenager waiting for a prospective boyfriend to call her and ask her out on a date.

"Maybe you were too convincing," said Flash.

"You may be right. Maybe Charlie believes the decisions we made at Knockie are the right ones for both of us. Oh God, Flash, what have I done?"

"Honey, he loves you. You'll work it out."

"And in the meantime, I have an appointment with Caulfield to sign the final papers in about two hours. After that, we're going home."

"CC, come over here and sit down. I have a confession to make."

"A confession? I thought you told me everything, at least everything you were at liberty to reveal."

"CC—"

"I'm sorry, I couldn't resist."

Flash frowned. "I'm sure you couldn't, so come sit and hear me out." CC joined him on the couch. "You don't really have an appointment with Caulfield."

"I beg your pardon? I made it myself."

"I know you did, and you can go to his office if you wish, but you won't be signing that right of rescission paper. You see, darling, this has been a set-up all along. Your mother and I knew you were miserable. We also felt you would be happy with Charlie, so we enlisted Caulfield's help. We all came up with this seventy-two-hour idea. We thought by telling you there would be a seventy-two-hour waiting period where you had to remain in England, you'd visit those places you've associated with your father and Charlie, come to your senses, and realize your life is over here and not in Indianapolis. There are no papers to sign except the ones that say you'll accept your title, and there's no time limit for doing that."

"And what if I do go home for good?"

"Caulfield will send you a document to sign in front of a notary there."

"Then this trip to England was all a pretense? I could have stayed home and never seen Charlie again."

"That's right, and you would have never known how you truly feel and what you really want. You had to confront Charlie once and for all before you could get on with your life. What was it you said? Close the book? You owed that much to yourself, and to Charlie, for that matter, and if you weren't smart enough to realize it, then we had to figure it out for you."

CC sat quietly. "You know, I'm furious with you."

"I can see you are, darling." Flash grinned, realizing there was no more fight left in her.

"But what good is any of this going to do me now? Charlie doesn't seem too eager to return my call."

"Maybe that's because he's not at Glencoe."

CC sat up straight. "Then where is he?"

"Would Suite 622 at the Ritz be close enough?"

"What?"

"When I saw how miserable you were last night, I sent the plane back to pick him up."

"Then he wasn't out jogging?"

"Nope, but at that hour, I assume whoever answered expected that's where he was. He's right here."

"But what if I'd decided to sign those papers this morning?"

"Then you never would have known that Charlie was in London. Caulfield would have given you a paper to sign and this whole scheme your mother and I concocted would have been a well-kept secret."

"So what now, Flash?"

"What do you want, honey? What will make you truly happy? "

"I'm not sure. What about my career? You know how much I love running the Knights."

"I know, and you've achieved everything you set out to do. You've broken the barriers and women are now working in baseball management. What else is there for you to prove?"

"I could be the first woman commissioner of baseball."

Flash smiled. "Or you could be the Countess of Litchfield and Lady Timperley."

"Yes, I could be."

"And be happy."

"Right."

"Then I'll leave you to make your decision. I'm going downstairs for breakfast." He hugged CC and took the elevator downstairs.

CC walked over to the window and looked out over the streets of London. *Can I really become an Englishwoman?* she asked herself, but she knew the answer without giving it any more thought. *I don't know, but I can be a wife to the man I love.*

She went to her room to shower and get dressed. If all went as she prayed it would, she'd call the Turners and submit her resignation when it was a decent hour in Indianapolis.

✲ ✲ ✲

Thirty minutes later, CC nervously knocked on the door of Suite 622. It wasn't long before Charlie opened the door. "I hoped it would be you," he said anxiously. "Come in." He stepped aside so CC could enter.

When he shut the door, he turned to face her but said nothing, realizing that it was she who had to tell him what her decision would be. "I love you, Charlie," she said. "I didn't realize how much until last night. I don't want a life without you."

Charlie walked toward her. "After the fiasco at Litchfield, I never thought I'd hear those words."

"I never thought I'd say them, but I'll say them again. I love you and want to stay here with you; that is, if you still want me."

"You'll give up your career?"

"The only career I want is being Lady Timperley. There, see how forward I am? I've asked you to marry me."

"You only beat me to it by a few minutes." Charlie dropped to one knee. "Carolyn Charlotte Cleveland, Countess of Litchfield, will you be my wife?"

CC laughed. "Not if you call me Caroline Charlotte Cleveland. You can call me CC or my lady, or, even better, Lady Timperley."

"So you accept?"

"I do, but with two conditions."

"And what might they be?"

"First you have to tell me the story of the MacDonalds. Every time you begin, we're interrupted."

Charlie laughed. "That's easy. What's the second condition?"

"You have to learn about the game of baseball, we have to start a group of Little League teams over here, and the team you coach has to be called the Dukes of Earl."

Charlie laughed. "It's a deal," he said as he swept her into his arms.